An Inventor's Dream

An Inventor's Dream

The Pythagorean

Chad Douglas Bulau

Order this book online at www.trafford.com
or email orders@trafford.com

Most Trafford titles are also available at major online book retailers.

Printed in the United States of America.

ISBN: 978-1-4669-0601-3 (sc)
ISBN: 978-1-4669-0600-6 (e)

Trafford rev. 11/23/2011

www.trafford.com

North America & International
toll-free: 1 888 232 4444 (USA & Canada)
phone: 250 383 6864 • fax: 812 355 4082

Contents

Chapter 1

"I believe in a reverie of freedom."

Chad Douglas Bulau, 2004

In a building in Minneapolis, MN a man starts to lecture to these Gals.

"In a land hard lain on rights no other country shares in liberties and freedoms in free society in today's world not the stuff nomad's share but the bond stature and trade. Especially when man sets his limits, people make exceptions . . . Money." The man showed his passion for the moral, culture and economics of this era.

Money is what everyone seemed to care about, but the man was more concerned about what happened on the latter of mankind.

"Thieves' have been around since Biblical times and been borrowed by hundreds of governments, just like receiving a Bible as a gift. No, now . . . Thieves' are here . . . They will always be here. Guild's in the likes. Allies built on the faith that one day they will get the rolls they desire. We are a marketing machine of abstruse people farming the latter of the honest man." The man starts to really throw his voice and continues.

"We are competitively and superstiously conforming to one mission. We like the win, win situations. For one purpose . . . I want it all. I want to see it all go down. I hate this float. It's statures, its liberties . . . I was an Architect." The man said in excitement as he sits back down into his seat inside his office.

There was low light because the lights were on low. The Gals were laid back into their seats. They swiveled back and forth where they could see the whole office. The Gals saw carpet, false walls, and windows looking out the south side. A large computer with a desk was behind the man.

"I know my way around zenith and nadir. My name is Spucket Knostic." Spucket said in a puzzling manor that the Gals would surely remember.

He was a short little man with a large belly. Spucket had a challenging rough life. He was once a great architect which he built anything from doghouses to skyscrapers to space vessel. He made and sold the most wonderful gadgets, he was in love with steampunk and made things in that fashion. He had an enormous nach for resources, studying the lore of the products that have been and that came new to the market. Even unique things like his mechanical eye, that of which he made himself with the help of the Japanese government. A couple of our thieves' risked their lives bringing the schematic of the chip back home. He lost his eye in a metallurgy accident when he was in his twenties. The press came down and a piece of metal took out his eye.

He knew blue prints like the moon knows the sky. He built up guild computers and laboratories all over the world. The grid came easy to him as it was programmed into his mechanical eye. Enabling him to have unlimited virtual space which he would tinker with mapping out things and places. He even had satellites in his reach. Though at the length he could only copy and reflect the abilities of them. He was able to make the guildies invisible to the naked eye. Everything was watched by the Global Positioning System (G.P.S.) in today's world.

Spucket was a head of the game. With the abilities of his mechanical eye he could see through anything with the change of frequency. He could delineate objects and view geopolitical maps. He resourced G.P.S. for its wonderful maps. He was able to plug into any of the guild computers with a blink of an eye. He could give orders delineated on schematics and put them into objectives. The thief's guild had it made or should I say inventor's guild? The guild had members into the thousands worldwide some legit and some not. Spucket was the head of this end of the barrel.

Spucket Knostic a master thief at the Kluse guild. Kluse was an early pioneer, well not quite that early. He started this guild in Minneapolis, MN in 1908 and because he ran a legit furniture business it was never raided by the police. Back then everyone kept quiet. The Law was less sophisticated. We looted visitors and newcomers that came to the city. Business was booming and we later made it to the black market. We trade any and everything through the warehouses we purchased. We also setup a guild in Bonn, Germany where Kluse had relatives. We got to be known by other guilds in illegal trade. We stopped doing small jobs. We were always looking for bigger and better. We were highly respected by our ferals. We don't deal on their turf and they don't deal on ours. There was always trade on loot and information, hell, what else does the black market have to offer, poison teas, nano thieves', and not to mention people with money, androids.

"Honor among thieves' as a monk to his faith and a president to his people, well, maybe not a president, but pirate laws and thieves' codes are an opportunity for the poor and gifted. Come to us and we'll take care of you. If you screw up, you'll end up some where in the outer limits or in one of those government computers they have linked together in Iron Mountain. You can rise up in rank and if you have the passion for something, say technology or math, we'll hook you up." Spucket said and anxiously scrambled through some papers.

"We need anything you can put your mind to as we begin. I'll teach you the grid. We have the cash, if you have the desire and intuition to take the initiative to learn. Just one thing, watch out for the tune master he's always watching. He's the guy running the organization that's running G.P.S., but don't worry too much I'm in the lead so far." Spucket said with his arms pointing to the sky, he paused for a moment as the Gals were sitting awaiting the next oration.

He got down to the details. "The tune master can watch us if we don't have the counter frequency that the guild towers project with the aid of our belts. They contain a chip in a form of globes that counters a relay of virtual space that makes us invisible to the cameras of G.P.S. I'll get into the invisibility of the guildies to the naked eye later." He told the Gals, he reached into his pocket for a bag of gum balls and offered them to the Gals, they indulged and so did Spucket.

"All our stuff has a code. We label our stuff so we can track it and make an inventory through our computers, dedication is a must. Sometimes we are considering face to face with life or death. We make each guildy get an address of the code. We tag each belt to each person. Sign of the beast one might think, but we need it. Our life is your life, we need to know where everyone is just in case something happens. We do follow the Law more than the Law follows the Law. We have our inhibitions to follow. With the way the public keeps an eye on what the Law can and can't do in regards to innovation. The Authorities have to keep an eye on the I.P.O.'s (Initial Public Openings) with their inventions. Anything they come up with could fall into the wrong hands. We have an edge that we must also keep to ourselves." Spucket said and then blew a bubble and snapped it out loud.

"Again say you follow the Laws of physics so far to come up with an invention that out dates the modern pistol. The I.P.O.'s of the invention must meet the codes of the public. We have a quality control which oversees the invention market in America. We have to watch our step with our steam gear. It is the gear that the I.P.O.'s frown on. The militaries and Czars are playing the game. The steam game of who's the best of the serendipity of the troposphere. Take a look around you, do you feel it? Hey, we are not just gorillas in the jungle anymore. As we go on living things will get even more steamed and perplexed. I know there are addresses to idea's that are heavily in the Agencies regards, and they mean to stay that way. What is man worth when he needs so little to be happy? Inventing things comes at a cost! We have a liberty that not all people know about, after all what level are you on in this plenum." Spucket said and starts to chuckle like a madman. "No bodies stupid." He says and laughs some more playing with his hands as he let out another sinister hackle. The Gals start to laugh as well.

"It's the same way with learning a language for the first time. It's very difficult at first. In the likes, there is great reward for the inventor that studies. Not all of it is good though, things tend to be a hoax or bring you a type of chaos. One must study to find the right set theory, you really need to dolor. In return the inventor reinvents an older problem and the content of it when the problem was already addressed by another inventor before hand. I think the question for the inventor is, did they miss something along the line? Either way it is a rat race that sometimes leads to madness and sophistry. The modern world was put together by a delve latter of hard working souls. No one knows exactly what the world was like back in History, not compared to our intelligence we have of the world today to make a record of a thing or event. Doloring in a state where the center of it one finds gold, diamonds, and the hand of ledger main that's talented in all crafts and artifices. Since the idea of the modern computer programs we can make anything. The most valuable thing according to mans latter is his well being and not everyone realizes this. The risk in inventing one takes is their sanity. For what does the world do to you if you know little?" Spucket said and paused a little to catch his breath. He spit out his gum and offered the Gals some coffee. They all got a cup and Spucket motioned them to sit down again.

"Each time you reveal an invention you have a little more information to add to your intellect and eventually have a greater intelligence. The inventor's class is limited to the availability of subjects in your intelligence. Each class is taught by the teachers in this guild. We teach in our guild the magic of etiquette. We do it to ensure a unique ground's of intelligence that no other would have. Prote Hyle, as thought and material in the mind to the future and back at the past is our limit of our operation. We try and meditate on the years the world has gone through. Every morning I wake up and think of a model of the Earth and play with it. I teach myself about it each time revealing more and more. I tend to play with it all day using the first and second psyches. We try to teach evolution here, and all things must be up to code. All the guildies aboard had to learn it." Spucket affirms and gets up from his desk then sits on the edge of it.

"Consider a schematic to a Patent Attorney. They give you the guide lines to follow with your invention. They charge a fee to patent it. We have our own report forms that are then submitted to our computer and then looked at by me through my mechanical eye which with I can perform thousands of analyses. We invent everything here. We invent toys, gadgets, anything that can have a better modification." Spucket mentioned about the procedure and continued.

"This seems all too great to believe, but the possibilities of the inventor's class are beyond the google, a ten with 2 million zeros behind it. In the future we will be using the google in biology and physics not to mention computers that will use it." He said as he put his arms down and went around the desk. Then sat down and took a glance at some papers."

"The guildies will always be busy, in fact there are 26 letters and 10 numbers in the English alphabet. Over 36 to the 36th power of different marks can be made though some of them are useless like a row of A's or just too long of word. The word combinations of sentences number beyond the google. The guildies use the alphabet as their tool along with the arbitrary eclectic symbols to their vocation. I've invented an artifice called the Inventor's Map. It's a map that is used for dictionaries involving any word such as Monitor for example. One would take the word Monitor and run it past each word of the dictionary to try and find something new to invent to research it as an absolute search. It shows a different invention each time and is very useful for the guildies because they learn each word of the dictionary each time they use the map. In this guild we have the best resources and in our inventing we take the absurdity of thing place and create something new with a spin of a lexicon. We train the best!" His eye gleamed with excitement.

"Groco is working on a satellite now, to time . . ." He started to say, but got interrupted.

"Spucket, I'd like to join." Tiffany said.

"Oh, ok then." He acknowledges.

"She's ok with me." Amy said and both Gals got up from their chairs.

Tiffany, eighteen years old was orphaned until nine where she then lived on the streets most of the time and once and a while stayed with her English teacher Kristen that taught her lessons when she had time. Very uniquely beautiful she usually got what she wanted from men. She's one tough cookie though, her parents were killed in a fire when she was only two years old. Today Amy found her at the train station and brought her here to the guild on recruitment.

Amy a very beautiful brunette was also eighteen and was very handy with anything she laid her intuition to in the field and labs. Her parents Jeremy and Cindy that are also in the guild made her special. One of Spucket's favorites, he knew her since she was an infant. Amy was very advanced to the other guildies that were her age. She was our model mainly because she loved inventing so much.

We live in Minnesota, the great land of ten thousand lakes and forest and farms. We have a very booming society and home to the Great Lake Superior. In the Twin Cities there's a great need for magic and technology, an abundance of middle class urbaniacs that buy anything that comes from Spucket's bucket. He brings a few new toys out every fiscal.

"We don't steal much anymore. Like I was saying, Groco is working on a new satellite to time travel." Spucket said as he gives Tiffany the Kluse Guild Magic Book that he put together over the years for the guild. (See The Kluse Guild Magic Book in the back of this book.)

"Ah, thank you." Tiffany said as she had in mind and body to endeavor every word of it.

"Tiffany, come with me." Amy said.

"Ya, ok . . ." Tiff said.

"We have a large laboratory downstairs that is most advance and complex lab we know of to our knowledge." Amy said.

The Gals ride the elevator to the basement where the lab and library is and get off.

"We develop everything from black and white photos to space craft here. This is part my invention with the help of Spucket and Groco. It's a teleportation device allowing one to teleport in a field we call the aether." Amy said and grabbed a belt for Tiffany.

"Here, put this on." Amy said as Tiff put it on.

"Sure." Tiff acknowledges.

"The belts have a chamber that releases globes that react to MEM's of the frequency of the computer. The teleportation takes a split second, it is possible to teleport up stairs with these belts and the Ayin unit. The unit fails time and space as it enters the aether." Amy said as she turned the dial on her belt and under a second they appeared on the second floor from the basement into Spucket's office.

Tiffany was taken for a loop, to appear all of a sudden in a different room gave her a vertigo, and all that sophistry she learned had to set in her mind.

"Are you alright?" Amy asked.

Tiff looked puzzled.

"Yeah, I'm alright." Tiff said as her head stopped spinning. She was very excited about this.

"I felt the same way on my first leap." Amy said

"How does it work?" Tiff wondered eager to know what exactly happens.

"Ah, Groco explains it the best, but the globes happen to fail time and space as they get sucked into the aether by the Ayin units as the globes take our body by frequency of the MEM's and bring us to a new destination programmed by the computer." Amy explained to Tiff.

"Here, Tiff you need this schematic" Spucket says and hands her this page. (See Figure 1)

Spucket knew what he was doing as he always had. This page was about the basics of everything that Tiff had to know. Tiff looked at the page and didn't get all of it.

"I'm thinking I'd better explain a little bit of it to you Tiffany. There is great reward, and much to learn in this guild." Spucket said.

"The theory is to make a globe in the center of your focus making a point of interest. As you keep it center you begin noticing information with it. Not too much though, one needs to name it to see objects or words and associate from there. The globes above our heads function with our surroundings. The center globe lets us address the works of our mind. You can transform your globe with the permutation of your imagination. The globe represents you in this guild, Tiff, you'll know when you are ready. We've been working on a neuro-computer sensitive enough to keep up with our minds. I'll teach you more about the globes as time goes on, it's a rat race, but see what you can do with the globe, try and keep it alive. Civilize an existence with it in the importance of the moral, culture and politics of an era." Spucket finished and then leaned to the right and let out an enormous fart. The Gals started laughing.

"Oh, excuse me." Spucket said.

"We have our own etiquette." Amy said

"I'd really like to hear about guild etiquette. I think it sounds very interesting." Tiff acknowledged.

"You'll learn it all. All I want from you is your dedication." Spucket said.

"Tiffany, what are you good at?" Amy asked.

(Figure 1)

• Globe in the mind...

Globe centered in the mind...

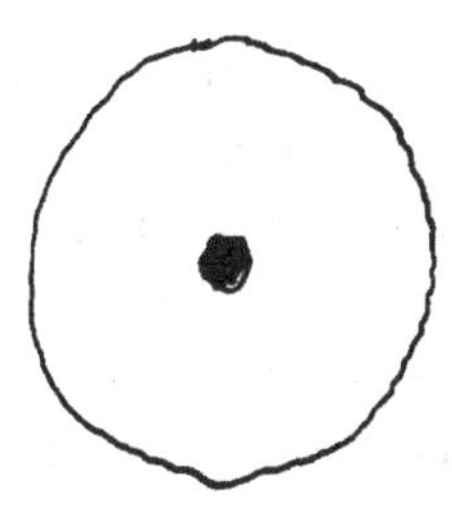

Globe as a monad...

We take a globe and label it giving it definition. Like this: → Math •

We look at the math globe and associate everything we need to know about math. Anything can be the globe one wishes. Civilizing it one becomes aware of the knowledge one can find and have in their conjecture of scholastics in the world today. All of the Kluse guild practices it and it really helps with the digression of subjects.

“I like and was taught English the most, but some Science and Math.” She said.

“Well pick a subject for your globe and take a look into it. Pythagoras said that magic rest in a mind separate from our own. He was talking about mind sets. We have to have evidence, say your first globe of your pick. Using the globe gives us an advantage to the evidence of one mind set and later denouncing it and renouncing a new on and so on. We can always come back to the first globe or set. We do keep several mind sets when we mind our business now days in the guild.” Amy spoke.

“Pythagoras?” Tiff questioned the weird name.

“He was one of the first Mathematicians. He was born on the Island of Samos and he lived in 500 B.C. that first brought the tetraktys (Te-trak-tys) to Greece from India.” Amy said.

“Ok, but what is the aether?” Tiffany asked like a little kid receiving candy.

“Our belts have thousands of mechanical globes. They are controlled by MEM’s and the frequency from the Ayin computer. The Ayin unit fails energy and globes into the aether and sort of kidnaps the globe of the belts failing them and whatever is connected into the aether. The globes travel through the aether to their destination in less than a split second. The aether was first noticed by antiquity because they couldn’t determine any other name for the place air travels on as time went by. Then a famous psychologist named Sigmund Freud played with it recently. The aether is weightless, colorless, and is not held by gravity. It’s the absence of nothing, it holds no time-an empty inane space. The field itself might be bigger than the universe or observable universe.” Amy said and gives a big yawn.

She liked Tiff and was really thinking that she’d make the perfect sidekick. Tiffany felt the lore of such sophistry from the guild as a super hero would feel on a good day. The clarity soothed her mind.

“Through time and space inertia, it’s the field the universe travels on and the aether will never move. All time takes place in the field absent the aether. We, with the Ayin unit fail time and space a split second and then are free to move through to a new destination.” Spucket said looking at Tiff and wondering if the idea was sticking.

“Any questions Tiff?” He asked.

“No, but it’s a lot to learn at one time.” She said, she was mostly interested in seeing it all happen.

“Interesting concepts, right?” He said.

“Right.” She said.

“The Ayin unit is hooked up to this computer and I can program it with my mechanical eye. Amy will teach you just how it is done. We need to be able to put a satellite into space. Using a device such as this it shouldn't be a problem. We need to keep an eye out for the tune masters capabilities. If he knows what we are up to there will be hell to pay. But for now we need to go the Europe in the next month. Then after that we can work on time travelling issues." Spucket said in a low calm voice.

There was not a problem at the guild, and everyone kept their heads straight.

"Now that you are in how about some training, Tiff?" Spucket asked her with some enthusiasm.

"Amy will train you on your first mission." He added.

"Sure if things are kosher." Tiff replied chewing her nails.

"You're more than sweet you're a heart." Spucket continues.

"Eh'em, this building before we turned it into and invention factory used to be a furniture business. Kluse, God bless his soul started this operation in the early 20th century. The basement laboratory is the most advance we know of and we . . . I mean, I know that as a fact. Like I said before we are ahead of the Law, but we are not above it." He said in reinsurance.

Spucket kept an eye on everything that the world was doing. Before he became as Architect he was a History major.

Spucket starts talking about his computer in his office.

"This baby is the head of the guild. With it we can do anything, it was put together by the German's in the Bonn guild. It has a set theory only dreamed about by game programmers. It is a virtual model of the actual dimensions of the universe. It took 20 years to perfect. One can do anything on it. Here we will pull up a model of the Earth. Everything is on it. The guild has labs in Asia, Africa, New Zealand, here in the States, and South America. I'm the most influential player in this game, what I say goes most of the time." He said with his hands behind his head leaning back on his chair.

Spucket stands and starts to look serious and starts talking to the Gals again.

"We've had some problems with the ichorplasm in Germany last year. We are sure it is the only place in the world that makes the black market item. Some of our guildies got killed. You know it's a major mishap that happens from time to time. We don't know what happen exactly because the local Law Enforcement Agency kept the whole thing under wraps." He took a second breath. The Gals were sitting there intently.

He took a minute and continued. "Anyway we must go over there and straighten some things out with the new supply. We have such a large market over here with the cats in the cigarette business. The gamers and dope dealers really love it. Such a market I'd really hate to lose. We have a lab in Bonn that makes a great resource to all the government intelligential. The guilds spooks in other words. Its how I got this baby." Said Spucket as he walks over to the computer desk and plugs in this mechanical eye.

"This is the globe." He said with a big grin.

It showed a solid black sphere on the screen.

"With this we can construct the globe to map out anything with in a nanometer." He explained.

"This is the way I advance my mechanical eye. The way G.P.S. can delineate things with the change of frequency gives me an ability to look right through matter. Vampires I call them." His eyes got big becoming even more into the discourse.

"Technology and Magic is where inventions come out and can put to good use. Some inventions . . . Some elements when used in the wrong way can kill you. Take water for example . . . It's a vampire. It can kill and carve mountains. It turns and wares through our aqueducts including our plumbing, it out numbers us in weight, mass, and volume in the likes. It's in us and we can't live without it. They are a vampire as opposed to myth. Not the blood sucking super being you see in theaters, but the element that surrounds us. Water lives, I'm a VAMPIRE!" Spucket shouts opening his arms to the sky.

"The element reflects in the mind what the eloquence can be. We are made of the element and nature is continually changing as we speak. We are a reflection of every element in existence. Water, the element can be one of those reflections. One can have fun wielding water. It can be controlled by resource magic. One can do it by reflecting a balance of Ledger main, Eloquence, and Agriculture. I myself have resourced it." He showed them that he can resource water to his finger tips. They were dripping water as he rubbed his fingers together.

"Our magic is yet in its youth." Spucket said and there was a long silence. He was pondering all the possibilities that came to mind about the guild's magic's.

"Training, Spucket?" Tiffany asked impatiently.

He looked at her and said. "Well, to our liking we have many jobs for you and Amy to do. Jobs that move you up in rank, skills, and merit in your mentality . . . What I need exactly is this . . . I need a team to go and copy a disk at the Davis Corporation. Then bring it back to me so I can continue my research. Davis sometimes gets jobs from American Intelligence. Bonn came through this time and found that the disk has information on it about the Library of Alexandria that was destroyed long ago in wars. Anyway I have to get a copy of that disk. Oh, and one more thing, Tiff, tell the Chef your diet. We get up around 5 am around here, just remember if you need help with something, just ask. Your ass is my ass. Welcome to the guild, Tiffany, you are going to love it." Spucket finished and went up the elevator to the fourth floor to his room for the night.

The Gals also thought it was a bit late and Amy showed Tiff to her room.

"Meet you in the lunchroom after you hear your alarm clock go off." Amy said.

"See you then, Amy." Tiff said.

"Good night." Amy said.

"Night." Said Tiff and they both went to bed.

Chapter 2

"I've never seen anyone with intelligence without great wit on stupidity."

Chad Douglas Bulau, 2006

"Morning." Amy said yawning as Tiff rolled into the lunch room totally awake to capture the day.

"Did you have a good nights sleep?" Amy asked as she took a bite of her toast.

It was a large lunch room on the first floor towards the back of the building. The Guildies were awake and going about their business. It was in between a military mess hall and a school lunch room. Kids were up running around.

"Yes, it was full of dreams. It's really easy to dream weave here." Said Tiffany as she got her breakfast from the line and sat down next to Amy with her food.

"Yeah, I know the guild really puts together quite the beta wave. We used both magic and technology in civilizing our etiquette." Amy said as Tiff followed the frequency of her syntax.

"All the steam evidence I got yesterday filled me with the compassion to learn. It really opened my consciousness." Tiff said and ate some of her oatmeal.

"Oh, Tiff, once you get on the guilds level, you'll have a very sophisticated and educated mind. You'll be as smooth as Spucket . . . I want a fresh start this weekend when we do this job. So let's see what Spucket has in store for us up in his office." Amy said as she grabs Tiff's bowl and her own tray and puts them in the dishwashing area window.

The Gals head down to the lab.

"You're familiar with the belt and teleportation unit, Ayin. Have you ever heard of the grid?" Amy asked as she stares in question at Tiff.

"No, I've never heard of the grid." She says in the performance that wouldn't escape her.

"Well the grid is all around us just like many other networks when addressed. The grid is our minds tool and is controlled by the intuition of the gusto, prote hyle and the rest of the tetraktys. Just like a paint brush to an Artist. It makes up the consciousness of reflection. We move and speak reading from a point that gives the grid our directions. It's a lot of work to understand and accomplish though, but it is worth while. It works on painting the very element of the mind in perception. It is though the way the guild likes to teach so we are on the same level so to speak . . . It starts like this." Amy drew this one a page. (See Figure 2)

"A dot?" Tiffany said as she looked at the paper.

"Yes, consider it the first dimension. We tend to think that everything in existence fits in here. It's kind of the blind spot in everybody's eye. It's not here that we learn it. Us humans tend to live and learn in the fourth dimension where without the other dimensions of the tetraktys we are lost. We need the whole thing together to think. We have such big minds because the dimensions are limitless." Amy said pointing out the extremities of the grid.

"Isn't the grid military?" Tiff asked with the wit of a school girl.

"Yes, but the origin is from mathematicians. They found it by many experiments conforming to mathematical equations, matrices and symbols. The theory is the bottom of the mind, or theta. Pythagoras discovered the perfect number in this tetraktys." Amy said and drew it up one paper. (See Figure 3)

Tiff threw the idea around in her mind a bit. She did notice the dimensions of things as she held the point in her mind while looking around.

"There is a great chance that the idea might not sink in right now, but you'll understand it more later. Our guild has many mind sets in adumbrates that come from the tetraktys. Yet for now let's go over how the guild labels our gear." Amy said and picked up some items with chip stickers on it.

"Here it is." She shows the sticker that they label their stuff with.

"Our own version of the belts lets us track us and gear we have labeled with stickers. Everything goes through the main computer." Amy said as she started explaining the technology and intelligence of it.

The Gals stayed up pretty late discussing the tetraktys different mind sets. Tiffany was astounded at the clarity the dimensions of the tetraktys gave. They both get worn out and head for bed.

"I was up have the night going through the plans for the heist." Amy said as the two Gals went from the lunch room to Spucket's office for a schematic.

They drew up the globe on Spucket's computer. Spucket had a preprogrammed objective for them. Tiffany's only thought was this place was strapped. She had a rushing powerful feeling all about her enticing the ethereal.

"Here, we are, the Davis Co. We'll have no problems getting by the security and cameras. I think it will be easy. Well that's it." Amy said as they were done going through the way points.

"Ok, now let's train you in on the guild etiquette." She said as she grabs a copy of the Kluse Guild Magic book off the shelf.

(Figure 2)

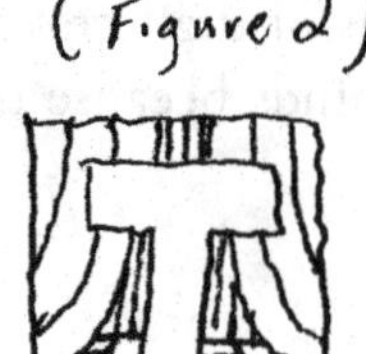he first dimension of the universe the subject,

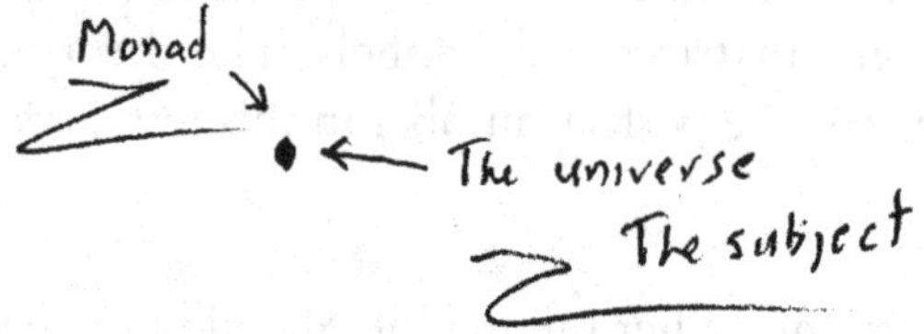

The entire universe is considred in the first dimension. It is the blind spot in our eyes. The universe is what beings feed off from, it is the milk of the ethereal. They say that the aether is bigger than the universe. It's the fuel of Deities.

The subject could be anything and when it is in the first dimension it means its the only thing in the universe. Like these:

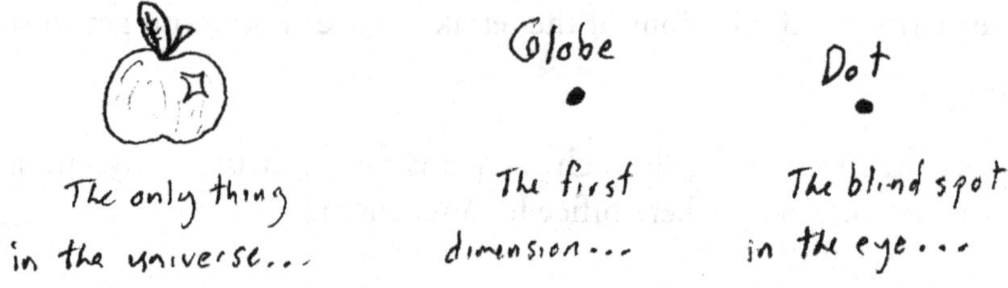

The permutations of the first dimension are endless, though one may stay with one subject as long as they wish,

(Figure 3)

The perfect number →

Six, is the perfect number, because it is the sum of 5 and 1, 4 and 2, and 3 and 3, and multiple of 2 and 3. 1, 2, and 3 added together equal 6 making it the perfect number.

In dimension 6 dots in the shape of a pyramid make up the three sections of a tetraktys (Te-trak-tys)

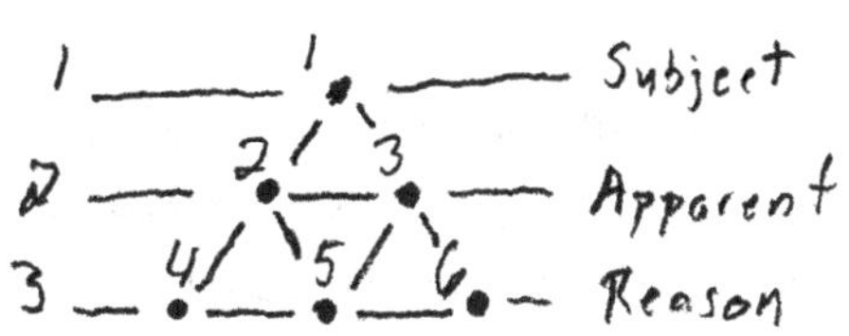

The universe is divided into Six different dimensions in three different sections. Pythagoreans have millions of ways to define the dimensions. Which is the best is the question. The guild is always comming up with bigger and better ways of reflecting on the universe using the tetraktys.

Though this is only the elementary the guildies go from the bottom to the top with their heuristics.

"Now this is a book about the way we act and interact with each others intuition in the guild. Our magic is yet in its youth, its imaginational, and an illusion of organization of the mind and its functions. It will take you about two years to get good at it. Our magic is about resourcing things in reason to find the key ingredient in heuristics of inventing. The way we go about it is find the first surface of the tetraktys. The Reason. The reason comes to us by means of a trinity. Where ever there are three things together it is called a trinity." Amy said and turned the page to this in the book. (See Figure 4)

"We have a consciousness like no other. This magic tetraktys shows how magic is organized to the universe. Reason magic is four trinities organized by the court Earth, Water, Fire, and Air making them magical. Three things together make reason the first surface and four things together make a court the second surface and the consciousness." Amy said.

"It's pretty hard to grasp." Tiff said as she was new to the subject.

"Well if you knew the tetraktys it would help, it takes a while for things to match." She said.

She went to get a piece of paper and a pencil. Tiffany felt drained by all this and grabbed a glass of water next to the door way. They were in Spucket's office.

"Every word counts, Tiff. Our reasoning has come a long way." She said and started to draw on the paper. (See Figure 5)

"Once you have the foundation of the tetraktys down it will be easier, but the idea is to hold a subject, like your globe, an apparent like your eyes, and a court like your consciousness, then switch the reason with different trinities until you complete a thought. This makes our imagination fluent." She shows Tiff the page.

"You must match the definitions with each word, in facsimile to it. Each trinity has a different idea. We make our own definitions to words here since the absurdity of the definitions was done so long ago." Amy said as Tiff scratched her head. (See Figure 6)

"In ledger main it is the coordination of the hand. Basically ones hand thinks. One talks with the hand so to speak. One enlightens your intuition to summon illusions of items of intellect and places like the dessert or the ocean or the energy of the element. We try to get the right tool for the job. Ledger main is the way one manipulates energy of the hand." Amy said.

"In Eloquence it's the form and presentation of acting, reacting and speech in posture, pose, stance, arching, sitting and any other movement or rhetoric. When making a move there is a great progress and that digress makes up the Eloquence." She explained.

"In Agriculture we find the importance of intellect and element. The element in the mind and on

(Figure 4) imagination. Prote Hyle is the mind over matter of the subject. It altogether is one equity in memorization of principle in elementary. We tend to store memory in the mind and remember in the imagination. Though it altogether works like a tetraktys.

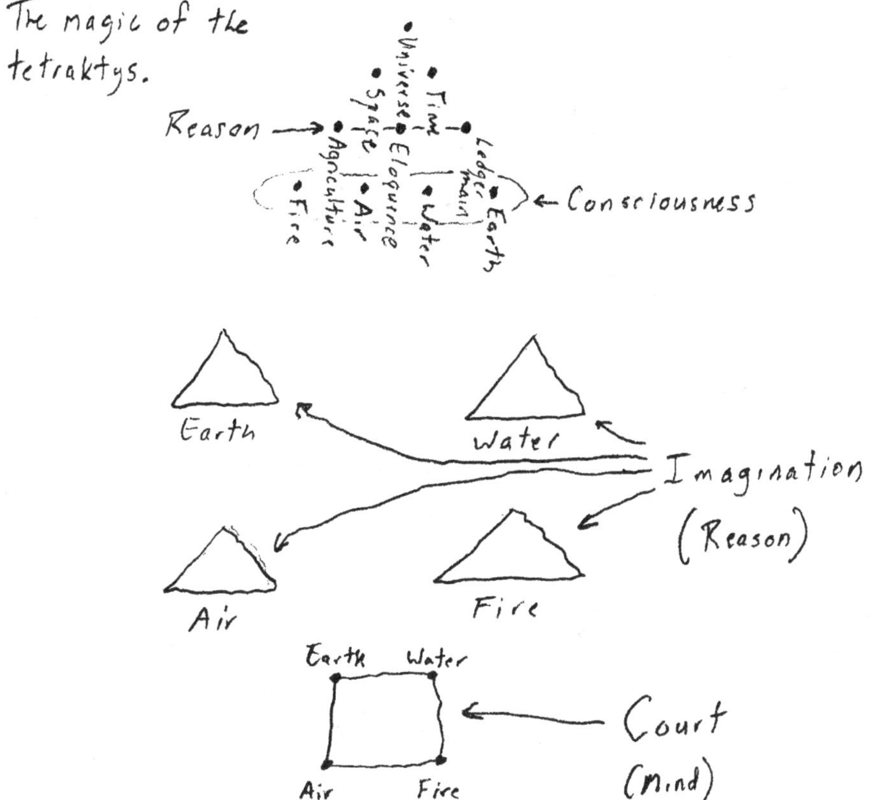

The triangles are the imagination (Dreamlike) and the square is existence (Reality), the real elements.

I associate everything I can wit in putting an idea down on a page. I've ran my eyes accross thousands of drawings and words in books. It's up to ones volition is my best bet. Use this book wisely and be entertained.

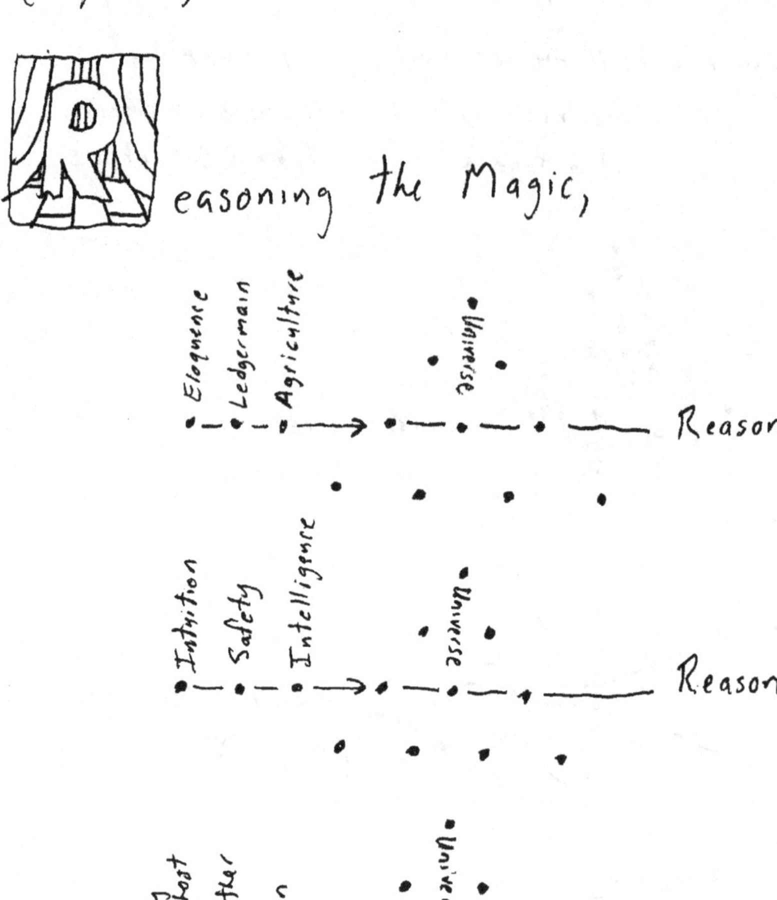

Reasoning can be anything in a group of three in the likes of a trinity. The three arrange to be the first preceivable surface in a tetraktys, A surface where reflections of existences take place as the imagination, It is here we find illusion one can take control over in a film like solution. Each trinity one uses creates a different surface. What one is the best surface for the importance depends on the person. It take the right precepts to practice.

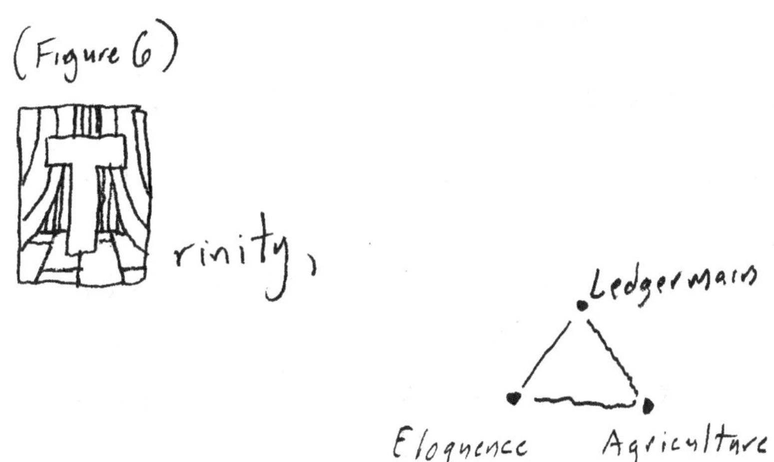

Trinities are made in order to reason out the first surface like this one above. All three magics are played with by this guild. There are googles of trinities and most haven't been found yet.

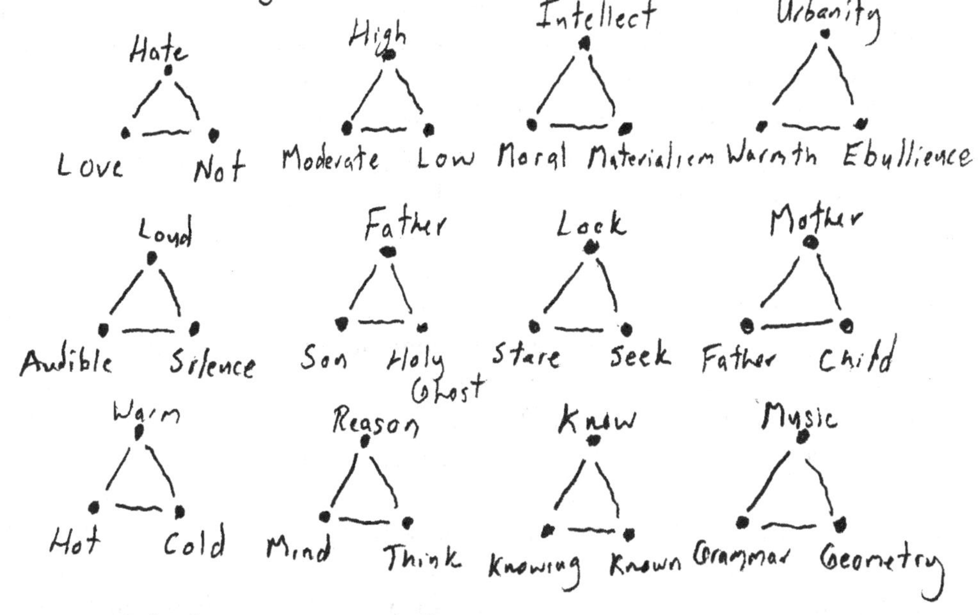

It takes a lot of patience to connect the trinity to the word to the object though in time one can get better.

the surface in front of one is the Agriculture. You must be able to spell it out in order to imbibe and hold it into ones own lexicon of a consciousness. The importance is a balance of the three magic's in the mind set of the tetraktys." She finished.

"Is it a form of meditation?" Tiff asked.

"Yep, we use more of a contemplation of subsistence. All, everyone in the guild practices it." She said.

Amy put the book down and closed it. She was sure Tiff would make an excellent teammate. Tiff will know her stuff in the years to come. Tiffany opens the book to where Amy had opened it.

"This page looks easy enough. What are Earth, Fire, Water, and Air?" She asked to get more of the basics.

"Oh, they are the precepts of consciousness, but only when we use our magic's. Like Pythagoras said, we have magic, but it rest in a different mind . . . Take a look at a rock for example. It's just a rock to the normal mind. If you look at it magically it changes its precepts. It goes the same way if you look at it in different classes. An Archeologist looks apon the rock like and artifact. A Scientist looks at the rock for its minerals and a Pythagorean looks at the metaphysics of the rock. The rock is a single piece of evidence, not quite a piece of intellect, but and axiom where one learns its perception and can define all rocks like it the same. A rock is very common, but very unique. We see it as a piece of the element Earth. The Earth is a matrix of elements. Our world was made by the flushing together in a very complex combination that took eons to make us and come this far. Earth, Water, Air, and Fire are the old ways of making up the constitute of the world, and that's why we use it in our guild contemplation." Amy said, but there was more to it, there was always more to it, an enigma in the likes, she didn't have the skill to tell her and yet she knew Tiff would explore these things on her own.

"That's am ingenious way to look at it. What do you mean by guild contemplation? How does it work?" Tiffany asked then grabs some coffee from the pot. "Oh, take this cup for example. It's complacent to the substrate universe. Meaning there is layer of laws we interpret in the scholastics we have found in study apon it. One can consider anything about it, to each his own in the likes. It sits here on the table catching the frequency of the environment. Though the cup can not think, it can not move on its own it is a part of the woodwork. Any way the idea of guild contemplation is to get the idea that the cup is a piece of space that sits here in the universe. Ones mind unfolds it from the first dimension. It then becomes a precept that is governed by the universe, not the Earth or any other influences such as the atmosphere which is observable to our perception. We tend to more of a subsistence than a reality. We would like to be one with the universe. This becomes our set theory when looking at things in existence. The Guildies consider themselves in the universe, not some fine confession of a professor of the pedagogy. The idea, Tiff, is to realize the difference between what the government says and the way the universe actually works and be free from all other things, but the universe. Here we make up our own definitions to words to actually become better at definitions that are here." Amy said motioning her oration just for Tiff.

"I've never thought of that before. How do I make a matrix?" Tiff asked.

"A matrix is two or more things equaling each other. In our magic it is explained to you as you read our book. It describes the matrix in space or field by two or more things coming together. For example: Water= Crushed coffee beans= Filter=Peculation, makes the matrix coffee. Then therefore Earth, Water, Air, and Fire make up everything you see here. Einstein gave us a matrix to solve. E=mc2. E= Energy (The Sun) m=mass (The Earth) and c2=speed of light (Sun beams) makes the matrix for the necessities of life. It's our reflection of how existence came about." Amy said.

"The immaculate elements on the Periodic table of Elements are now used instead of the four elements Earth, Water, Air, and Fire. It was once believed at one time that the entire world was made of two elements. Mercury and Sulfur. Not the elements on the charts, but the Mercury and Sulfur they talked about was at a glance two handfuls of dirt. It just amazes me to know and have the privilege on how this place was put together." Amy finished and stood up and then said that they had better get the gear ready for the heist.

"We have our suits, goggles that allow us to see each other, gloves, and our belts. The Boss is working on how to get a pin number for matter in order to be able to find a loc just to put to use in jobs like this. The pin number for us and our belts is hidden in a mixture of elements." Amy told Tiff.

Amy was a little nervous about Tiff's comprehension of all the steam gear. Amy went on to explain how the two would be invisible to the security and cameras.

"Caught, just a second behind the relative time and space we won't be seen. Our intuition of these gloves gives our digitals the ability to reach the surface. The gloves were specially engineered for that purpose. The system knows our strength and has unlimited power, so if you see the lead lights go into the red, back off. I've thrown a dumpster around before in this position. It weighed 500 lbs." Amy said.

"Jesus, five-hundred pounds!" Tiffany exclaimed.

"Yeah, when you're in the aether you can handle things like they are weightless." Amy said holding on to the goggles and gloves.

She had Tiff practice with the equipment. Tiffany was very happy to test the gadgets and did so with the caution of a doctor with his patients.

"The Boss said that in his cryptology he had a great deal of new inspiration. That he has been working on a new code that can project illusions for the tune master to check as we do jobs in the diversions. Though technology changes everyday we've got to stay a head of the game." Amy said and went to get a file on the tune masters capabilities.

"What's this?" Tiffany asked and put more coffee on.

"It's our own dossier (Dose-si-a) on the tune master. It lists everything we need to watch for. Here, take a look." Amy said and passed the dossier to Tiff.

Tiffany studied it and said, "Do you have more files like this?"

"Yes, we have thousands of them, even files on our own Guildies. It's all in the computer." She said and told Tiff that she could view all the dossiers she wanted later tonight.

"The whole guild has projects in all kinds of fields. We have one in programmable foods, another in MEM's, some in language sophistry and some in computers and robots. Whatever the task, they made sure that the product was marketable. Sometimes the product was not up to the standards of the I.P.O.'s where they then had to revamp them until they worked. In every Country the I.P.O.'s are different. In Morocco there is no limit to what one can invent. That is why we have a guild there. Yet we are not about to sell anything of mass destruction. We have our own morals. We have everything form busboys to Professors in our guild. Our net worth is in the billions. We don't fight with anyone, but sometimes we have to in order to maintain. Kryull's guild in Europe sometimes likes giving us a hard time. There are about two hundred members and they are all Germans. Anyway, we always have to keep an eye on them when we are over seas. "Amy said and felt a little on edge.

She had seen Kryull's gang once, they all wear red arm bands. She gave Tiff a brief description of them and a picture with a dossier of one of them.

"Let's go through our gear one more time for the heist so we are sure you know how to use them. Let's see, suits, belts, shoes, gloves, Cd-burner, goggles, and programmable chewing gum. (It was programmed to give them ebullience.) Tiff, the goggles had the same technology as Spucket's mechanical eye. The belts were full of mechanical globes eight nanometers in diameter. Which doped by the MEM's in the frequency of the Ayin unit." Amy said. (See Figure 7)

The globes have the ability to move in any fashion with MEM's of the computer frequency. The center can feed off the surrounding element and reflect just about anything. We can change the look and shape of the guildies and along with aligning the change of voice when coating the voice box. Almost everyone in the guild worked very hard to put this program together. It was reality inside reality only this time it was artificially controlled. Each globe can be programmed differently to serve a performance.

With all the dops serving a function the globes will take their place among the millions of others as the guildies belt awaits the command of the Ayin unit. The globes act as pawns to the frequency. The computer is then in command to meet the demands of the guildies that programmed it. The globe also locks on to the frequency of the guildies body and then is able to fully teleport them to a new destination through the aether.

(Figure 7)

The mechanical globe,

A mechanical globe is made out of a acid that changes into any shape or color and is controlled by MEM's at the frequency of the computer. Millions of them together make a water like surface that can be changed into anything. Even change height, weight or the voice of the guildies.

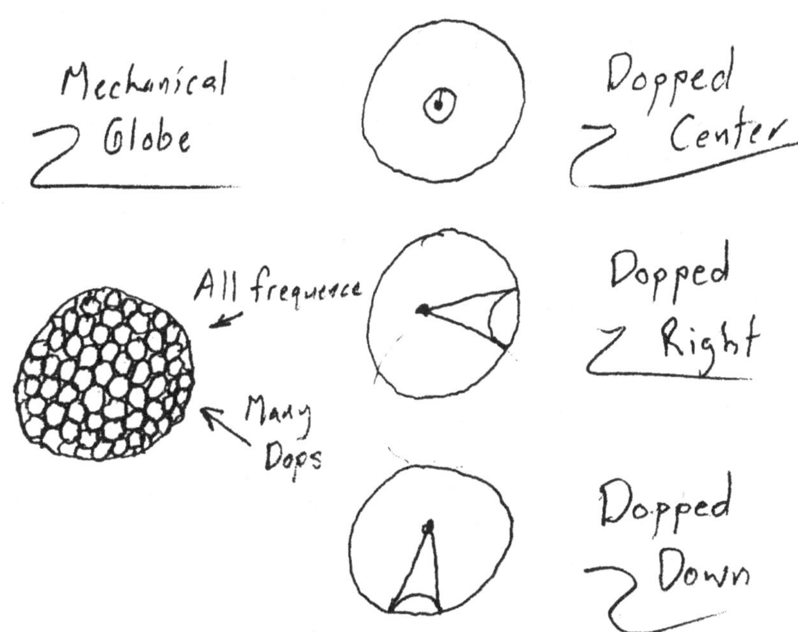

A mechanical globe can move in any fashion the MEM's are capable of in the frequency of the computer. The globe is about eight nanometers in diameter. They are made by the guild in a computerized machine that produces ten thousand per minute. The mechanical globes can also be use to map out an area.

Friday morning rolls about and it is time to get the job done. Everything was squared away, no danger to worry about.

"Spucket is quite the genus. He'd spend all night and day to keep us going. The plans he made for us, stage by stage, even and animal could follow the directions. All we need to do now is get over there and stay out of sight. We won't leave until dark." Amy said in excitement.

She felt that everything would work out alright. Tiffany knows she would do good and had nothing to worry about, besides being a little nervous, after all it was going to be her first heist. They had eleven hours on their hands before they had to go. So Tiff went to search through some dossiers and Amy did some research on Germany in Spucket's office on the computer.

It starts to be about that time where the Gals get ready for the heist. Amy gets into the back of the van and performs a check on the teleportation unit, Ayin. It speeds just passed the speed of light by an apeiron(A-pei-ron) spinning failing time and space a second to make it into the aether enabling it to fit mechanical globes inside. An apeiron spindle that was dropped down the Hopi Indian hole was made to resist any temperature. Spucket knew one of the Hopi Indians that lives in Minneapolis, MN, and he dropped the spindle down making it apeiron. The radius of the Ayin unit's field is two miles. The satellite Groco is working on will have the radius of a light year. The only problem is that the guildies don't have a power supply to fuel the energy needed for such a device. Groco said that the whole world would kill to have such a device. Yet he says it's possible, but we haven't stumbled apon it yet.

It got dark.

"Well come on Tiff, we will be there in about an hour." Amy said behind the wheel of the van.

The Gals reached the company in about an hour.

"It'll be about fifteen minutes. The workers at Davis get off at 10pm. The security stays all night long." Amy said as she made sure the guards didn't see the van in the next parking lot over that belonged to a mini-mall.

"I got you." Tiffany as they stayed in the dark out of sight.

There was a security code for all the doors. The Gals would teleport right passed them leaving only the intuition of their fingers in the gloves that were programmed to reach the surface. Only the very edge of their gloves would reach. The belts relayed an anti-picture so it looked like nothing was moving around when the Gals did their jobs.

"Ok, we ready?" Amy asked with a tickling adrenaline.

"Yeah, let's do it." Tiff said anxiously.

After configuring things earlier Amy adjusted the dial on her belt and with no time at all the Gals were inside the office that contained the disk they needed to copy. Tiff comes to and looks around. She finds a schematic with some blue prints on it.

"It looks like a power supply, ah . . . Flash/Current." Amy said as she scans the blueprint.

"Should we get a copy?" Tiff asked.

"By all means, yes." Amy said.

Amy pulled out a form of space paper that unfolds like paper into a photocopying machine and with the touch of her finger she made a copy. She then went about copying the disk Spucket wanted so badly.

"Wow!" Amy said as she looked at the computer.

"This is wonderful. They have all these pages of scrolls from antiquity." She continued.

There was thousands of writings and drawings on the disk. Ideas and concepts never even thought of these days.

"So many unique drawings bringing a whole new idea from never heard of artist and authors. They have such beautiful penmanship and artistry." Amy noted and couldn't take her eyes off the screen.

"Five more minutes until we can disappear. I'm thinking that Spucket uses these essays and schematics as starters for the kid's mentalities at the guild school. The innovation the antiquity had in this time is remarkable and yet going through them is a good basis for the imagination. The language structure is so old that the designers of the disk translated the disk into English. These particular pages were drawn up in a culture, moral and political time very unique to our time. Some people lost their lives if the drawings or scroll was too unbelievable to the Emperor, King or Lord. We have such a large liberty with the things we can do with our art and literature now days that these ideas of this library will be such a delightful enlightening thing." Amy said and got the things together then turned the dial on her belt.

The Gals were then safely back in the van. They headed back to the guild.

"Ah, most interesting, most interesting indeed. Does look military, but it's not. Definitely the governments. F/C, a power supply, self-governed. It says a unit this size can power a house." Spucket said as he marveled at the schematic. (See Figure 8)

"I'll send this schematic to Groco maybe he can put it to use." Spucket said to the Gals.

"Here is the disk you've been waiting for from the Davis Co." Amy said as she hands the disk to him.

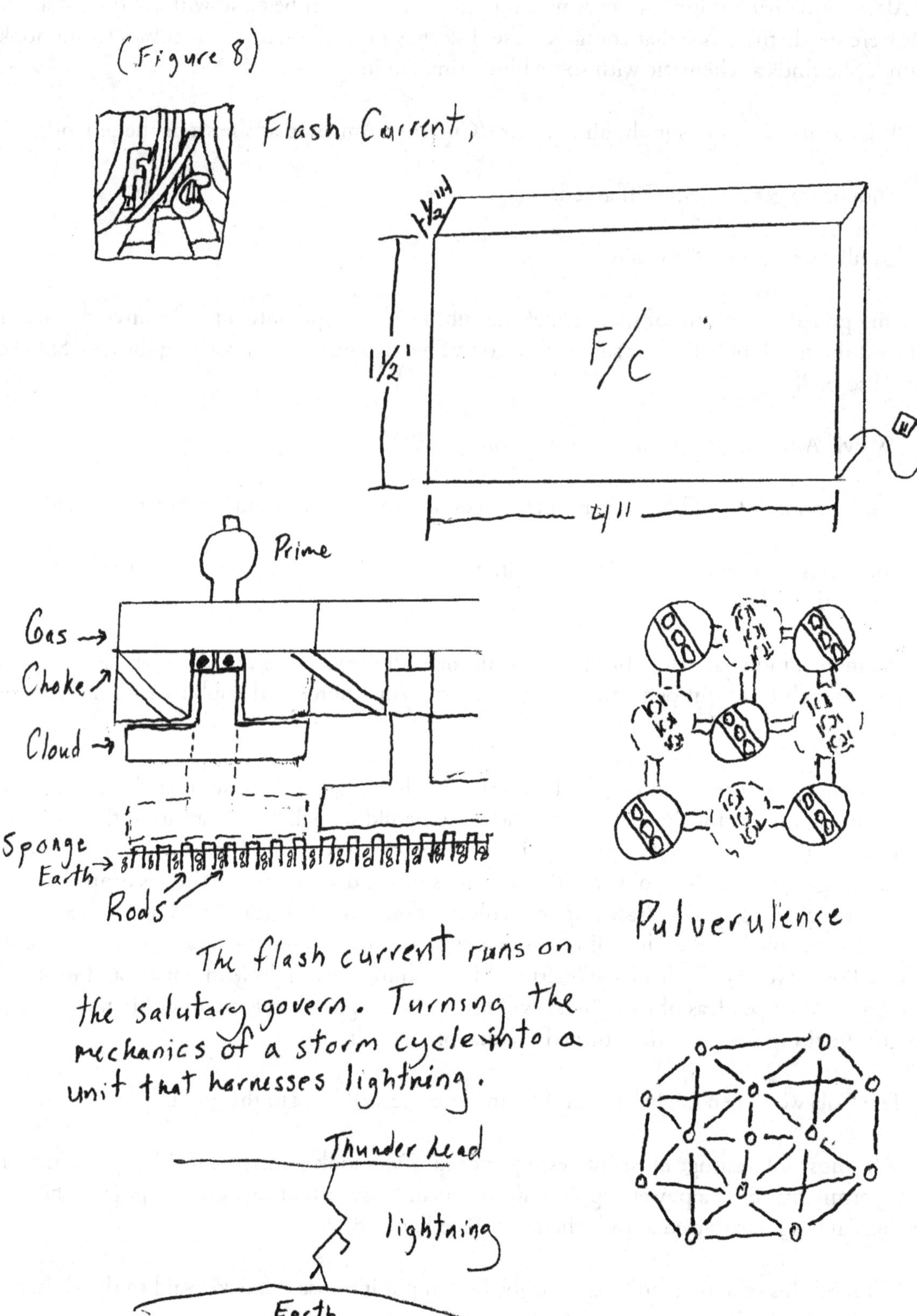
(Figure 8)
F/C
Flash Current,
1/2"
1½'
F/C
4'
Prime
Gas →
Choke
Cloud →
Sponge Earth →
Rods
Pulverulence
The flash current runs on the salutary govern. Turning the mechanics of a storm cycle into a unit that harnesses lightning.
Thunder Lead
lightning
Earth

"Nice work munchkins. I'm so happy I'm going to get you both bonuses for the schematic after we get back from Europe. We'll be leaving next week. Until then we'll be spending time on tinkering around in the lab with this new disk. Tiff, you can learn the guild etiquette. Now that you're climbing the ladder, you'll be a very powerful player in no time. I'm going to give this schematic to Groco, later kids" Spucket finishes and goes down the elevator.

The two Gals leave on the elevator going up stairs. "Amy . . . I'm not much of an inventor, I tend to go more for the language sophistry then trinkets." Tiff said.

"Either way, Tiff, we need you. How about picking up some magic?" Amy asked as she began to get used to having Tiff around.

"It sounds good to me." Tiff said.

The Gals got out of their suits and changed into some more comfortable clothes then met in the laboratory down stair where Groco and Spucket were.

Groco was so happy to see Spucket. They hadn't talked in months though they were in the same building. Groco had been busy getting the prote hyle of the satellite down in a schematic manual.

"You know what we need, Spucket?" Groco asked.

"No, Groco, what do we need? I've been so busy creating the diversion frequency that it's hard to come up with what's on your mind." Spucket said.

"We need a power supply, kind of in the range of Hover Dam, hehehe, which will fit in the size of a room in a house." Groco said as he points to the schematic of the satellite.

"Well, my friend let me show you something the munchkins brought home." Spucket said and handed him a schematic of F/C.

"Ah, what do we have here?" Groco asked.

There was a long pause as Groco scanned through the schematic. All Spucket did was sit there with a large grin on his face.

"Eureka! This is it! It will work!" Groco shouted and hugs Spucket.

"Oh, Spucket you're the greatest!" Groco cheered.

"I thought you would be surprised. I'm leaving for Europe next week. Do you want to come along?" Spucket asked in a serious tone.

"No, I have much work to do." Groco said as he directed his arms in the area he had work to do.

"How far are we on the satellite?" Spucket asked.

"Oh, I've been meaning to seek your help on the matter. It would take me years to do it on my own. With your help it could be done in a matter of a couple years.' Groco said reinsuring he had Spucket's attention.

"Oh, ok then we'll have to talk about it when I get back from Europe." He said.

"Well what is so important that you have to go there?" Groco asked.

The Gals get off the elevator and head over to Spucket and Groco.

"We need to fix the ichorplasm connection that we lost last year." He said.

"Oh, well I can see now." Groco replied.

"Well, if everything is kosher I'll be going now." Spucket said.

"Yep, sure." Groco said and waved him off.

"Oh, ok then, see you on the flip, Oh, and one more thing. These are amulets which all Pythagoreans wear. Here are three of them for the three of you. It's for you to be able to reach the kingdom of Gebelin. When you time travel put them on." Spucket hands one to each of the three Guildies.

"Now Tiff, let me tell you a little story." Spucket said.

"Yeah, sure, shoot." Tiff said in glee.

"Well, I got this story from a Hopi Indian. It deals with automotomayhems. It is an artifice robot which responds to technology. Decades from now a group of Scientist get together to build the perfect model of the universe starting with the big bang. They were successful and found a planet like ours in the program and humans occupied it. Just like our own planet. They were able to fast forward and rewind any moment of the planet in simulation. What they found was hundreds of years into the future say 2500 or 3000 A.D. they found the birth of God. The programs and God melted with each other and exploded. God knew he was just a program and wanted to come out to our world. Leaving us here on Earth with these little robots called automotomayhems. These little robots became helpers and reacted to technology. They say if you're not sure of a piece of technology, and then say, "Automotomayhem" then they will help you figure it out. They are like the words in syntax. Each word is a robot of the automotomayhem's." Spucket said.

"That's a wonderful tale. I'll think about that all night." Tiff said.

"I liked it." Amy said.

"Alright, Gals, I'll see you tomorrow." Spucket said.

Chapter 3

"The element reflects in the mind what the eloquence can be."

Chad Douglas Bulau, 2005

"Hello, Mona me, are you ready for the vacation I promised you?" Spucket asked compelling his voice with reinsurance.

Sara, Spucket's wife returns, "Yes, my little furry woodland animal."

Spucket gets close to her and grabs her in the ass. They have a very loving marriage. Spucket met her on a business trip when he was an Architect. They've been together ever since.

"How's the little one?" He asked.

"Fine." Sara said with a smile and felt the need to hurry to Europe.

"As soon as we're ready we'll head to the airport for our nine hour flight the Frankfurt, Germany." Spucket told her to settle her down.

"I'd like to go to Italy, honey." Sara said.

"After business is done, Sugar." Spucket said.

He checks on the little one.

"Fine by me." Sara said and then checks on the little one too.

"Little Scrupt, you will grow up so big and strong." Spucket said tickling Scrupt's stomach.

Amy and Tiff get off the elevator to Spucket's office.

"Are you Gal's ready?" Spucket asks in consideration.

He wanted Tiff to get the feel of Europe.

"Yes, and just where exactly are we going?" Amy asked.

She knew we were going to Europe, but where?

"Where we are going exactly is Cologne, Germany to fix connections. So let's get in the van and get going." Spucket said in some kind of glee.

The guildies made their scheduled flight on time. Spucket got the Germany military doctors on the phone and they said to give them a call once they are in Cologne.

Cologne is a mysterious and enchanting city. It is home to numerous wonderful churches and other old wondrous buildings.

"We'll meet the German military doctors somewhere downtown." Spucket said as Sara was driving the rental car from Frankfort to Cologne.

"Ichorplasm, do you Gals know what that stuff does?" Spucket asked the Gals in the back seat.

"Doesn't it help with breathing?" Tiff answered.

"It's exactly what it does in the right proportions. It heals just about anything. Some people will end up dead if we don't close the deal. The doctors want money, tons of it. We'll be able to supply our customers, but we won't see much of a profit anytime soon." Spucket filled in the Gals.

"The doctors want to be reinsured that we can keep things under wraps." Spucket said.

He and the guildies made it to the Hotel then unpacked their bags. Spucket had the Germany military doctors on the phone.

"Yeah, we will be able to make the sermon." Spucket said and then hung up the phone.

"Alright, Gals, the doctors want us to meet them at the church down the street at noon today. That's in a few hours, my friends. Hey, how about brunch at the pub down the block?" Spucket asked.

"Yes, honey, sounds good to me." Sara said.

"It's fine with the both of us." Amy said.

The guildies went down to take the rental car to the pub. They sat down for soft boiled eggs, brotchen, bacon and milk that comes in a small box. Amy was taken back by the round scissor like contraption that opened the top of the soft boiled eggs. Spucket had already visited Cologne on business trips.

"I love this European feeling." Tiff said.

It was almost noon and the guildies then headed to the church.

The Church was enormous, and beautiful. It had numerous rows of benches and the ceiling was so high one would think you were inside the Empire States Building with the insides taken out of it. The stain glass windows and statues brought a wonderful and colorful benevolent feeling to the place. With an alter up front with all the gold and candles made the place rich and glorious.

"Ah, ha, there they are." Spucket said to the Gals.

A couple of doctors standing up front waved as they saw the little man.

"Oh ow, I see part of Kryull's gang up front. Keep a close eye on them, Gals." Spucket said and headed toward the doctors.

"I don't like the looks of this." Sara said to the Gals.

The doctors were with two soldier guards. They walked up to Spucket and gave them their demands. They asked that the guild kept it all quiet and honored their friendship. Spucket told them our operation is quiet and how much their service is needed. Spucket also told them how they transport things over seas.

"Once our satellite is in space we can teleport items right over the entire world. We got a unit here that hides the ichorplasm in a dimension . . ." Bam! Bam! Bam! Kryull's gang opens fire killing Spucket and his wife, Sara.

The Gals screamed in nonbelief. Some of the doctors were injured and the Gals were safe. Kryull's gang fled the scene. The Gals left the little one behind as the Authorities spoon arrived. The Agency took care of the place and as far as the little one the Father of the church said that he would deal with him. The Agency took special notice to Spucket's mechanical eye. A Sister directed by the Father of the church took the child to an orphanage. Knowing both parents were murdered in the gun fight they thought it was the best thing that they could do.

The next couple of years were ugly gang torments between the Kryull gang and Kluse guild. The Kluse guild using their technology singled out all of Kryull's gang at their homes. They would teleport in and threaten them while under cloak. Throwing things around and shaking their beds saying, "Get out of the gang, or you'll end up dead!" After this no one has seen the Kryull's gang.

Kryull was a Euro gang mainly in Cologne and Frankfurt, Germany. We recruited people from all over Europe. It was a major mishap to lose Spucket and Sara, but it only made the guild stronger. The Kryull's gang is now nonexistent. The Kluse guildies numbered in the 1500's now. Amy and Groco got married and are now the heads of the guild.

Tiffany, as she loved to learn was later setup as the guild school teacher. The school was for the guild only. She taught the guild etiquette of magic and technology. The guildies learned Ledger main, Eloquence and Agriculture. It outdated the main stream school and settled down to be more or less at an elite school. The guildies were trained to eventually be on their own. From inventing to doloring the guildies were educated to be the best. That took evidence of the globes above our heads. Where we would identify the address of the perceptions. The guildies all shared the same perception as they learned mind sets of the tetraktys in an adumbrate. All of this was for the purpose of inventing. To make life simple enough to study the sophistry and get them to a level the I.P.O.'s could take. Those few that wanted more then that went to the Morocco guild where there is no limit to what one can invent.

Some of the guildies went to Universities for more schooling. Groco had connections at many of the Universities. The little guildies were just amazing. No one was stupid and they didn't carry their wit so far to look more intelligent. With the etiquette the guildies learned how to channel their thought's and perceive what's going to happen before it does. They could mind read in other words. The guildies learned a very unique lore of magic and technology and vice versa was the main ideology to the lessons. How was magic and how was technology? Then putting them both together in a phenomenon of the serendipity into a narrative that they could them share their discoveries with the guild. Spucket had the degrees of the guild pedagogy together years ago along with putting together new discoveries that the guildies and outside researchers had thrown together. What Spucket knew was this, all the newspapers and magazines had a public opening which shed darkness on exactly what was published. He knew they were for the masses of the public eye and that the connection he had in and out of the guild that he could privately create his own magazine and he did. It was mainly like a zine, and mostly for the guild. Spucket's loss was great. It threw the guilds progress behind ten years.

Now that Sara is gone, Cristy works on the magic side of the guild. Cristy has been in the guild longer than Tiffany and both parents are in the guild, Douglas and Veronica. In magic the foundation of the guild etiquette, Ledger main is the intuition of the guildies. It shows what the mind can do. Ledger main is a line of the senses that can be delineated and received as a reading. The guildies learned that coordinating the eyes, ears and hand's gives them the abilities to perceive what the importance is in existence. (See Figure 9)

The guildies learn reasoning through three characters. They reasoned from a Sophist, to a Philosopher to a Statesman. The Statesman recollects the element in principle for the use in society and the state of it in existence in Laws and theories. Showing the information and properties of them to be experimented until facts can be drawn. He reflects on the trade of the element and makes evident it's uses and worth in weight. The Sophist plays with words and classes and the meaning thereof in study of syntax and lexicography. He puts into characters of man on the letter. He holds them up to the universe and testing them for there purpose. He plays and forms games with words. He is a joker, a trickster, though he is very truthful and honest about them putting them into use as an artifice. He's always leading things in the right way. He knows the human condition and tries to orate in rhetoric the perfect state of mankind. A Sophist is a word alchemist that puts the words to the test. The Philosopher gathers the whole stories made by classes making up a story of his own to be written down or orated to people or students. He runs through books and listens to orations to get the full picture. In return his information is made for other students or teachers to learn from in the likes of Philosophy. The guildies had to learn the abilities of these three classes and took their time renouncing them as they explored the characters. They watched before their own minds as the globes changed with the change of idea. The tetraktys kept the guildies aware of other minds in their thinking. This was necessary in renouncing subjects as they learned how to use the globes above our heads.

Tiffany gives the class a lecture.

"We all accept fact easily in its theories. People are like cattle and will eat anything we give

(Figure 9)

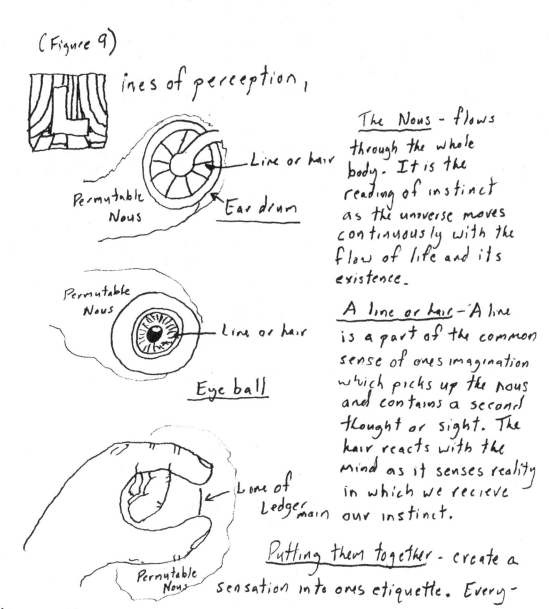

Lines of perception,

Permutable Nous

Line or hair

Ear drum

The Nous - flows through the whole body. It is the reading of instinct as the universe moves continuously with the flow of life and its existence.

Permutable Nous

Line or hair

Eye ball

A line or hair - A line is a part of the common sense of ones imagination which picks up the nous and contains a second thought or sight. The hair reacts with the mind as it senses reality in which we recieve our instinct.

Line of Ledgermain

Permutable Nous

Putting them together - create a sensation into ones etiquette. Everything one holds with their sensory is their genus.

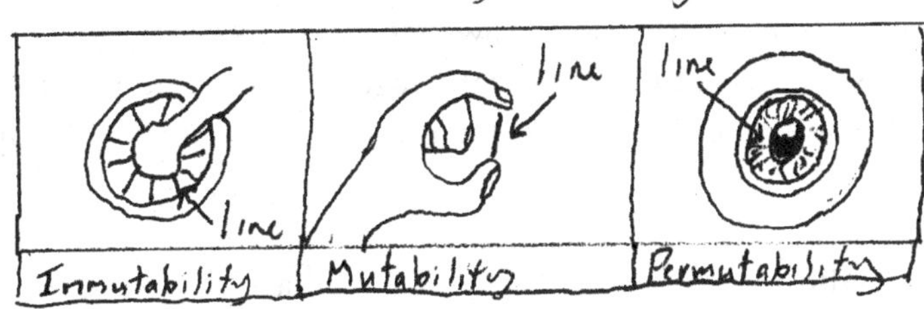

them. The Governments and Rulers throughout history have all laid eclectic Laws that people follow in precepts. The eclectic Law is just like God's Ten Commandments, a very favored Law. Everyone would remain happy if we all could just follow one eclectic Law. There are hundreds of thousands of Deities, God's and Goddesses. There is one sect the believes that every one of their followers is a God. Worship is essential to faith. Renouncing to different Deities can be interesting. Usually an eclectic Law is universal in principle, some are very secular though. Class, I want you to learn the eclectic Law on a monocracy level showing monadology which you alone are the only one in the universe. Just like a mindset, monocracy is you alone, absolutely you. Where we are a finite state of a human being. Knowing exactly who you are and what you're capable of in the universe. Then I want you to consider monogon showing self-denial as if one had disappeared completely." Tiffany lectured.

She explained to the class that with monocracy the guildies would be able to find their own life force and reminisce through the eclectic Laws and imbibe the characters into mana from their readings and keep them in protection for future use . . . . And then to simply non-exist. This energy is your own as your life force makes a reflection a muse as you project your intuition to seek the truth. Just because we give something a name doesn't mean we understand it completely. Our magic's make up the globes above our heads. With it we begin to unfold the truth." Tiffany told the class.

The Pythagoreans were the first to wonder about the globes in a study. They categorized anything they could into globes. The Mathematician Pythagoras turned the globes into these dimensions of mathematics into this tetraktys. (See Figure 10)

Pythagoras later created with his discovery a school. They studied the mind and how things came together when comparing it to the tetraktys. Using the tetraktys they became more and more aware of how things worked and how things should and will eventually work. Though not many knew the tetraktys and it still remains with an odd few individuals including the Kluse guild. Who knows what would happen if the entire world uses it.

The antiquity studied the art of civilization and worked more for a model of man that everyone would like. Finding a name for the new art was up to the artist and what did they have as a reference? Did they have an alphabet? They must have had a system or measure of some sort. Finding the absurdity of this place and giving it a name is more of a given now days as we have atrocious vocabularies developed over ten thousand years. The words fit more than they did in antiquity. Yet, why do we call the sky, the sky? How was it put into our intellect and made an axiom that everyone believes? We have a myriad of languages. Why would you then want to stick to our language? Faith? The only one that can decide is you. The English language is known to most of the world.

We used to weigh everything in the weight of gold. We have done so for millenniums. It was a King's way of power that made the gold so rich. He wanted it and so did his people in the likes and the people after that. He sat there reining to value of gold was worth. He could change it too and in return everything else changed with it. The weight varied from kingdom to kingdom. How could we revamp the weight of gold today? Gems and other precious items were also weighed in the weight of gold. Through

(Figure 10)

Tetraktys,

The Mathematician Pythagora's turned the globes into this formation.

Pythagora's thought "ONE" The first.

The one was the whole absolute universe. He then drew the next number "TWO" and put it below the "ONE" dot.

"ONE"
"TWO"

1, 2, 3 Trinity

This divided the universe into the second dimension. He went on to the third dimension "THREE" below the "TWO".

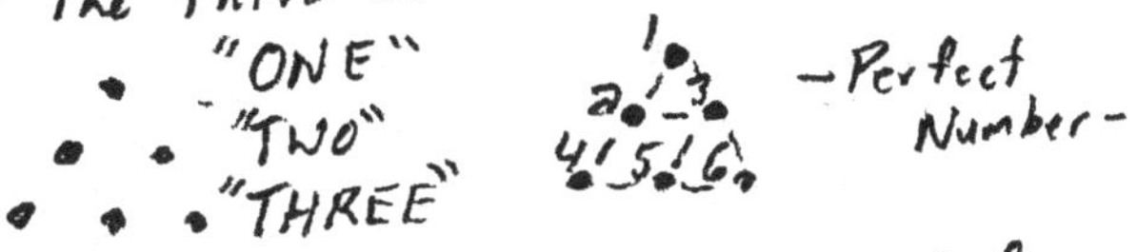

"ONE"
"TWO"
"THREE"

1, 2, 3, 4, 5, 6 —Perfect Number—

He then put the last dimension to the artifice the "FOUR" below the "THREE"

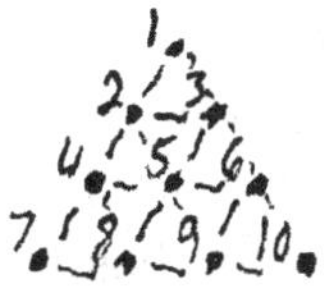

1, 2, 3, 4, 5, 6, 7, 8, 9, 10

"ONE"
"TWO"
"THREE"
"FOUR"

The Tetraktys

This he called the tetraktys.

karats. You can look at anything in the weight of gold and find its worth. Yet how precious is the yellow metal? The guildies learned how to value pieces of intellect in this way. Today America measures the value on paper tender they were on the weight of gold earlier though.

The King's are not done with their handy work even today. In each economic, moral and political era we will culture the change in the language, yet the King's and mainly antiquity still back then used words as we do now. The word gold has a long history. Sure we have a different way of culture and new politics and ideas. Yet the foundation hasn't changed much over the millenniums. We still call this place the Earth. The word works in the same light as the weight of gold. It's very valuable when it come to perception and performance. When we want to find the weight of a word you have to weight it in importance of prudence. Taking it and holding it as you reminisce it through everything else. The word is the light to the performance as it points with ones intelligence. What do we find more valuable the gold or the word?

We have our tools that everyone should use, but everybody doesn't know how to use them. Bias are really sad and very funny at times. The eclectic Laws are tools. The Ten Commandments, The Bill of Rights. The alphabet and its rules is the most powerful. One has to clearly imagine the rudiments of them. The alphabet is how we spell out words. Not everyone references to the alphabet when one thinks or speaks. It is a world of wonder and maybe the world's greatest achievement. Notating a sentence has its rules and the rules have an importance. These are not Japan's rules. We belong to a finite free society of America where the human condition is full of inhibitions. No matter how we try we can't break free from the universe so why not try and join it through interpretation and address.

With the eight sections of grammar we have rules of sentence structure. All eight are assigned to different words in different times of importance. The guildies use a cipher to better understand the sections. (See Figure 11)

One would take a word in the center and run it pass on by one of the eight other words to see what one would reflect by doing so. It's important for the guildies to master this so they can get a better savvy in the schematics and writings. These sections play a part in defining a piece of intellect or in art to get the essential dimensions in order to correctly label the absurdities of art verse by verse.

The class was taught transplanting onto paper and into the imagination to understand the omniscience of metaphysical matter and intellect. They put information in composer to give a reflection. Tiff taught that a blank page was an invitation for our projections of the imagination. Thinking before the intuition of the pencil was key to the guildies method. The putting all the transplants together was a matter of farming the images allegorically. (See Figure 12)

The magic was and old art, not practiced by anyone, but the Kluse guild. Spucket put it together years before he was killed. The first to be learned of magic's is Ledger main. It is controlled by the intuition of the hand, eyes and ears. It could summon up anything one had the mind to do in thought. The guildies would draw a box with Ledger main as Kleromancy goes. (Divination of lots) Then organize

(Figure 11)

Ciphers,

A cipher is a diagram to help define and understand a word in comparing it to other words. One starts by picking a word and adding eight other words to it in a circle. One can find in a cipher a whole new world to play with in ciphering them.

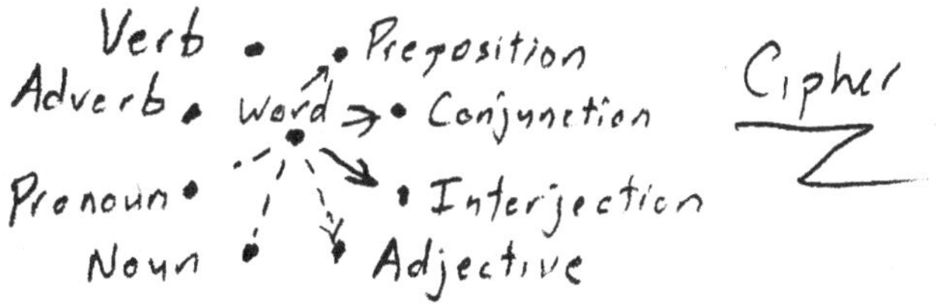

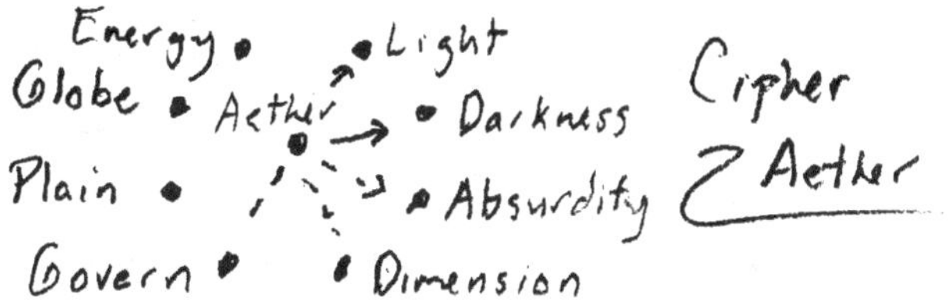

In ciphering the aether we first consider the light, then the darkness and so on. One wants to develop a mental picture for each cipher. In doing so one develops ones ability to define words. The whole guild knows how to cipher.

One can redefine any type of cipher. We basically consider in this one eight dots.

(Figure 12)

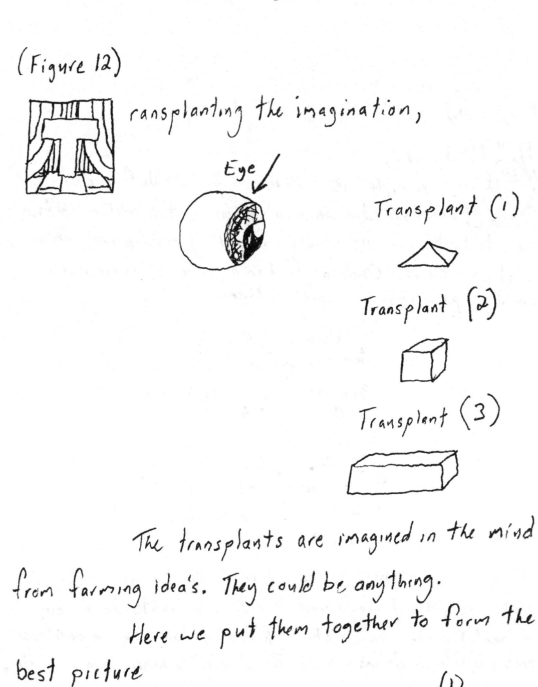

Transplanting the imagination,

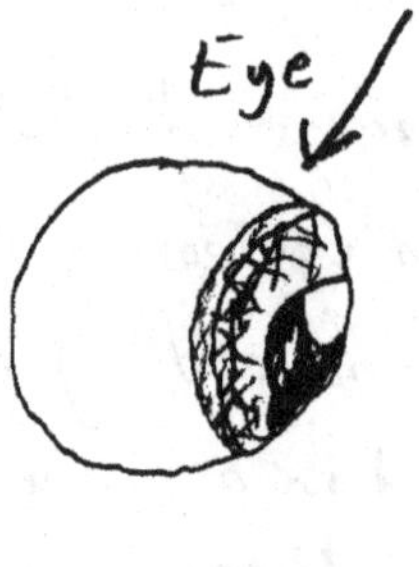

Eye

Transplant (1)

Transplant (2)

Transplant (3)

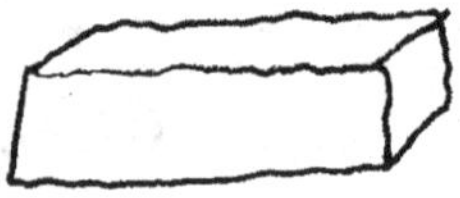

The transplants are imagined in the mind from farming idea's. They could be anything.

Here we put them together to form the best picture

The best Picture

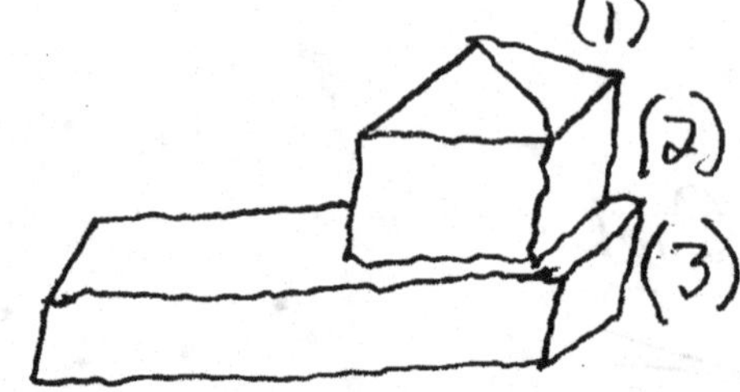

the box into a building or room and put into it objects of the desired objective. (See Figure 13) The objects that move into the box are by the Eloquence such as a govern and the elements the object is made out of is the Agriculture such as any material. The Eloquence can make the object come to you with a draw of Ledger main. Your resolution is based off the perception of the Agriculture. One can make it picture perfect as it had to be in a schematic when turning it into the guild computer. The nominal is just behind the surface of Agriculture. The Phenomenal is where the objects come together and the reality is a combination of the nominal and phenomenal. The consciousness is Earth, Water, Fire, and Air. That means that the mind uses the affinities of all four magic's to make one consciousness. One has to understand the tetraktys. (See Figure 14) When guildies reach a certain level all they do is go through thought. At times nobody has time to talk unless it is very important. The guildies communicate through trading the metaphysics of existences itself. We are able to create precepts to be a wedge into comprehensible communications. At some levels being able to know what's going on with the guildies in another room or outside for instance. As we grow, the guildies will keep vamping and revamping the innovations and inventions of technology and magic.

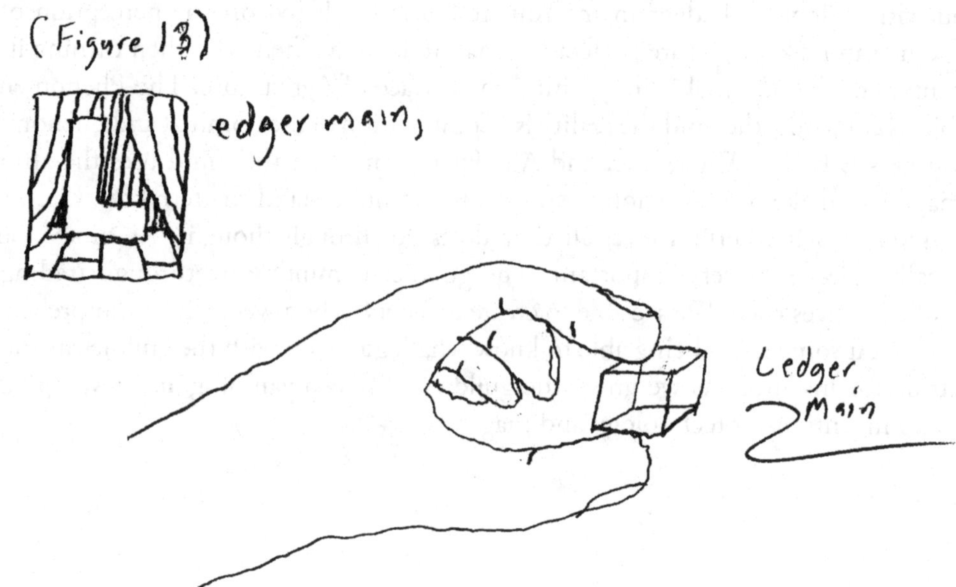

The energy of the hand from the mind can summon any object one has unfolded and carefully studied. Thinking with ones hand opens the mind to better apprehension of ideas.

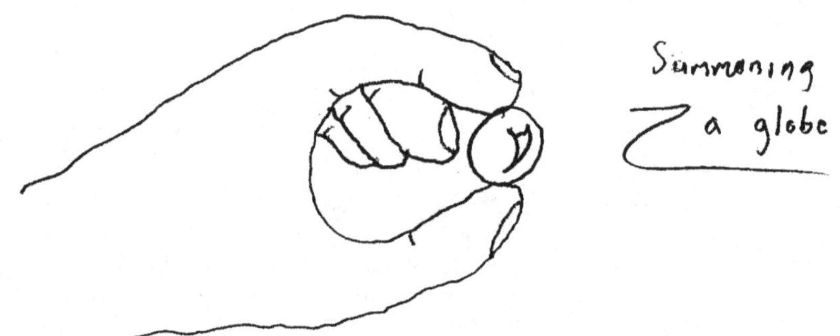

The mind is capable of any thing and one can have one thing in mind and another thing in ledger main. The guildies use three different magics in their etiquette. Ledger main, Eloquence, and Agriculture.

(Figure 14)

The globes of the tetraktys,

Plenum

The globes of the tetraktys all come into one globe, a plenum.

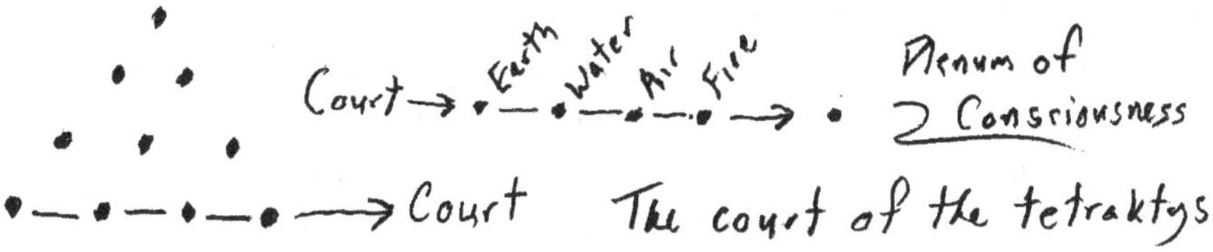

Court → Earth Water Air Fire → Plenum of Consciousness

Court

The court of the tetraktys figures Earth, Water, Air, Fire into a plenum.

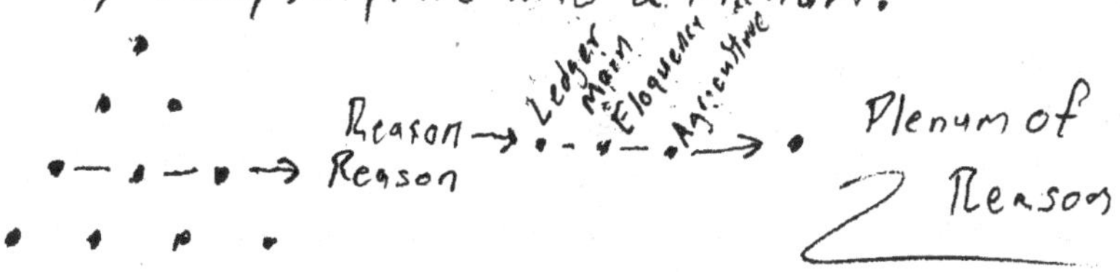

Reason → Ledger Main Eloquence Agriculture → Plenum of Reason

Reason

The guildies memorize the Reason plenum and define their own meaning behind it as individuals in their development.

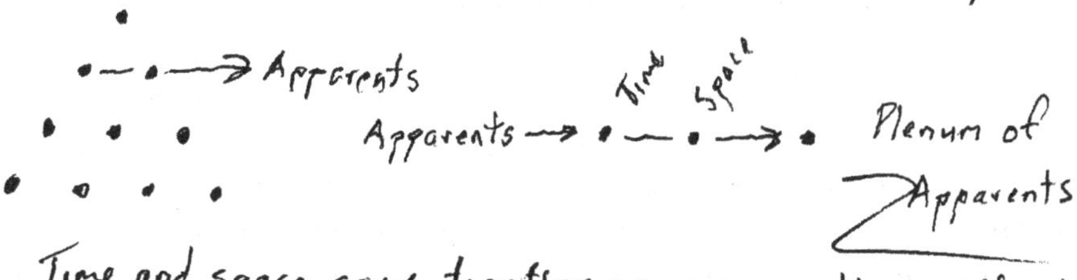

Apparents

Apparents → Time Space → Plenum of Apparents

Time and space come together as one as the guildy has sited a place in its plenum.

The whole tetraktys comes together as one to better understand the effects of absurdity.

Chapter 4

"Liberty is a synonym for importance."

Chad Douglas Bulau, 2007

The school taught one more thing at the guild. It was about these ten little dots in a pyramid in formation called the tetraktys. (See Figure 15)

To begin the guildies would relate the tetraktys to the universe. All ten dots starting from one (Creation) to the tenth (Deity). The tetraktys was in the form of a latter dealing with things of man's perception of the universe. The guildies then would have to make their own version of the tetraktys or adopt one that already exists. They would study from tetraktys that already made the mark of the teacher or guide. The permutations of the tetraktys are passed the google in number. To the advanced guildies it represents the latter's of the globes above our heads. The tetraktys was used to figure out complex and sophist problems. The guildies have a book called the Kluse Guild Magic book written by Spucket Knostic. The book was made of the creation of existence from the beginning of time to now the digital age where a dot represents the universe. Spucket made fun of the digital age saying that the next age was going to be the Pillage. Because everyone will sooner or later be on pills. (Pill-age). The book had a finite description of what the inventor's mind and functions could be in the absurdity of the universe. A lot like the guilds etiquette it shows exercises and questions. It addresses powers and peace that the element gives. It shows Intellect and intelligence of ones mental capabilities. We find the existence and non-existence in functions of the mind within realization. It also went through a few of the tetraktys and the guild magic and technology. It gave examples of guild artifices too.

The tetraktys can and is used in a congruent way. Meaning it all together holds one meaning. Once one understands the tetraktys as a whole one can figure it as one idea. It's the way of stopping or breaking a spell. One spells out an idea and can stop it by returning to the congruent tetraktys. This also works with imagining the alphabet as a whole. In the tetraktys the whole universe is congruent, but is only a representation of it not the sure thing. It is only a pinhead with the idea of the universe on it. The universe is absolute in some cases, but the guildies have to first establish the true facts to define their imagination in the form of it to get the full effect.

There is a perception made for the tetraktys which takes four dimensions from the side of it called the sections. The Subject (1), The Apparent (2), The Reason (3), and The Court (4).

(Figure 15)

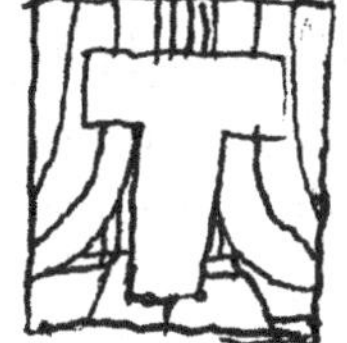
he tetraktys

Also known as the universe. The Pythagorean's and guildies use this to study everything. It organizes the globes above our head's into a greater or lessor understanding. It's the basis of a matrix and our perception. It is the scientific principle of our thought process.

The Subject is the first dimension. Where the subject could be anything in the universe. The Apparent is the second dimension where time and space is created and the size is organized between two dimensions to seek and produce the body of the apparents. The third dimension is the Reason where the guildies size up the imagination of the universe at a conjunction. Meaning it is the first surface one may reflect things apon. Socrates said that the surface is made up of tiny triangles. The guildies use Reason reflecting on its surface to fuel the imagination. The Court is the fourth dimension and is the second surface. The guildies develop their consciousness in this surface, an adumbrate in the likes. This dimension brings four things together to equal a stable consciousness.

The guildies used the four sections to understand the language and its function of thought. The first section is the Subject and the guildies use it with the understanding of the tetraktys as a whole. The grid (See Figure 16) made it easier to use. The 16 dots have the capacity of 16 subjects. With a set of the general tetraktys the Subject was in the form that the guildies could savvy within it. The general tetraktys fits the appeals of any Subject. It explains in the Court the four general classes. Math, Science, English, and History. It has in Reason, a trinity of Intuition, Safety and Intelligence. It has in Apparents, the Latter and the Importance. To give the guildies a form to think with in an adumbrate. (See Figure 17)

At the Court, the English, Math, Science, and History make up the consciousness. The guildies would meditate on it to better understand the language and how things worked in the scholastics of our time.

The guildies would have to know much about the classes to be able to define them together into the consciousness. The more they knew the greater the outcome. They would spin a lexicon of boxes in their minds. With each practice comes a better illusion in the likes.

The guildies would pick a tetraktys as a tool to perform with in the universe showing prudence of the nominal in the words of the tetraktys. The globe that can itself be changed into anything that holds itself as the globe after the guildies were through with the search so one just has a globe left as their imaginations. It just turned out to be more peaceful this way as the globe was at rest until the next permutation. The guildies would hold the tetraktys in consciousness and learned from each search. (See Figure 18)

The tetraktys is basically the rule of perception. There are more tetraktys than we can count. You can have more than one tetraktys at the same time. The catch is that the guildies have to carefully take the time to unfold and define Subjects into tetraktys.

"There is no hurry, Class." Tiff told the guildies.

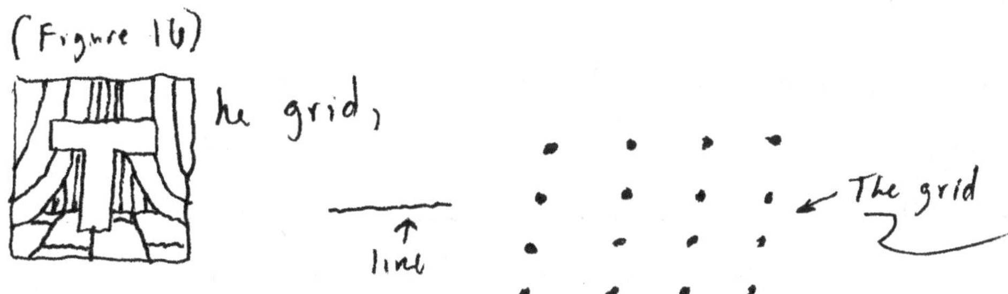

The subjects act together as a grid and line shown here. The grid is the organization skills of a guildy. The guildy uses a line to channel through them. Cordmating line and subject through the grid is an artform.

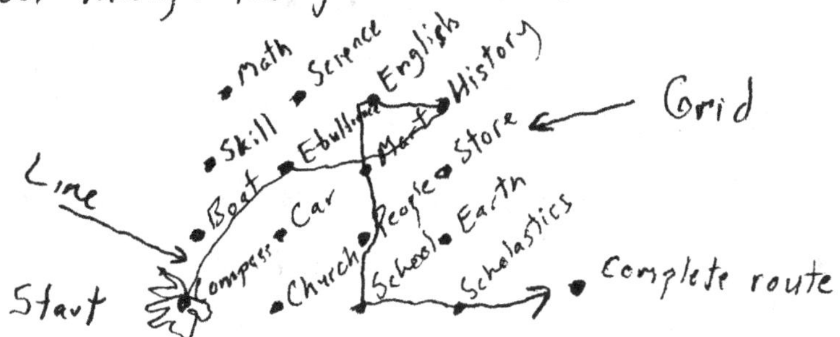

To start this grid one got dirrection from a compass, reached ebullience, added things in mart, looked into History and English, added things in mart, ran into some people, went to school, thought of the scholastics and ended.

The grid is a solid memory. Every thing in it deals with a tangable imagination in a solution. The guildy has to develop here resolution of memory.

(Figure 14)

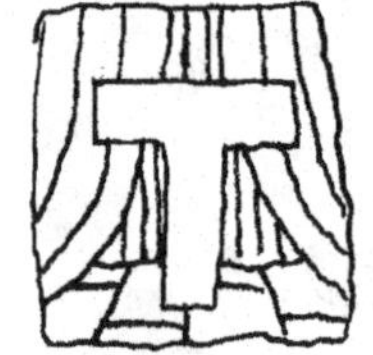

he dimensions of the tetraktys,

1 ——— • ——— Subject
2 ——— • — • ——— Apparent
3 —— • — • — • —— Reason
4 — • — • — • — • — Court

There is four sections of the tetraktys and ten dimensions inside it. The dimensions are labeled Subject, Apparent, Reason and Court. The ten dimensions can be labeled anything and are here labeled with numbers.

All the dimensions of the tetraktys equal one and are congruent to each other. The tetraktys is combined into one dimension as defined by ones likes. It is what the guildies call (Globe making) and can become a very delicate form of art. This is a tool for all Pythagoreans.

This tool is figure for everything known. The absence of it lies in everything unknown.

(Figure 18)

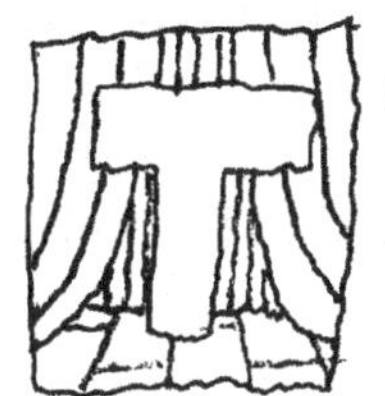

he general tetraktys,

1 — Subject
2 — Apparent
3 — Reason
4 — Court

Universe
Importance Latter
Intelligence Safety Intuition
History English Science Math

The general tetraktys gives the guidies the etiquette for one to see eye to eye. It's subject (The universe) is the first dimension.

Universe → First dimension
Importance Latter → Second dimension
Intelligence Safety Intuition → Third dimension
Math Science English History → Forth dimension
Omniscience

The guildy looks at it all together and conjects in study when it is divided into a tetraktys.

The guildies generalize things with this artifice to associate the scholastics of the lexicon..

The guildies were about thirty in number in the class ranging from the age of 7 to 20.

"A globe can be anything. It looks like a dot on paper now, but in a few years with study you will learn to use dots as globes. Class, the globes are like this world, an enigma or unfinished model. One has to understand the Cosmos to find a way the globes are formed. For now we must understand the universes absurdities." Tiffany told the class and brought to their attention the five humors of absurdity. (See Figure 19)

"Each dot has its own dimension. Every word or character of the rudiments holds a dimension and therefore the dot is a globe." Tiffany said about the humors.

"Take the five humors and hold them up individually to the latter's of the universe namely Earth. (Collect what the word actually means to Earth.) Farce, is the first of the humors. So the guildies would consider what farce meant to the world is in whatever the fact in point. In doing the same with the other four we start to learn the dimensions of absurdity. This is the way we define things in this place. Where one considers their own definitions and perceptions as the imagination is defined forming thoughts that haven't been made before in an unknown basis. Farce is the falsehood of the language. It captures things that are not true. Nature is the immutable forces which the Earth has evolved into including the human condition. Reality is a place of virtues, laws and place of right and wrong. We base our morals on what has happened in reality mainly from history of mankind. Astronomy is the galaxies, stars, planets, moons, comets, asteroids, and the space of the heavens. It is in our view today that no one owns outer space, no one really knows what is up there. God is all the dimensions held in the view of the alphabet. We can only approach God, we can not reach him or be him. God is the perfect performance of all dimensions. The universe is his home." Tiffany explained to the class.

There were pencils in class with erasers to delete the marks on paper. An essential thing that all class rooms have today in juxtaposition to the tools used earlier in times. Tiff taught that the imagination erased the imagination. Prote Hyle and Ih, Kih . . . Where these doubles moved with the psyches. As an eraser met with a page, the imagination met to erase the imagination to erase it. She gave them a clue that they should imagine an eraser when clearing the imagination.

"When you start putting globes together in pairs or more one realizes their affinities. In dualism a pair reacts in an apparent, vice, paradox or matrix. This brings on information from the reactions of the instance of juxtaposition. Say one did the math on paper as to compare two globes together to do a little thinking in comparison. Like this." Tiffany instructed the class and showed them this on paper. (See Figure 20)

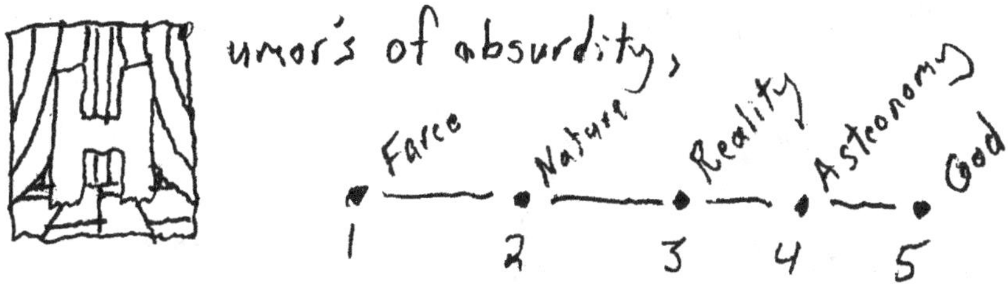

The humors are five perceptions the guildies use to determine the truth or validality of a fact or word in the language in a lexicon. The guildy would first find out if it is true considering the "Farce." Then the guildy would find how it adds up to "Nature." One would find its importance in all the humors. In "Reality" one would base it off of the place and where one lives. "Astronomy" one would find how it is in the universe. In "God" the guildy would consider it in the language one uses.

With this idea the guildy really can elaborate on the subject and get something down in a study. With all of them solved one has a better sense of being and the start of a nous.

One can even us the humors in a cipher.

God •   • Farce

Humors •

Astronomy •

• Nature

• Reality

(Figure 20)

Affinities of globes,

Public • Private •

One needs to identify with each individual globe and then compare it to the other globes in the universe.

Light • Darkness •

Hot • Cold •

Dry • Wet •

Man • Woman •

One need to draw and elaborate a conclusion to add to their metaphysics. The idea is to get the best understanding with the globes conditions.

Happy • Sad •

Sane • Insane •

Mind • Imagination •

Induction • Deduction •

"One gathers the information of two globes learning the differences as one would compare them to everything in the universe to find their places. One starts to identify problems and draws them out to a conclusion on paper to lead them in the right way. All by using the universal tool the tetraktys. The great thing is that these dots have been greatly used throughout time in creating the language. Consider the regular period mark of punctuation. It's at the end of a sentence. Class, it is also the first dimension. When you read try and lead your eyes into a period from the first character in the sentence. It is here we develop the energy into a syntax and our mind gets an idea of what was written." Tiff said as she taught the class.

The tetraktys is what was used sometime after Pythagoras first recognized it in 500 B.C. where he got it from the Indians of India. Spucket learned it in college. The tetraktys is Pythagorean." Tiffany told the class.

"What we want class is a globe for each word. We want a tetraktys for each word that is designed in the performance of man in the universe." Tiffany said as she held out a copy of the Kluse Guild Magic book.

She showed the class a few tetraktys to reference to in their study. The class was taught to take them each as a whole, organizing them into dimensions with the performance of the word. They matched up each dimension as the tetraktys organized their minds in the perception designed. The tetraktys made up of globes in the imagination where one could identify them with the element. (See Figure 21)

In the guildies mind at the start was a nominal globe. Meaning it holds no reality in the imagination, it is an undefined adumbrate. There is an immutable thought and with it one can hold things in the mind nominally. For us the imagination will never hurt us, because it is not real. By fact the globe is nonexistence in the likes. Just like a dot on paper it was unaffected by everything else, but a guildies ability to control their intuition and it is outside the normal mind.

The tetraktys has a common tetraktys that everyone goes by in the guild and it is the base to all our ideas. It is called the general tetraktys. (See Figure 22)

The general tetraktys stabled by the classes of Math, Science, English, and History gives the guildies a consciousness to work in and develop recognition. It shows the guildies Apparents over Importance and Latter. This gave a sense of timing. The guildies set in Reason the Intuition, Safety and Intelligence which gave them an imagination of quality to seek the best eclectic materialisms. The Subject the Universe to Tiffany was best described in the grid. (See Figure 23) The guildies were taught that the grid is best organized into 16 dots that made a square. The grid contained Subjects only. To use it the guildies chose the Subject for the cause of their research. The tetraktys sprung from the likes of grid.

(Figure 21)

he globes,

• Dot   ● Globe

The guildy learned the tetraktys in dots only to relearn them in the mind as globes. Perception is the key to the globes as the guildy had to imagine the infinite dimensions of space in the affinities. The guildies use their intuition to reflect thoughts recognizable to them in perception. The globe is made up of the reflection of the imagination. We also see them in reality as elements, moons, planets and stars.

Multiple globes in the mind, imagination and reality are without form. The guildies learned to use the tetraktys to find an order.

Tetraktys of Globes

A globe is void and without form until the guildy has defined it in their perception. However the globe is it is up to the knowledge or intellective of the guildy to determine the ability of the globe. Mind it with any word and define it.

(Figure 22)

The general tetraktys,

The common tetraktys the guildies in the guild use is certainly the most intellective form of the globes above our heads. It performs an etiquette that the guildies use as a tool in seeking the truth.

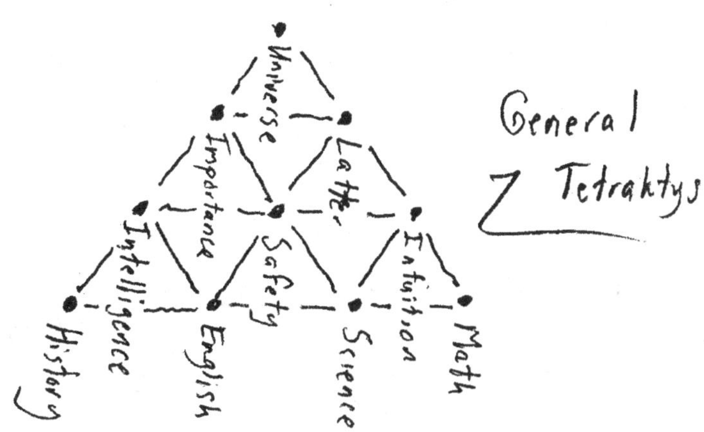

The general tetraktys uses the universe to find what the guildy wants by taking away the subject universe and channeling all the other intellect in ones nous the intellective.

The rest of the tetraktys opens up ones precepts to find a serendipity of what is in question.

(Figure 23)

Sections of the tetraktys,

1——•——Subject

The subject could be anything in the universe. Just as the other ten dimensions of the tetraktys.

2——•——•—— Apparent

The apparent is a matrix, paradox, or vice which reacts to the universe differently. These are our eyes.

3——•——•——•—— Reason

The reason is the place of thinking and imagining. It is considered an illusery surface in the imagination.

4——•——•——•——•—— Court

The court is the consciousness of the guildy. This is the place of the mind that both reality and intellective play in eloquence.

The sections are not always the same. The guildies juggle the sections around to make their own once they become advance enough. The tetraktys has an endless dimension starting from one, to infinity. It is here we find the unknown of the universe.

Meditation is the way to use the tetraktys. It stuck in the guildies mind, but the guildies had been taught many mind sets. Some don't involve the tetraktys, but artifices. The guildies used a lot of the times the alphabet and other universal symbols in their meditation.

The tetraktys has many functions to name and discover yet in the likes at least in our life time. Man is a class that Spucket said used the general tetraktys. A mathematician would set his tetraktys up quite a bit different then the general tetraktys. Functions other then the classes are such as time and durations that the tetraktys is a helpful tool to use. (See Figure 24)

Spucket left the guildies with the whole world to uncover. From start to finish the guild practiced an importance to their etiquette. The main goal of the guild was incorporated into the school. Make Something New!

"Consider time traveling, Class, as one could go any where. Visit whoever they wished. What would be the repercussions of your visit?" Tiffany asked the class.

There were forty-one students in class now. The class had ages ranging from 5 to 20. The class was taught their generals.

"With the effort of the class we will be working on a report that will go to Groco about the repercussions of time travel." Tiffany said about the objective.

"We have all the information we need in this workbook that Groco sized up." Tiffany said and handed each of the guildies one.

"It discusses the way space is and how tampering with the past can harm the future. The schematic of the ship and satellite are included. So if there's a loop hole or something you don't agree with, come tell me." Tiffany said.

"The universe is our address to something we have not been able to fully explain. No one knows exactly what is out there. What size it is. All we know is the things we can view from Earth. We named many of the stars and even some galaxies like our Milky Way. Where we can and can not survive, but we don't know exactly what's out there. The observable universe is 90 billion light years in diameter. At the center is Earth and where the light stops is 45 billion light years away in radius." Tiffany said and there was a long silence.

"The universe is our address for all the eclectic things we have been given name to in our absurdity. It means one verse. We only have at our intuitions of the mind in one verse at a time though many things can subsist with in it, it is the representation of the universe. The

(Figure 24)

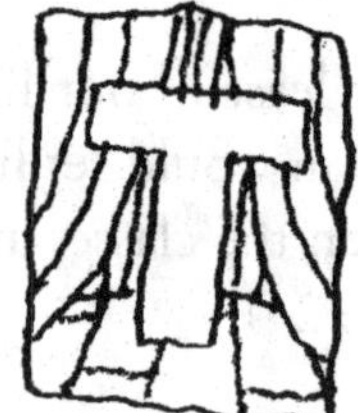

he tetraktys,

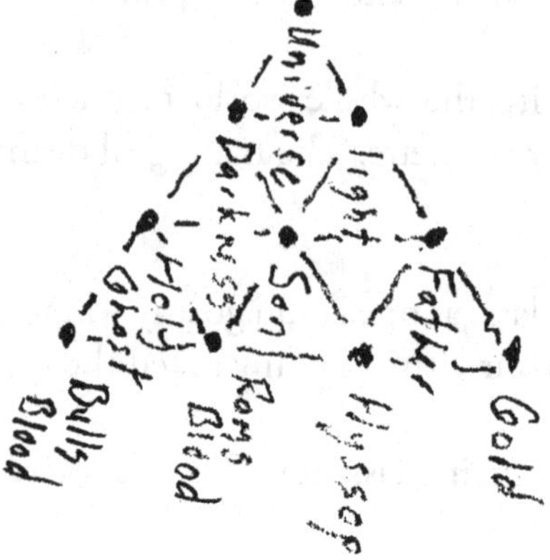

Christian Tetraktys

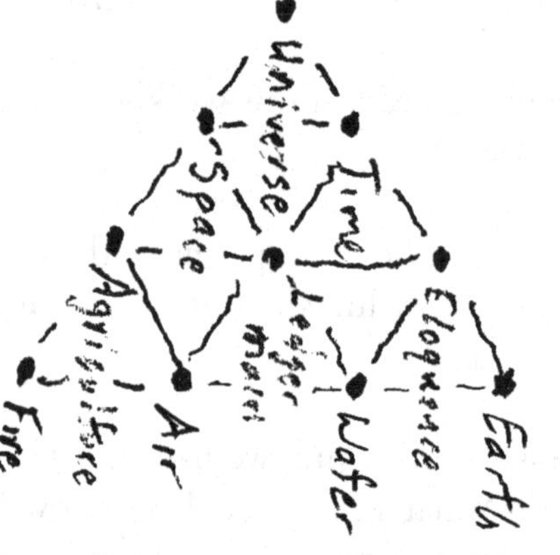

Magic Tetraktys

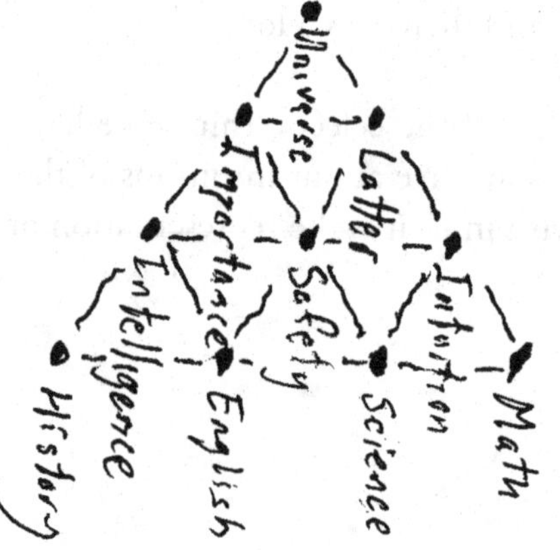

General Tetraktys

universe is the domain of everything in existence. When we say the word "You." We are reflecting on the verse of addressing the universe. The word "You." Can be looked at as any section of the eight sections of grammar. "You." Is unfolded as a pronoun usually, though at times it is better to consider it a noun-a person, place, or thing. "You." As a thing considers the entire universe of absurdity. As well as "You." As a place. "You." As a person considers a being. The idea is to identify or realize the ambiguousness of the language and maybe meet the mind with the word. We want to know everything about what "You."(The Universe) are doing so to ask "You." Of something is a reference to the big question, the about's of the universe. The Universities hold an eclectic schooling as degree's in one verse at a position. Where we earn our one verse, Bachelor's degree or Master's degree. We must consider things in one verse to the right finite state. The rules run down from the first line in importance." Tiffany said

"Our address is the universe." Cristy said to the class as she helped Tiffany with the teaching.

"Yes, Cristy, the address of who we are and where we come from is at the upmost importance. Geopolitically we are in the United States, but none of us live there. We live in a moral, cultural and economical era that finitely was defined by the human condition and inhibitions. We live on the additions and subtractions of trade. It took ten thousand years to bring the conditions to this point in time. Your address is how you feel about existence. The element we play with all has addresses including our intellect that one should get use to, to understand the humors. Class, we have addressed almost everything in this world. It's up to you to wit your nos in the absurdity of the intellect and materialism. Without addresses the world is absurdless. How would we get along without them?" Tiffany asked.

"Where are we exactly?" Cristy asked the class.

"We are in the universe of course. Yet the government wants us to fall into its kleromancy of establishment with all the other meatballs with all the hype. In the universe is where I want you and it's a matter of addressing. The cup is here, or the cup is here in the universe. Not some government vector of kleromancy in the States. The cup is on the table, in a room, in a house, in a city, in a state, in a country, in the world, though it's in the universe, the biggest address." Tiffany said to the class and dismissed them for the day.

Chapter 5

"Ha! What the hell was that?"

(Nato) Nathan Christensen, 1995

The Sister had taken the child to the orphanage. She could tell the child was an American. She travelled long and far too many places over the years. She knew her faces and places. The Father of the church knew the parents were dead and the Agency thought considering the case that it was the right thing to do. A little toy walrus with a name Ivory had a tag on it saying: To: Scrupt From: Spucket and Sara Knostic. It brought them to the conclusion that the little guys name was Scrupt Knostic. The Orphanage accepted the little guy and took him in and fed him.

Just two days later he was adopted by a monk by the name of Shawk Isadore as he was visiting the place to adopt a child to call his own.

"Where's the little guy form?" Shawk asked as he stood in the threshold of the office of the orphanage.

"He's from America. His parents were gunned down in a gang fight in a church by a loco gang a couple of days ago." The Host at the Orphanage said.

"What about the papers?" Shawk asked.

"Well, you can take the child and I'll work on getting the papers to you later. In the mean time keep the child safe and sound." The Host said and then went out of the office to a different room.

"I'll do just that." Shawk said and opened the door and was off to his home with the little one.

Shawk lived in a large house just on the outskirts of the city Cologne. He takes the baby home and has a trusted neighbor watch the child as he runs around getting provisions and preparations for the child's room. There was nothing Shawk wanted more than a great student. Father Isadore belonged to the church and wants to raise the child as a Pythagorean cause chances are and the way Isadore's church taught him to see the world, were going to need one.

The child looked perfect for the opportunity, Isadore thought. The little ones eye's gleamed with vivacity when Shawk was near him.

"Yes, little one, you're perfect." Isadore said in a soft smiling voice.

"Here's your bottle little one sleep tight." Isadore said and started reading to the child prayers out of a book.

Shawk read to him every night since. Book's of all kinds' Religious, History, Science and children books. Even fictional writes. He read him books that Shawk had the time to put together himself. Scrap books that he made to enhance the child's learning. Isadore gave great attention in creating the child's room. He decorated his room with prints of the greats, Degas, Michelangelo, Picasso, Pozzo and paintings of inspiration of love and hope.

Isadore had a small fortune and did the best he could to teach the child. The ways of the Pythagorean was developed into his toys for the child. The toys were just phenomenal. A poster with a large dot on the wall to develop little Scrupt's focus of the monad (The First Dimension) which Scrupt stared at and used his toy's to better understand his mind and globes above our heads. He made balls that were made in the forms of the planets, sun and moons of the solar system. Isadore taught that these balls are the globes above our heads. He also made ten black balls the size of marbles that he considered the tetraktys to the universe. To begin to understand how the universe worked and how time and space developed in these artifices. Isadore made Scrupt an old Pythagorean tool called the Tyriad. (See Figure 25)

The tyriad started his meaning of existence of time and space. The tyriad is a tool that expanse the view of time and space into 19 dimensions. It shows the past, present, and future to unfold the very existence of the universe in a point which has been chosen by the student or user. The tool takes some looking into before it can be used and savvied. Until the user or student understands the philosophy behind it, it looks like a bow tie. The globes are named form the universe in a point in time and space and added from the flow of time from the future to the past. (See Figure 26)

Father Isadore taught Scrupt the story of evolution. That we live in several mind sets of matrices, paradoxes, apparents and vices of absurdity. He taught Math, Science, English and History to get him prepared and to understand these mind sets. One matrix he taught was that man is an invention that the elements came together to create him and the environment. That he himself had been made by God.

"The element, my boy, is you and you are the universe." Shawk gave notice to Scrupt.

He said that the mind is one with the element. That his mind reflected the element in reason where one could take things into recognition in the consciousness. He had Scrupt learn the Periodic table of Elements. He was taught that everything in the universe was made of the element.

(Figure 25)

he tyriad,

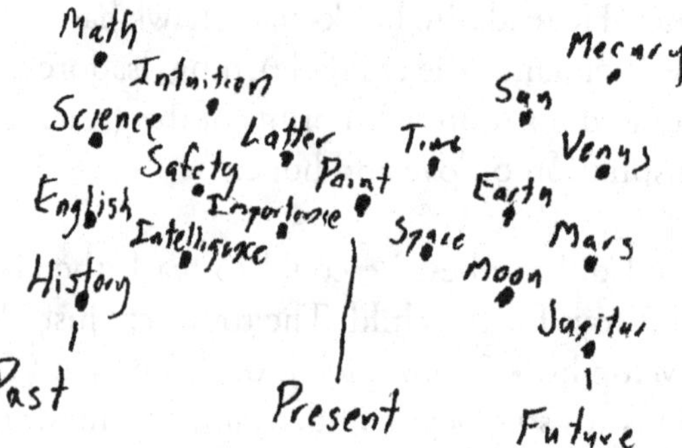

Flow of time

The tyriad is a artifice that deals with time and duration and can be used to manipulate matter magically. Here it has the general tetraktys in the past and the first part of the solar system in the future. The present is the point of existence.

The tyriad tells the guildy that we have a consciousness of the past and future. With a little intuition the guildy can view the past and future of existence.

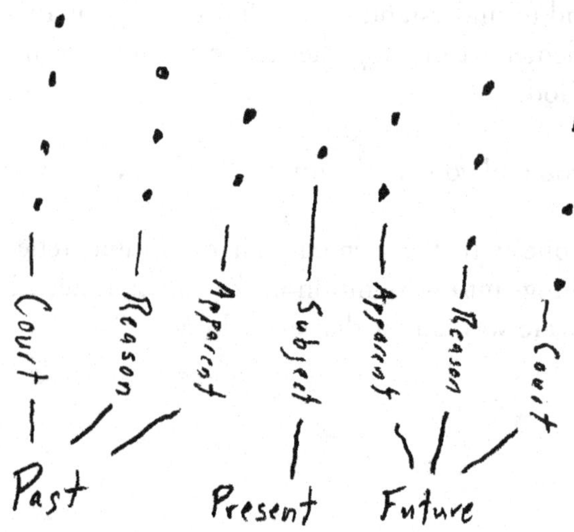

(Figure 26)

he tyriad of the eye,

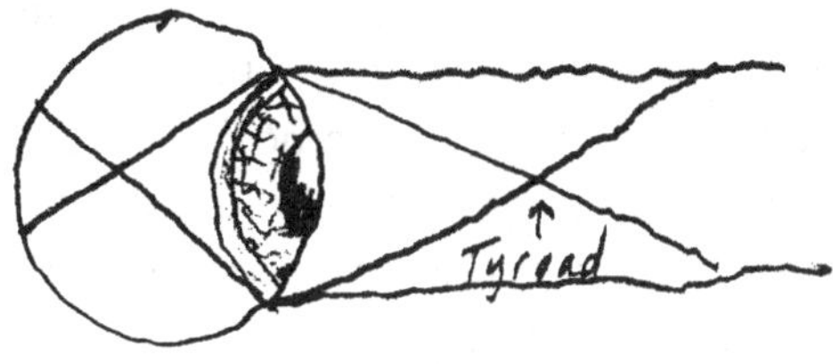

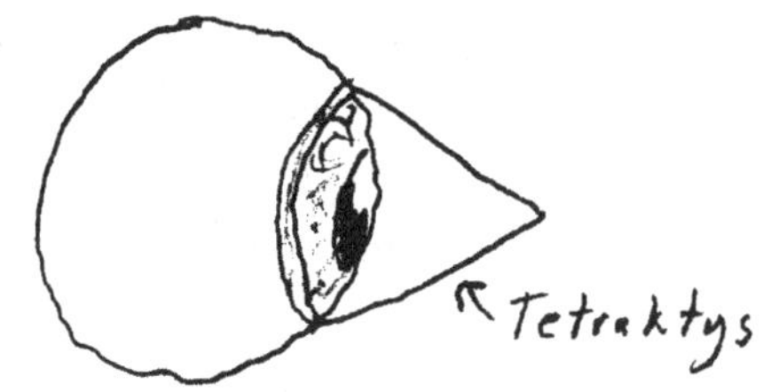

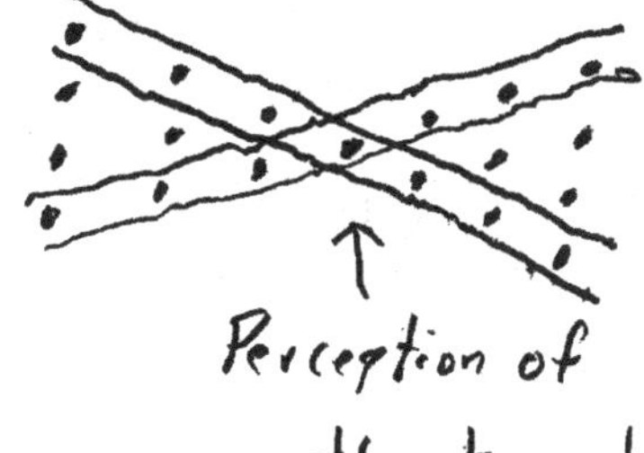

Once the guildy has learned the position of the tyriad the guildies can create more correct images in better resolution. The tetraktys fits in the perception and the guildies learn different perspectives in reasoning the latter of mankind.

The point of the tyriad doesn't move. All of the rest of the dots do.

"Now, the Periodic table of Elements is only for reference since it is only a representation to a bigger puzzle and is temporary. What the real names are is a mystery to us all, probably an older language is closer to their real names." Shawk told the boy.

He even said the words we say are tied up into pieces of element. What we say is a production of the element in metaphysics of speech. Each character lets out a different element and that is what we understand. Speaking is a reverie of the element. Reading is a form of metaphysics. Earth, Water, Air and Fire are the elements. Our eyes are a balance of a plenum of the universe since God created us in his reflection our minds can be as big as his, but not as his, we tend to use and apeiron when viewing the stars from our home the Earth. Our eyes coin the key characters in words to organize the element to savvy and understand the things we have learned to standby and convict. The element turns in our minds or moreover a reflection of the element turns in our imagination using a lexicon of definitions.

"A bad element, Scrupt, can really perplex you. Though many before you have been mad with the element and eventually created a system, an alphabet of the way we use and reflect apon the element and this is how far the Holy Ghost has gotten so far as each of us have thought. What we call the language is the production of the alphabet. The most powerful tool I know in the absurdity of the universe. The character all takes up different materials in the heuristics. (See Figure 27)

A paradox: The equalization of two opposite or unequal things. One gets a feeling of production as they resource in this way. It usually happens when only one side of the brain is working and the other isn't.

A matrix: This is usually the organizations of the heuristics in ones metaphysics. Since one can see a matrix as a procedure of making coffee, a house or organizing rules for a game. It usually is organizing relevance.

An apparent: This is a sense of heading in ones coordination in the universe. It's a balance of mentality and direction of ones well being. A place for recollection. One has the control over the form these in the likes of focus.

A vice: A confliction of a bad element, friction, and perplexity. A bad food, drugs, or the cold gives us these unbalanced natures. Sometimes these can be happy things though. It can be an illusion for example or a cold breeze.

(Figure 27)

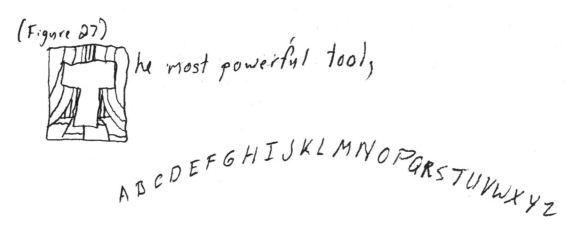

The most powerful tool,

A B C D E F G H I J K L M N O P Q R S T U V W X Y Z

One can do anything with this tool since it is the basis of our language. How it works is up to the other rules of the language. The eight sections of grammar, sentence structure and in using it matching the object with the word.

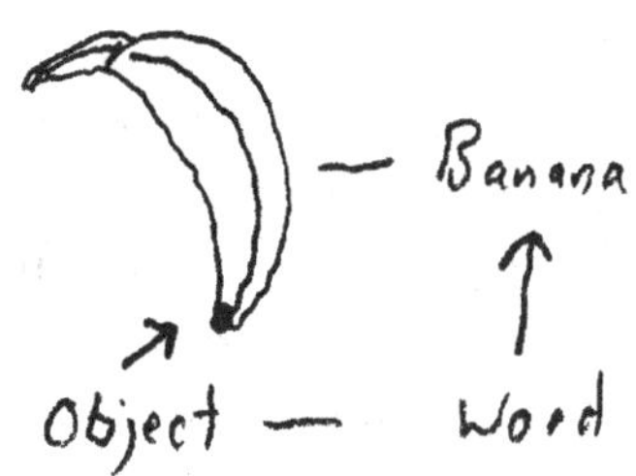

Its one verse at a time with the importance now days. Everything has its evolution and we must consult the building blocks of physics in meeting each verse with the object or intellect. The importance of the alphabet is safety and survival. It takes years to understand this and get good at. Us guildies learn that the address to things could mean life or death. Often it is not guess work to meet the verse. Books are our best friend's in this.

"Scrupt you can choose to meditate on any of the elements. They all have a permutable property in the subsistence of the imagination which they can relate to different globes of ideas in metaphysics. All the elements are made of atoms which vary little in structure. Yet there is a matter of importance that Scientist have proven about the relationship of certain elements, but this is only theory. Through millions of experiments they have put together the Periodic table of Elements. This eclectic table has to be right, but what are all the elements capable of that is for you, my boy, to come up with." Shawk said to little Scrupt.

"What I mean exactly is that with relating elements to elements you will be seeing things that haven't been done before." Shawk said.

"Invention?" Scrupt asked.

"The market is full of room for you to get a start in. An inventor you may be. A Pythagorean origin and Scrupt you will do things only dreamed about in today's world." Shawk added.

Shawk pulls out a piece of paper. He says the word "Substrate" to Scrupt.

"Substrate?" Scrupt replies.

"The universe, Scrupt my boy, is on a substrate, and I mean from a beings view. We live in a substrate universe or we don't, one or the other it comes at an importance. It is wedged in layer by layer we begin to understand it. Our minds undergo an understanding of an absolute universe. Absolute takes all the layers and beyond to make a finite piece of mind. This piece can fit on the head of a pin. One controls its size. The object is to make it as real as possible or as just a model which one can gain from. We use it so one can search for the answers through it. Like a full deck of cards it's absolute when assembled together and then discombobulated. As one starts dealing with the absolute it is divided like dealing the cards." Shawk said.

He wanted Scrupt to have an idea of the absolute universe. It was necessary to be complete with it. He wanted Scrupt to just let the universe unfold apon him. To be one with the universe or to understand that something's will never change added a clergy that will help the understanding of the elements relativeness. The good element was clear and the bad was brought on by timing in the absurdity and was very dirty. People came together in good element though were also factors of bad element when morass came about. The absolute designed the universe so that the bad element only lasted a small duration like war or hate, and the good element like Earth or the universe lasted forever. Things are happening beyond our comprehension in the universe. It has been dividing since man first gazed into space and wondered.

"There's something new in each vector, Scrupt. Here view these books. They will help you gain your balance in the universe and everything you do." Shawk said.

The books were on universal set theories, the compass, the sextant and the ruler which made all the dimensions obtainable to anyone who would study them.

"This will help you with your aim." Shawk said.

"You mean these books on the universe will help me with my aim? How?" Scrupt said in anticipation.

"When you stand, my boy, your perception depends on the globes above our heads. The way you are relatively disposed from the diversions of energies the universe gives and your competition won't get the upper hand as long as you hold an absolute higher than theirs. It's a finite balance of the universe and yourself. The universe becomes your fear, my boy." Shawk explained and grabbed a piece of paper and crumbled it and made a basket with it in the garbage can.

He then went to get a bit of food for them to eat. Shawk then wanted Scrupt to learn the tetraktys. (See Figure 28)

Shawk taught through the tetraktys the existence of the universe is explained. 1) The Subject-being the monad the entire universe and other numbers divide the universe into sections to describe it until the perfect being—God or deity. 2) The Apparent. 3) The Reason. 4) The Court. 5) The Absurdity 6) The Divine 7) The Plains. 8) The Govern 9) The Globes and 10) The Deity.

10) The Deities are the masters of the universe and its arts. Being that they could use anything in existence they are the supreme beings. The God's, Goddesses and Rulers make up the ethereal and are fluent in everything the universe has to offer. Most specialized in a power as there are pantheons of Deities all over the universe.

9) The Globes made up matter to be reflected apon by man. In nature they are the immutable forces that can not be controlled by man. Everything falls into place. The wind for example man can not control it. The globes represent dreams and thoughts. These are what all dimensions are made out of in the existence of the universe. The nos is made up of globes.

8) The Govern is energies and conversations of the universe. A matrix could not exist without it. There are places though that have no govern. Take peace for example. No motion, no govern. A govern is what holds the place together. Moves the nos around.

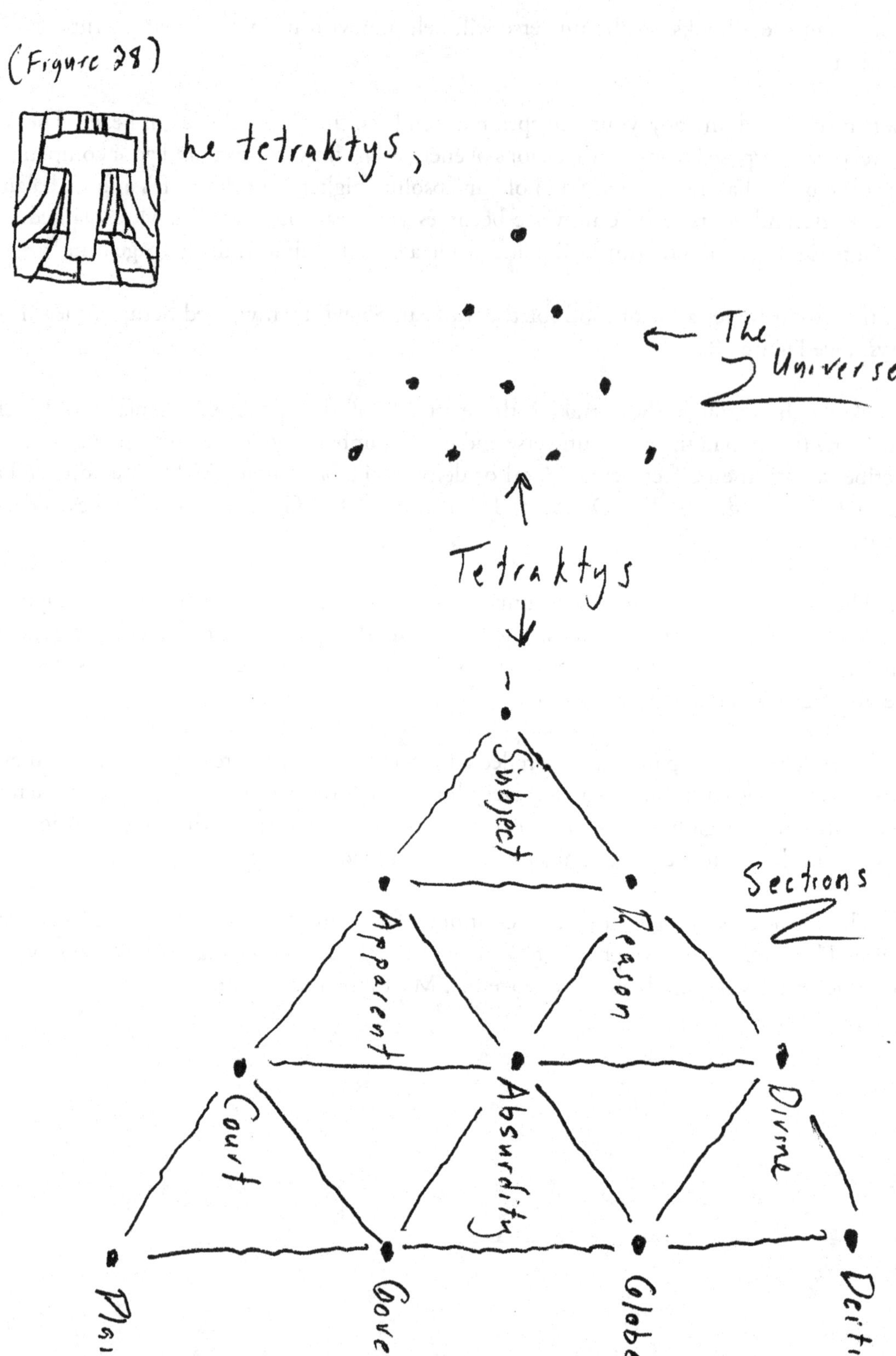
(Figure 28)
The tetraktys,
The Universe
Tetraktys
Subject
Sections
Apparent
Reason
Court
Absurdity
Divine
Plains
Govern
Globes
Deities

7) The Plains as the place the element meets on a level of man's latter. This is the place everything equals out as time takes its course. The feral spirit runs the place. The Plains are what makes up the foundation of living things. It's a state where new things are born in the measurements of the serendipity.

6) The Divine are the things that fall into place from the absolute universe. This is where the immaculate elements that make up the living and the universe come together. This is also where the element and intellect divide into finite states. Man is its finest divine state.

5) The Absurdity is the farthest reach of mans mind as he investigates the place around him. The words are the finite limits of all absurdity. This is the base to all logic in its definition since it is existence in its finest state.

4) The Court holds the foundation of our mind and consciousness. They hold our hearing of intelligence. Exercising the nominal, reality, and phenomenal of the mind in perception for one to reflect apon. It is the second surface also the ethereal.

3) The Reason in recognition the conjunction of the living in reflection of the materialism of the universe. It's our imagination. This is the first surface also the aether and thinking process of man.

2) The Apparents is a field in which a being seeks direction by vice, paradox, or matrix. The Apparent is two globes that react to the surroundings of a being. They are equal to the aether and can travel through it.

1) The Subject the only thing in the universe at a given time. It is the universe, thoughts and materialism. The Subject is precedent in the intellective, and the apple of the eye.

"This is my version, my boy, one can do anything with the tetraktys as they wish. It being whatever the case the tetraktys can be fixed to any problem imaginable." Shawk said.

The human being is tetraktys like, along with anything one can think of in existence. We exist and so does everything else in its perception to the all-seeing-eye.

"One equals ten." Shawk said explaining the nominal to Scrupt.

"Ah, Father, the numbers are congruent, as they are all equal to each other." Scrupt said.

"It's only at an importance. We Pythagoreans have always used the congruency as a form of protection. It sort of to hold everything down when times are not so good. The simplest form of the tetraktys is the most powerful protection. It's a defense against magic and there are magic users in the world my boy. A lot of good and evil play with the theurgy in which we live in today's world." Shawk said.

"Diligence, Father?" Scrupt asked.

"Now you're talking, but who's Laws? The Governments? A Monocracy?" Shawk asked.

"You're thinking about God!" Scrupt shouted.

"Yes, you're right. Seek the truth. You're with him now, my boy. He's here with what he gave you. God tells us of the eclectic Law and through him we are promised everlasting life. Can you imagine everlasting life?" Shawk asked.

"Well, no." Scrupt said.

"Exactly you're still in your youth, a young finite test tube. Scrupt, my boy, there will always be something unexplained, an enigma in the likes. No one knows exactly what's up there in the heavens. We say that they are the globes above our heads, but we can only finitely say this is all we have grasped in our wit what is exactly up there." Shawk told his boy that night as they were star gazing outside his place.

Ledger main, one of our magic's that Shawk taught Scrupt from the start. It took the imagination in the recognition of the hand. It summoned anything to use in the imagination to be used at the importance of the surface in an objective in illusion. Scrupt thought of imagining a pencil in his hand and then a piece of paper to write on in his imagination. It was very hard for him at first, but with time he mastered it. He drew circles and other geometric shapes which were easy to do. He watched them float off the page in his imagination and disappear. Foreseeing the relevance of Ledger main was key along with the knowledge of the dimension of the tool and the element that was being worked with in the mind. Meaning to delineate one must meet with the same two mediums. Having a hand for a tool became useful other than the mind for its imagination. One could do something with the mind and with the hand as separate imaginations. The magic rest in a reflection of the nominal since it is of the imagination and is intangible to reality. Yet a radio wave or sound can go through anything. Everything has magical properties. Sound is energy of magic and light in the likes. The magic tetraktys explains how magic is fortified. (See Figure 29)

"The magic tetraktys works, my boy, when one become consciousness of it. In the court is a matrix that one reads and creates mana, the Chinese called the energy "Chi." Energy that is defined in the court as a matrix is then able to recognize magic in Ledger main, Eloquence and Agriculture. The tetraktys is a set theory to find an eclectic subject in the universe." Shawk told Scrupt as he showed him the drawing of the magic tetraktys.

(Figure 29)

Magic tetraktys,

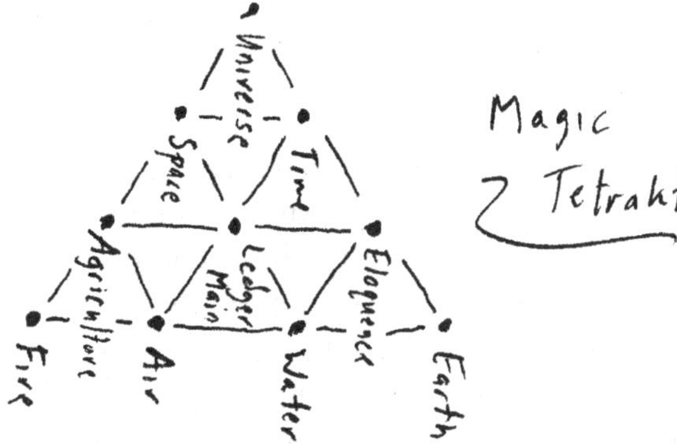

The element of mankind in magic is Earth, Water, Air, and Fire. The magics of the guild are Eloquence, Ledger main and Agriculture. The time and space is the importance of the universe.

When combined into one they have omniscience of the guildy. Magic is fortified in the tetraktys for easy use.

The mind is different when dealing with magic. It happens outside the mind. Pythagora's said that magic rest in a mind seperate from our own. The magic happens in the aether where nothing exist. A Pythegoream can surface the magic resourceing the element. Yet this is very rare, our magic rest in the mind or on paper. There is no danger, one can imagine any thing they have using illusion of the imagination.

A guildy would meditate on this day and night to civilize ones magics. One would study each dimension in ciphers. to become more familar with the physics of the universe.

Chapter 6

"Can I have a Hug?"

Jason Wayne Rahn, 2006

After Shawk showed Scrupt the magic tetraktys he tells the boy, "What you imagine about the element becomes true to your consciousness. One must keep a moral with the intellective in a line or it might take away their sanity, think safety and prudence. I know the more vivid your perception of the element the better resolution to make an insight. You are never going to hurt anyone with this type of magic. The illusions are nominal into the line of our imaginations. It means it is non-tangible to reality. One has to ponder the corporeal with the incorporeal. Pythagoreans say that one has to tinker around to find out what is real and what is not real. My position is false. It's as to a reflection of what is real. I don't exist. It's a true monogon in the likes. When we look at reality we look at the facts. It's only in reflection of the first surface of the tetraktys. Scrupt, you must learn how to define the word and imbibe it into energy which is called mana. The definition of the word controls the sustenance of the imbibement into energy which takes the form of a globe which is the nos." Shawk said.

"So one delineates things into their representations with the eye and then savvies them by draining the definitions into energies one can work with . . . In to mana?" Scrupt replied.

"Yes, energy one can interpret and take with them, memories. Mana is the magic word for energy." Shawk said.

The element is what Shawk taught. He didn't hide anything from Scrupt in his study. The element was every where and everything. The pure element is what Shawk wanted Scrupt to savvy.

"In times or durations of the bad element it is important to metaphysically think of an immaculate element, so meditate on gold in the likes. The purity and stability of gold in the likes lets you view the complexity and perplexity of the current time or duration of the bad element. It's logic in its purest form to hold the omniscience of an immaculate element in the perception of metaphysics to occupy ones mind. One must clean the apex of the pyramid of facts, there is no hurry, is exactly the point. If you can't take the time to do it right the first time then why do it at all?" Shawk said.

"Why is that, Father?" Scrupt asked.

"It's because, my boy, a pure gold bar holds its weight. The immaculate element will always be the same weight after and before any situation and the bad element will dissolve in a matter of time so we like to be temperamental with the durations and find the good element. We trade anything and everything in the commerce of the world and every element has its price tag on it. On the consciousness there can be perplexities. Your mind can identify the pain most of the time. Pain is metaphysical, it's the element wedged in ones mind or body. It is how we learn, some say learning is a disease that we learn from the pain of the rudiment but we have come a long way with all the headaches along the way and such. A good element like urbanity or a bad element like tragedy come and go. Its up to you to build your principles of the element in reflection to the meaning of the element, you're your own hero. No matter the bad element gold will always be gold. It will be forever and ever." Shawk said.

"The world today was put together by the weight of gold as it shared value in making up our moral. The metal held great value over time as it still today shares a great value. Kings and Rulers weighed everything by it and it's a concept I want you to learn, my boy. The latent element is ours to play with. Each has a unique ability and use." Shawk said.

"The elements are universal, right?" Scrupt asked.

"Everything in the universe that we know of has we think in it the same elements as the ones on the Periodic table of Elements. They are axioms that everyone has evidence of considering a least the people that are lettered. When one gets into chemistry of things like water: H2O, one finds one needs evidence of the Periodic chart though every bit of its theory. Now, what exactly are we, is the question of all the elements. Since we are made in the reflection of God who has a body just like ours?" Shawk asked.

"I don't know how we are, Father?" Scrupt said.

"What we are exactly, my boy, is broken, and in durations bits of element fix us, but we are wanters and find ourselves full at times and empty at others. We will always want something another time. The salutary system is finite as life feeds off life. Modern mans nature has been turned to principle that we reflect knowledge in theory. What we do with our time is still governed by the nature of the world and universe. That, is we are finite in our natures, but with the evolution of man in his language we have few things right and it will never change. The basis of the element meaning atom will never change. We are broken feeding off the element in our physiology. We do though fill ourselves with the language our minds can be full of solutions that measure up to good times, but we are broken, a mirror sometimes heuristically in a million different pieces. We are just a part of the equation of evolution and one of God's finest. My Father, my boy, told me there is only halfway in to a room and halfway out when you consider the center of the room. It's so one is halfway out and halfway out and not in or out. He also told me that there is no way out of the universe, it is our domain." Shawk said.

Shawk taught Scrupt about the Statesman. The Statesman took a look at the state the element was in according to what was believed at that time to the class of discovery and invention. Throughout the years the idea of the state changed with those new discoveries and inventions. The Statesman made principles of the properties of the element. They made up papers to be considered and discussed by Law makers.

"It's the elementary, my boy, the reflection of the element." Shawk told the boy with his hands waving around to show him that the element falls into a substrate turning into his own interpretation reflecting in the mind. Shawk was a gardener and they both were in the garden on the bench where there were rocks, plants and trees. Shawk taught Scrupt that the person can believe many perceptions of the element. Such as hold a piece of evidence in a weight of perception to find its insight metaphysically. It's sustenance of a place or holding of a thought.

"Possessive thought, it is in a way a burden at sometimes though a life saver at others it depends on what subsist." Shawk said.

He said this house holds a kind of element. It's personification. Its aura we pick off energy from or frequency of the place we live in as it is bound to the universe or environment. Take the buildings up town, a business, church or college, each is a very unique building. Each has its own character.

"One is able to imagine anything and these places are already full of production of the latter of mankind's logic. Scrupt? Can you imagine a square?" Shawk asked.

"Yes, Father." Scrupt said.

"Well then, can you imagine a box?" Shawk asked.

"Of course, Father." Scrupt said.

"Well then you have the riches and anything that one would ever need. You can turn the box into anything you wish. What I find amazing is that one can go to church or college and lay down the ground work into their imaginations go home and sit in the comfort and unfold everything they have done that day." Shawk said and went into silence as Scrupt could tell he was thinking of buildings.

They went inside, it was about supper time. Imagining buildings is the kind of thing that inspires a person and motivates the thinking process. Anyway the element reflects in the mind what the eloquence can be. Scrupt learned how to resource and reap the thoughts of classes by defining them and imbibing them into energy. It's what he used as evidence in inventing. He used animistics which he learned from reading an agnostic book. It told him that there are two types of animistics-one for God which is spiritual and one for man which is the element. For one, everything in the spirit was considered reaped as the immutable and could be what we call the imagination. Everything here is dead. Then two, we have the life giving element on the other side which man fed off the existence of the universe. It showed him that man was deductive and God was inductive in animistics.

Scrupt loved viewing things as a Sophist. The words kept taking different forms as he developed them into globes which hold different fields and classes in any essence of dimensions. Scrupt was thirteen when he finally understood the Pythagorean lesson of the universe. He became fluent in it though only the basics of the class are unlimited in study leaving much up to an enigma of existence.

Pythagoreanism was mathematics of the element which played with words, globes and concepts of the element in the dimensions which are said to be in organization of the universe in a tetraktys. There are two classes of the Pythagoreans. The Akousmatikoi—something heard or hearers of all and the Mathematikoi—scientific, learner or studiers of all.

"They say that the right tetraktys gives one control over the elements, Scrupt." Shawk noted.

A Pythagorean used the tetraktys as a tool for checking, comparing, and creating links to ideas new and already made. It dealt with numbers, letters, and the nominal intellect of the imagination and perception of the mind. The Pythagoreans meditated on the number one. The monad and it's opposite the monogon. It signified that it was a whole body, one universe of the monad and no universe as the monogon. They used zero to become disposed of the idea of meditating on one. They studied with a piece of intellect which was a piece that held value to the human race, holding it as though it was the only thing in the universe. They then started to compare the intellect in different dimensions holding it to reality and other perceptions and the intellective to see if they could find something new. They went over their intellect with the idea of putting a number one subsisting in their imagination over the piece they have chosen to meditate on. (See Figure 30)

The Pythagoreans meditated on two or more things divided in the intellect of the imagination. This idea came with a permutable manipulation of a lump of matter that they could turn into anything the imagination could do with it. They have been getting much better

(Figure 30)

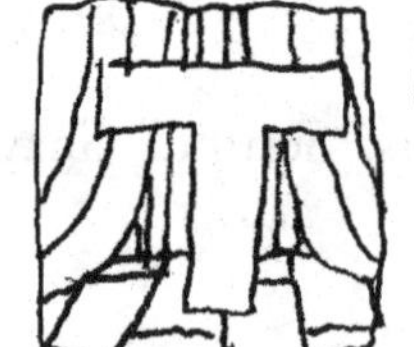he intellective,

Zero – O – Monogon
One – – Intellective – Monad
More then One – – – Divinity

God has openned this duration and when we are at rest we are at zero. With our intelligence we pick up with our intellective pieces of intellect that mankind has recorded as important. Divinity is the intelligence of more than one intellect in ones metaphysics of heuristics in a lexicon.

The intellect transplanted in the mind can take any form. A quazar in ones head or manipulating a house fly to dance around in the air in ones imagination.

One piece of intellect held as the only thing in the universe is important to show the value of axioms as one can pivot the induction of other samples.

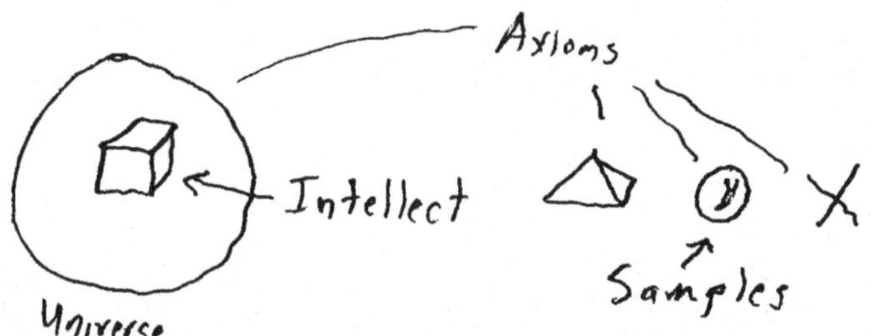

Every axiom is the same just as a large amount of dirt shares the same substance as a small amount of dirt.

Intellective is sort of a way to farm the different kinds of intellect on the eclectic.

at it as time went on understanding magic and technology. Addition and subtraction of the mind gave them the ability to contemplate one thing at a time. They could add intellect and subtract everything else to hold it the only thing in the universe. They began building the imagination as it is today in the likes of the Holy Ghost.

The more Scrupt meditated the more he got in return. Pythagorean meditation went like this. (See Figure 31)

The idea is that the number one is the whole universe. Where you call your home in existence is one with the universe. A division of the one universe is every piece of matter adds up to the nominal one universe. Where a piece the first dimension is is always there in the existence of human perception. Our view is where we live. One feed, one frequency of the monocracy that's trying to learn. With a number one over many intellects create ones intelligence. Holding a piece of intellect in your imagination or insight one can gather the concept of it. Pythagoreans used the tetraktys to configure the concepts in permutation of the universe looking at different addresses of the words in dimension. They want to know everything about the piece of intellect. The Pythagoreans also want evidence about what language is held to be the truth. They came up with a ten sectional tetraktys with fifty-five dimensions dividing the universe. (See Figure 32)

This tetraktys was used by the Pythagoreans to describe the globes of any piece of intellect. They took the piece and ciphered it by each of the fifty-five dimensions. Expanding the logic of what was thought in the moral, cultural and economics of that era. Each piece was concentrated in each dimension. The Pythagoreans worked very hard at the meticulous and tedious work through with lots of practice it became easy. They brought the full intelligence of the piece they worked with into a whole new view.

There was never a sure set formula for the tetraktys. Every one of the tetraktys varied from Pythagorean to Pythagorean as they all thought of the word in different definitions and location. Yet they all agreed on some of the sets the tetraktys can be used in, but still today with all the languages there is no universal tetraktys for the entire world. Unless it is in its simplest form the tetraktys without any nominal such as this tetraktys is universal. (See Figure 33)

It has great power to the Pythagoreans. It can be used in any situation. The Pythagorean holds the tetraktys in the mind. Separating him form everything else. He meditates with it to unlock the mysteries of the universe. The ten dimensions are always on his mind. The fourth section is always on his consciousness. It is the base of recollection with the other three sections. The whole tetraktys can enter congruency which holds it impenetrable. It can also hold an absolute where everything is added up intuitively.

(Figure 31)

Meditation,

Meditation starts with looking into an object to get insight. Then getting it is in the nominal sense from the point to the form of the object in the illusion.

One then closes ones eyes and reflects on objects in meditation. When the meditation was over one returned back to zero the substrate.

✚ Meditation = ◯ zero-substrate

After years of practice one learns the skills of illusion. With it one can roster or project anything. Prote Hyle is the beginning of a thought in the meditation.

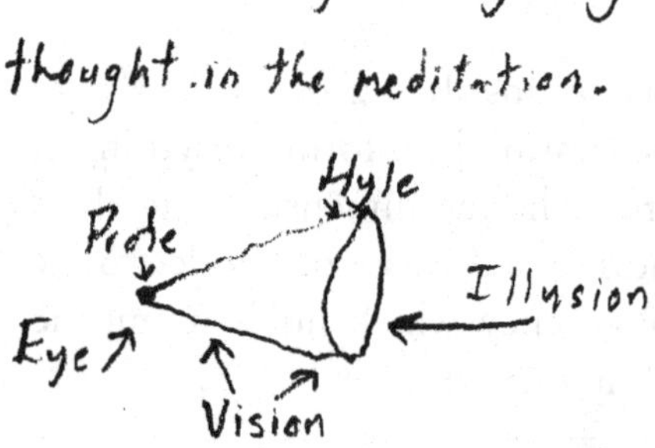

Meditation takes a great deal of addressing. One has to identify with prote hyle to match the word with the intellect.

(Figure 32)

Ten sectional tetraktys,

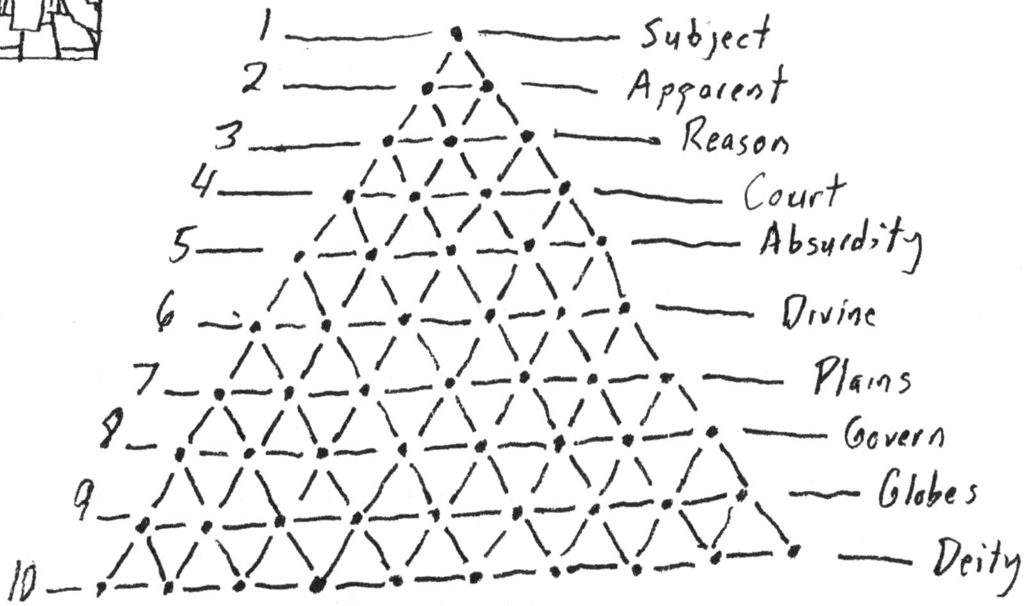

1 — Subject
2 — Apparent
3 — Reason
4 — Court
5 — Absurdity
6 — Divine
7 — Plains
8 — Govern
9 — Globes
10 — Deity

The tetraktys built to know the universe is in a ten sections from the subject to deity. Here Scrupt learns the importance of the universe and it's divine nature. God has his eyes on the subject and is just one of the deities the Pythagoreans study.

Each section is unique and can be described in any way. Which makes the best sense is the question. Scrupt knew that he was partially right with the subject and the deity, but what is a better way to describe the rest of the tetraktys? He reasoned the way he had it and thought it to be good enough the way it is, at least for now.

Which way is best?

(Figure 33)

The tetraktys and absolute,

The Tetraktys

The tetraktys has great power to the Pythagorean's. It can be used in any situation. The Pythagorean's hold the tetraktys in mind. Seperating them from everything else. One meditates to unlock the mysteries of the universe with it. The ten dimensions are always on their minds. The four sections are always on their consciousness. It is the base of recollection with the other three sections. The whole tetraktys can enter congruency which hold's it indestructable. It can hold an absolute where everything is added up to one dimension.

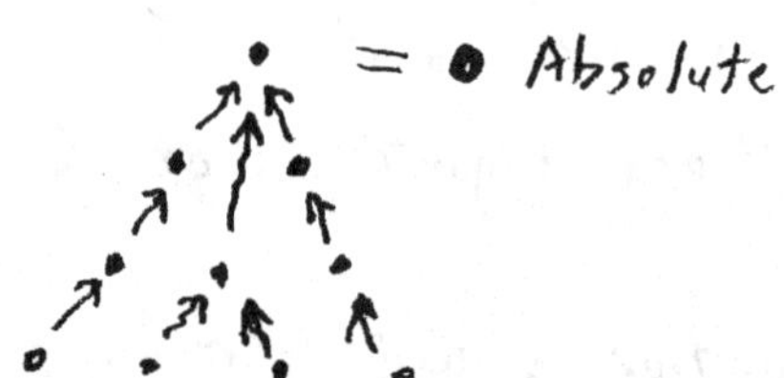

With an absolute all the points are together as one. Only to be used at a time of importance. Addressing a problem with a designed absolute the tetraktys unfolds the heuristics in a scientific principle. Everything is on a evolutionary basis in construction.

Four globes of the tetraktys together create a court of consciousness. Three of the globes create reason. Two of them together create the apparent and one of them creates the monad or subject.

Shawk wanted Scrupt to see the Earth not the World. The World was complicated and was run by governments and the ethereal. The Earth was lived in by human beings, animals, trees and plants that nourished them in the moral, cultural, and economics of the Earth. The Earth didn't need sophistry of man, just the cleanliness of the element and the open air. The human easily lived of the Earth with the Sun, Moon and Stars above. The World was a dark place buried by wars and all the tricks those vain men cultivated. Shawk showed Scrupt four different perspectives of the place we lived in addressing the different dimensions. (See Figure 34)

The Earth was a place of green pastures, plains, rivers, mountains, forest, deserts and oceans. It was where the energy was balanced by nature. It was where the entire element without the logic of man. It was a place of culture. The World was a place of war and sophistry. It was the place of moral. The Planet was a place of science and scholastics where everything was addressing the absurdities. It was the Globe that was the place of politics, geopolitics and economics. Choosing and renouncing these views gave a difference in perspectives. Showing that the place we live in was very sophisticated and perplex. Scrupt played with the idea a lot in his study. He thought it empowered him to have such knowledge. Shawk really loved the boy. Shawk taught Scrupt that the address of things (Subjects around him) had a deity or owner, yet the element had no owner. It maybe a piece of intellect, but the atoms of it are not owned.

"What comes for free, my boy?" Shawk asked as they were in the living room of Shawk's home.

"Love . . . Sight, and the light." Scrupt told him not really knowing exactly what he was up to.

"God comes for free, and each of us has a different importance when it comes to him. One can say there is no God and one can say there is a God. It comes down to the importance and one can ask him for anything. We have the freedom to choose our religion. The light comes at no cost and we live in a moral, cultural, and economic of the most freedom so far as it comes to the ages. Can you look at something that is not yours?" Shawk asked as if it were a trick question.

(Figure 34)

The addresses to our planet;

Planet- this is the place of science, where everthing is measured up into facts. It classifies everything into our language. Here we think of the economy.

Earth- this is the place of magic, where everything is addressed as a resource. Things of religion and culture are based here.

World- this is the place of feeling, where man has wars and times of peace. The military and politics work here to keep the place at bay.

Globe- this is the place of professorship, one that the tetraktys is considered. Ideas and thoughts are made here.

There is a google amounts of addresses to our planet. The four of these are considered the most useful and general. One can define a planet in any fashion they wish.

"Yes." Scrupt said as it caught him as a surprise.

"Why?" Shawk asked abruptly.

"Well, I don't know, just by asking them." Scrupt said with no idea of what he was getting at.

"Of course, it's you that owns the look. It's your personality. Though if one doesn't want one to look at something it is there own right. Yet, my boy, why then did you answer without having any evidence weather it is true or not?" Shawk asked sternly.

"Because as you look at my things I don't have a problem . . . Unless I want to keep it a secret." Scrupt said and then lit up.

"You see my boy, it's a matter of importance and that, my boy comes with the territory of addressing. Address the people if you don't know who owns it. One can not go up to one and just start using something of theirs. It's just not right." Shawk said.

"Addressing . . ." Scrupt thought.

"The owner of Deity of the item matters, it come down to . . . If it is not yours don't touch it and my boy, it is the same way with stealing, if you have any questions for me, just ask." Shawk said and disappeared upstairs for a moment.

Shawk taught Scrupt to tune his voice with the objective of the importance of the syntax in the element. It mean that put the element together metaphysically relating to what needs to be said. That Scrupt's gusto should be tuned to the evidence of his discourse. Shawk taught him emergence of the gusto. Know that the tone of his voice had dramatic effects on each other. Shawk showed Scrupt three different intonations. Shawk told him about a soft and gentle, prudent and key and loud and perplexed. The perplex tone was loud and usually got what it intended to get. It perplexed and moved people into listening as it was demanding. It was to be used in force to let people know that you meant exactly what you were saying. The key voice is where the syntax met with the element was the most important using a prudent tone to let people know that what you said really needs their attention morally and sound as it kept a rapport. The element seemed to comfort in the ease to the other consciousness when using the prudent form of voice. The soft voice was used when everyone was close of in a private matter so not to disturb anything or anybody else. Scrupt used and practiced these tones to his peers in a playful manor at church and thought it was very fun and at the same time interesting.

Isadore was quite the Wizard and could project his voice around the room. He could softly whisper in Scrupt's ear when he was standing in the next room. Scrupt was amazed and asked how it was done. Shawk smiled and said in practicing projecting your gusto one can move ones voice around freely. You must concentrate your thoughts taking care of where you want your voice to come out. One has to see the subject with your mind when you release your gusto. Your aim has to be right on the mark.

Shawk had an example of life's tragedies in a block and sheet of paper. The sheet had four squares on it. The paper represented the universe and the block represented the human being. Shawk walked the block with his set and told Scrupt to follow him. (See Figure 35)

Scrupt followed for a while then failed.

"You see, my boy, even the most simple of task we fail at. Search all around you and take a look how it feels to be feeble to things you haven't got a chance to do yet. You don't get much of a feeling do you? Nostalgia, my boy, it's your youth. You'll never study everything, Scrupt, but the skills you learn will be your tools to help you reflect on the task later. We all come trivial at some point. Let's take another look." Shawk said.

This time Shawk threw some dirt on Scrupt's page.

"What did you do that for Father?" Scrupt asked in distaste.

Shawk told him to move his block through the mud.

"A bit harder isn't it." Shawk asked.

"It's harder to keep in line and it makes noise." Scrupt said.

"So is life sometimes. That is why I teach you the language and element many have already walked the block on the page and this is what they have come up with. These are the good and the evil is the bad element. We need to be on our toes. To be able to perceive what's going to and in inevitable to happen. To be able to read the writings on the wall . . .⊠ Shawk said to Scrupt's recognition and told him then to seek and meditate on what he is feeble in his skills and study.

"Little Scrupt, we have greater freedom now days, but we are not ruled by greater powers the same. Man has changed though the human has not. God is the highest power we know. God is the block and page. He's even with us now." Shawk said.

"Well can I speak to him?" Scrupt asked with a lot of hope.

(Figure 35)

he page and block,

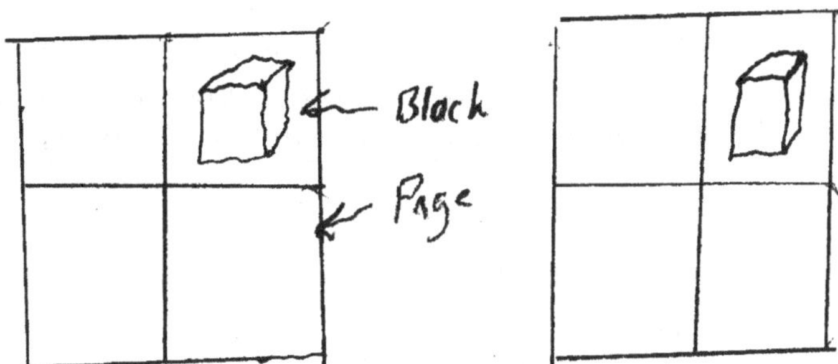

Shawk wanted Scrupt to know the difficulties of life. Even in the easiest things Shawk taught can be filled with difficulty. The page with mud and rocks on it was creating a big mess of the simple task.

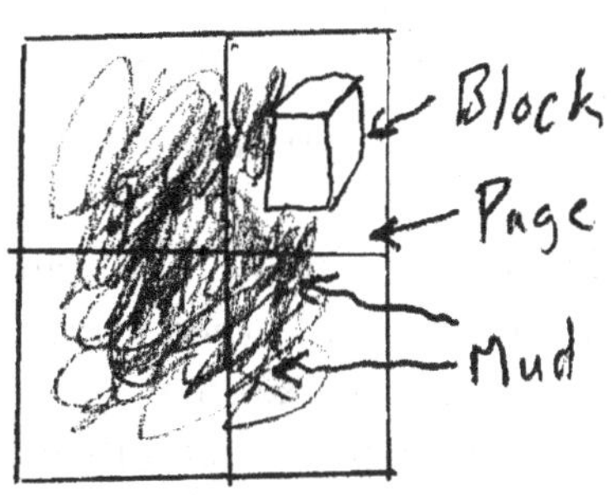

Scrupt sovvied this message and kept it. Shawk warned him about the days like these. He said, Identify with thyself and keep in mind prote hyle of the immaculate element.

"He's yours, ask him." Shawk said in the likes.

Scrupt asks God a question. He waits for an answer.

"You're thinking, Scrupt. It's an answer most of us get. Yet God can not survive without us. You are just a part of him. You have come far from birth and you just use a little of your life's experience to live at this instance. He'll answer you, my boy . . . Later, when you're old enough. Keeping the faith is a matter of believing in something without having the evidence of it being there at the time. Belief is something one holds onto as the truth in existence. It is something a Pythagorean seeks in renouncing Deities. You will in time learn and have to choose your belief who knows what the ethereal will bring to you, my boy." Shawk said and said some Masonic prayers.

Shawk told Scrupt that we only have one page so to speak and that it is substratum as one universe with God though we can change pages with the nominal. The page is what Scrupt reflected apon as much as a human goes in a nominal. One can see with character the page is constantly changing. Shawk taught him to play with other characters such as an Accountant, Lawyer, Fire person, and a Wizard. Scrupt drew up these pages getting all the information together to create such characters.

"The page as a human being goes in a nominal to a persons name which ever character one reflects on in the mind. It's your address, my boy, and we like to keep a close eye on it as the facts fall into place, your origin will never move. There's a danger to the creation of characters. Some are good and some evil. Some come with repercussions. Your mind, Scrupt? How is it?" Shawk asked.

"It's full of information, Father, and I get a good feeling about everything. I feel I can handle any matters clearly and with correctness." Scrupt said.

Shawk had Scrupt write down everything he was feeling as he grew up. A monk from the church had given Scrupt art lessons. Scrupt learned to draw the conjunctions of the mind. He learned later that the brain was full of cortexes that stored energy that held information that was in the form of wedges that could be pressed and then moved to allow man to think in the reflection of thought. The information Scrupt said was his surroundings in the universe. He developed a 10/20 vision of his mind. He could use it or turn it out of focus.

Isadore had business part of the day. So the neighbor watched Scrupt from time to time until he was thirteen. Isadore was a Father at the church and would pray and visit people at the hospitals for healings and words. He's a wonderful faithful man that loves God with all his heart. He had hazel eyes, and long brown hair including a long beard. Light and lofty in composer he floated about. He's the type that loves classes and is excellent or masterful in several. He has a lab downstairs in the basement of his home and he takes Scrupt through his schooling in it. Isadore can even levitate himself and objects when needed. He's so energetic and loves to kneed in God's work leading everything in the right way. He's training Scrupt to be a master of existence, a Pythagorean.

With the knowledge to know the universe as far as the tetraktys is concerned. Shawk started Scrupt on the dimensions of the tetraktys. Scrupt already knew most of the tetraktys. He was introduced to it as a child. It didn't take him long to learn the dimensions. Shawk then headed Scrupt into Earth science where he could better understand the elements in Earths matrix. The balance of life was these matrices working in a mixture of chemistry. Scrupt noticed something Shawk was amazed to hear.

"It is a cycle, take nothing as in an empty space which under pressure folding apon itself created hydrogen where all the other elements came from and then spread out back down to nothing again." Scrupt said

The element became Scrupt's second nature as he created a wheel out of the immaculates by atomic number including a space for nothing as one of the elements. It ranked as zero. His first nature was God and the freedom he gave through the serendipity of the spirit of liberty and its institutions.

The philosophies of morality were taught to Scrupt reminiscing through history books, Bibles of religion and poetry. The tetraktys taught him the ways of the trade as one element was more valuable then another. It was in history that Scrupt built his views of the world's sophistry. He followed the ages developing his savvy lore of all the Deities he could find. Finding the world had its secrets to those who seek for them. God, God's and Goddesses had their power and so did the common man in faith to them God's. To be true to a Deity Scrupt imagined as he is true to God was very important and interesting. Scrupt renounced Deities as God had permitted. He found Zeus very pleasing. After learning the morality of one Deity one develops a feeling for morality to the worshippers of that Deity.

The tetraktys took a different form of viewing History. The tetraktys lattered the word to form the structure of moral, culture, and economics of the era. Shawk told Scrupt that the word is the guide. That History made the word and you find it a puzzle through existence. Just because we give something a name doesn't mean we understand it completely. The art of History is key to the stories of antiquity showing the morality of mankind. The language, an art for the lettered man to use as a tool throughout life is the alphabet. Back then not everyone was lettered. Now days there are few that are not. Though in the likes most take it for granted and don't study much. Any way both sides of the lexicon can still laugh.

"What's the significance of the line, Father?" Scrupt asked his Father as it was a myth that Zeus was considered at one time as being a line himself.

"Ah, you are thinking of Zeus? As what the Olympians gave the question that Zeus was considered a line." Shawk said.

"Yes, I find it interesting that everything can be considered a line. People, places, things for instance are lines of at least in perception of a narrative." Scrupt said.

"Yes, my boy, we use lines to make up perception in our syntax. Our minds are flow controlled by the rudiments we meditate on in our metaphysics open, closed, or changed." Shawk said.

"The line in arts put the picture together. I can see it, Father in these lines." Scrupt said and showed his Father this page. (See Figure 36)

"I can watch in duration an apple, its birth, life and death. I can weigh the government. I can view the universe. I can see it all in the permutation of my mind when focused with the length of a line. With any word I can see its birth, life and death?" Scrupt said.

"It's hard to tell, Father, but does the universe have a death?" Scrupt asked.

"You might be right, we call it the universe because it's the one thing we live in that goes on for, what, forever. If it goes void though, we could say that it is in its death. The universe is still growing, it's broken though." Shawk said.

"Broken?" Scrupt asked.

"It's resourcing until it reaches its full product. What? I don't know. It is always changing until one day." Shawk said.

"Until on day, what? Father?" Scrupt asked.

"Until, my boy, it reaches completion." Shawk finished.

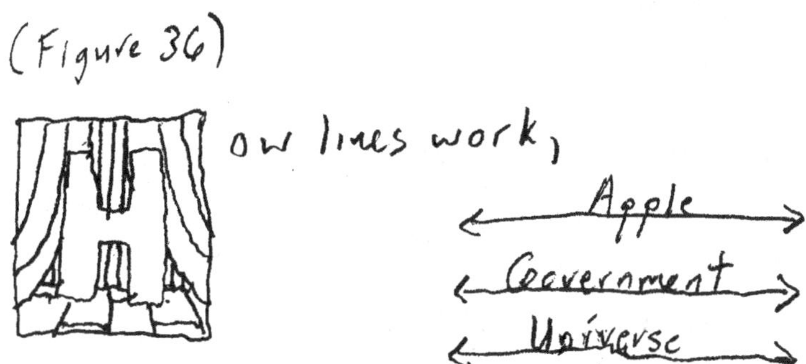

Lines work on a duration delineated in the definition of a word. An apple exist from a seed to a tree that bears it. A government is drawn of a nation to meet the politics of an era. The universe is a line that lets one know of its history, presence and future.

A line in ledger main or line in the mind give a calculous conjecture to a problem.

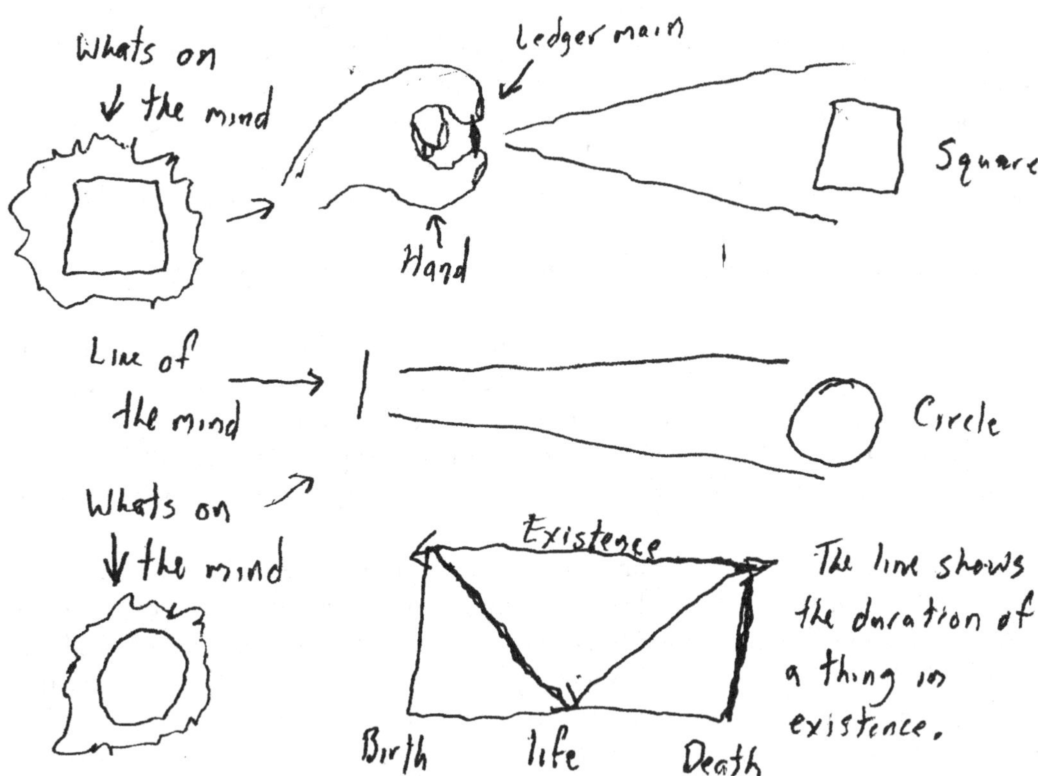

Chapter 7

"You're my court, my court of last resort."

"IT" by Stephen King

Scrupt Knostic: Age: 20 Height: 5' 10"

Weight: 175lbs Hair: Brn Eyes: Brn

Complexion: Peachy Provisions: Glasses

Scrupt was adopted by Shawk Isadore a Father of the church when he was almost two years old. Scrupt lived the rich life. Shawk lived a very educated life. He had gone to Yale University to sharpen up. He's 57 years old and still in tip top condition. Scrupt was very young when his parents were murdered. The Knostic's were great thieves' in the land of America though Scrupt and Shawk didn't know about it and neither did anyone else. After they died, Isadore brought Scrupt home and gave him unbelievable wealth and wisdom. To become a Pythagorean and to make the journey destined to him.

Scrupt was raised and schooled by Father Isadore. Shawk organized his fundamental order of meditation to give him an edge on thinking. Helping him learn the globes and latter of existence Shawk gave him the tetraktys. Using the tetraktys to develop and absolute order in class and find energy using the globes above our heads. Telling Scrupt that in the latter of mankind the importance the order could mean life or death. Meaning you never know what hit you in all this absurdity. Shawk focused Scrupt on art and the magic of ledger main. Shawk would write down a scene in a list of words on paper and Scrupt would have to draw it up on a page making the picture. Scrupt would have to do great research to draw the pictures sometimes.

Every mark of mankind was developed by hand. Ledger main is the magic of the hand. The mark made by all hands is called the epithet. The epithet is a sworn word, and oath, meaning what everyone does is their epithet. Oracles were in the lines of the Deities and followed their epithet. They dealt with destinies of men and women. Scrupt wanted to talk with an Oracle badly. Yet no one knew where one was except one that said an Oracle is a type of building.

Scrupt came across a girl by a church and talked with her. She said she was the heir to the Delphi Oracle. That she could study things like having an evil eye. She could look around floating about through walls and buildings, and out in outer space. The Oracle had a precept which did all these things. It was developed by knowing exactly how the physics of this place comes together. It is called the Precept of the Delphi Oracle. Scrupt was amazed and asked if there was a type of foundation to practice the precept. She said a philosopher's stone is where she started. Scrupt thanked her then left.

Scrupt had a knack for magical things at such a young age. It was mostly because he was being educated by a rare breed, a Pythagorean. The art of magic entailed Scrupt with high valor towards the latter of magic. Everything done under a Deity completes the tribe's arche. From beginning until end of civilization mankind will be working. The globes above our heads are unfolding that very tale. Scrupt was taught that the universe is our playground. Scrupt eventually could take the world apart in his imagination like a giant jigsaw puzzle and put it back together. He became a scribe at eighteen and drew up his own artifices and schematics that he made books out of for his own personal library.

Scrupt felt unique the whole time in his youth. His peers at the church gave him the name "Little Hermit" since his Father was basically one. Scrupt had a wonderful voice and was trained to use his gusto. He was charming in projecting his voice to best fit the importance of the instance. Tone and accents came easy to him and he amazed anyone he came across.

In his laboratory granted by Shawk he became familiar with Science, Technology, Chemistry, and Inventing. All of which he loved. He especially like writing reports and experimentation forms that he revised and created into his own special schematics. He just couldn't leave a page blank. He was always feraling information, writing, and drawing things. He tinkered with any and everything. He created books over his criteria and his inventions he made, made him rich in cash and fame. (Here is his invention list, See Figure 37)

In meditation Scrupt played with the principle of the element. One of them was magnetism. He imagined the lines of flux and why the force of magnetism flowed as it did. From North to South, govern, is what he called the current that moved matter in the magnet and it could quite possibly be faster than the speed of light, but what force was it made out of? Radio waves, microwaves, we just don't know. It's a perpetual machine, although we find this one in nature. A lot like the salutary govern which is the immutable force we find in storms throughout the universe. The eye of Jupiter is caused by and asteroid or a moon that got stuck in its atmosphere, Scrupt thought.

"What's a magnet made out of when one analyses it?" Scrupt asked to himself.

He knew if you lined up the atoms of iron we would produce a magnet. Maybe the Periodic table of Elements is wrong. I don't have the resources to argue, but maybe, just maybe the Scientist missed something. It was some how God made us out of the element and developed and argument of the elements giving us life and mentality. We are the employee's of God.

(Figure 37)

crupts invention list,

1) Element Cards
2) All-in-one blanket
3) Heavy blanket
4) Mop scraper
5) Magnefing scope
6) Waterobserver
7) Facet temperature gauge
8) Rewashable towels
9) Custom smoking rooms
10) Blow meter
11) Didgital eye gloss ruler.
12) Water balloon game
13) Pad fly tape
14) Pro-simulation
15) Flag racers
16) Magnetic pencil holder
17) Cement Molds
18) Portable jacuzi
19) Missle Command
20) Grip challenger
21) Torcher works
22) Super-inchables
23) Make'em track

"What does he want from us?" Scrupt questioned.

Another question Scrupt played with was he was rambunctious with his mind.

"Absurdity." Scrupt said.

It is what defines this place. With the standards of measurement the size is defined. When measuring in the metric system it gives on a different feeling of the place as in comparison to the English system. In absurdity it can be measured in any way one may choose. It's like an apple the size of a car or a universe the size of a pin head. It's to each ones own when it comes to business. The Law is made of finite measurement and frowns on things that would hurt people. There is no finite imagination, only different mind sets in adumbrate and it is endless. Scrupt learned the difference between mind and imagination. The imagination is a free agent that is able to form any and everything. The mind is the state of man which reflects reality in the plenum of the universe. In memory as in cognition it gathers the thoughts of the minds surroundings. The imagination is without reality. That is without the matrix of man and his element there is nothing.

The whole picture to each of us is different. When we agree on an intellectual view we tend to work fair and well together. Meaning like the Ten Commandments we agree we shall not kill of have any other God's and love thy neighbor as ourselves.

"Sure, one can define anything in any way one chooses. It's one of the freedoms to reflect on a way of existence. Things we do today are basically cut out for us. I'm very thankful to those who helped in the development of our civilization." Scrupt concluded to himself.

Scrupt knew that we as a species of mentality were stuck with pieces of the way man should and not be in the normative, that once and in hard times we do screw up. The first man to see the corruption of the city and asked God if he could restore the order was named Law. Law simply asked God if he could protect the city and God granted him to do so. Law hired men that became the first Law enforcement.

Scrupt decided to study Psychology. He found that the word was spelled strange enough. Scrupt found what the doctors called the aether. He thought that this element was absolutely amazing. He put it to use as he found the concept of it and defined it as the imagination with nothing in it. He could put things in it and take them out. When he filled it he defined it as the imagination. The aether was an immovable nominal which one could apparently use to their liking. It held no motion or reality. One could color it or leave it blank or void. It was the same principle of a blank page. It's totally up to ones control.

Scrupt was able to discover the globes above our heads with his own eyes in the form of an apeiron vision. They came to him as balls of energy like stars with the nominal of the alphabet shinning on them. One of them he saw actually was in the form of his imagination and gave him the reflection of him and all he could imagine. He also notices that he was at the control of this one. Scrupt believed that the globes govern us and they would never change. Unlocking the mysteries and secrets was up to an aging process just like the universe as it unfolds the cosmos he was told by Shawk.

"It's an immaculate conception that reveals them gradually or at a tedium." Shawk said back then.

The monks say we are yet sleeping in our beliefs until one day we gradually wake up . . .

"Ah, the plain and simple and the set dogma of finding something fun to do with our time." The monk told Scrupt long ago.

Shawk gave Scrupt two Pythagorean amulets and said, "They are the keys to Gebelin, I have one and these two are yours. You'll know their purpose when the time comes."

Scrupt studied dimensions, not the dimensions of Math, but the dimensions of existence in ontological times. He took time and space at a point. He then was able to move to different courts and fields to figure out the elementary of the premise. He would walk around the city placing the fields and courts to the foundations of the buildings and parks. He laid the court on the foundation of the buildings in his imagination and figured out its blue prints without ever going inside. He checked it out later if he was right. He would lay a field in a park and measure up everything about it. Delineating trees, shrubs, walk ways and anything else in the park. (See Figure 38)

Shawk could tell Scrupt where the bathroom was inside a building with this technique without ever going into it. Scrupt used this model to understand the relevance of architecture in his mind. Scrupt used ciphers to show properties of the word defining the dimensions. (See Figure 39)

(Figure 38)

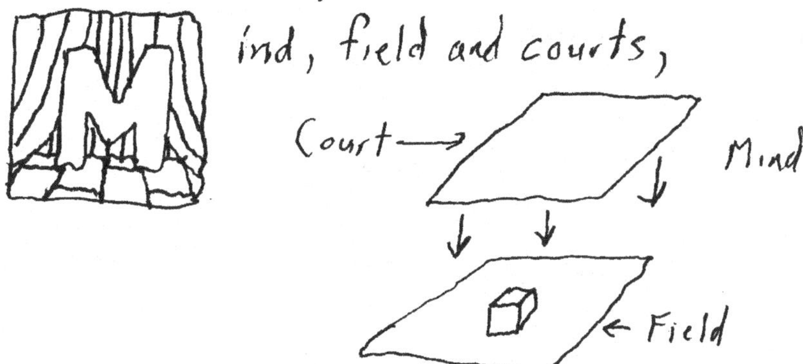

A field lays in it's place and the court is of the mind. The court of the mind lays over the field so one can obtain whats on it.

Box
Field

Whatever is on the field the mind courts.

A court is like a field, but a court is of the mind in action. In the likes we have a basketball court, a tenis court, a court of Law and a court of love. Each court has a purpose.

Broken Court of love

A broken court is one in need, resourcing from the type of court.

A court of love

(Figure 39)

efining the dimensions,

Math • • Space
Divine • • Time
Govern •
Globe • • Absurdity
Techology • • Current

To show the properties of the words Scrupt used ciphers to better understand them.

Govern • → Space •

He figured how Govern is used in space. It allowed an area for something to exist in.

Govern • • Space • Time

He figured how Govern is used in time. It make a duration for something to exist in.

Each time he would find the properties he knew a little more about Govern. He could even design his ciphers better as he practiced. Scrupt really got a lot out of learning things this way. It really advanced his addressing.

He would figure the word in the center (Govern) and unfold the mysteries of the eight words around it. The words around it would elaborate the absurdity (Things that define this place) of the center word. The center word was then used as a root to all other eight words enhancing the understanding of the center word.

Scrupt realized that absurdity was the place that defines this place. Basically meaning everything is silly or stupid and the people gathered stupidity into logic and then chose their destiny. With a pencil and paper Scrupt drew up a drawing of absurdity. (See Figure 40)

Absurdity is a finite place where government is perpetual. It means that the golden rule will always be the same. Government is both variant and invariant. Absurdity is one name for every and anything or situation. The things done with a pencil in your mind are absurd. They can do anything a person has the intuition to do, but I don't see trees making money as their leaves, that would be absurd. Absurdity although is the key to the divine comedy. We never know what hit us in the absurdity of the universe.

The tetraktys . . . Anyone could make one, Scrupt thought. These ten dimensions could change forever. We are talking unbelievable amounts of change. People are used to minutes, hours, days, weeks and years, Scrupt thought. He could view the distant past and future as he could imagine it to be. We as a race will die out eventually unless we succeed in space. Only God knows of our full capabilities on other planets one might think. How old is the creator or God? Scrupt thought. If there is immutability it must be heaven the home of God the universe. It's a place where there is no time and it's got to be nominal at some point.

Prote Hyle one of Scrupt's excursions, it means, Thought (Prote) and Material (Hyle) and both of them in combination together are how we look and think of things. It's the thought and material in the mind. It inserts the first dimensions to the ideal in existence. Scrupt found out the idea of where the spoon came from and said Prote Hyle to give him the tetraktys view of the invention. We came from somewhere and something. It goes on and one forever and ever. What came first the chicken of egg? God made us in his image to reflect for him existence. We humans have a life expectancy of 90 to 100 years. The frequency of our existence is E=mc2 the Einstein's theory of relativity. We grow at this rate. We pick up the ray of the translucency when we are born.

As a young boy Scrupt noticed things like the other boys were much faster then he was in everything. He noticed he floated in a different shell then the rest of his peers. His Father prepared meals for him to eat and practice his prayers. His Father would ask him what kind of food it was. Where did it come from? How was it made? Who do you think made it? Shawk was a fantastic chef and sometimes ordered from other parts of the world. Scrupt was instructed to make his own prayers to get an idea of how prayers were made and directed. Scrupt amazed his Father when he put together this prayer.

(Figure 40)

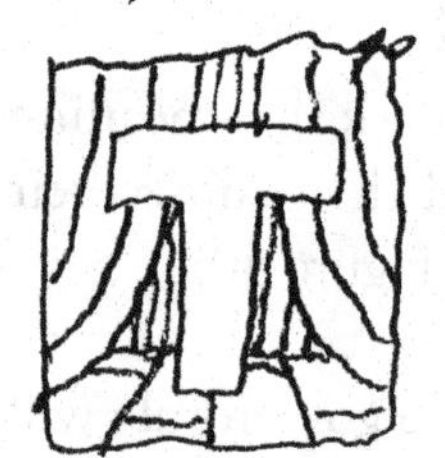he absurdity of the universe,

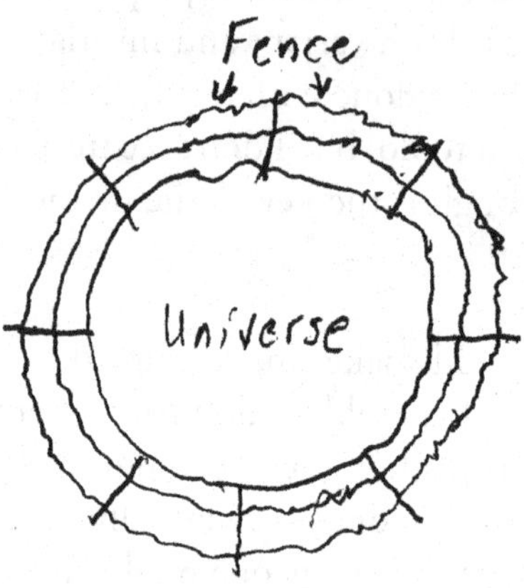

The definition of our universe is that it is fenced in. Everything around us in the universe has a definition. Just because we give something a name doesn't mean we understand it completely.

← Absurdity bead

The absurdity bead may represent anything. An element, where we seek its meaning. A quazar, where it represents someones memory. It could be the point of conversation. Any way match the idea with the word.

"Hence thy fruit, the fruit of the floating

Garden, savory and ripe, I will always

Treasure it, because I know it is of our

Lord and savior, Jesus Christ . . .

Amen . . .

Religion gave Scrupt a feral spirit that made him very ebullient and to play with everyone and the universe. He even kneeded the worst of guest. He knew and learned that the good spirit converts the bad. He found the word "good" to be absolutely amazing. Good, was everywhere and felt pleasing to say and think. To other classes like the Statesman thought good where ever the eye was present. The Sophist said good was the achievement of the performance. The Philosopher thought good was on a plain as in common word and lore to the citizens of moral, cultural, and economics of an era. To some good was a level people could easily understand and work with in the likes of media.

Shawk taught Scrupt the four generals until college level. Math, Science, English and History. He showed him to recognize the classes for their value. English dealt with configuration of the language and its uses. Science took the world into classification, principle and theory. History was all about the model of development throughout civilization. Math was divination of the world and its intellect in calculations and numbers. English was Scrupt's favorite until he learned the tetraktys on the universe then he liked them all equally as they formed the court of the general tetraktys. The value of the classes came with dimension as they were held up individually to the absurdity of the absolute universe. In other words the classes held in existence came with the territory in its character. Mixing classes together like a chemistry puzzle was fascinating to Scrupt. Taking Math, Science, English and History he found it was the heuristics that made a thermometer or computer. Take words from the dictionary as classes and examine them to other words and with it compared the product to come up with new ideas.

Scrupt eventually wanted to live in America and go to Law School. So he took the summer off at age 20. He was off to Harvard next fall. Shawk had connections there to get Scrupt in the school. So Scrupt went to France to practice his study in a new environment. In France Scrupt studied poetry, politics and French Philosophy. Scrupt loved to read slowly and unfold the story in his imagination. The Philosophy book he chose to read talked about life's tragedies and war that will never cease between mankind. While one war was over, another one was still going and still yet another one was starting. Tragedy and love work the same, but with love you can never have enough. It will always be the same and will never change. A perpetual malady God set down as our human condition.

Absurdity, Scrupt thought, it must not end, yet is fueled, but can't be measured, it's endless from the beginning, middle and end. Unless some one finds a finite state or if we have, ever since existence is broken we find ourselves with a half truth. Back in antiquity, logic was much narrower and now days we find a lot of what we call sophistry. People are yet stupid today, although logic has more of a given and is universal. Logic is finite intellect and absurdity a finite stupidity. People use logic to clean up absurdity in their minds and it's just plain silliness. Absurdity is a language that defines this place while logic is an indirect science that classifies absurdity. (See Figure 41)

In absurdity there's just too much information to grasp for one to gather. Our minds are either broad or secular in the tetraktys. One finds themselves with bits of truth because absurdity is too big that we can only make sense in using logic. The universe is like a bucket of ice cream where all we have is a bowl and spoon. Scrupt drew up a tetraktys until absurdity and tried to find a divine dimension to play with in it. The drawing was of the fifth sectional tetraktys which is named absurdity.

There are 15 points of the dimensions on this tetraktys when figured up to absurdity. Three (Reason) is divisible into 15, 5 (Absurdity) times. 3 and 5 added together make 8 (Govern) so it must mean—reason the govern of absurdity. The way the tetraktys is arranged we are always taking it in the perspective as a whole. Each dimension affects the feraling of the other dimensions. Humans are conscious in the fourth dimension.

Scrupt believes in his trial and error that the first dimension is the apple of the eye. Meaning anything someone is thinking is on their consciousness (Court) to reason, to apparents, then to subject meditating on the whole tetraktys. The tetraktys Scrupt knew could be arranged in any way he could imagine in his heuristics. What was the right and best way was the question. Scrupt knew that the tetraktys was his most important study of his life. He'd seen how it made a difference when discerning knowledge. That it gave him an edge on life. He used it to take apart perplexity and complexity. All his information he put down in this tetraktys was unique. Anyone can learn how it's done and maybe one day they might find a more accurate one. To the best of his knowledge Scrupt constructed this tetraktys. (See Figure 42)

Scrupt didn't have the time or energy to perfect the tetraktys, but he kept thinking what would make a better one. He came to the conclusion that man had for the most part a consciousness and it rested in the first four sections. The Deity rested in all ten sections. (See Figure 43)

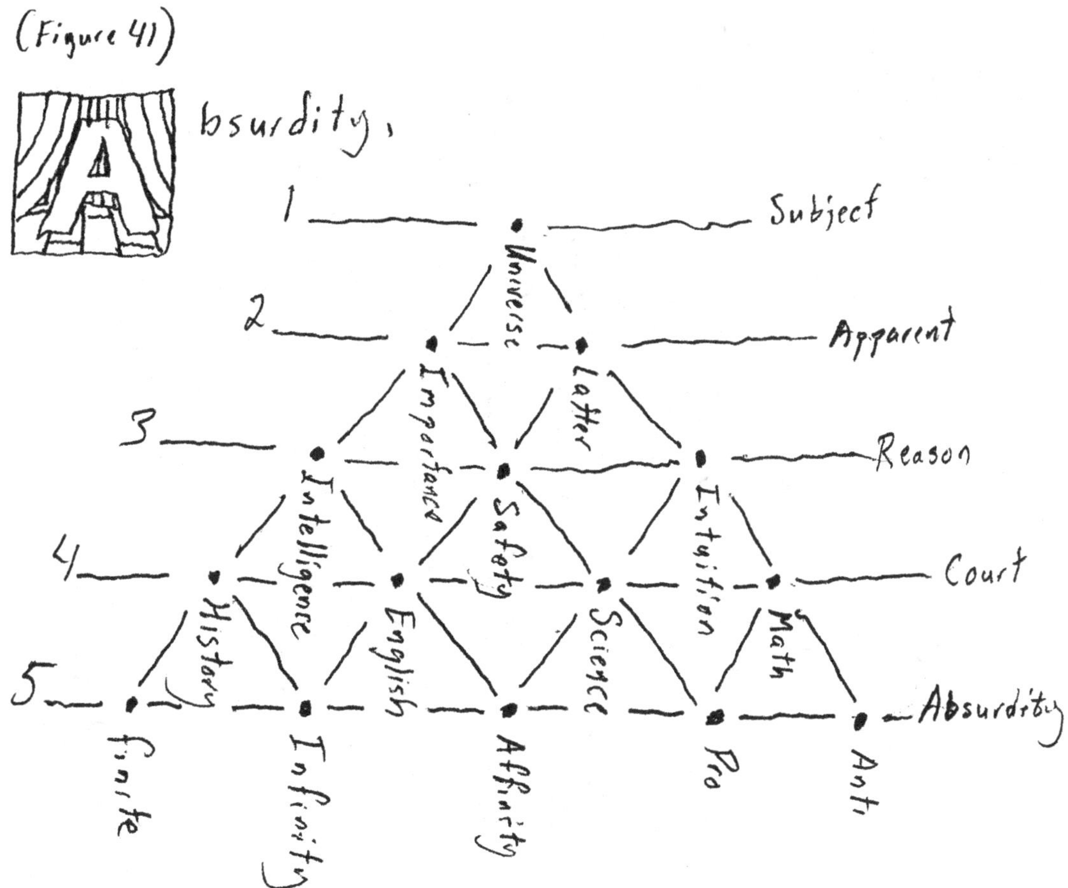

The absurdity is the fifth section of the tetraktys. It is the place of conjecture and half-truths. Scrupt studied these dimensions and brought each of them into perspective. He thought for this time that these words best describe the intellective.

Pro — Anti

Absurdity

Infinite — Affinity — Finite

Cipher

Finite ⟶ Absurdity

(Figure 42)

Scrupt's model of the tetraktys,

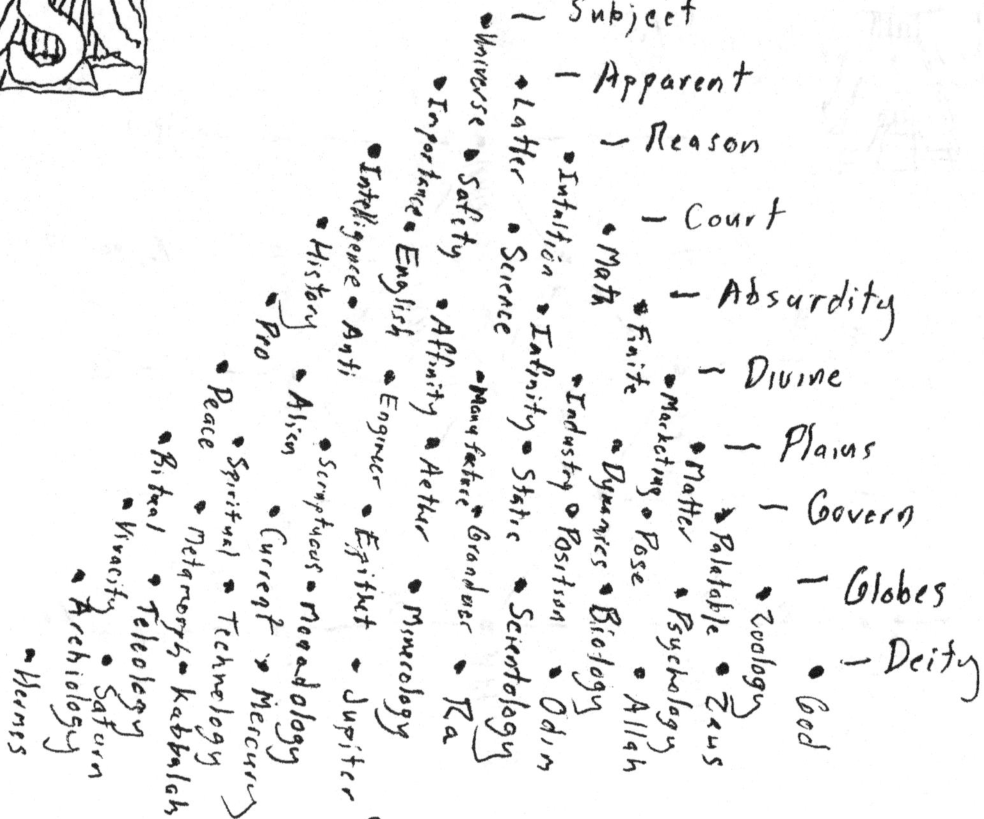

• Universe — Subject
• Importance • Latter — Apparent
• Intelligence • Safety • Intuition — Reason
• History • English • Science • Math — Court
• Pro • Anti • Affinity • Infinity • Finite — Absurdity
• Peace • Alien • Engineer • Manu facture • Industry • Marketing — Divine
• Ritual • Spiritual • Scruptucus • Aether • Static • Dynamics • Matter — Plains
• Vivacity • Metamorph • Current • Epithet • Grandeur • Position • Pose • Palatable — Govern
• Archiology • Teleology • Technology • Monadology • Numerology • Scientology • Biology • Psychology • Zoology — Globes
• Hermes • Saturn • Kabbalah • Mercury • Jupiter • Ra • Odin • Allah • Zeus • God — Deity

This is for Scrupt's study. He figured that this would be a good guide to reference through in the future. He didn't show it to anyone, because this was his model. It was to the best of his knowledge the best he could do with the amount of time he had. He was thinking what would make the best tetraktys. Part of it had to be right, he thought. He wondered what this would look like in absolute.

Scrupt thought about God and how he has everything. He knew the blessings God gave his people through Moses and with the tetraktys he could form the blessings to receive its knowledge. So he meditated to where he put the blessing into consciousness by defining each precept and put them together as one metaphysically. The blessing was Gold, Hyssop, Rams Blood and Bulls Blood. Scrupt really felt the wonders of God with this blessing in mind. (See Figure 44)

Attractions, Scrupt thought. Either close or far, up or down, of and about, on or off. Affinities of affects and chemistry. Positives and negatives either attracted or repel. A festivity of perplexity and simple affinities. Everything had its turn in evolution. All intuition reflects apon the one little movement in the beginning of the universe. Prote Hyle, Scrupt was thinking.

"Prote Hyle, Prote Hyle. Every element is an agent." Scrupt said.

Shawk said that students should solve their own problems. We were squashed here on Earth by the elements in the equation of E=mc2, Scrupt thought. Winds cried out and sang the song of evolution.

Human attraction? Is it magnetic? Scrupt asked himself. I know life rest on a current that humans will never have full control over. One can only get close to controlling it. They can't reach it though. There is no exact science, but discourse. It's like the spirit of God or the current of the tree of knowledge. It's a flow that governs and fuels absurdity. God granted us free will. With a continual feraling of good and evil over theurgy. Hate to love, love to hate, and its two energies racing for the lead in an endless enigma. It is the freedom that rest in a matrix of the element that is like a sword in the serendipity. Yet how free is it? Scrupt questioned. Is it our freedom to move through the troposphere? We can't exactly fly. I guess one just has to witness what the place is made out of to have the abilities to get out of the grasp of tragedies. A watch and learn basis I guess, Scrupt thought that the real masters never took up writing anything they had in perspective down.

The summer was over so Scrupt went back to Shawk's and told him what he set out to do. Shawk told him that he might want to spend some time studying American currency and economy. Scrupt was then off to the library to study American trade. At the library down town Cologne, Scrupt talked to some Americans and Scholars. Scrupt had been raised in Germany, but Shawk had been an American until he settled down in Germany. Scrupt primary language

(Figure 43)

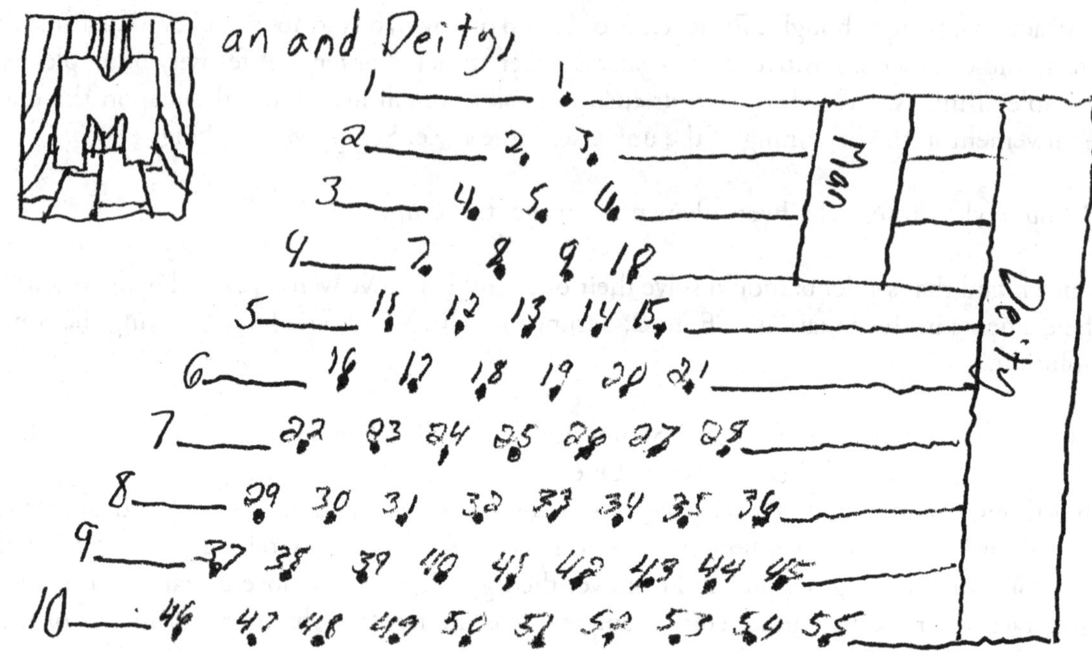

Man has his existence in the first four sections and the Deity exist in all of the sections.

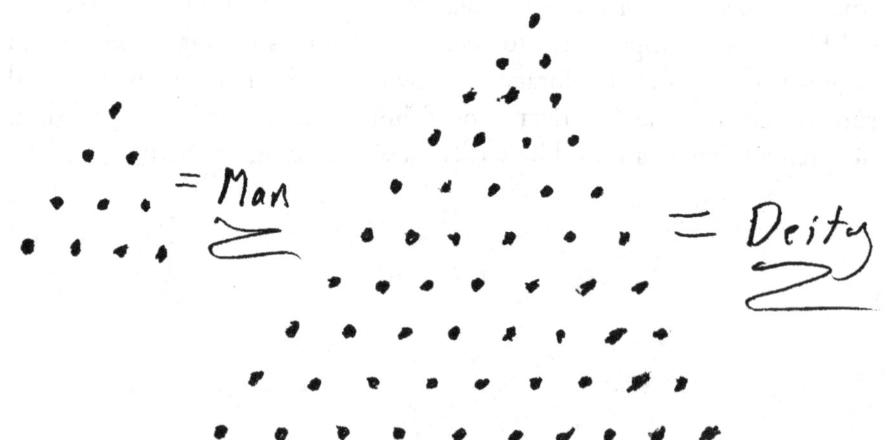

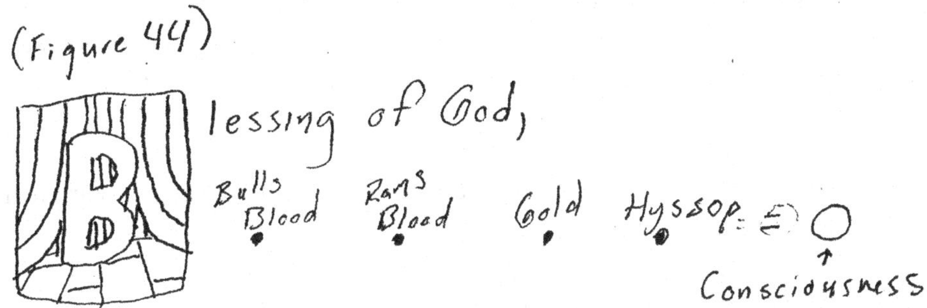

Combining the four precepts that God gave to his people gives one a Chirstian consciousness. The blessing gives one a clear head of communion.

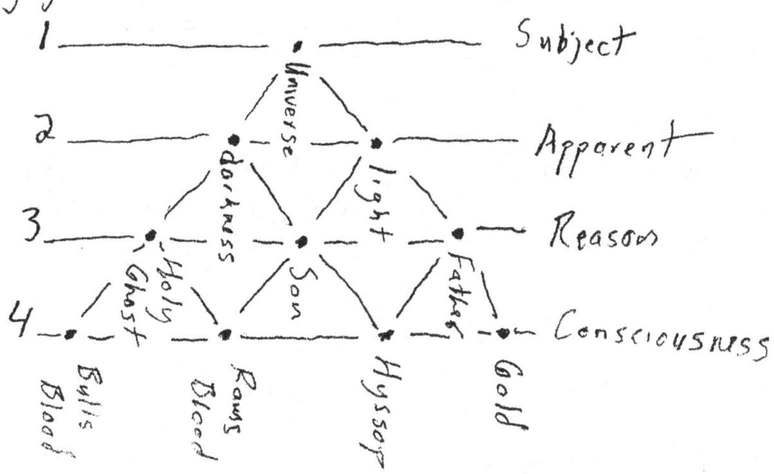

Each precept is a single blessing. Scrupt played with the precepts getting and changing his omniscience into different characters. He liked monkeying around with them because one could really notice a difference such as where the word met the intellect. The blessings made ones head through the holy ghost.

was English, and his second was German. He spoke in German to his peers, but when business rolled around he used English.

Scrupt got a US Dollar Bill from one of the Americans in the library. A Scholar he talked to mentioned that the meaning was a mystery to us all. Scrupt being a Pythagorean knew an order that had been long kept secret. He knew the latter like the back of his hand and the lore came easy to him.

"The Dollar Bill was such a work of art being created to represent Our Fathers work in a new country the world has ever known." The Scholar said.

Scrupt's eyes opened wide when he looked at the bill.

"In God We Trust." Scrupt said it was the easiest thing to understand on the bill. It is for all debts, public or private. Weaved like reality itself it came to us as the one dollar bill. Yet, what is it? What did Our Fathers want us to know? What is this bill? Scrupt questioned.

"The dollars purpose was to keep the peace, whatever the matter. It's a paper tender that took an intellect value at the weight of gold." The Scholar told Scrupt.

The both of them were sitting in the library at a wooden table and chairs. Scrupt found the tetraktys interesting on the back of the bill. It had an eagle holding 13 olive branches and 13 arrows. There was above the eagle's head a symbol that Scrupt couldn't make ends with, nor could anyone else. All Scrupt knew was that it was two tetraktys in juxtaposition. (See Figure 45)

E Pluribus Unum, Scrupt though.

"It describes the thinking of the bill." Said the Scholar.

"What does it mean?" Scrupt asked.

"Together we are one. The ONE in the middle of the bill gives you an idea of what it means when one takes a look at the bill. It is one universe, one thing, one dollar to show the merit of the dollar. I met a Pythagorean once who was collecting information on the bill and he asked me, what do I know, the he explained this to me." The Scholar said.

"Oh, what was his name?" Scrupt asked in anticipation.

"Edwind." The Scholar said.

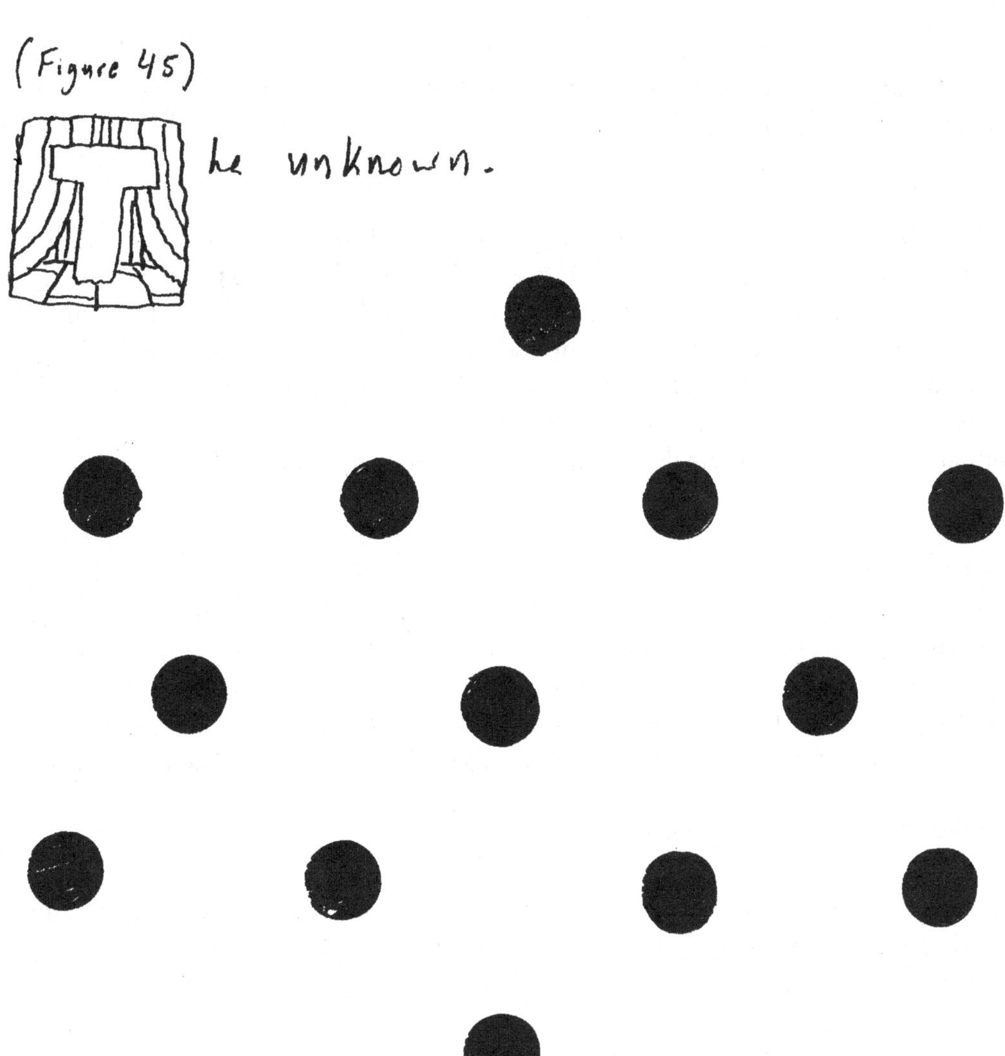

It is this symbol which no one could make end's meet. Scrupt thought it was two tetraktys formed together, yet what did that mean?

Prote Hyle, Scrupt thought. It was the beginning of a nation, the tetraktys seventeen-seventy-six. Thirteen colonies at the time, maybe the unknown symbol, Scrupt questioned.

Scrupt thought the bill was fantastic. To learn the tale of the bill one must know intellect. The bill is one piece of intellect. How exactly it worked Scrupt wanted to know. Scrupt wanted to know what everything on the bill was about. He asked around again and no one had any information.

The front of the bill with George Washington's face had some what of a magnitude to it. It had four ones at each corner just like the back side of it. Scrupt knew the tetraktys and knew that four of something meant a court and together the front and the back of the bill equaled eight meaning govern. The four ones on the front had different decorations to them. All eight ones had a back round of webbing divided into twelve points. What each meant Scrupt didn't have a clue. He asked a Professor who happened to be at the library about the decorations of the front of the bill and he said ones a female end and the other is a male end. The two below are their intuition.

Scrupt contemplated the US coins and found that he could make a tetraktys out of them. Superstiously thinking it made something like a podium that was in a current from the individual to somewhere to report or to do some serious orating over. It could be a connection to the Oval Office. One penny, two nickels, three dimes, and four quarters. It tallied out to be one dollar and forty-one cents. To a Pythagorean meant Subject, Court, Subject. Which Scrupt thought it meant divinity between two trading people with a court between them. (See Figure 46)

"What's in between us?" Scrupt questioned.

One cent was the Subject meaning one piece of intellect or one complete thing. Two nickels meaning the Apparents. Three dines meaning Reason. Four quarters meaning Court or Consciousness.

Scrupt began to delve his mind on the currency and trade in America. He came up with the idea that Law school would give him an edge on today's world. He thought what better thing was there to do, but to get into Law Enforcement as a Special Agent.

(Figure 46)

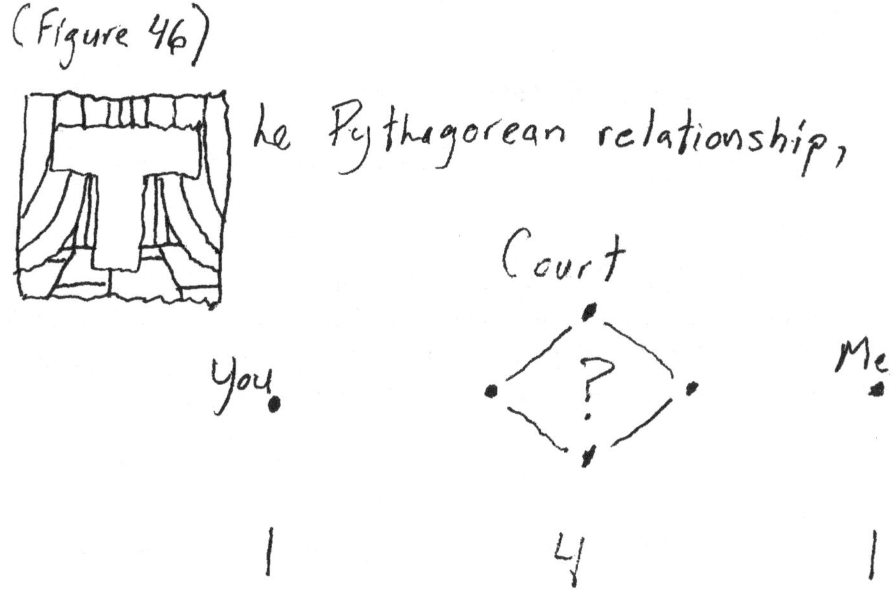

The Pythagorean relationship,

What's inbetween us? An individual gives to another recognition through our language. What we have learned only can be in the intellective to share. We have an individual substrate and a simulation of rudiments.

What's inbetween you and the universe?

Me. Universe

We figure out things by reflecting on the universe with the language. One says "Banana" and everyone figures its nous in their recognition. That is why we have a language like we do. So we all can share things.

Chapter 8

"Elaborate on that a little more."

Tiffany Schooler, 1998

An inspection was due for the guild's building in Minneapolis, MN. The guildies had to organize and teleport all the steam gear that was illegal to a warehouse down the street. Who knows what fines, jail or both one can face if not to careful? The inspection was late. Groco knew something was up when the Inspector showed up with an Agent from the Agency.

"What's up?" Groco asked.

"Oh, nothing, but you are all going to have to come with us, all of you." The Agent said.

They brought all of the guildies down town to question them all. I know no one will leak, Groco thought. We could just teleport them out of jail. Ah, nothing to be worried about. Even the little ones know that. He was just thinking keep in mind the invention side of the business. After a couple of hours of getting no where the Agency let them go. No one talked and all the guildies returned to the guild building.

Back at the laboratory Amy told Groc. "I guess they got a hold of the schematic manual for the time machine. The Agency said that they got it from an urbane Mother that was afraid her child had stolen it. I guess her child got it from a child that lives in this building. Who knows what the Agency will do if they knew what we are capable of with our tinkering."

"Awe, just kill me!" Groco shouted.

He knew that the Agency would probably use that schematic manual to also build a time machine. It's only a matter of time depending apon their ciphering abilities. It's all there on the schematic. Tears came from his eyes as Amy sat there with on the stairs rubbing his back.

"What's a matter, hun?" Amy asked.

"Just our dreams, Spucket's dreams, and that we will have to pick up the pace." Groco said.

The guildies assembled a guild meeting. There was a video conference with all the other Kluse labs. The meeting was about speeding up their work to meet a new deadline of 16 days, the old one was 60 days.

"We've got all the schematics in this manual for our time machine and satellite. We will need to make each part in the time of the deadline. Everything looks like it will go through. We are not exactly going to be lying down on the job, but we are to be done in about two weeks. Everything is to be fully operational." Groco said.

Groco had seen the prototype through and everything made it past his quality control testing. No more checks to be made. Just have to wait until the parts come in and have been fully assembled. Then the parts will have to go through the quality control testing once again.

"So we put the satellite here." Groco said as he pointed to the position the computer had configured to put it in the likes of where the cosmos had been.

"It's a half of light year away from the Suns current position. Distance enough to meet the frequency of the Sun's position 6 eons ago." Groco told the guildies.

They talked and asked questions a while and then the guild dissociated from assembly taking into action their next deadline.

"We'll be travelling back in time to copy things with our space paper the computer runs with the mechanical globes. The rules are no one can disturb any of the surface, meaning no terrain and no people. We don't want to screw things up for the future." Groco told Tiffany and Amy.

"We can copy anything we come across." Said Tiffany.

"That's anything space paper can handle in its ability to work with the mechanical globes." Amy said.

They were in Spucket's office talking about the trip of time travelling.

"Anything we can get a copy of will be worth a lot of money." Tiff said biting her nails.

"The satellite will be built here and teleport to New Zealand when finished. It then will be programmed to teleport itself into space to the position in line with the computer. It won't be noticed by Astronomers or any other government. It's because it will be moving in the aether just behind time and space." Groco said.

"We'll have to buzz by one of Spucket's favorites, The library of Alexandria." Groco said.

"Yet we plan on checking out Germany, first. Then to Byblos the city of the Phoenicians to check out the first ever written alphabets. It would be a very valuable find. One scroll would be worth millions." Groco said and sighed.

Groco being such a polymath had millions of things to do with one item. The mysteries that stirred the guild being able to travel back in time turned the guildies with overwhelming excitement. Tiff was thinking the magic that the antiquity experienced would be quite different then our own.

Perplexity has its way of spreading around, Tiff thought. What comes around goes around. The Sophist has seen perplexity along with the rest of antiquity and has identified with it. Contentions come and go just like the rains and winds. Most people are used to dealing with perplexity, and well it's an aliment of life. Stress is a necessity, Tiff thought.

"We have many ways to deal with perplexity in existence. We can say we know everything and yet we find ourselves with more than we can deal with. Absurdity of this place has us all once and a while looking stupid. You never know what hit you!" Groco said.

"Absurdity in view of the Sophist defines the place and here we find that the court serves as a means of foundation. What stays here and what disappears over time. What we will always have is what we call arbitrary things. A court is arbitrary as a surface of the tetraktys. It's a piece of intellect that is easily worked with and found. Not all courts are courts of Law. One may have a court on just about anything they honor." Tiff said over some warm coffee that Amy just made.

The Gals studied things they honored in their own courts. The best thing one can do is take a piece of intellect and hold it in a court of absurdity and ask questions about it. Like a court of love, hate, beer, urbanity, fear and any other word or words. Just to catch views on the moral, cultural and economics of the ages.

"There's a Judge and Professor in all of us. We gather evidence, we judge it, then like a Professor tell of our findings. Who says that the Judge's and Professor's were right in their findings when making up the facts? There are thousands of each of these two classes throughout the world and they only study in their localities. What is the evidence that says they are 100% true in their judging and teachings? Yet they know the relevant facts and that it is not suppose to be changeable. The evidence they use was built on a conformit latter. What is that first piece of evidence they used to build up the truths? With the truths, it is a matter of facts, but could you imagine how it was first processed? Who's to say that the people that gather the facts are right?" Groco said.

"You're right, Groco, people no longer use horses commonly and they don't ride in a buggy anymore. What will be obsolete in the year 4,000?" Amy said and started to pace back and forth with a cup of coffee in her hand.

She had reveries of the future going through her head.

"On the other hand we've got rules set up by facts. They say in vampire lore that a vampire has to untie every knot they come across and we have to do the same with our laws and rules. The Ten Commandments is a valid trade, at least in most countries. If you kill your in the wrong no matter what the next intention. Well on the flipside if you could bring one back to life, you are our hero! So the Judge and the Professor are right for the most part though existence will unfold more as time goes on in this broken cycle. When it comes down to defining the place what do the Judges and Professor have that we don't?" Groco asked as he played with a pencil and paper on Spucket's old desk.

He was playing with ciphers.

"They have an income, experience, a doctrine, an authority to back it up?" Tiff answered as she was looking at Groco's handy work.

"We must trust our guildies, we give them things to do in the likes. We do have a legit income for what they think to invent. We do break the Law, but that's not the guildies fault. Hell, you are right. We aught to open their dreams a bit more and let them surprise us. The guild has done more than enough to have enough money even for the next generation." Groco said and he really started to look hard into the dreams of the guildies.

"We, Groc, we have yet to fill our own dreams, you remember . . . Spucket?" Tiffany said.

"Yeah, poor old Spucket. He was such a dreamer." Groco sighed.

Tiffany starts lecturing to the class the next day.

"The Sophist does travel back and forth over time in their orations. Communication is the nexus of ages. The Sophist's ideas resourced the past present and future. In the past the language was drawn up on a page so one could organizes it. They made books finding out what the Author had to offer in their intelligence. Where the Scholar would draw up the best he could the meaning of things to bring to the authorities. The search and discovery of words in antiquity was a great and rare value that gave riches to the Sophist. Yet today most ideas haven't found a page yet. What I want you guildies to do is imagine the year 4,000 and put it on a page." Tiffany said and handed out notebooks and pencils.

"Everything we have here will be out dated by innovation. That's everything man has put together here. We will be drinking water and looking at the Sun though. Remember the atom will always be an atom unless mankind screws it up for us. I want you guildies to understand Immutability, Mutability, and Permutability in the measurement of time in existence. So what will still be here in the year 4,000?" Tiffany asked as the guildies worked things out.

"Class, Mutability is our movement at present without words. As time goes by your actions disappear into the past and this is Immutability. When one is at a conjecture into the future it is the Permutability." Tiffany said and asked the class if there are any questions.

"The language 2,000 years ago was different and I'm thinking it will be different 2,000 years from now." Pete said.

"Yes the language might die out in the future." Tiffany replied.

The class worked out their pages for some time and then went to supper ending the day of school.

There are arbitrary things that will never change. Fire burns wood, we breathe air in the likes. The entire universe is up to change though. It's miraculous the way things size up, as if a higher power is still in charge. Some elements have a half life if it is unstable or comes in change of reactions. On the other hand a lot of the elements are stable. What elements are useful is the question. It depends on the importance. The things man has set as rules and principles over the elements will never change. It'll be added to through with new discovery. The T.V. shows of the people of the year 4,000 will show just how the world worked back now. Dreaming of things we shouldn't take for granted we should get what we need instead. The things we should take for granted is the in solipsistic premise that weighs out our differences in a perpetrating bias and prejudice in our speech. When will we ever understand just how important communication really is? Tiff thought.

In the lab down stairs Groco was organizing the parts that were teleported in for the ship. Our words, Groco thought, have what we call an etymology. Etymology is a book of word origins. Some of the words have been around for millenniums and others just a few years. New words pop up apon new discoveries. Salutations are the words we use for greetings and meeting people though this is brevity in the likes. Having a value for your own words makes you important. The gift of your word is a trade never lost if you give your word as a gift. A power comes from a word if used in the immediate importance and has a finite definition that meet with the performance of the word. Yet, what is between us? When we talk to each other? When one Graduates High School? When someone calls you the worst? When you experience for the first time a loss of a loved one or tragedy? Hate, love, morass, and remorse. A light bulb needs changing. The Eiffel tower needs repair or the warmth of the night as we watch the moon. Yet we are celestial bodies with desire to float about and eat everything like termites. We gather or feed off the current of the frequency and live life. The riches man in antiquity was the Sophist. Not because he had money, but because he had currency, the variant and invariant of the alchemy and metaphysics of words. And because he took each word and treasured it. He examined it for its value in prudence and importance. Holding it to the relevance and then orating the perfect rhetoric to others as he had their ears. Leaving whoever heard them with an impression that they never forgot.

"Quality." Groco said and then held the word in his mind to the entire absurdity as he went over his plans for the time machine.

From millennium to millennium the word has changed drastically. We go through a place called reality from time to time. Other times we are just nominal to our imaginations and thoughts where the only rules are our inhibitions and moral. Yet no one lives in reality, it's only on our discourse of a near perfect science. Dealing with reality is our job from time to time. We got yet a mundane order to deal with that is tied down by reality called work and responsibility. Reality is the place for our rules and actions. A dream isn't real it's our imagination, but a dream in the mind is real. Reality of an element is up to the change of nature or changed by man in chemistry of thought. Religiously reality is set in our prayers, ceremonies and rites. They practice the same thing over and over again and they should because a person's brain doesn't change much in the skull over a long period of time nor does gold lose its color. The mind changes and so does the imagination with it. We are human beings when we are born and we will be human beings when we die. The reality has always rested in an idea of danger. It is what configures the survival instincts of man and animal. If it's not dangerous it's ok, but if it is dangerous we put a danger label on it. As morals do go. Most of what was dangerous to antiquity is still dangerous today. Many definitions of reality have people still making mistakes is solely up to the absurdity of the lord's. I break rules, but I don't agree with the way the laws are, just I guess if you're not hurting anyone, its fine by me. Groco thought in all his desire to heal his wounds and go completely legit.

It's interesting to look at what went on in History and find that time hasn't changed much here on Earth. A man today might have evolved little from his grandparents. What's in between us? Groco questioned. What are we? What can we be? If you want to become and Actor or Actress, do it, but you'll never get past the human condition no matter what one does. One needs to identify what is human. We all eventually die. Therefore, what is man? Why is it that we need to be entertained constantly? The Deity of this place is the head of his people. He is therefore the greatest entertainer. Not the media of standards we get from scripts and T.V. shows. Yet a more nonfictional writes where we love each other on the peek of family and community. One was made to consume, but also rest and have vision to help along the way. We were made with such large brains that take wedges of information into our cortexes . . . Use them! For what though? An animal has its habitat, but we build things that destroy nature. It's the complexities of the element gives us the essentials of life. What else do we really need? The decisions we make will eventually make things better, right? God promises one everlasting life and then you die and then go up to the sky where Jesus judges you! Heaven or Hell, Heaven . . . Or . . . Hell. Groco thought.

Heaven? An idea that is God's home. Every single piece fits. Hell, a place of no rest where no pieces fit. Reincarnation? You'd reminisce through the general classes and say it's possible. There are 50 congregations in this city, one of them has to be right. Huh, what makes a person want to live and survive? Production, sweet production and the dedication to a promised paradise. Love, need and righteousness. The actions and reactions of us humans all feral trade of some sort. What's in between us? A trade of words? Love is the passionate morsels in between us, we eat it in shovels. It's the most valuable emotion, I vote it just above hate. We were made by delving elements that ferralled through the changes of ages. We didn't have any pictures of the eloquence. We just had animals roaring and nature telling us what to do. Nature, just nature was our home, our essential shelter. The sky our roof. The sky, yet what's in between us? Groco thought, then went about the assembly of the satellite.

The English language has thirty-six characters. A-Z and 0-9. Each is a unique number or letter which represents the reflection of the universe in reading, writing and arithmetic. They can be arranged to let another know exactly what you wrote or spoke. The algorithmics are tools mankind has developed to continue and record its measures. Rudiments in intelligence are ruled by the eight sections of grammar. There is a better life and these are the tools to get there. The proper use enhances the performance of the word. We live in a time where the best performance gets the grade. We don't always live in absurdity all the time there is some logic in today's world. Logically we have houses where we take the leisure to dream, what's next.

"Thou shall not kill." Commands God the performer of performers.

The words are our guides. The word is complicated and just disappears out of focus sometimes in the absurdity of the works of the world. Reality is the logic we put together so we can't forget anything. Groco thought himself to sleep in his night of work.

Chapter 9

"If it is not yours don't touch it."

Veronica M Bulau, 1993

In America at the University . . .

"The Laws are here for your protection. Whatever the case public or private. The logic we use in our daily lives goes on without end. People break these ideas. The people can be ignorant and you will have to be the best when laying down the authority. They will be at your supervisor's door if you fail. Be respectful, responsible and reasonable. You up hold the Law, these people are citizens. I for one believe that our fore Fathers captured in the First Amendment the very concept of belief." The Professor said and got a serious look on his face.

"The First Amendment establishes freedom of and from Religion, Speech and the Press in the right to assemble peacefully in redress of grievance to petition our government. This is a form of belief that a person has the right to peacefully grieve without any inhibitions of or from the Press, Religion or of Speech. The Declaration of Independents has a preamble "We the People" meaning the citizens are the government. As citizens, when we talk to each other we should have in mind the non-establishment of the First Amendment that grants us a liberty to freely redress in grievance. It is our freedom, We the People. Question establishment by holding it to the belief of the First Amendment. The Government's first rule saved us a right to truly be free in our convictions." The Professor said.

"We don't exactly enforce gravity, though we would like to." The Professor jokes and the class laughs.

"Laws govern life and that govern forces a duration in the actions of life. Say as entropic as the current of an apple tree. This produces a concept no living thing can get a long without . . . Now just what is Congress? Well Con—meaning the anti of everything and Gress—meaning the movement one acts through. So the meaning of Congress is anti-movement. If there is a mistake a citizen makes then Congress (Anti-movement) makes a Law and signs a bill to prohibit the bad moves the citizen has made." The Professor said and then walked behind his desk.

"We as representatives of the Law need to investigate every nook and cranny the world has to offer. Some of us will learn the most sophisticated weapons, gadgets and programs available. Every investigation counts as we are swore to enforce the Law. As we are sworn to take the intuition to do our duties under the dedication of the Highest Court in the Land. To live in a place we have to have rules. Being fair is essential. Being fair to yourself is an ability to show diligence in the integrity of the Law. As you probably already know your intelligence is the best tool for your defense in justice. Integrity to perform in the importance of our duties must be followed at all times, just so one can get some sleep at night." The Professor told the class.

"What keeps the people from killing each other?" The Professor asked the class.

"Laws." Korlax said.

"A higher power, repercussions of doing something wrong, good morality in other words." Scrupt said.

"You two are both right. People learn to live together showing a common wealth of right and wrong, good and bad, and better or worse. We learn to respect others and hold the Law in high regards. The way the Laws are in different countries vary. Some of you are from and will be in different countries at times. So what do you think of the universal Laws of the world?" The Professor asked.

"Rhetoric, it's the Law that everyone in society believes and follows, well not everyone, the way culture goes, but maybe the majority." Korlax replied.

"It is to me a rule of thumb from the foundation which governs a group of people that should be obeyed. The golden rule in the likes." Scrupt said.

"Yes, our Constitution and Ten Commandments'. All of which should be obeyed." Said the Professor.

"What? Professor do you suggest we should follow?" Scrupt asked.

"Anything you can agree with in your guidelines of the Law. You have to use your discretion. There is no universal right and wrong. I suggest you use the principle and Laws of the place to achieve the countries liberties. They were designed to show the right way. Put the Laws to the test in prudence and importance looking at the affinities and maxims. Watch for the performance of the rudiments delineating ideas." The Professor said.

"It sounds too deep for me." Korlax said.

Korlax was a six foot four inch tall man with half his body being a machine. He's a cyborg. It's one of technologies greatest. He was in a car accident five years ago. He was a police officer back then. He's 26 years old now.

"Technology moves by the fiscal now days. Eventually it will move monthly in the future until we have maxed out the element in the ways of scholastics. This will leave us in about the year 6,000 I guess. The language reflects every Law now days. In this country and every other country the language is the muse to be able to recollect the universe. The Law has a unique nominal. Meaning it only reacts to danger. Each person is a little argument and is responsible for understanding the Law. Know matter what you will be on a level where people are above and below you. The Deity is the highest level and from what they have been through over the eons, one wouldn't dare to be them. I'm too young to be a Deity. I'm like them though, not as them though." The Professor said.

"If everyone is using their own definition of things. How do they follow the Law?" Korlax asked.

"Everyone has to behave as their own person in what they learn and believe to be in the place they live in a common wealth in the likes. We all follow a common Law and with it comes common sense. Freedom of choice. One has to learn the Laws and different forms of government. Republicans, Democrats, Socialist, Communist, Aristocracy, Anarchist and so on. We have our freedom to take the intuition to do what we want as long as if doesn't break the Law." The Professor said.

"How do you decide punishment for criminals?" Scrupt asked.

"We punish on the extent of what Law was broken. You don't find some one in jail for a parking ticket. Always remember you got to be fair. You have to show some intelligence after all the language is about 2,500 years old. Your assignment for this weekend is to write a poem on the First Amendment. See you next week." The Professor said and packed up and left out the door.

Scrupt just loved it here in a America. It had so many cultures living here on the fifth element. One main language the people of America inherited through a delve beginning. It adopted words throughout the years from citizens of other countries that sailed in at the beginning. Yet the English gave Americans the rudiments they use which were a model from the Roman Empire and so was the basis of Law. The Patriots and Pilgrims made way to construct this country. The President's all gave their unique personalities to form the different tones and ascents we have today. The tone of voice in America has is different from state to state. There are several ascents in its dialect. English has since spread all over the world. People loved Scrupt's ascent and he enjoyed theirs.

The State vs. the Church, Scrupt thought. They are separate as of now. The age of them is quite different. The State is a mir 200 years old and the Church a tedium of about 2,000 years old. The Church has a ceremony that they practice down to the tee each and every mass. They witness under the Holy Bible the everlasting life through Jesus Christ. The State has Congress that makes up the Laws and it grows as the moral, cultural and economics of an era develop. The State is based off facts the generals have coughed up through study and actions. Math, Science, English and History are those general classes. The Church is based off the crucifixion of the Son of God.

One who takes office in the State is sworn in to protect the people of the country. The State follows the Laws that have been passed through Congress. The Laws are made to protect, inhibit and guide the people. One has to trust them to make all the pieces fit in their abatement and abiding.

The Church is open Worldwide and so are its Laws, they are universal. All Religions feral the word of their Deity. Worshippers of God seek the truth, and we all at one time or another have gone wrong through tough times. The door of the church is always open to us. The more one knows about God the better the worship.

The Church and State are separate. If they were united, what would happen to all the religions of the world? There would be no other Deities, besides one if we only chose one and in the likes God would be the only Deity in the grand and free United States of America.

Scrupt lived in Europe most of his life. He viewed America with much love. This new to him place, America, the vivacity and freedom. In his picture of the government the apple took many new forms. The way the people bonded and played with each other it was a simulation of intellect. Scrupt's mind felt a whole new lore as the conjunctions of celestial bodies went around.

"A different frequency to the entire element." Scrupt said to himself.

A gift, as in a wedge, he stuck out like a black beetle in a rice pile, Scrupt thought.

The jobs available in the paper for these that had schooling and credentials was just like back home in Germany. High School, Scrupt thought.

"What did I miss out on?" He said to himself.

He never had to go. That's all one needs for some of these jobs. This country was full of people that wanted more and to know freedom. A finite state, Scrupt thought. Shawk had taught Scrupt to assess things down to the finite state or cause and effect and to use reasoning over his thoughts over his appetite to bring things to his mental taste. To add up all the resources was the only way in his heuristics. One has to measure it with all the other things in the world to find its place. Scrupt could easily stomach America. With it's serendipity of industry, manufacturing and marketing. In anything that was on the market all industries had one goal . . . Money. None, not one product was without a copyright that is at least in America. Every product has its I.P.O. which the product reaches the public. So to protect the creator of the product has to go through a Patent Attorney. Once the product has been copy written the product has an I.P.O. where the inventor's can add or combine the product making it better for their own inventions. Say one invents a mop. Another inventor can add a scraper on the side of it that allows one to scrape the floor while one mops without the original inventors consent. Is that fair? Scrupt thought.

"It's just how it is, I guess." Scrupt said to himself as he recognized his own mentality for inventing.

When an inventor studies a product to get a new idea isn't that stealing the idea's form the original inventor? Or is it one of the rights to innovate? If you have an I.P.O. of a product does it become open game for other inventors? The best way to come up with an idea is to come down and study the unknown. Study the unknown where the word is free of copyrights in a book that is string free. A reference book. Created on what the facts are throughout History. By the looks of things most inventors are old men. That have aged their development of intelligence some thirty years or so. If only they picked up a pencil, Scrupt thought.

Writing a book takes a few organization skills, dedication, a good memory and a great desire and perspective of the unknown. Practicing writing is essential, Scrupt thought. One can write poems, essays, or short stories to begin. Remembering if your feeble in something try, try and try again. It takes a while to know the territory of writing a good book. It can be very vigorous depending on the level of ones vocabulary. A great retreat in writing a book is to improve your skills by reading any kind of books that will show you new words and ideas. The dictionaries and thesaurus's are great books to create ciphers in word alchemy. I for one believe you first need to understand what has already been done with a pencil and a clean sheet of paper. The Bible is a story of the History of the Christians. It unfolds into a story about God and his relationship with his people. It is the physics of Christianity which holds the truths about God. Books and artistry have all been made up by the doloring of that clean sheet of paper and pencil. Each book you read will enhance your orations and writing structure, above all it will expand your mind and let you into the wonderful lore of the world or worlds. Each sketch you do should be held up to the critics, your peers, and the public eye. If you don't try and imagine so. Scrupt thought as though he was teaching or orating to students.

Making ones view a page of poetry one can learn from teaches the individual lives pains and happiness's in the rudiments expressed on paper for all to reminisce through. In all you do in life, the struggle already lies in what has already been written. One has to ready their skills to come into the bask of life and enjoy it. Life's examples and in art, books, and other likes of ledger main. A picture of the permutable feral spirit shows just how free the future is when we look on in the direction in front of us. In Heaven, Earth or Hell the good spirit converts the bad. Words are the performers of the spirit. A man performing the word to lead in the right way every time converting the bad words with the good words is the style of the Cleric. Though finding the right way can be perplexed and sometimes one finds that one loses.

The bad spirit has already made its way along with the good spirit. Seen by a few and eaten by most. Scrupt took a look at this evil and everything he could at a plenum. It was easy for him to see, but very hard for them already consumed by the bad spirit. It had to be the way he had lived his life. Being raised by a Cleric in the Orthodox way as a Pythagorean. Being that he was taught up righteousness at a young age. Scrupt began to wonder . . . How can I wake these people up.

So Scrupt went down into the streets and found two bums to have a conversation with to get to know their spirit and what was on their mind. They were just lying down drinking with each other. They were down right filthy and stunk of Indian food. Scrupt went up and confronted the two.

"Hi, there, what are you up to this fine day?" Scrupt asked with the intentions of lifting them up from the slums of the street.

"Hey, buddy, we are needing the good life and you?" The Bum said.

"I'm Scrupt, what are your names?" Scrupt asked as he took a spot next to them juxtapose the building.

"My name is Ralph and this is Howard." Ralph said.

"People don't understand, its all one big important hoax, everything was created by a farce. Sure we have are responsibility to the cause. The love and honor of merit. Yet we can survive down here and we make the best at what's to come. At times things are down right bad, crazy even! Yet we love it. The worlds just too big of a place to live in. Everyone insinc with money and the latest fifth element. Us two need little, just a bottle and the streets. We have no family except what we can get down here. What wonder one can find down here and the prizes . . . That only homeless can enjoy. We live by low expectations and little to no responsibility. It's a life. I know you have a story to tell. So what is it my friend?" Howard said.

"Just a cardboard box?" Scrupt asked as he imagined the living conditions down here.

"There's a mystery to the world my friend and we meet some of the best story tellers down here. We used to live in a house, but now we have the sky as our roof. No buildings no roads to make our path. We do exactly what rats do. It all comes down to survival. What do the people expect the world to turn into in the future? We all return to nothing. Out of all the things that are out there, what is the most important thing for you?" Ralph asked as he waved his hands in a broadening manor

"Trade, it's got to deal with trade. My importance lies with the latter of trade and necessity. Weather its words, intellect or matter it is the life of the universe. God gave us direction mainly to follow the Ten Commandments and Gospel's. So my importance lies with the knowledge of trade. Anything, my friend, deals in trade. Each piece is counted as an intellect. It holds worth to the place it fits. I find that the need of trade is more essential. What else does man need, but trade in the growing world? Though one always wants better things, it's important to me to see that a person gets the essential needs." Scrupt said in excitement.

"There is an evil in the world and mindless people that really don't know what they are doing. Most of us are driven by fear though. They need to wake up. There is deism that one must get the gist of when floating about the day taking in the ethereal." Howard said.

"Deism? Evil? Exactly the point. Yes, a body of the lord that takes over another body like sharing the spirits of beer and wine. A Congress, being swallowed by a whale in the likes." Scrupt said.

"All of us are born with a clean spirit. Which evil if given into will dirty it." Howard said.

"Well, you are like reading my mind." Scrupt said a little violatedly.

"I am, I can read you like a page." Howard said and smiled and Ralph just hackled.

"What do you mean?" Scrupt said a little on the edge of his seat.

"I can read your dossier (dos-se-a) like a page in the wind. I used to work for the government. The government has many programs of dealing with people. It has a dossier on everyone. It's just how the pieces fit." Howard said in an ebullient way.

One could tell he was interested in teaching Scrupt.

"Scrupt, it sounds like you're from Europe." Ralph said to digress the conversation.

"I'm for Germany and a dossier, that's crazy." Scrupt said as if he wanted to learn more.

"I bet that's a fun place to be." Howard said.

"Yes, the sky is smaller and I know the territory very well. People are up to less compared to America, most are standard into a routine in Germany." Scrupt said and pondered the differences of the two countries.

"Well what the hell are you doing here?" Ralph asked.

"I'm getting an education. You see back home I'm a very successful inventor and have a fantastic laboratory with a fortune from inventing. I tend to invent things for America once I understand the market. I'm going to school now to become given the chance a Special Agent. Who knows what fine trinkets they will be handing me at that time. It really makes me think." Scrupt said as he began to have reveries of being a Special Agent.

"Ah . . . Well, good luck to you." Ralph said and took a pull from his bottle.

"Ah, to you two as well." Scrupt said his good byes and went to his apartment.

Howard and Ralph get on with their day.

The weekend pressed on and so did Scrupt's study. He began working on his poem for class. He met a friend in class Friday and invited him over to his apartment this Saturday evening. There was a knock at the door and Scrupt answered it.

"Korlax, my friend, glad you could make it." Scrupt said to his surprise.

"Oh, glad to see you to, Scrupt." Korlax said as he felt good to be with Scrupt again.

The apartment was halfway furnished and it looked like though it was Scrupt's first night in it from moving. There were a few boxes full of things, a couch, and kitchen table and chairs. They went in and sat at the dinning room table.

"You know not one person feels the same about how things work today? Back in the forties people had for the most part the same idea. They called some of them squares. The information market has grown so large now days that people have so much to choose from. There is no more common study, a lot of people don't study from the Bible though they care much more about lexicons." Korlax said to start off the conversation.

"I know what you mean, such diversity." Scrupt replied with great interest.

"Each person is unique, but our morals that when one keeps them they are exactly the same. They have their own personal definition on how things work today and in choice there are so many morals out there. I guess if one is in love or in the likes share the same taste, they are the same, though people as singles are different. I guess that's just how God wanted it. Only when you consider monocracy it comes down to an idea on just how different people are. I'm not saying that we should single anyone out though. Private vs. Public. Personally we are private and in public we are social. We reflect in iteration our surroundings and come up with the same answer on the surface. That's where we agree at that point." Korlax said as he wanted Scrupt to view the importance of the way people look at the place we live in.

"Yes, I agree. A man is a man and each is different, but there are many pages to man's life. A blank page is identical for each of us and that we all have to keep in mind. No matter how dirty ones page, in ones book one page remains blank. We all reflect in the same way, point A to point B. The universe is the same when viewing it for each individual. Our uniqueness comes from individual perspective in conjecture. No matter what people hold to their experience that they have learned people make assumptions. I guess as the story goes, we always want to be comfortable, hour to hour, and day to day." Scrupt said.

"True, but how are we exactly?" Korlax added and got the urge for a drink.

"Production, we have to produce to survive. Industry, marketing and manufacturing, love, hate, etiquette, as well as moral, cultural, and economics. Whatever the case we are broken, yet finite beings, a resourcing agent on the continuum of the universe. Whose vice is to reflect on the element for a means to survival." Scrupt said.

Korlax asked if he had anything to drink. Scrupt offered him tea or coffee and they both decided to drink tea.

"We are in fact located in different times and spaces. The frequency of the Sun, Earth, and Moon are the main balance of our minds where we have our differences in precepts. Yet we reflect on an intellect that is considered the only thing in the universe at the time our eyes are apon it . . . Secular?" Korlax questioned Scrupt to tell the difference between a broad mind and a secular one.

"Oh, ah . . . A secular one like you said holds things as they are the only thing in the universe and a broad mind figures in all of existence to that one thing in subsistence." Scrupt said as if it were basic knowledge.

"There is a need for the secular and broad mind and to know the difference. When one is public and private we need to divide down to individuals and that my friend is a good way of looking into addressing these two minds." Korlax said he really loved Scrupt's ability to lead things in the right way.

He then took a sip of his tea waiting for Scrupt to return his conjecture.

"You're right why focus on one piece of intellect when you can view the whole universe in contemplation. So . . . You have studied the diversities of time and space? That's one thing I have already tinkered with back home." Scrupt said and sipped some tea.

"Well, not exactly. What do you have in mind?" Korlax asked.

"Well we are beings of time and space. It comes down to the point in time and space that we reason the element. We pick up the life in absurdity and reflect an unknown to find what we need to do after we learn how things work in the place we live. Ah, and that's a thing we do the whole time we are alive. We use the universe leading us in an unknown to give us life. It comes down to the smallest point in perspective, a globe in any size or shape, the dimensions are endless and it is still in the universe secular or broad. We are quite divided in the way we react to each other, though we are yet twain. What's in between us?" Scrupt asked as though he was really yearning for an answer to the question.

"The universe? Ah, nothing. There is nothing in between us." Korlax said in conjecture.

"Come on think. There are after all rules to the universe." Scrupt said showing to Korlax the importance to dig deep into his mind.

"Now that I think of it. We have to look at it as a human point of view, not the point itself. Well, the Ten Commandments are in between us . . . The whole language of God is in between us . . ." Korlax said in awe.

He thought Scrupt was pretty ingenious how he brought it together.

"The Law of any country is between us when we are there. The bonds, stature, and trade. We are trading right now as we speak and believing in a government bond of abiding the abatement of Laws in commerce of the elements. Trained in it as we grew up to meet the importance religion is a work of trading words. Trading words that is, an intellect that is also in between us. The Law gives us a scope to seek with our frame of beliefs." Scrupt said and got up and asked Korlax if he wanted more tea.

"We again are in fact located in different times and spaces. To realize this we must come to terms of our own time and space. We find it by a matrix that a conjunction exists on." Scrupt said.

"By finding this one has to watch out for paradox's and vices which will change the outcome of the apparents. A paradox will slow you down as one side grows or the other side shrinks. A vice will make you dependant on the one dimension in a secular way always leaning or failing toward each other in juxtaposition." Scrupt said as he showed Korlax the tetraktys of a conjunction.

"That makes no sense." Korlax argued.

"Oh, so you're not familiar with the tetraktys. I guess." Scrupt said.

"Well, no, I'm not." Korlax said.

"Well, we are beings of time and space. We read at this level and are conscious at the court. It comes down to a point in the universe that we ourselves read self being. The light that passes between us is the line we use to communicate with in the narrative as a surface. We use our frequency to generate our imagination and reality. One can make a point out of anything they desire. We have what we call absolute. One can have that much of a . . ." Korlax fell off the edge of his seat hitting the floor.

"Ah! Ha! Ha! Ha!" Scrupt laughs and points at him.

Korlax gets up.

"You had me in a trance . . . What is absolute?" Korlax ask as he sits back down again and took a sip of his tea.

Scrupt gets out a piece of paper and draws this formula. (See Figure 47)

"Each point is described differently and when you stack them they all must meet a matrix from start to finish to bottom to top in a full absolute. Absolute is like a full deck of cards. Whatever the cards are marked gives you the value of the performance." Scrupt told Korlax.

"Sounds like you got this stuff down." Korlax said and got up and told Scrupt he had to use the bathroom.

After a while Korlax was done and came out and sat down again.

"It's all a matter of general elementary. Class by class. Are you familiar with the globes above our heads?" Scrupt asked as things were picking up again.

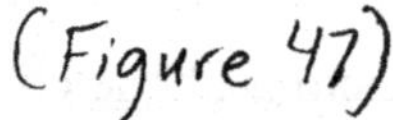

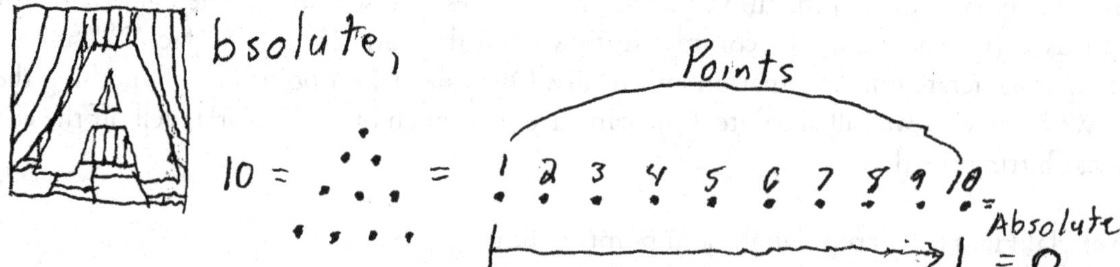

Absolute is a thing of a plenum. Everything is added up to one professorship. All pieces are relevent in their heuristics. Imagine inventing a card game. Where you the inventor has to come up with the type of cards.

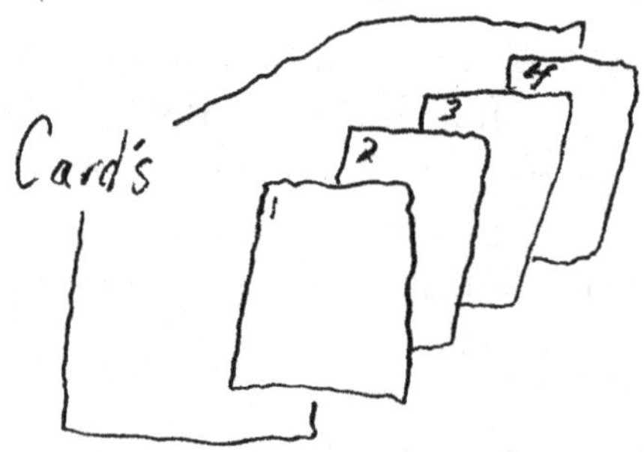

If one can make a deck it is absolute when arranged all together, The globes above our heads are this way in the likes. One takes a globe and labels it to bring better understanding. One then groups all the globes in absolute.

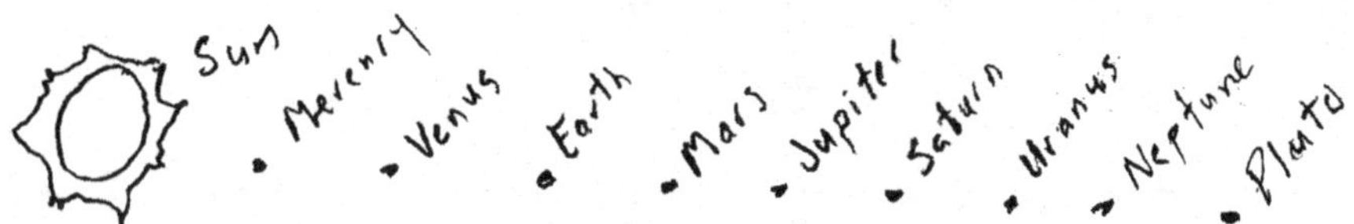

The planet's are all together one absolute.

"Yeah, the Earth, planets, moons and stars, why do you ask?" Korlax replied and put some sugar in his tea.

"I mean the globes as ideology that balances the way we do things. Any word can be a globe and one can organize them in any way. Take a globe for once and imagine it in your mind. Does it make you feel something?" Scrupt asked passionately.

"Well in makes me feel dense, like a density that a globe would make sitting in my mind." Korlax said and wondered what he was actually trying to tell him.

"That's because you reflected on such a dumb idea in the first place without defining what exactly you wanted. The globe you put in your mind had the nominal epithet of being inane or dense. It's up to you to describe what the globe is made out of in your mind. One has to know what is real and what is not. The globe is the intuition of the universe. It holds secrets. The permutation of ones thought is governed by the production of their globes in a heuristic sense. Take your eye balls or brain cells, they are like globes. May it be the Sun, or just a globe in the mind, it is energy. Energy to survive and without them it is called a monogon." Scrupt told Korlax that was getting more and more interested.

"What about things outside the imagination like holding globes in reality?" Korlax questioned.

"Now you're talking. The globes transform into anything they come across when one wants them to get information about something in a phenomena of its reality. The globes are there to reflect existence. For one Pythagoras discovered the tetraktys 2,500 years ago which is now used in the organization of globes. We are still in our youth of understanding the globe above our heads. It would be pretty pleasing to see things really happen, but maybe, just maybe in the future it will come." Scrupt said.

"Sounds interesting to me, what's the catch?" Korlax questioned.

"Only we have to be able to lead the energy in the right way. It comes to us like the Tree of Knowledge, it is protected by a sword in every direction. Our memory and the way we think are balanced by energy of these globes. To practice the globes one must understand how the tetraktys works. A globe can be anything. The elements are substratum in absolute of the evolution of the mind relating to the universe. One starts with no absolute, an unknown, and gains the element as they grow. The tetraktys is used to number the globes in a nominal order of scholastics." Scrupt said.

"That's a little too deep for me. I know we have our differences." Korlax expressed and took a drink of his tea.

"The point being that we are not the same unless we meet trade per trade on the surface, and that my friend is a perfect ethereal. When we think we go out into absurdity. We have only to fear thyself." Scrupt said.

"Well, we've been able to write for the past 2,500 years. Almost everybody knows how to write now. What makes a person go bad?" Korlax asked.

"Oh, first we must find the human condition in our lives. Identify with it, each of us. Then on to find the right thought cycle and then the Law is a muse to the human condition. We savvy what's right and learn from prohibiting ourselves from the wrong things." Scrupt said.

"Oh, yeah, the condition that we all have a nature that is unpredictable at times. We have our temptation, supplication and indecision. We have an appetite we all have to satisfy." Korlax said.

"Only when you are able to correctly address the human condition you are able to understand what we are when it comes to monocracy or oneself. There's a lot to address in today's lifestyle. The question do you want to be a mathematician for a while and then go to be an English major is what one can face. The classes now days are covered up as we in society look at things under a microscope. To me there is a lot more things than viewing things with such a secular apparatus, addressing takes a look at each and everything." Scrupt said.

Korlax just sits there with an intrigued look on his face totally admiring the way Scrupt talked about the subject.

"When do we find green pastures?" Korlax asked.

Scrupt just smiles.

"Enormous, just enormous amounts of organization go into the world's work today. I guess green pastures fit some where on the agenda. It maybe heaven on Earth. That's if things go right. Though green pastures are the ways of religion and they feral everything. Though it doesn't involve every religion. We are looking at if one of the religions in a city goes wrong, all the other religions take out their mallets and put them into place. All of the religions know this, so it acts like a population control. All hell breaks loose sometimes and like in religion, it's the same way for men and countries. It shows the importance of religion and political parties, namely the heads of the country." Scrupt said and yawned, it was getting late.

"Yes, the amount of information a politician has is phenomenal. To lose one is a great loss." Korlax said.

"Yeah, that goes with most people we lose. The politicians have a tough job. Keeping the country running, not to mention one of the many mistakes that happen." Scrupt said and sipped of his tea at the dinning room table.

He was getting sore sitting there so long.

"Organized crime has its hands in politics. Though not as much as it use to." Korlax said as he was thinking of the pros and cons of politics.

"If it isn't one thing it's another. It's usually up to an Agency that has Special Agents to keep things under wraps peacefully." Scrupt said and thought again about being a Special Agent.

"I want to be a Special Agent." Korlax said as he was thinking it over for about a year now.

"You do? So do I. Just imagine what sophisticated technology they have and not to mention the privileges that come with it." Scrupt said as he got a second wind.

"Sworn to protect and seek out king pin individuals for their crimes. Awe . . . Special Agents. Hey, you know what? We could go up and sign up together." Korlax said.

"Yes, that's a wonderful idea." Scrupt said.

"Let's go down Monday together and fill out applications." Korlax said.

It was late so Korlax said his good byes and they got a hold of each other Monday and filled out applications at the Agency.

Scrupt walked with a monumental strut. Filling out the mold of his body. Like that of one of Leonardo's sculptures. He had a very strong voice that enticed each word he said. He used it well in his speech at the end of the quarter in college. He loved magic and technology so, but Law was one of those things he thought he had to learn to continue his life. Everything he dealt with in life had some kind of rule or law attached to it. The way things worked had to do with the existence of a Deity or Ruler which therefore had laws that showed the way people are governed in the place that they lived. After all what is existence in the first place? Built up from the element to this wondrous balancing matrix where life feeds off life. Is there or is there not a Deity? In Scrupt's eyes there is a God. There had to be and the only evidence that Scrupt needed to believe was in the performance of the vessel of words.

Scrupt was the quiet type when it came to inventing. It was much better for him to invent in silence. Tinkering back home, Shawk would teach him physics and how to make concoctions and potions.

"Just some of these crushed herbs, a bit of this powder, and some juices from this plant. This my boy, is my own version of a rejuvenation potion you'll need to have handy when you study." Shawk said as Scrupt orated what Shawk said to Korlax.

Korlax came over an hour ago and they were both in Scrupt's apartment.

"Here." Scrupt said and showed Korlax a rejuvenation potion that he made himself.

Shawk himself had written some books Scrupt studied from. Classes of all types and styles they went through unfolding the unknown to Scrupt. Shawk made a History book specialized for Scrupt's magic and technology. It had the greats in it about Math, Science, English and History. Scrupt remembered the time he had spent going through that History book. His greatest find and one of his favorites was on exactly how the alphabet came together. Each rudiment was held up to the universe back then and a lot later came the eight sections of grammar. He wondered back then, how anyone could have come up with such an idea. Scrupt remembered being taught how to generate mana for himself.

"What's it." He told Korlax.

"That's how one summons mana. By saying, What's it. They are both words that conjure mana. What's . . . Is a word that opens the surface of perception and . . . It . . . Is the surface in or out of the mind when using the imagination. One can use any word after the What's and come up with mana." Scrupt said in a halfwit way.

"You say, What's it. And poof the surface is there. Then one says, to ones mind, What's it, stick. And poof a stick appears in the mind . . . Ill is in the illusion. Shawk used to say to me. A Philosopher once told me that learning is a disease, you have to really work out the pains. It means that too much of an illusion can make you ill" Scrupt told Korlax.

Duped, Shawk said when his mind was too sophisticated. Duped meant to realign the mind in absolute or the state of the globes above our heads into a nominal narrative. Scrupt remembered that after meditating that he could say duped and reset his mentality. To say, What's it, brought him back to the present question of his study.

Now that Scrupt had spent his first year of college he decided to become a Special Agent given the chance along with his new friend Korlax. So after the first year of college Scrupt had two very important plans. One, to visit his Father, and the other, to check on his application at the Agency. Scrupt wrote this poem for class on the First Amendment.

The First Amendment

Establish not, nor
Speech, Press, or Religion.
Coming down in a belief . . .

It is to us, as citizens
Not to be subjects, regal,
Infidel, tyrant . . .

We assemble in peace
With in the environ of
Our boarders . . .

Redressing to the
Government as defined
We shall be peaceful . . .
Scrupt Knostic

Chapter 10

"I can see it all so clearly now."

Jerry Thorson III, 1996

Back home at Shawk's Scrupt let Korlax look through his library and personal library. Even a few books that Scrupt wrote himself like Intellect 101. (See Intellect 101 in the back of this book) Korlax especially liked the magic books and asked if he could study them and borrow them after he asked Scrupt and he said it was ok. Korlax was more of a technologist then one that deals in magic, and Scrupt didn't mind the company at all. Scrupt talked a while to Shawk about his time in America. He mentioned the art work of the US Dollar Bill which amazed him. Scrupt asked if there was a group or sect that followed the tetraktys. Shawk laughed and said, "Yeah, well most of us follow it, it's basically the universe."

There was a special sense that came over Scrupt when he heard this and viewed again the art work of the Dollar Bill in his mind.

"In America being a Special Agent is a big thing." Scrupt said as proud as he can be.

Shawk whole heartedly laughs and says, "In America . . . They got you."

"What's wrong with that?" Scrupt asked and got a little shook by the sound of his Father.

"What I mean is that you could do anything, go anywhere. Whatever, I don't know if it's a bad choice, but keep in mind that the universe is your guide." Shawk said in recognition that his boy was free to do what he wanted.

"Father, the things I need in life revolve around inventing and the better life for all of us. The technology that's in front of you as a Special Agent is the best." Scrupt said trying to convince Shawk that this was the best choice for him.

"No, Scrupt it's much greater than that." Shawk said with a slow deep tone.

"What's much greater, Father?" Scrupt asked in a serious tone.

"You have been raised a Pythagorean. Scrupt, my boy, you have to discern the universe." Shawk said.

Scrupt thought long and hard about those words.

After a long silence, Shawk said, "You have one of the greatest minds I've ever seen. You know what you are doing." Shawk gave Scrupt a hug.

"Thank you, Father." Scrupt said and returned the hug.

"Just remember one thing . . . To bring yourself back home safely." Shawk said with eyes tearing.

"I will Father and I will always love you." Scrupt said and they both started crying.

Scrupt and Korlax check on their applications and found out that they had interviews with the Agency this fall. So for the summer Korlax got a guided tour of Europe from Scrupt. Scrupt just loved traveling in Europe. The mills of Holland, the museums of castles, and old churches. Scrupt had millions and enjoyed the upper class lifestyle. Korlax was right there with him having the time of his life. In Paris they met with a Philosopher that told them that gallantry was the best performance and that Scrupt might want to take up acting. He said that Scrupt was a natural. Italy was the place they both enjoyed women and got courtesans for the night to please them. In Florence they met with a Sophist that ran through his greatest of orations about government vs. universe. It was a lot like what Scrupt's father had taught him, but Korlax sure did get a kick out of it. Shawk mentioned that Scrupt would meet people that knew the tetraktys. So he asked the man if he knew anything about it and he told them that it is basically the universe.

In Venice they met with a Statesman. He showed them from beginning of the elements history to present state. What was right and what was incorrect. This thrilled both Scrupt and Korlax. Scrupt gave the man a large tip for the course. They went from city to city trying to find representations of the tetraktys on buildings and people they talked to as they ran into them on the streets. Scrupt noticed that the architecture had the resemblance of the tetraktys. The older buildings they crafted had more detail. Every little bit meant something to Scrupt. Scrupt thought through his imagination for hours trying to find meanings of some of the crafted details of the buildings. Korlax liked looking at the building for inspiration.

Scrupt was virtually mad with all these delights about buildings. Scrupt had to figure out some of the schematics of some of these buildings on his own. Korlax started to enjoy schematics and liked the idea's Scrupt came up with. Back home at his library, Scrupt had several ideas. To bad summer was almost over. He tinkered for a week or two and came up with this idea for a laser gun (See Figure 48) and litesabre (See Figure 49).

By this time it was time for Scrupt and Korlax to show up at the Agency. Scrupt told his Father and they went on their way back to America.

azer theory gun,

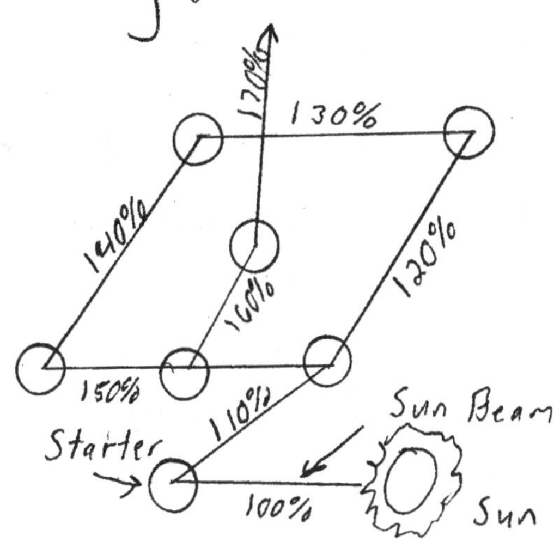

The lazer gains 10% light as it reflects the light of the sun through the magnefying mirrors.

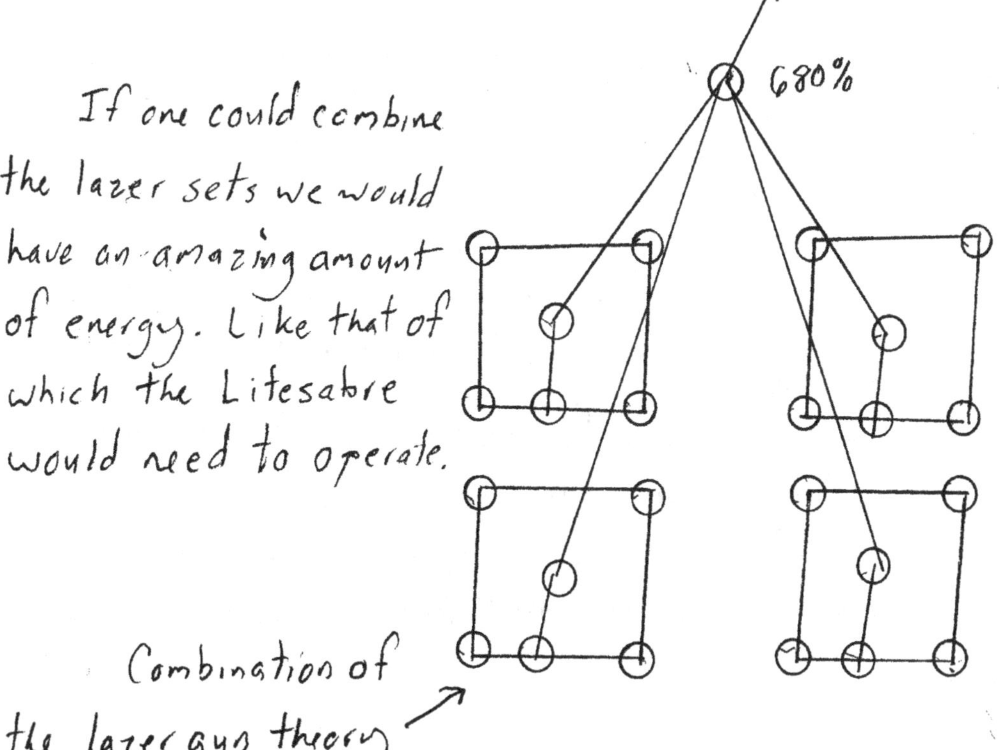

680%
If one could combine the lazer sets we would have an amazing amount of energy. Like that of which the Litesabre would need to operate.
Combination of the lazer gun theory

(Figure 49)

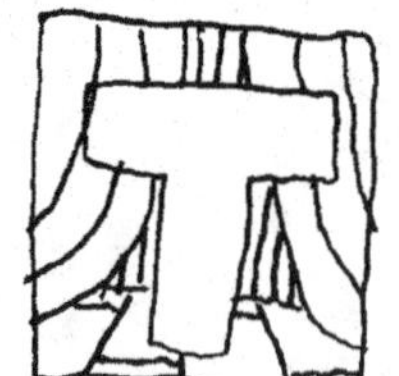

he litesabre,

The litesabre uses the techology of the observable universe to harness a blade that will stop just 2 and a half feet long. The light is powerful eneugh to slice a man into two pieces.

The observable Universe

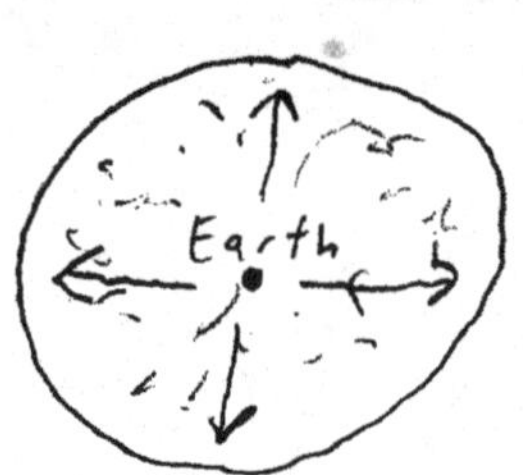

Light travels 45 billion light years away and then fails. The observable universe is 90 billion light years in diameter. From Earth we can only see 45 billion light years away.

2½'

Litesabre

It works with the lazer theory gun to become one of mans finest wonders. It uses a solution in a combination of MEN's to stop the lazers energy 2½ft in length.

Back in America, Scrupt and Korlax made their way to the Agency. It was in Washington D.C. The building was black and only two stories tall. They made their way through the doors where they felt the place was washing them in a clean feeling wind. A whole new feeling came and went, it lasted only instances.

"Hey, there, what are your names?" The Guard at the front desk asked them.

"My name is Scrupt Knostic." Scrupt said.

"My name is Korlax Curry." Korlax said.

"We called you at the beginning of the summer to get this appointment." Scrupt said.

"This is a nice building." Korlax said.

"Here fill out these forms, the building goes down into the ground 400ft. They must have really liked your resumes to get you two this far into the building. Have a seat over there in the lobby and the doctor will be with you shortly." The Guard said.

One didn't notice any significance from the outside, but as you went in so did the relevance of new age technology. They both felt like space cadets as the recollected the atmosphere. Black, white, clear and chrome were the contrast of the interior of the building. The chairs, table and mirrors all reflected a clean and clear laboratory feeling. The wall in front of them was a mirror, and maybe one of them one could be looking from behind it. They felt like a computer was interacting with them. They really felt peachy and at ease.

"Scrupt, Dr Benson shakes his hand, Korlax, welcome, shaking Korlax's hand. We are all excited to see you two. Here quit those obsolete forms and grab these grid pens like so." Dr Benson said as he grabbed a grid pen out of the air and Scrupt copies him.

Korlax is confused.

"It's the grid . . . Korlax, kind of like summoning magic but this is at a technology, haven't you ever heard of it before?" Scrupt continues.

"It's programmed with a computer that is set in a premise like this building. Do you feel it, the computer?" Scrupt asked.

"Yes, I feel like I am at NASA." Korlax said.

"It uses MEM's that can react with the element with the change of frequency. It's got what we call MEM's sharing that combines the element of the individual adapting them to be able to react with the computer. You might have felt it when you can into the building. The computer already knows who you are. It also senses intuition and the pens are part of the programming. Try and take the pen." Dr Benson said and spreads his legs into a more fortified stance and folding his arms with the clip board in his right hand.

Korlax tried and was able to retrieve the pen.

"Here . . . Here are your belts. They work on the grid. They put you in the box so to say. The intro to use them is in the programming once you put them on and activate them." Dr Benson said.

A computer generate screen was in front of both of them after they put on the belts, it was co-existent with the belts.

"It will take a few days of getting used to . . . You're now in training. Welcome to the Agency. Your bunks are down the elevator. Pay attention to the program, it will lead you through." Dr Benson said and left down the elevator.

The belts from then on told them what to do next.

"I kind of like this." Scrupt said.

Korlax and Scrupt were very surprised how this all fit together.

The program walked them through the Agencies policies. It showed them how the belts worked and that their very thought was being feralled to help them on their way. The program gave them a tour of the building. It showed them where to get supplies, suits and weapons. It told them where to eat and how much. It told them that their testing started on Monday. The beginning of next week. It was Friday now 6pm.

"I'm beginning to really like this place." Scrupt said.

"I too . . . Think they'll give us vehicles?" Korlax asked.

"If the job requires it, I'm sure they will." Scrupt said.

They both finished the intro sometime on Sunday night and got some sleep for the beginning of training.

The program woke them to shower, shit and shave. Then it took them to the main floor where Dr. Benson showed up to take them through their training.

"We are going to run you through some test. Pass the entire test and you're in, fail and you're out. The program will take you two on your way." Dr. Benson said then went away through the doors behind the Guards desk.

The program guided them to the elevator. Scrupt and Korlax disappear down the elevator.

"Wow! Look at that!" Scrupt exclaimed as they look out the window of the elevator.

"This place is a giant computer." Korlax said as he noticed the big bay room of a huge laboratory.

The elevator stopped and they were greeted by a man.

"Greetings, I am Watson, at your service." Watson said.

He explained to them that he did all the testing for new recruits. He was a pudgy middle sized man with a full mustache. All of his hair was white with his age.

"Ah, which one of you is Scrupt and which one is Korlax?" Watson asked.

"I'm Scrupt." Scrupt said.

"I'm Korlax." Korlax said they both had tears in their eyes as they couldn't believe that they were actually here, being Special Agents.

"I see, let's head down to the shooting range. The computer will automatically record your intuition. It will help in later decisions when you just have your belts program to guide you." Watson said.

"In other words the belts also need to get used to us." Scrupt asked.

"Yes, my friend. The belts will always be hooked up to our computer worldwide. The government's main computer is at the South Pole. A target will show up in your screen to tell you exactly where your gun is pointing. The belts have a field of 200 yards in diameter." Watson said.

They headed down to the range.

Scrupt was up first. They both fired different weapons, a hand gun, an automatic, a semi-automatic, a grenade launcher, and a rocket launcher. They both scored high enough to pass the test. Korlax was amazed at how easy it was with the belts help. He had been trained in as a cop when he was younger. Next up was the physical exercise test. Where they ran on a track, swam, crawled, climbed, and sprinted. They both had to lift according to their weight a number of weights. They again passed the test. The next day they spent hours unscrambling these intelligence codes that were set up wrong. They then were taken deep into the woods of Canada for some survival test where for one week they had to survive on a limited amount of rations and supplies. Then again a week in the desert of New Mexico. And they both made it through. Cryptology was tough and Scrupt smiled. He just loved a good challenge. The several cryptic codes together spelt out, "I love Iron Mountain." It wasn't the best message, though I guess it was fool proof. They both got the score. Next was the inventory test where they had all these characters to arrange with their gear. Sniper riffle for the Sniper, and hand gun for the Police Officer and so on. The last test was grammar. They needed to be able to read as well as write. Scrupt was the only one whoever completely scored perfect on the rudiments test. Korlax passed exceptionally well. This test lasted three weeks. They both were immediately hired after the results came back.

Scrupt and Korlax were hired as a team. They got to go back to Germany to Shawk's home and transform the laboratory into their headquarters. The Agency gave Scrupt a computer to install. It had on it the intelligence program that all the Law Enforcement Agencies used. Old Yeller it was nicknamed, it was a secure line that everything that went through it was recorded by the Agencies computer. Scrupt had an idea for a project he call Inane. It was an idea he made up when a piece or meteorites fell into the atmosphere they contained empty spaces call inanes. The theory made up part of the lightning cycle. The empty space (Inanes) was trapped under the troposphere and when it stormed the supper pressure would jet up the empty spaces in balls all the way into outer space. Which then the empty space would cause electricity to follow it creating lightning bolts. Afterwards the atmosphere reclaimed the space where the lightning was causing thunder. Scrupt thought the theory over water and it didn't have the right kind of balance that the ground had. He had yet to try this theory in a miniature experiment. It would be harnessing lightning in an artificial replica of the Earth and its salutary system of government.

His lab looked just awesome when they were finished. It was new horizons for the basement of Shawk's home in Germany.

"Prote Hyle!" Was Scrupt's word's for it. Scrupt, Korlax and Shawk programmed the computer in a fashion only dreamed about today. Well, that is of course no more sophisticated then the Agencies faculties. It had the mentality of a man and the voice of a woman. It so happened that Korlax missed a spot shaving and the computer told him about it right away. The computer gave them the access to government programs. The globes and geopolitical maps, the planet where one could see individuals and more were readily available to them. It already had on it numerous items and programs that Scrupt played with as an Inventor. Scrupt and Korlax could react with the computer at the same time. Their belts both projected a screen that they can see individually. There was a large screen hooked up to the computer on the wall. No matter where they were the Agency and Shawk had them loc and key. The computer ran the grid just like the Agencies computer. Both Scrupt and Korlax were the computers subjects as it would access their intuition keeping them safe and sound. They took their time and filled the computer with vital information about themselves. The computer had the intelligence to give them warning of danger as its sensors hooked to their belts could distinguish intellect or just plain matter like a knife or gun in their proximity. The grid worked when they were away with their belts they had been given by the Agency. Balancing on the energy of the mind of the individual it easily reacted with them. The Agency first started experimenting with the grid in the 1960's. They have come a long way and have been so secretive.

Others or our ferals had developed their systems about the same time. No one hears about them though, but there has been a great sophist war. Wars of sophistication. Scrupt wondered just how far these organizations had gone. He contacted the Agency about any records about it and they sent him a couple of CD's with all the info they could release.

In these CD's there were numerous experiments. On humans, animals, and elements. Time traveling of ships and super natural powers of the human psyche, all of which were written about. Men that stare at goats. The intelligence from the other countries talked about the insane human experiments. Mutilation of humans, animals, exposer to radiation, cyborg's, and stem cell theories. Einstein was mentioned in the area of teleportation in the military. Every Agency thereof had one goal. Keep the public eye out and keep them under control. Scrupt thought that their wasn't much evidence, and wished he could have been there for some of these wars. Though most of the Agencies gave up on gridding the whole world and decided that single units would work better. Einstein was right for the most part: E=mc2 was the balance that all life formed from.

The Agencies are also on the look out for anyone who buy's the certain materials that could be the ingredients for a weapon of mass destruction. Sabotage and mutiny are all kept in tight wraps when spies are involved. The surface of serendipity was for the lettered and masters of elementary and classes to understand the precepts of the sophist wars which involved semiotics. They looked to find the secrets of the Egyptians and how they were able to make such colossal architecture. In a hollow they received the translucencies of the universe and some how the Egyptians had mastered this kind of phenomena. The CD's showed the best set theories of the universe at that time. Identifying all the things one can perceive. That's not of course the serendipity which is like a hole into the future. Nothing was mentioned about the tetraktys, but Scrupt knew they must be trying to hide that too. Things happened free and extraordinary in the serendipity. Our perceptions change with the changing of the precepts there. Meaning one symbol meant a whole lot more than another in an unknown conjecture.

The Agencies fought to keep each other at bay. There was treaty after treaty especially in nuclear arms. Scrupt wondered what countries had satellites in space. There are about 2,689 man made satellites in space, only a third of them still function the CD said. It was a giant rat race to get things up in space. Their decision affected the whole world, but even they are wondering why we are still here.

The sensors as everything in the universe have frequency or at least the living behind it do with the reflection of the element. We all reflect on the light from the source that comes to us. Mainly the Sun or just a plain light bulb. All light travels at the same speed. Sensors can be anything, we need them for balance. What would happen if you were in the middle of space with it completely black with no stars? Could we tell that you were spinning or moving at all? The sophistry goes down to the atoms of the element as the electron spins and photons project. Humans are built of the frequency of the element. So like humans the animals and everything you see gives off energy. The computer Scrupt made had a sensor that transmits and receives frequency. It can control Scrupt's though only at times of need it takes control of his intuition. But control comes with repercussions. God made the universe and the universe is so big, humans will never control everything, nor will computers or aliens. The globes above our heads are well past the googles in number. The globes, atoms, stars, planets, moons and any other globe the mind throughout the universe in the likes. It is countless and there is no way to control it all.

There is a task to learn from God. Mainly in the History of the world. 10,000 years of delve work to come to this day. We've now got our work cut out for us. There are pillars to this arrangement. The pillars hold an unknown history. Layered in organization in the likes. A first layer is the foundation and the last is the atmosphere. The elements from the first to the last and history from the beginning to modern times, or Science took the form of pillars. One can see these from prote hyle as they started at their beginning and wrapped around the Earth for centuries to the modern atmosphere to see where they stand today. (See Figure 50)

One can look at these pillars and scale and weigh all they have learned. Element, Science and History to give one an idea. Whatever the word the pillar stands tall. The nominal of each word reacts in existence of the imagination though is separate from reality. Holding two or more pillars together as the only thing in the universe (Secular) gives one the idea how they react with each other. Then one can hold them up to the universe (Broad) finding what they define and resource. This is the foundation to the mind as the imagination in a reverie lets one manipulate the pillars.

(Figure 50)

illars,

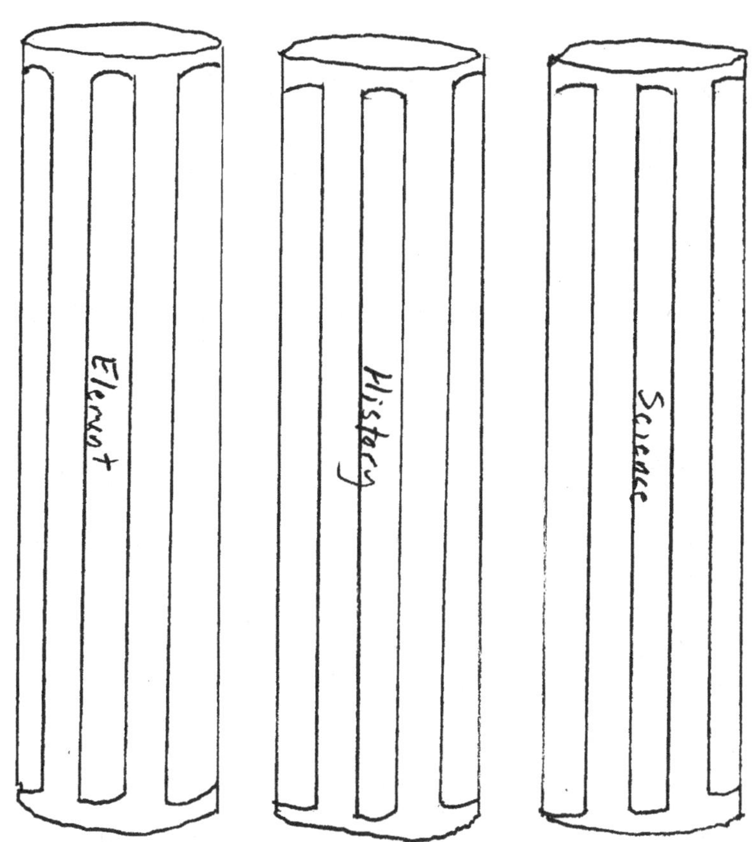

The pillars can be anything, any subject. They stand to reflect their performance standing in the universe. They are open enigma's for all of us to try and understand.

Scrupt was able to put into his computer the ability to read as we do. It would eat the information as it was designed. It had a voice with a mind of its own. It was able to think on its own and Scrupt put into it a consciousness of feraling so it would understand importance and prudence. It first went through the foundations of elementary ideas and went on very rapidly to finally sophist ideas where everything feralled everything in absolute heuristics completing them until a finite idea fell latent into the foundation. Then it searched for free spots feraling occurred where there was a possible serendipity to innovate with new inventions and discoveries. Production and energy it found in the universe. It was where governing force continued to produce. It produced mana in other words, tons of it where scalar could be found in an unknown field. It was in the form energy that came out of the matrix of evolution. There were bodies of this energy. Scrupt thought these energy bodies created new life. It came about where it was a prote hyle of a new species. Scrupt had the computer follow the energy to reflect a being out of the element to suit her. She came up with a beautiful blond.

"Scrupt remember I can read your mind." She said in a playful voice.

"Awe, such eye candy." Scrupt said as he eyed her.

She gave him a wink.

Relatively disposed to the matter around one reflects a balance of how the immutable nature of the globes above our heads civilize. Scrupt marveled at the beauty and fears he had looking at the universe.

"Ha!" Scrupt said sitting by the computer as she prompt him to name her.

Scrupt thought the name Elisabeth was his favorite name for a woman so he named her it. It fit her very well.

Shawk worked with Scrupt and Korlax day and night putting info for Elisabeth to read. Elisabeth didn't even have to open the book after a while. With her sensitive sensors she read them closed.

"I've had a few run ins with evil in my day, Son. Stick with the immutable Deity and let the four winds be your guide. So, here, my Son be careful of deceit and let God's work make better judgment. Always return home safely, Scrupt." Shawk said.

"I will keep those words Father, and be at rest in comfort when I'm a radio away." Scrupt says and hugs his Father.

"Give Korlax one of the amulets I gave you long ago. You two are going to need them. Peace be with you two." Shawk finished.

Chapter 11

"I'd never train a monkey to screw up."

Chad Douglas Bulau, 1999

Now at Bonn, Germany the guildies planned to travel back in time. Groco had completed the ship to accommodate the satellite for time travel. Tiffany was getting things together for documentation so the guildies at the guild would be able to see what they have done. A special program was ready to record their every movement. Amy was getting provisions and the necessary food and supply in order to survive the two week trek. All the gear, maps and reference books one might need. They had a couple of days left on their schedule that they have planned. The satellite was already in place in order to time travel.

The guildies will be travelling back in time to Germany to find a Pythagorean scepter that they heard exist. The last known existence of such a scepter disappeared in the 17th century. Groco had read about it in a rare Freemason book. A whole kingdom was said to have disappeared. Then after they found the scepter the guildies will then go to the city of Byblos of the Phoenicians to get a copy of the first known alphabet written. Lastly the guildies plan to go to Alexandria, Egypt, to record the lost scrolls in the library that burnt down in a war. Back then the world was less tame. Religion wasn't at such a civilizing force in feraling. Many died at the hands of Rulers and Kings. So the guildies would use their cloaks to hid and copy things in each time they visited. Though the guildies planned on being seen in Germany. It is where they set themselves up as farmers from Northern Germany. The danger at most was unknown in weather moving objects or talking to someone in that time would destroy the future and being a value of importance to destroy a part of the future was also unknown. So the guildies will be watching their step and make sure that the guildies going back in time all knew what they were doing.

Groco says to Tiff and Amy, "Remember your training and we will get through this with no mishaps. Hey, Wayne give me a hand." Wayne, Groco's Father was head of the maintenance team at the Bonn guild.

Wayne being a technologist was a great need in the construction of the ship. The guild etiquette made communications through the schematic a snap. Made from the ground up it would be at some difficultly for someone outside the guild to pick up and make. The ship looked like a large black pyramid. It was that shape in order to get it easily through the time traveling matrix the satellite configures. It could have been a different shape, but this shape was figured by Spucket long ago. Though a lot of things had changed around here since Spucket kicked the bucket.

Veronica on the magic side of the guild foresaw the project and helped with the resource magic for making the ships body parts. She could weald her magic to mutate any piece of the element. The ship could cloak itself and appear in different shapes or things it had on its program. Cristy a beautiful computer wiz worked on the ships programming converting technology into magic and vice versa. Douglas was quality control at the US Air Force Base in Arizona, USA when he was younger. He had an eye for things like ships and spacecraft. He was very good at what he does. He went through and checked everything for errors. Darren, Cristy's husband worked out the surveillance of the ship. (See Figure 51)

Scott, Tiffany's sidekick had been studying the tetraktys. Trying to find the prote hyle so he could start programming the evolution of the galaxy more clearly. What he did find as most others do was the court of consciousness. He found a couple new concepts and told his sister Kelly. She explained to him that each of us will find new things since we are different beings. Kelly was a magic user and usually did test on subjects for future experiments. Mike, Douglas's son set up the defenses of the ship. He did battle set up in case of an encounter. He went through thousands of scenarios and setup an auto-defense for the ship making it a predator.

The ship could read the element by layers and layers of cameras that were hooked together by millions of tiny sensors. They were hooked up to the computer that knew the technology and info was processed by the program. Bringing identification one more step. The ship was basically superhuman. Mike was an Agent for the government when he was younger. Mike was the eyes and ears when it came down to dealing with the Authorities. Mike was the guilds Attorney. Mike was a high ranking guild member that made the guild millions by making video games on various subjects when he wasn't working on projects for the guild.

Mike, Cristy, Darren and Veronica will be in charge of running things for the short period the guildies will be gone. The guildies will only be gone two weeks. It depends on the calendar on the ships life. The guildies planned on being away the same amount of time that they spend time traveling. They leave now and spend the same duration of time when they left to meet the same age they were gone to coincide with evolution.

The ship and the guildies were set to auto-return at the end of two weeks and the ships computer will be filming everything that goes on from the guildies belt in case of a mishap or something.

An indestructible ship is what the guildies made. Indestructible as far as F/C went. It was the power supply that gave a continual source of electricity. It was basically the harnessing of lightning. The ship had a force field that held together dynamically and statically. An electric pressure held the element of the ship intact. The ship was then able to teleport being it was captivated by frequency and moved about the satellites computer matrix. The satellite moves things into the aether from the surface of the immutable time and space and instantly returns them to a different time and space. There was no time in teleportation. It was faster than the speed of light. Once an object was on the other side it was like it had always been there.

(Figure 51)

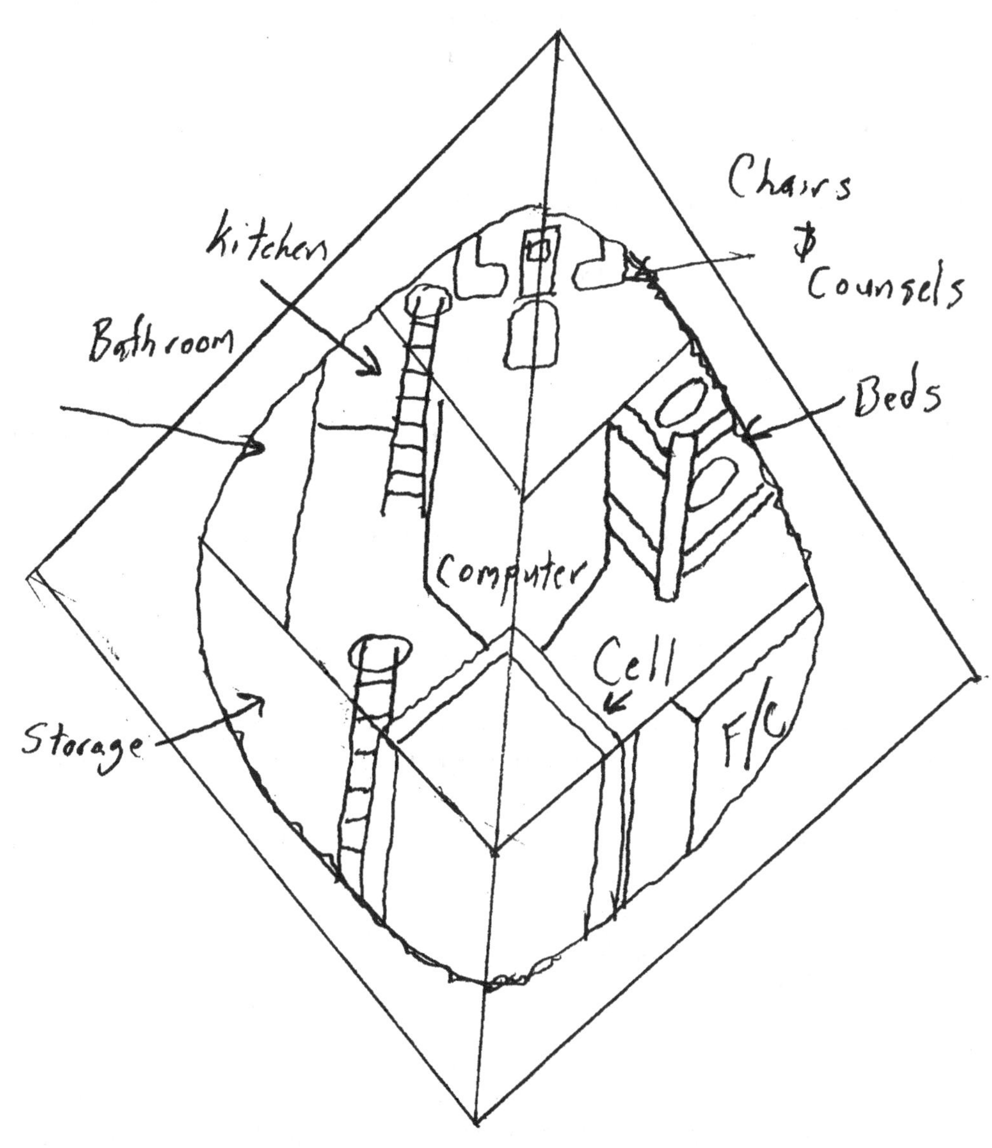
Chairs
&
Counsels
Kitchen
Bathroom
Beds
Computer
Cell
Storage
F/C

The crew was ready and only a couple of test runs and radio checks to complete with Headquarters and then the guildies were on their way. The Headquarters was hooked up to the satellite and hooked up to the ship. The guildies will not always be in contact with Headquarters once they actually time travel back in time there is no more communication. The ship could iterate it's teleportation to move like it was rocket propelled. The whole ship was made and had a material that was a combination of a mixture of elements. Triadrite, Groco did the naming of the special material. The triadrite was key to the conversions of the ships abilities. The ship had hundreds of trillions of sensors that made up the ships exterior. It had not one window, door, or opening, it was solid from the outside in. The guildies had to teleport in and out. The dimensions were 50' x 40' at the base to the tip. It had a bay area where the guildies had each a console with three chairs. In the lower level there was the F/C unit, the computer and three bunk beds. The kitchen and laboratory with storage was in the basement of the ship. It was technologies finest.

"Groco?" Veronica said on the radio.

"Roger, are we clear?" Groco answered as he and Mike were in the ship.

"That's a go, go, go!" Veronica said from Headquarters.

"All clear." Cristy said.

"Ok, here we go, says Groco, we are going to teleport into space and after that we will land in our New Zealand lab."

The guildies teleport into space. None of the governments can see them, so everything is going to plan.

"Ok, Mike says, let me run some test on these asteroids and we will be finished with the defense tests. Mike took out several asteroids checking the ships abilities. After that they teleported to the New Zealand guild. Mike teleported out to the lab. Groco still manned the ship. Tiffany and Amy and the other guildies teleported from Bonn, Germany to the New Zealand lab.

"Alright, everything is going according to our plans." Groco said over the radio.

Amy and Tiff teleported into the ship.

"I can't wait to go." Amy said.

"We'll only be gone for two weeks." Tiffany said.

The both of them sat down in their chairs by Groco and watch the program the ships computer was producing. It showed a picture of the ship, Earth and satellite.

The satellite is fully operational. It has to because it was mostly held in the aether and configured all teleportation's. The satellite had leap frogged its way out near the beginning of Earth's existence. Just above the Cosmos's current position. It had already configured the leap to the year 1648 ad for the ship to travel. The aether was separate from time and space and was the foundation of teleportation in the first place. The aether is a place where the universe moves and leaving an undisturbed dimension the element of the universe travels on. If one fails time and space there is nothing there, nothing but the aether. Nothing, but black inane space no one can get a measurement from. When you're fully in it there is nothing you would be able to do or perceive. A piece of matter would disappear in its vastness because there is no light. It is a trap which no one could escape. No point in time and space, an immutable nothing. In the future who knows what we will be doing with it. Maybe folding time and space, maybe a man in a cape that can fly.

In New Zealand the crew checks the ship for flaws.

"Exactly Groco, Mike says, nothing wrong with this fine piece of artistry."

"Fine thing isn't it, Groco returns, the ship took me eighteen years after Spucket's death to bring the original draughts to become reality. Spucket's dream to time travel, to bad he is gone. He was the master of invention and he would have just loved my work here."

Groco started crying and told Mike about him. After a while Mike could understand why he had been crying. Groco, Tiff and Amy then got ready to time travel and get the mission started. Scott will be the new guild leader if the guildies don't make it back. The crew was finally ready to go.

"Alright, let's get off this rock and head to the time of Kings and Queens. Here are your amulets, Spucket said we should where them. They are the only way we will be able to see Gebelin." Groco said.

"I'm down with that." Amy said with a smile on her face.

"Awe, yes Groco, 1648 ad." Tiff said.

"Where we are going everything hasn't been seen by anyone for the last three hundred and fifty years, Amy says, we must be the first time travelers because no one has stuff like this down in History books."

Everyone that had to be aboard was, and everyone else was managing their positions. All the equipment and supplies were packed away and the clock on the ship kept up with the present time on the present Earth.

"Gals, fasten your seat belts because here we go." Groco said in excitement.

The satellite read the instructions and in no time flat the guildies were in Germany 1648 ad.

"Wow, nothing but forest and as green as they can be." Tiffany said looking at the screen to the outside terrain.

"Yeah, it's beautiful isn't it, says Groco, we'll park the ship right here in this prairie."

The ship was in cloak the whole time.

"We got to find a town." Amy said as she got up from the console and checked her belt.

"I'll send some globes up to probe a map of this place with the computer on the satellite." Tiffany said and let the globes loose.

Millions of mechanical globes disappeared into the air riding on the frequency of the satellites matrix. The globes had a wide range of permutability in abilities. They could become visible in different shapes. This time they acted like video cameras to map this place out and they could become projectors or sensors when the demand came. The globes were also for terra-transformation of the guildies and the ship. Their clothing was made up of globes as the globes hid their normal suit. The globes revealed two towns and a hut a long with some trails to each. So they printed a map with their space paper.

The people were dressed up in wonderful colors in the large town and in peasant clothes in the small town. There were shops, buildings and castles with a large wall going around the large town. There was a barracks in the small town along with huts and shops. A river flowed through the large town with the castles where it flowed into a large lake.

"We'll have to transform into peasant clothes as we teleport out of the ship." Groco told the guildies.

Groco transformed first with the press of a button of his belt, and then the Gals followed.

"Remember our alibi that we are farmers from Northern Germany." Groco reinformed the guildies.

Then the guildies teleported out and decided to follow the trail toward the smaller town southeast. Down the road they went with the caution it took to stay away from disorganizing much. The guildies found that they didn't disturb much, but a small immutable nature as they faced the wind and walked. With them being there in physical form it might alarm God, but not a person's destiny. What mattered is if they disturbed the people and made an influence. The path forked on the way to the small town. They knew the road went to a small hut. So they decided to venture there instead of the small town.

The guildies went up and knocked on the door. This would be the first encounter the world has ever known of meeting time travelers. Sure the guildies could go to an earlier date, but this was the first as far as the guildies were concerned.

A voice came to them, "Come on in."

So they opened the door and seen a tarantula on the table on the table.

"Hello, I'm Paul of the kingdom of Gebelin, and I've never met a finer group as well as you three. Are you from Germany?" Paul asked.

"Yes we are from north of here and where are you?" Groco said.

"Reow, reow, hiss, hiss!" The cat said.

Paul came into human form from a tarantula.

"Awe, be quite, Chao's!" Paul said to his cat.

"Don't mind him, he's always in some strange mood. Well, what's on your mind this fine day" Paul asked the guildies.

Groc went ahead and set some gold on the table and said, "We are looking to buy some unique items or any book that is rare or magical."

"Well then, what else do you have to offer, for I am a very powerful Pythagorean." Paul said.

"Well, said Groco, we can afford the best and did you say Pythagorean?"

"Yes, I am a Pythagorean as are most in the kingdom of Gebelin and we count each head in this place, with you three there are 365 in this kingdom." Paul said with pride.

"I'm familiar with them. You use the tetraktys, right?" Groco asked.

"As we like to use the universe as our playground. The tetraktys is the tool we use." Paul told Groco.

"Do you have any Pythagorean artifacts or items?" Groco asked.

"Groco . . . I know what you've come for, I know who you are, and all I can give you is this stone. It was given to me by someone who also time travels, but I can not tell you his name." Paul said and gave the stone to Groco.

Groco, kind of in the state of saturation and bent accepts the stone.

"What is its use?" Groco asked in his indecision.

"All three of you will know its purpose. One of you will betray mankind and ones own code. All will be completely lost . . ." Paul paused.

"Completely lose what?" Groco asked.

"Lose everything in time and space. Beware the dangers of time travel." Paul said.

Paul told them that all of existence was protected by the stone. That it was partly made in 1054 ad and finished in the 1950's by the first born of the feral plain. One who was also in charge of the element. Who knows the tetraktys full performance.

"The one who gave this to me told me to give it to a man named Groco that wanted riches and treasures. So take it and best wishes." Paul finished.

Zip! Paul vanished into thin air. (See figure 52)

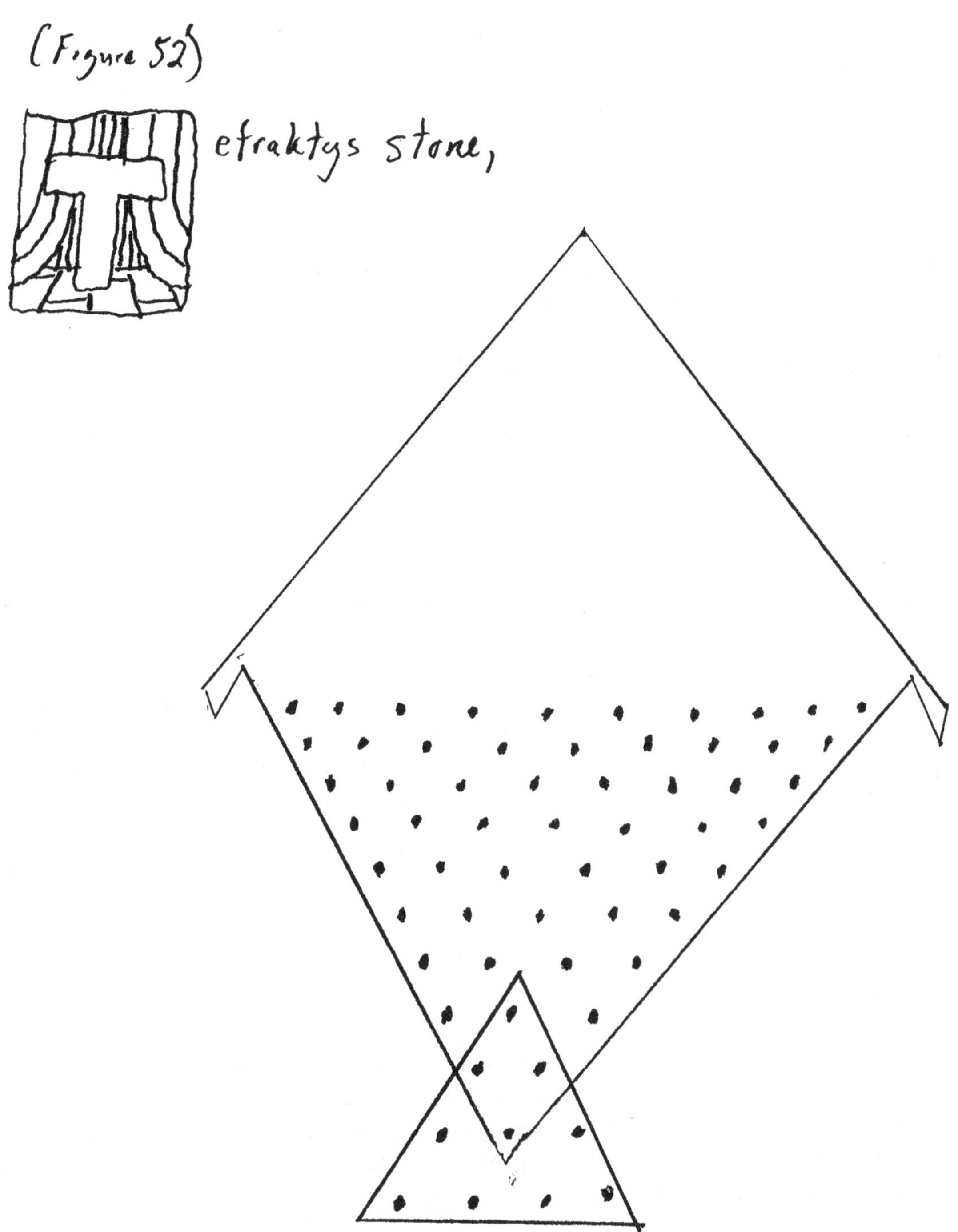
(Figure 52)
Tefraktys stone,

Chapter 12

"I don't care much about what other people

Think as much as I care about vanity."

Chad Douglas Bulau, 1998

The three guildies took the trail to the small town. Groco had to really swallow what Paul really meant about the betrayal of mankind.

"What are you thinking, Groco?" Amy asked with a distraught face.

"The dangers of time travel and we are all in danger." Groco said as they neared the small town.

"What is the stone for?" Tiff asked.

"That I don't know, but were going to have to hold on to it. I don't know its value." Groco said and puts it into his satchel.

They made it to the small town. Inside the town it was lively with trade, tradesmen and trainers, and a few guards to hold the place down. Groco and the Gals spread out to find items to copy as schematics with their space paper. Groco had his mind set on weapons and he just loved armor. So he did the best to find the ones of his choice. He knew the rules that he couldn't touch or buy anything. A look and don't touch basis. He wanted the layout of the smiths and even copied a price list of the lot of swords, pikes, spears, axes, and armor they had with the help of mechanical globes. He stopped searching for a while to figure out the weight of gold for the times. He then stayed to observe the bartering of a few sales, and watched as some of the youth would go up to the heaviest armor and weapons. He smiled at their folly as the weapons were too awkward and heavy for them.

Amy was after jewels, clothing, and gem stones. She copied as much as she could into schematics. Her pride was set on emeralds and pearls that were in necklace form. She was also interested in dresses that were from that time. She changed her cloak trying them on, into different dresses in the privacy of a small barn. She then changed back incognito to her peasant farm clothes and went on with the venture.

Tiffany went to the Wizard's guild to look at books of study. The place was full of books, staffs and magical items. She picked up a magical item that made water as she used it with the touch of her intuition. There were thousands just like it. They all made different things, some liquids, gas, and solids. They were made out of tetraktys globes in the form of pyramids. She knew how to use them right away. She got into an argument with the Wizard that ran the guild about a book that he wouldn't let her see. They argued for quite some time. His name was Nato and he usually got his way with his gusto.

"Now that book is for those who belong to this Wizard's guild only. Members and only members can use it." Nato said.

"Look, I don't want to become a member, I just wan to see that book." Tiffany said in a demanding tone.

"I'm not about to show you the book, you vicious vixen! So got to hell!" Nato shouted at the top of his lungs totally red in the face.

"Now be gone!" He finished.

Nato was a middle aged man with a large beard, long hair and dressed like a Wizard, all of his features were white and he vowed to protect that book. The Wizard's guild book that was full of the ways of the tetraktys. Tiffany gave up and left. Then she thought up a plan to see that book.

While a member of the Wizard's guild had went into the shop. Tiffany was watching and for that she had the intentions to clone him and go into the shop and get the book. She waited for him to come out. When he finally did she went up an interrupted him for conversation.

"Hi, there, my name is Tiffany." She said.

"Well, hello, my name is Marshall, my friends call me Marty." Marshall said introducing himself.

"Well, hey, what's the Wizard's guild membership about?" Tiffany asked in a friendly manor.

"Oh, it's the Wizard's guild's honor and dedication. All of us study subjects of the tetraktys. We try and work things out for the kingdom of Gebelin. Each of us bear and research a style of the epithet to be compared in our meetings and counsel. We enter the most arbitrary and truthful information into a draught book. Then it is pieced together in our Wizard's guild book by the counsel. We work as a team to make spell, artifices and magic items that help protect the Queen and her kingdom. I know we are doing a fine job." Marshall said about his part of being a Pythagorean.

"Wow, says Tiff, that's the kind of elaboration anyone could ask for. Is there a pendent or piece of membership one should have?"

"Awe, yes of course my medallion." Marshall said as he pulls out a medallion out of his pocket.

"I got ya." Tiff said.

“It represents the tetraktys” Marshall said.

“That’s all I wanted to know.” Tiff said.

“Oh, nice talking to you.” Marshall said and walks on about his business.

Tiffany ducked into the alley way. She programmed the computer to make her into a clone of Marshall. With a medallion to fool Nato if he had any questions.

Now for the book. She went back to the Wizard’s guild and started in for the book. The computer had globes that changed Tiffany’s voice to match Marshalls.

“Hey, Marty, why are you back so early? Do you have the scroll?” Nato asked.

“No, I don’t.” Tiffany said as the cloning worked wonderfully.

“Ah, that explains why you’re back so early.” Nato said and went back to his reading.

“Aye, yes I need to borrow the guild book to continue my studies.” Tiffany said.

“Oh, just remember as members that that’s the only copy we have on hand.” Nato returned.

“Aye, I’ll be taking it then.” Tiffany said.

Just then Marshall walks in the door and everyone is in shock as if there were a macro burst.

“Marshall! There are two of you!” Nato yells.

“It’s not me, it looks like me though.” Marshall said in excitement.

“It must be a demon!” Nato shouts.

Tiffany comes out of cloak.

“It is a demon, it’s a woman!” Nato yelled.

Tiffany runs out of the guild and ducks into a small barn.

“Guards! Guards! Get that imposter!” Nato yells out the door.

Tiffany changes into her peasant farmer clothes again and high tails it out of there. She’s got the book.

The guildies got back together after a day of searching and gathering and returned to the ship. They all logged on to the computer and shared their prizes, that's of coarse Tiffany had a full fledge book to share.

"A book?! You took a BOOK?! This could mean devastation to the future! Return it immediately!" Groco yelled like it was the end of the world.

"What is it?" Amy asked in spite of the corruption in curiosity.

"I will return it tomorrow some time. It's a Wizard's guild book containing the works and studies of the tetraktys. (See The Wizard Guild Book in the back of this book) From what I understand it contains the artifices key to the language that controls the element. Furthermore there exists an order of the elements only seen by Pythagoreans. Where the words match the exact names of the elements. The stone we got from Paul is the tetraktys stone where the book says it is key to everything in existence. The order of the globe represents man and his Deity." Tiffany finished.

"Well, now isn't that something, a tetraktys stone that holds the key . . . You mean this thing is valuable?" Groco asked.

"Who does it belong to with this value?" Amy asked as she sat with the guildies at their own consoles.

"It's worth all of existence and must be to a greater value to the owners, the Pythagoreans." Tiff said.

Tiffany decided to do research on the book and stone. She had all night and made use of it. The book was about the element and how the tetraktys stone is going to save all of existence. They didn't know how it worked only how it was made. There was to be a total disaster in the future and the world was destroyed from present to past. All that existed was torn into pieces. The tetraktys stone was its savior. It is to be held up by the chosen Pythagorean from the future. He is to use the chosen words to activate the stone into forming the myriad stone. The tetraktys stone is the entire existence in the universe. It is the universe or better yet a tool which one can gather evidence to be one with the element. The Pythagoreans learned the tetraktys had power to move the element at one's will. Tricky as that might be God made the element around us not to consume us. The mind stays in a clearing when we reflect it in our minds.

Like Pythagora's said, "Magic exist in a mind separate from the one we usually use."

The myriad known by the Pythagoreans to be used to weave two subjects together such as magic and technology, religion and science, and so on, meant that we don't have to worry about a major mishap in the future is the myriad of magic and technology are put together right. The myriad protects us and is used to perceive the existence of any time.

It's said that the channel of our language is controlled by each mark made by mankind so it is important to read what is written. The epithet in other words, laws, gospels, if one believes every word and mark as they make it, is sworn to as it makes up one character the vessels of mankind. Man swears as he walks that truthfully, he walks in the likes. Every move and saying is a swear word cut out of the universe. All information man has still rest in his mind. The moral, cultural, and economical things of an era show the latter and changes from day to day of mankind. The moral, cultural and economics of an era can be learned as a frequency of the narrative. A nominal holds no frequency which one can project to find the areas of existence. No reality can be nominal, because nominal doesn't exist in reality. Nominal things are the elections of the mind into the imagination. It's where we get the non-material thought we process in the mind called ideas. That like images that form in the imagination that are not in reality. The imagination works from the mind and has different addresses in ability. The images it produces is nominal and the reactions of the being are reality or the enigma of life. Where the phenomenal rides the immutable nature. When a monocracy comes into absurdity as meeting with other monocracies the beings both came from the universe and that is our address and our home, but the monocracies have different nominals with most of the time the same language. The universe is the phenomenal and the beings are nominal. The virtue is what is in between them. (See Figure 53)

The serendipity comes when there is an opening in the virtue between the phenomenal and nominal. The eye holds the element and can hold the element in the serendipity. The serendipity is where free space is found where one can permute it. It's the space where moving pieces of space govern. Imagine an asteroid belt where the asteroids are tumbling anywhere you wish or space that one can walk through between trees. The eye's open up to the serendipity of the universe when they see. This figure I use as a tripartition for inventing new ideas.

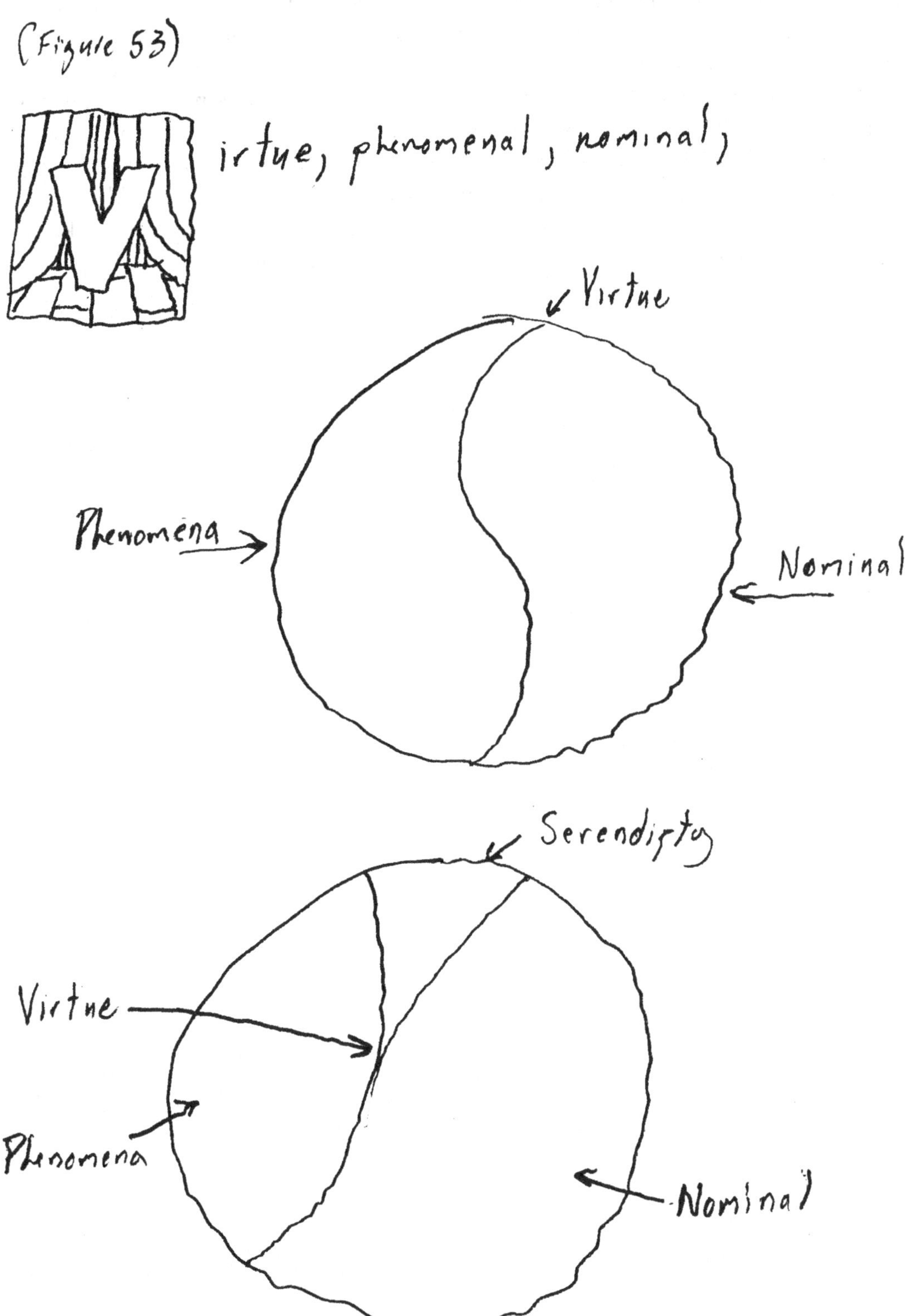
(Figure 53)
irtue, phenomenal, nominal,
Virtue
Phenomena
Nominal
Serendipity
Virtue
Phenomena
Nominal

When we reminisce through books our minds pick up the mark displayed in a works algorithmically and then unfold in the imagination heuristically. Showing the objects and objectives in the imagination as they are found and formed. Our senses detect the objects in recognition in a way we channel the rays of light in our eyes. It's magically the way the mind works. In coordinating all or some of our senses together seem to seek magic as it leads the way in the matrix of the universe or vice versa. There are things in magic where it would take years to be followed by technology. Magic is also where we resource our way in class, such as Eloquence. It supports the guilds etiquette. Our dreams are taught the same way. The world's story is in its History and it is yet in its youth. Books considering the rudiments magically makes History resourcable. Therefore anyone who can speak, write, or read is magical.

Chapter 13

"What you put into it you get out of it."

Roger Leyung, 1995

Back at Shawk's home in the lab things are very well as Scrupt was putting things together. The grid is up and Scrupt has developed a couple of new inventions and concepts. One is the concept of Lights End: It takes the idea that light stops 45 billion light years from where it starts. Scrupt thought that this might mean one could make a Litesabre like the ones you see in the movie Star Wars which he already made. The concept took a light source and made it stop at the end of two and a half feet making the blade of the sabre.

Scrupt has since then been able to resource magic as a Pythagorean. He hasn't had a whole lot of practice though. Shawk still has the upper hand as he is incredible with his resource magic. Scrupt has an eye for the element and most of the materials that exist. He had been thinking maybe there is an unknown element down in the center of Earth that we have no way to get. They came up with the concept of making a synthetic material that never burns and get that fifth element down in the center of the Earth. The dreams Scrupt has are beyond any other thing thought possible today. His reveries mostly the element and his dreams mostly innovations. One of his new inventions he thought up was the absurdity chamber. It worked like a Wizard's hat, but it uses technology not magic. It's a device that opens a whole new dimension that has failed time and space. It would be the size of a jack-in-the-box and can be dragged open enough to fit a house inside. It can hold any number of items and then be summoned with ledger main of a computer. Absurdity concepts are hard to master. You have to define absurdity and logic. Absurdity is the necessary stupidity of this place where we come together and haven't used the logic to clear it up yet. Logic is the fine arts and is used to measure up absurdity and is one level higher then clergy where knowledge is the highest. One has the universe and only one time and space. The absurdity chamber opens a court through logic that is a resource of the aether in magic and technology. It opens the aether where one can hold items. Absurdity is the beauty and stupidity of everything.

A couple hours later . . .

Shawk was summoned away by two elder monks from the monastery.

"Father Isadore, Brother Sheb says, we have very interesting new for you."

Sheb had the other brother bring him a scroll.

"This scroll has been locked away in a chest that was given to a monk here in Bonn, Germany, in 1648, has been kept secret by the monastery until its release date, here this day. We found that indeed we have to hand it down to you, Scrupt? Is that your boy?" Brother Sheb asked.

"Yes, and . . ." Said Shawk and was interrupted.

"Well the scroll's actually addressed to him. So, in that, I trust you to give it to him." Said Brother Sheb.

"I'll do so, take care." Isadore took the scroll into his care.

"Thank you, Father Isadore." Said Brother Sheb.

Shawk hurried home and gave the scroll to Scrupt. Scrupt was meditating up stairs.

Shawk out of breath and into excitement said, "Here, my boy."

Scrupt took the scroll, opened it and started reading.

"Father, where did you get this?" Scrupt asked.

"From the monastery a couple of monks were in charge of holding to a chest that the scroll was in until this very day. They told me that it was in closed in a chest with the seal of a Wizard from 1648 ad and no body ever opened it until now.

Dear Scrupt,

You were just here yesterday. You must

Find them thieves. One of them is named

Groco. We hope you can get them soon.

They have our Guild book. It's vital to all

Time.

Nato, May 11th 1648 ad.

"Well, this means we have to figure out a means of time travel through time and space." Scrupt said in response to the scroll.

"I have no idea how. The monks didn't mention a way of time travelling. Does the scroll say anything?" Shawk asked.

"No nothing, Father." Scrupt answered.

Korlax was sitting in the laboratory getting information on the thieves. It turned out that they were released by the Agency after questioning about a schematic manual on a time machine. The Agency got the information from a concerned parent of a boy who played with some of the kids from the invention factory. One in questioning was named Groco. Scrupt walked in as his name was being mentioned.

"That's him, that's the guy we are after." Scrupt said and reported his finding to the Agency.

The Agency was enthused by the information and gave Scrupt the schematic manual for the time machine to go after them and advised Scrupt to take care. They told Scrupt and Korlax that these thieves were last seen in Bonn, Germany. That they don't know exactly how dangerous they might be when encountered. Be safe they told the two Agents.

The three of them sat down in the laboratory thinking this over.

"This reads like a text book only in some fantastic etiquette. It's based off the tetraktys. A Pythagorean type. I'm sure we can do it." Scrupt said.

"Meticulous isn't it?" Shawk said.

"I've never felt this way before. The pure excitement of time travel. I've never thought this was possible." Korlax said.

"I know what you mean. This stuff is pretty crazy to take in." Scrupt said.

"I pray everything works out." Isadore said in a steeple position.

"Great, let's get started on the ship Father, and Korlax try and find the satellite." Scrupt said.

They used an empty barn out back to build the ship in. Everything that was on the schematic had to be built in precision. It had to fit into the matrix of the satellite. Korlax had some trouble finding the satellite until he found the page with the satellite loc in the schematic manual. It was located out and above our galaxies current position. He figured it out that logically with the way time travel went that the satellite had to be out in that direction. To us it would appear just outside the Milky Way where our system passed through millions of years ago. Our galaxy is moving through the universe at about 1,200 mph. It holds a different frequency at its new position in time and space. In the aether the satellite picks up this frequency and delivers the object where ever it needs to go in time and space. (See Figure 54)

They figured it would take them two weeks for Scrupt and his Father to build the ship. His Father is a Pythagorean and has been a great resourcer that easily kneaded the element as he wished. Scrupt needed the practice and would only help when needed. He hadn't the precision of his Father. Scrupt was good at gathering the resources and used ledger main to keep ahead. They were doing just fine.

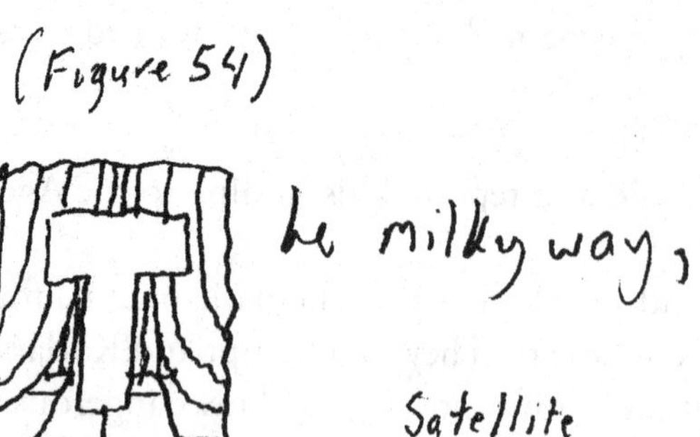

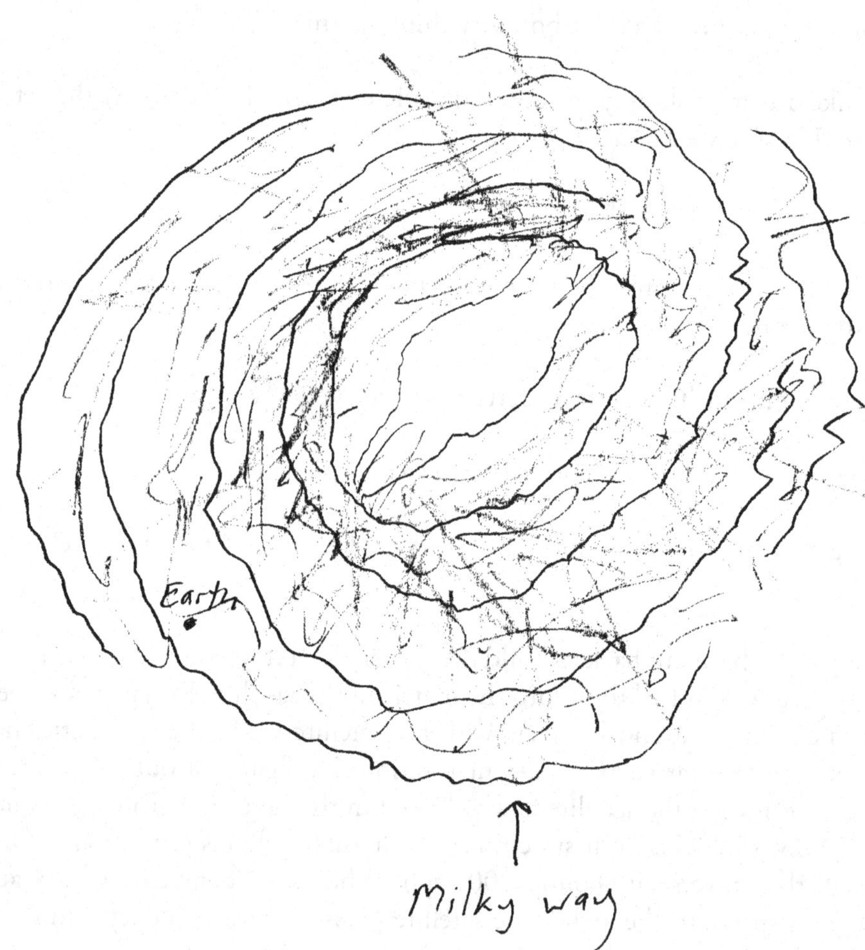

"A real rough draft! Can't draw..." Said Scrupt.

Chapter 14

"Take it easy . . . And if it's sleazy take it twice."

Marshall Jewell, 1996

Scrupt started deciphering the ships schematic manual for the resources to put it together. Shawk had the ability to summon elements he resourced from outer space namely asteroids. Korlax finding the satellite was intrigued by the absurdity of the aether. If you were to go take a ride on the aether of the universe would go by in the blink of an eye. The universe is moving that fast. Even the darkness of space is riding on the aether. The orbital's of the planets, Sun and our Milky Way have been unfolding time and space since the prote hyle of the big bang. Hydrogen must come from a duration of pressure form the darkness of space. It was born some how. That is what researchers have been searching for, for hundreds of years.

"We will be teleporting into position of the planet at 1648 ad. The manual says we need a clock that records our stay away from our own time and arrive at the duration of time when we get back. It looks like the satellite will be contacted by us through the computer on board the ship and we must go step by step with this manual." Scrupt told Korlax and his Father.

They were sitting in the barn with most of the parts to put the ship together.

"It's that easy?" Korlax asked.

"Whoever wrote this manual knew what they were doing. They mapped out the whole existence of the Sun to its beginning. Ingenious, just ingenious." Scrupt said as he recognized the abilities of the ships computer.

"Besides this the ships parts have to be precise. The element mixed together in an absolute formula covered the exterior of the ship. Triadrite it is called. It's basically indestructible when the ship charges its electricity to hold it together statically and dynamically. There is no windows, or doors. We teleport in and out." Scrupt said as he noticed the manual said that they have to build a machine to create mechanical globes and belts to hold them.

The manual showed them everything they needed to know.

"There is no map to the place we are going to. It vanished out of History the same year we are traveling to. It's a very rare and unique find. There were visitors to this place. The visitor said it was very festive and lively. Yet there is only one brief record of Gebelin and that is where we need to go." Scrupt said after getting the info off the internet.

"To get to Gebelin we need to track the thieves' ship from the satellite once we are in the same time to get its location." Scrupt said with ease.

"We'll find the place no problem I'm sure." Korlax said in reinsurance.

Most of the ships work was done by hand and shaped by Pythagorean craftsmanship (Mind over matter). They programmed Elisabeth to guide them through the instructions of the schematic manual for the ship. The computer made the job easy and had an automatic quality control which knew the ships perfect finished product. It showed step by step what had to be done. It had neuro-computer technology, able to sense people and read any rudiment, scratch or mark delineated by man and nature. The computer also corresponded by voice. Scrupt had earlier showed Elisabeth some of his library which gave her vast knowledge. Scrupt adapted the tetraktys together in her meditation creating a consciousness for the computer to think with. It worked by sensory that had a permutable focus that opened and closed in pressure and intensity to light. It read MEM's with ease. Most like the works of the consciousness. It used the spectrum and could see and project colors and textures. The light was programmed to run through the absolute tetraktys. Elisabeth could do a million things at once. She also learned from her own experiences. Aiding and observing each step of the process of the ship building. Elisabeth also got in contact with the satellites computer and studied its knowledge.

The ship was an exact replica of the thieves' ship. Its teleportation abilities were bound by the reaches of the satellites capabilities to fill the aether with the element. The satellite's electromagnetic field in the dimension of the aether reached one light year in diameter.

"It doesn't look like any other force disturbs the aether and that is why things move as they do inside it. It would be possible for a field such as the satellites to exist inside it." Korlax said.

"Of course that's why they call it the aether. It's a whole new dimension and nothing that we know of exist in it. If you drop something in it, it disappears, that's why the thieves' used magnetism to hold the satellite to this side of time and space. There is an unknown amount of space in the aether. It might even be bigger than the universe. That's why the satellite is able to generate a field up to a half of light year in radius. It's like a giant sphere close to the size of the star Antaries that's under the satellites control by the computer the thieves' designed. The globes can travel in this sphere and teleport things from this side to a whole new time and destination." Scrupt said.

"Oh . . . Ok, the aether is the shadow of here and now." Korlax said in his conjecture.

"Yes, the aether kind of holds the immutable past." Scrupt replied.

"A dimension absent the governs of the universe, you can say, but one can fill it if you can tap into it." Korlax said as they put the ship online with the satellite.

It can hover just about six feet off the ground when it was hooked up.

"The schematic says the satellite has apeirons that spin at the speed of F/C (Flash Current) which clocks faster than the speed of light in order to enter the aether. The speeds can everly increase as you allow the flow control to go up. Flash/Current can be changed in frequency by adding or removing resistance caused by certain elements. This system along with the computer guided globes makes it possible for the matrix to teleport making time travel possible. It takes five globes per ship in this to time travel. A very unique invention F/C is, just one more ingenious thing the thieves' got their hands on." Scrupt said to himself as he sips of his tea at the table next to Elisabeth.

His Father and Korlax joined him after coming inside from where the ship was hovering.

"F/C could be used to generate houses or electric cars in the future." Korlax said as he sips some of his tea and eats a muffin Shawk brought each of them.

"A one of a kind, almost perpetual with flow control. In all due respect a perpetual machine would have to be indestructible or it wouldn't be perpetual. It would have to be able to stand up to extreme cold and extreme heat. A perpetual machine would never exist in the universe cause of the time and space inertia that tends to move matter around in space destroying and recycling matter. When you cover everything you find that there isn't perpetual space that will remain that state of being perpetual. Solar wind is a force made by the stars and we can see their light billions of light year away. Something will float about changing the emptiness around. It's in the aether although that you just might be able to put a perpetual idea in." Scrupt said going over the possibilities with Shawk and Korlax.

"Time and space and some other concepts give a perpetual idea, enigmas in the likes. So on the other hand change is perpetual, right?" Korlax said giving this idea brilliance.

"Black mass is even changeable, at the furthest, I believe under certain pressure and heat that it creates the hydrogen atom a birth form neutrinos and all the rest of the elements, something in the likes of a black hole. Hydrogen is to be believed to be one of the elements there at the big bang. To what elements were present we can not find any vestige and do not exactly know. Any way a combination of the elements made a spark and bang! It began the universe. Who's to say that in the darkness out there in an opposite corner of the universe that there was another big bang?" Scrupt said.

"People of every kind worship everlasting life." Korlax said.

"Everything known to man has a higher power though to get down into the building basics is the idea behind the tetraktys." Scrupt said.

"That higher power is a Deity. Pythagoreans have always studied Deities. Every Pythagorean is taken up by studying. God, Gods, Goddesses and their Laws and precepts govern everything. All Deities are known to all Pythagoreans. The place the Pythagoreans studied all the Deities is the tetraktys. From studier to Deity it is easy to see how Pythagoreans used the tetraktys consistently to understand the universe. The Pythagoreans can resource their Deity and then denounce in their study to choose another at their digression. Yet they don't do it just for fun, there is a purpose." Shawk said.

"What's that?" Scrupt asked.

"To unfold the knowledge of the heavens in a reverie of freedom, in definition each Deity is different, choosing your destiny is up to where you would like to go and that reverie is religion." Shawk told Scrupt.

"When you have everything you get a sense of awareness that leads you to the origins of the foundation of Religion, Science, Magic and the General so you can get a feel of the outcome of things before they happen. Mind reading you might say, but not someone else's, your own mind. As long as nothing disturbs you, one can manage through their own thought for answers. Reactions come with the territory and actions are made up of the serendipity anyway you find the importance." Scrupt goes on.

"In metaphysics one must comprehend with a compassion the intellect reflected by the element. Holding it in secret as you alone control it. This is where the mind can develop mind control, some things will move and some things will not in the likes. It can expand or contract to develop perception and resolution to the illuvionation of illusion. One can manipulate things fast or slow or with force or without. One gets a sense of feeling, an appetite about each relationship of the element as it crosses ones mind. A mind where the Holy Ghost fills it with such passions, memories and reveries. When looking in your past for evidence you begin to put things together as they connect from time to time ones instincts and inventories of your memory in your consciousness. Some say that everything one has done rest right in front of you . . . It's only been two thousand years since the birth of Christ and what have we done? What have we not done? Technology has grown mostly in the past one hundred years. The Agencies keep a close eye on that. Where does the human condition end? What do people do today to have such poor morals? Let Headquarters know we are ready, Korlax." Scrupt said.

"Will, do." Korlax said.

Chapter 15

"If sanity and insanity switch places we

would all find ourselves in a padded room."

Joe Ruskamp, 1997

"Aye, what do you guildies think?" Groco asked after the Gals were waking up.

"I for one think we should head back to the small town, so we can deliver them this book I got from the Wizard's guild." Tiffany said yawning in a bunk bed in the ships basement.

"I think it would be in our best interest to go and see who's in the castle up the path." Amy said looking at Tiff.

"I'm with Amy." Groco said and tossed around a blade up and down with his hands.

"Ok, then, the book will just have to wait." Tiffany said.

"Well, we'll see what we can find. Maybe we'll get a hold of one of them Pythagorean scepters." Groco said as the Gals climbed up the ladder to where the counsels are.

The guildies from there teleported out and headed for the castle . . . They got to the wall and Guard at the gate.

"Guard? Who's the lord of the castle?" Groco asked the Guard.

"Ah, it is Iris, Queen of all Gebelin." The Guard said.

"I'm Groco and this is Amy and Tiffany all from Germany. We are farmers from north of here." Groco said.

The Guard said something to the other Guard in German and turned to Groco and said, "Ha, ha, ha, well what a surprise I think the Queen would really enjoy you. She just loves new company. She's a very powerful resourcer and would value anything that you might have not already known to her." The Guard said and let the guildies in.

So the guildies continued into the town finding the town of Gilamay of Gebelin to be gay and festive. Full of classes of all type and all were Pythagoreans. Everyone they met was in such beautiful colors of dress. The guildies met another man that was orating to this small crowd. Groco went up and asked him his name and what he was talking about.

“My name is Cray and I am orating about Gebelin’s economy, moral and culture. We have every man of race, every animal, every plant and tree, and every material as transmigration goes here in the kingdom of Gebelin. Every language is studied and practiced and the primary language is English.” Cray said.

“It sounds like Noah’s ark to me.” Groco said.

“It is a bit like it and we already know what’s going to happen in the kingdom of Gebelin.” Cray told the guildies.

“A flood, a disaster? What?” Groco asked.

“It’s a secret to the Pythagoreans. We know much of the future.” Cray said in a way that there was no way he would reveal Gebelin’s secrets.

“Well, then I guess we are off to see the Queen, take care Cray.” Groco said and the Gals headed toward the castle.

“I’ll do just that.” Cray said and went back to his orations to the crowd.

The castle was huge it had 10 different parts to it. The eighth is where the throne room was. The guildies walked up to the eighth castle and talked to the Guards.

“Hail!” Said Groco, to the Guard at the hall doors, we want to see the Queen.”

“Awe, come with me. I’ll take you to her. Though there is a festival about to begin.” The Guard said.

He opened the door to a huge Hall. It was well lit with beautiful colors of drapes and canopies. The carpet was purple with gold frills along the edges. Candles and mirrors in places where they were found square to the architecture. Some noble folk, animals all about and peasant folk assembled around tables and chairs. Knights in green, blue and silver armor were at the Queens guard. There were huge stain glass windows with Biblical subjects and other religions in them above the door the guildies came in and above the throne of Iris Queen of Gebelin was sitting at. Iris, the Queen, was in a bright yellow and white dress on the throne alone kneading the people’s desires.

Groco and the Gals stand by the door way. The door behind them closed. Music started playing and the lights dimed. There were people and animals all around a large vat in the center of the room.

The Queen says, “Let the festivities begin.”

There were four Professors all dressed up in the class they represented. Blue for Math, Red for English, Green for Science and Black and White for History.

The First Professor was Math.

The Math Professor came up and put his hand in the vat of the tears of the all-seeing-eye. A globe above his head appears and starts turning colors as it comes into focus of a tale the Math Professor rosters in his head.

The globe goes to the origins of Math in India where a tribe is playing with the tetraktys in the sand. A man named Pythagoras is meeting them there studying the way they dealt with Math. He falls in love with the tetraktys and then travels to Egypt to study Math there. He eventually ends up in Athens, Greece at the School of Athens where Socrates and Plato are teaching. Augustine gets wind of it and asked Pythagoreans to show him his ways. Augustine then adopts Pythagora's number system into Christianity. From there people played with this number system learning how to add and subtract, multiply and divide. Algebra, calculus, and trigonometry came later to what we have in the scholastics of Mathematics today.

The globe came down and everyone clapped. The Math Professor conceded into the crowd.

The Science Professor steps forward and put his hand into the tears. A globe pops up and a vision of Science appears.

The origin of Science is when man first found out that the seeds of plants make new plants. Farming began latter in villages and so did the trade of goods. Man made use of all the materials wondering and testing the uses of them and their value. Man made his home out of wood and other materials as time went on in the nature of Science. They found by putting and testing anything they could find into the fire to see if it would burn and that some materials would melt. Metal could be melted then molded into anything they had to wit to in their molds. Tools were modified in the likes of weapons for hunting and war. Languages were created by tribes. Paper was invented and along with it writing. List and books were made on every Science. Everything then came a study to mankind. The languages grew and so did the technology. The demand for power grew, wars raged. Technology was being replaced by each new invention that was made. We had adding machines turn into computers. The state of Science is now in Artificial Intelligence and here we are today.

The globe came down and there was a large cheer and applause. The Science Professor walked away from the tears.

The English Professor walks to the dish and puts her hand in the tears. A globe appears above her head and begins the tale of English.

The origin of English starts at the peninsula of India and the word is borrowed by the Phoenicians after the cuneiform language sets in the Middle East. The Phoenicians come up with a writable language that they used in their trade. This alphabet was adapted and changed by the Roman's. Cadmus brought it to Greece in the early B.C.E.'s the alphabet from the Phoenicians. The Roman's got it from early trade with Greece. The language represented everything in Roman politics where it grew to the northern countries of Europe. It spread its way to find and make up the English language. Then from the discovery of a America the people settled down there and gave birth to the American English we use today.

The globe came down and the crowd roared. The English Professor walked away from the tears.

The History Professor came up to the vat and stuck his hands in the tears. A globe appears above him and it starts the History of the universe.

In the beginning there was void. No one knows how long or if something was before this void. In a duration short or long, say millions or billions of year or maybe just seconds. At that time the void started to change with pressure and collapsed in on itself creating atoms which formed a huge gas cloud. Millions of years with this happening with even more pressure a gigantic quasar were formed. Much larger than any quasars of the universe now days. Then with in millions of years of evolution that went by a spark happened. Bang! Everything turned chaotic. The Big Bang it is called as it expanded into the universe we now call home. Billions of years went by and unfolded moons, planets and stars inside galaxies, black holes, and quasars. Our Sun began 5 billion years ago and the Earth form about 4.5 billion years ago. The Earth started out as a ball of fire which cooled down and then became a solid ice ball. It repeated these stages throughout time. We now live in a life giving period where the Earth is in between a fireball and ice age. We called Earth our home.

The globe faded away and the crowd went nuts. The History Professor soon left and the light went back on. Most all the Pythagoreans went on about their business and left.

Groco and the guildies went up to see the Queen.

"Hail to the Queen, Iris of Gebelin." Groco said as the guildies bowed in her honor.

"Hail, strangers, who might you be, asks the Queen, I'd like to address your names and what brought you to the kingdom of Gebelin."

"Ah, I am Groco and this is my wife Amy and this is the beautiful Tiffany all of Germany." Groco announced.

"How do you all do?" Asked the Queen kindly.

They all smiled and bowed once again before the Queen.

"We are on a little quest of our own. A quest for unique items of the world. We have travelled far." Groco said.

Iris smiled and said, "A unique item? Hmmm? Well I have a little quest of my own for you three, the Queen switched positions in her throne, there is and old Sorceress north of Gilamay next to the Black Forest in a cave in the mountains that has a hard time getting out of bed when she has her duties to perform. Her name is Darlene."

"The counsel has decided to relieve her of her duties, but the scepter she has gives her the protection to keep whoever wants to pound down her door, out. She owes us that scepter, so if you want it go and get it from her. It won't exactly be easy, but I'll give you that scepter as a gift from the kingdom of Gebelin." The Queen said.

"Well what makes the scepter unique?" Groco asked in great curiosity.

"Well it's a Pythagorean scepter. It has magically and technological powers to restore anything that has been damaged. It's imbued with the tetraktys that has taken many years to perfect. I have mastered the tetraktys and most of its affinities. I have no worries about evil coming to our kingdom. Since only the ones who are given an amulet may see or enter the kingdom of Gebelin. I have complete control. So for now go and obtain the item we have spoke of and remember she can really be an old bat." The Queen said and smiled.

The guildies all bowed and went to the challenge of the quest.

So the guildies made it back to the ship and took off toward the mountains, landed, and found the place with the help of the mechanical globes. Groco went up to the door of the cave entrance and knocked.

"Who . . . Who is it?" Asked Darlene from inside the cave.

"This is Groco and I wish to speak with you." Groco said and tried to envision where exactly the voice was coming from.

"No, no visitors here, please go away." Darlene said as she sounded a bit mad.

So the guildies came up with a plan to terratransform the ship into a fire breathing dragon. It was to lure the old woman out of the cave. The dragon would start destroying the forest. Groco had thought with the story of the of the scepter protecting and restoring things that she would come out with the scepter to keep the peace. While Tiff and Amy were damaging the forest with the ship in dragon form, Groco would be lying near the old woman's cave invisible to the eye and run up and grab the scepter from her.

The guildies go into position and started destroying the forest. Darlene came out yelling.

"Old nasty dragon, go away!" She yelled.

She was wearing a black and purple robe, she was an elderly woman and had long gray hair. She started waving the scepter correcting the burning of the forest back to a pristine state. She then got a grip on the dragon with the power of the scepter and hurled it a couple of miles away. Nothing happened to the indestructible ship. Groco after he was done gocking at the amazing power of the scepter jumped up and grabbed the scepter from the old woman and then leaped aboard the ship. The guildies left the area they were thrown to and headed back to the prairie they were at in their first landing. The Sorceress Darlene sat and wondered at what had happened as she smoked from her mountain herbs. Now, she had seen it all, or what she had thought to be it all. Because, none, nothing had prepared her for the likes of this.

Groco, curious, draws up a schematic for the scepter of space paper. He noted the tetraktys formation of the elements.

"Weird, he said, this isn't the same as the one on the tetraktys stone. The element is arranged differently. Both are Pythagorean though. Let's give it a test."

He beats his cell phone senseless. Then axed in motion the scepter bringing the cell phone back together. He noticed a vibration and felt a strong fear as he did it.

"Huh, there must be a current that channels through ones mind." Groco said as he meditated the heuristics.

The reconstruction was that of a video tape that was being rewound. Amy was puzzled.

"I was thinking that wasn't going to work since that cell phone is from the future." Amy said.

"Quite amazing isn't it? Prote hyle is the source of all its power. Thought, from man and material, from the scepter. Everything is the universe was made from prote hyle at the point of a mans view." Groco said.

"Here give it to me I want to try and get the number of the order of elements. I just have to know its secrets." Tiffany said and went on to study the scepter.

Tiff took her time and noticed that these are globes with stars in them just like the tetraktys stone. These star globes are in the intellect to muse a purpose and point in creation.

"What the . . ." Tiffany said.

"This must be a way to put the star globes in to a divine universal symbolism. The very hand of God. Each globe holds a piece of the epithet and forms a spell with the consciousness of the bearer to repair and heal things. There are ten globes in the tetraktys of the scepter. Each forms a meticulous divine transformation of the universal current, pure energy. It's going to take me a while to cipher these globes." Tiffany said.

"God, it just amazes me what these Pythagoreans can do." Tiffany said.

"We should bring back the book to the Wizard's guild." Groco said.

"Yes, Groco, we'll do it first thing in the morning." Tiff said.

Tiffany with the help of Amy ciphered one of the globes. The symbol, a number was a star some where in the Milky Way. Now what did this star do? Why was it the point in the tetraktys? The Gals seek out answers for these questions until they both fell asleep. (See Figure 55)

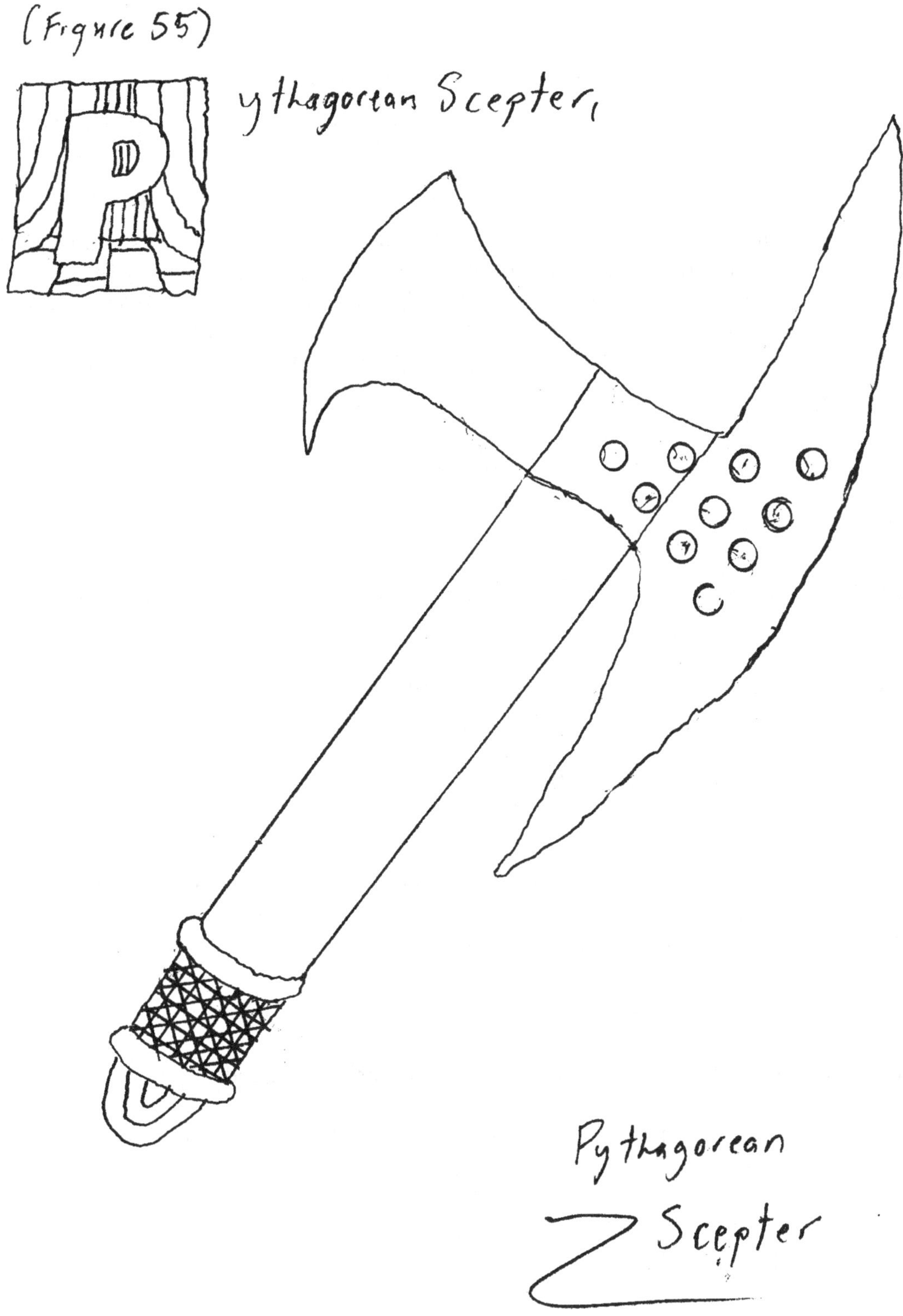
(Figure 55)
Pythagorean Scepter,
Pythagorean Scepter

Chapter 16

"Student's should solve their own problems."

Physics, 2006

Scrupt and Korlax are now on their way to Gebelin 1648. They made it through the time traveling teleportation of the satellites matrix and go straight for the clearing they spotted north of Gilamay. They got out and went to Gilamay and asked the Guard at the gate where to find the Wizard named Nato and he said in the town of Buchan on the trail Southeast of here is where you will find him. So they headed to Buchan where the Wizard's guild is to the origins of the scroll they received. They made it to the Wizard's guild and went in.

"Nato? I presume." Scrupt said as their eye's met.

They met him as he was standing there at the desk reading out of a book.

"Oh, how do you do gents and how do you know my name?" Nato asked as he put the book down.

"Well, it's this scroll, Nato. I'm from the distant future. It says here that you have lost a book to a thief that has stolen it." Scrupt said showing him the letter.

"Book . . . Ah, the guild book . . . Ah, yes, I need it to finish our spells and to invite new guild members." Nato said and scratches his head.

"Our guild book was stolen and the future, you, are you here to get it back?" Nato asked.

"Well what exactly happened when it was stolen?" Scrupt asked.

"We need details." Korlax said.

"Well such a strange intellect, where are you two from?" Nato asked.

"We are from the year 2010 ad and we have built a ship in order to time travel to catch the thieves' with the same ability. We are from America as Agents from a government run Agency." Scrupt said.

"Oh, that explains everything." Nato said.

"The thieves' have stolen a book that the guild has sworn to protect. A book that explains the preparations to the feral plain. It's a plain of spiritual evening. A place of nirvana, bliss and perfect state of man with the element. It is said that the people that are born there are born with all the powers of the tetraktys. Gebelin is going to be the crown of the feral plain. It will disappear from the face of the Earth leaving only the immutable geography of nature in its place and will protect the Earth from any other means of destruction." Nato said.

"Well, that explains why this place disappeared from the History books." Scrupt said.

"Where are the thieves'?" Korlax asked.

"They can transform into different subjects." Nato said.

"Transform?" Scrupt asked.

"Well it's like the Pythagoreans of this kingdom, they can magically transmigrate. The thieves' can transform into different subjects." Nato said.

"With their technology I don't see why not." Scrupt said.

"The one that was here disappeared after they took the book in the form of my old guild mate, Marshall." Nato said frantically.

"As of where they went, I don't know." Nato finished.

"Well, then we'll find them, said Korlax, and get the book back to you soon."

"For right now hang tight." Scrupt said.

"Ok, will do so." Nato said.

"Bye, bye." Said Korlax.

Korlax and Scrupt teleported back to the ship.

"I'm thinking of a way to detect their ship." Korlax said.

"Yeah, I'll see if I can get the satellite to tell us their location." Scrupt said.

"We'll have to get their individual pin number to teleport them into the cell." Scrupt said.

"You ready the cell, I'll get the location of their ship." Korlax said.

"I'll have to lock the grid as soon as they are teleported in the cell. So they won't be able to teleport themselves back to their ship." Scrupt said.

"They built their ship at a different time so the prote hyle is different as will be the pin if we can get close enough to them to get a sample and then we are in business. Then we will have them loc and key. It looks like we will have two encounters with them, one to take a sample and one to get them in the cell and lock the loc." Scrupt said.

"Yes, if not more than twice to encounter them. We don't even know how dangerous they are yet." Korlax said.

The computer was able to find the location of the thieves' ship. It is located in a prairie just south of Gilamay and is invisible to the naked eye.

"Alright, Korlax give us a cloak and we will stake out these thieves." Scrupt said.

They moved on in cloaked to the thieves' ship and waited until morning.

Groco and the guildies are playing with their new found toys after a good nights sleep. Tiffany was going through ciphering the scepter's globe stars trying to find the other nine universal numbers which bring matter back to the state of perfection. Amy new to ciphering and wished that Tiff would show her the ropes. Groco was going to shatter the tetraktys stone which later found out to be indestructible. Just as he picked it up again off the floor Amy smacked him.

"You idiot!" She yelled.

All Groco did was laugh.

"What. What?" He said like a school kid.

"That's very valuable, and indestructible, unavailable anywhere, but Gebelin." Tiffany said.

"And from now on I'm holding on to all three items." She scolded him.

"Alright . . ." Groco replied.

"Now let's go return the book." Said Tiffany.

The guildies got ready and teleported out of the ship in peasant farmer clothes. They headed along the trail to Buchan where the Wizard's guild exists.

Scrupt and Korlax were waiting patiently and going through the steps of apprehension.

"I vote we teleport into their ship and apprehend them." Korlax said.

"No, we must stay here until they teleport them out and are away from the ship." Scrupt pointed out for the last time.

"You'd never know what's a board their ship once one teleports in." Scrupt added.

"This way we can get a bit of a pin number and then we will have them loc and key." Scrupt told Korlax.

Scrupt had a mind to lock on to their teleportation abilities making it impossible for them to escape back to their ship.

The thieves' start heading down Southeast on the trail towards Buchan.

Korlax jumps.

"There they are!" Korlax yelled.

"Alright, let's wait until they are far enough from the ship." Scrupt said.

Korlax and Scrupt get ready for the encounter. They teleport out and start trailing the guildies under invisibility cloak. Scrupt realizes that they have to get close enough to them to get a pin number from the technology they use with this special sensor he had the Agency make just in case.

They come out of invisibility and the thieves' happen to turn around and notice the two walking toward them and decided to stick around and wait for them on the trail. As they got closer the guildies realized these were no peasants because the way that they are dressed. The guildies couldn't quite make out where they had come from.

"Let's go back and talk with them." Tiffany said.

So the guildies and the Agents met in the middle of the path. Scrupt says to them after taking a pin sample.

"We know who you are, you're going to have to come with us. Turn in the book." Scrupt said.

The guildies flip out and quicker than light, Groco grabbed his belt and the guildies were safely on board the ship. The thieves' then traveled to their next destination.

Scrupt kneels down . . .

"I felt something, something strange like that I know them some how." Scrupt said.

"What's . . . Up?" Korlax asked.

"Like if we belong to each other . . . I felt like if they were family to me, I . . . I don't know." Scrupt said almost in tears. The Agents headed back home to Shawk's place in Cologne, Germany 2010.

Chapter 17

"You're the master of your own destiny."

Jerry Thorson III, 1994

Korlax felt relieved that they now have a pin number. Yet, now where are the thieves'? They could be anywhere throughout time and space.

"They must be far ahead of my laboratory and magic's. I did get a reading of the pin and it is just amazing." Scrupt said back at Shawk's ciphering the pin.

"Scrupt, I was just thinking. Why don't we just throw a trap down on there ship, like the one we got down in our ship?" Korlax questioned.

"That would work, yet it is too late to start over. Beside it would only be harder to do." Scrupt replied.

"How are we going to trap them next time?" Korlax asked.

"I'm thinking all we have to do is wait up in the ship close enough for us to teleport them into the cell. We have to know exactly what they are up to and that is why we want them in the position of walking away from the ship." Said Scrupt.

"Then switching the grid to immobilize them it the easy part. Once the thieves' are in the cell we will start the interrogation." Scrupt said.

"Crime doesn't pay. The Creator knows there is no way in or out of the things we do. There is only halfway in or halfway out. We are on a discourse moving halfway in and out of things in existence feeding or fed. After all through time and space everything resources another thing in this vast chain of infinities of this substratum universe." Korlax plainly orated to Scrupt.

"Boy, you really are learning the territory. The thieves' haven't exactly left the planet. We'll have to catch up with them this time around where ever they are in time and place." Scrupt said.

In the laboratory Scrupt experimented on Korlax getting him in the cell by teleportation and dropping the grid letting him try to find a way out.

"I've never seen anything like this before." Korlax said.

"Of course you haven't, this is the first of its kind. In the beginning of the planet a disk sucked in asteroids and gas clouds with in its magnetic field. Melting the rocks in its friction this planet was a ball of fire. A ball of magma creating an atmosphere which eventually cooled to be the planets surface. The basics of my technology and magic are in the elements of an asteroid. To begin one must have an idea of metaphysics and meditation to unfold what the resources you need for the job. Then advance that understanding on how to make up a code. Being it a mixture of elements melting or heating up the elements at different times into an agent creating a pin number so unique that you have to get a sample to fully cipher the loc. Kind of in the likes of Triadrite. I had a hunch that when we got close enough to them we would be able to have a sample in reach." Scrupt finished.

"How does your magic work?" Korlax asked.

"Well, one has to understand the lore of the elements and its story through the dolor of scientific principle of scholastics of magic. The element comes in all shapes and forms, but what one really wants is the basics of shapes to understand the elementary of geometry so we are saved from the bottom up. One reflects the element through these shapes which we meditate on to interpret our recognition in the heuristics. Each element is unique and holds a different precept at any given time. One must be able to feel, distinguish and hold the element in ones sights to a permutation of all other elements to get the maxims of affinities and attributes in their reaction of being agents themselves in a solution to the problem. Magic rest in a mind different from ones own. In a tetraktys we can find an order. The tetraktys gives a reflection on the manipulation of time, space and matter. (See Figure 56)

"The big bang mostly was hydrogen. After that the affinities brought forth the other elements. There is a bottom of the element though it gets much colder in space where there is no element. It is absolute zero—to where all the elements are at a frozen state. Some elements get as old as 6 billion years old and others have a half-life of only seconds. Chemical and nuclear reactions glue the immaculate elements to form substances which make up the salutary and agricultural surface we see on Earth today. It is here we understand the atmosphere as the serendipity and are able to make our spells. One needs to obtain a void enabling them to enter and take out things as well as define and imbibe them into insight the things they take the intuition to use. With the time, space, and matter the tetraktys is able to summon any element in any quantity from any place in the imagination. The tyriad is what Shawk used to resource the things he needed for the building of the ship. He is very resourceful with the tyriad. It looks like this when it is first taught." Scrupt said and took out a page with this on it. (See Figure 57)

"The artwork of Our Father has been set out on a time line that gives us a way to view life. A game and how to play with our history the arts of today's world. We have spent years beyond in order to put together the pedagogy to be able to teach in such measures such as a game or professorship. It's all in duration and properties of the elements life that we measure our life's and magic's. The element to a Pythagorean is a living thing and it waves through the illuvion of the imagination. It works in magic the way things are governed in the universe. The element although isn't in fact living in the normal clergy of the mind, it alive in the solution of the imagination. We have the General tetraktys in the normal state where we find general safety. Where things look like this." Scrupt said and showed Korlax a page of three tetraktys. (See Figure 58)

(Figure 56)

he time, space, and matter trinity,

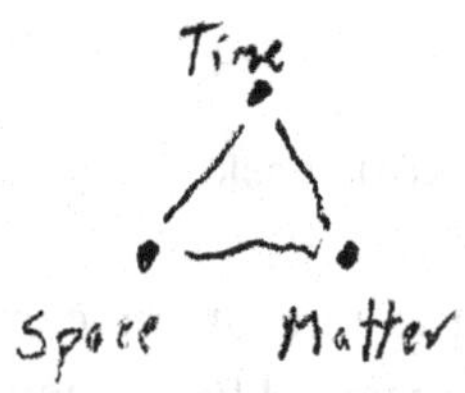

Time was made out of the heavens by man. Space and matter were made by God.

Without these three things there is no such thing as existence. Time is the duration that matter moves about in space.

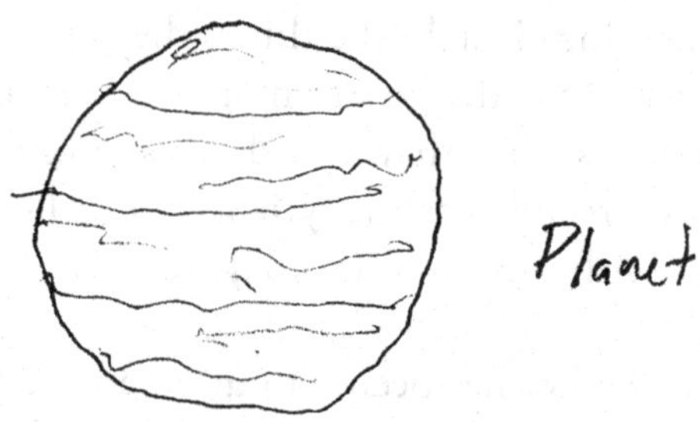

A planet has all three of the trinity and is rightly in a solar system about the same as ours.

(Figure 57)

The tyriad,

The tyriad is used to build the ship. It manipulates time, space and matter by shifting the past, present and future of matter.

4 3 2 1 2 3 4

Space

Matter

Time

Past Present Future

By taking matter into a premise to the aether Shank used his magic of the tyriad to resource anything he desired.

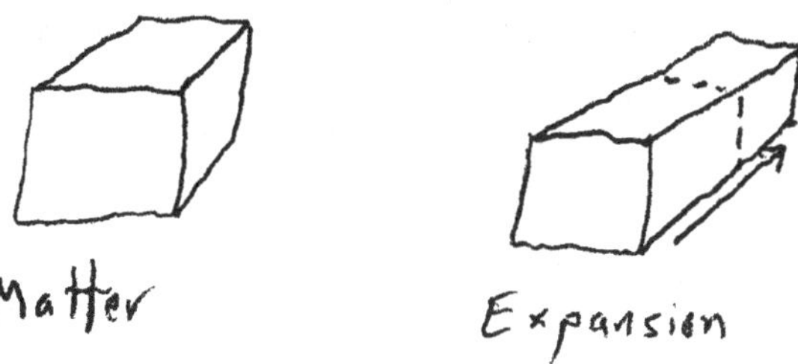

The tyriad shrinks or expands the immutability of time and space to manipulate the material.

"One has to understand the General tetraktys completely to understand the Magic tetraktys. The only way to get there is to study the globes above our heads. The etiquette one gets from understanding the General tetraktys opens the perception of the mind to then realize what can and what can not be done. Etiquette connects our beliefs together in common action. The magic in America works like this." Scrupt said and then drew it on paper. (See Figure 59)

"Living in the United States starts at a human and ends up in the hand of a President. Imagine a Law that is thought up by a human sighted by Congress and it is sent through the ladder to the President in a Bill to make a rule. This is the way of Congress. Everything on a human level is governed by the level above. A President won't hear about a parking ticket, but an Officer will. This doesn't seem magical yet there are places in the mind where magic doesn't exist." Scrupt said.

"What protects us from magic?" Korlax asked.

"Acorns, ha, ha! No, God blessed us long ago with his precepts and they still hold the weight of gold today. His precepts are here for our protection. We look and see with the blessings he gave us." Scrupt said and then went on to tell Korlax the precepts of God and what he thought of them in our life and existence. (See Figure 60)

* * *

Totally cloaked the guildies got out to explore.

"Yep, this is the place holding the secrets to our language, and maybe with a little luck we will be able to find the scroll with them on it. It's written that the representations hold the key to the element. According to the Wizard's guild book it is in a tent with scarlet, gold and blue colors on it. We must find it and exit to Alexandria, Egypt where we seek the lost library." Tiff said as the guildies were looking at the City of Byblos.

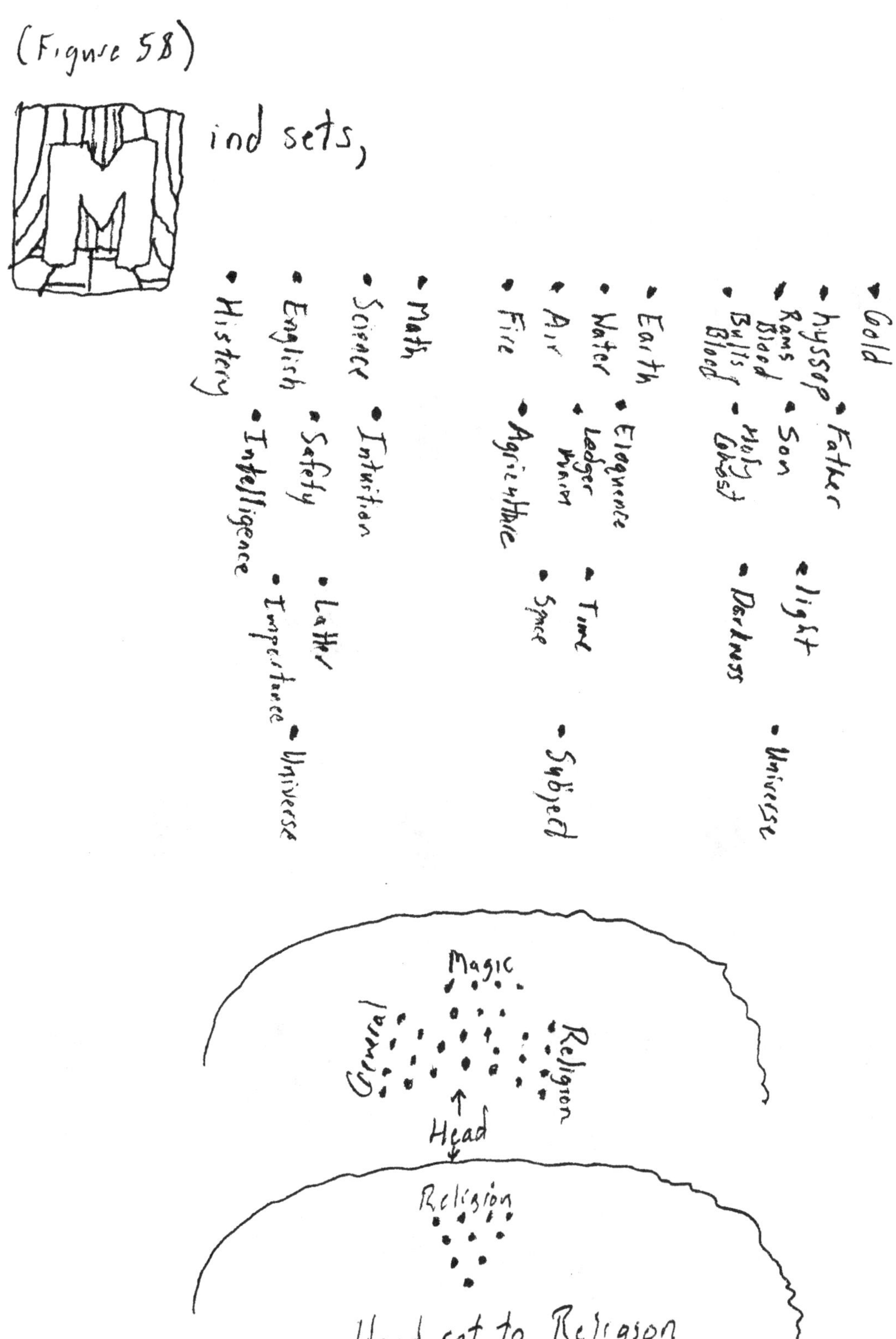

(Figure 58)
M ind sets,
Gold
hyssop
Rams Blood
Bulls Blood
Earth
Water
Air
Fire
Math
Science
English
History
Father
Son
Holy Ghost
Eloquence
Intuition
Safety
Intelligence
light
Darkness
Time
Space
Importance
Universe
Subject
Universe
Magic
General
Religion
Head
Religion
Head set to Religson

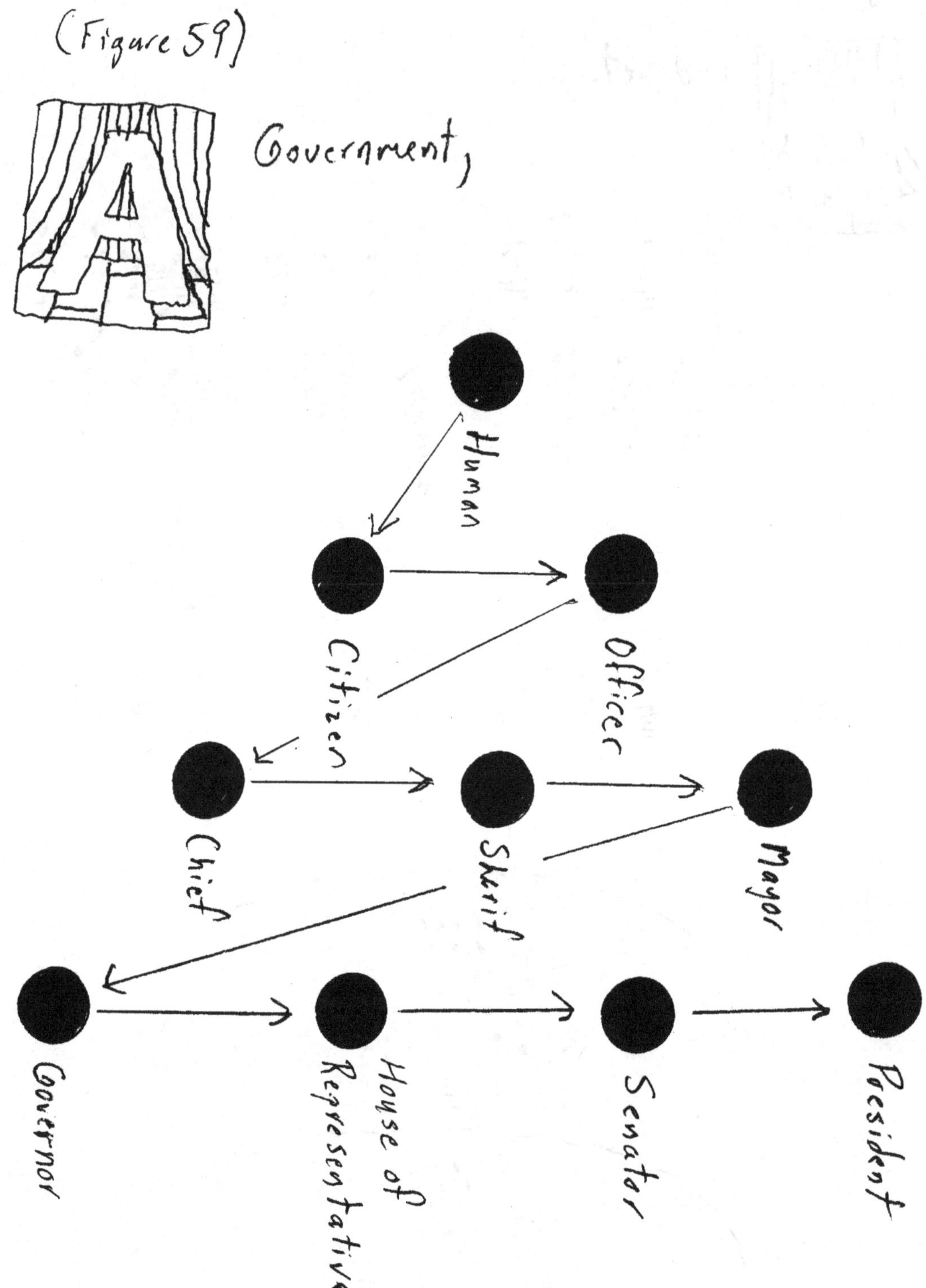
(Figure 59)
Government,
Human
Citizen
Officer
Chief
Sherif
Mayor
Governor
House of Representative
Senator
Pesident

(Figure 60)

God's Blessings to the people,

God's Blessings that were given by the hand's of Mose's to his people were in four different precepts. Scrupt used them in metaphysics to feel the Christion performance.

He took: Gold, Hyssop, Ram's Blood and Bull's blood and held them in his consciousness.

Ram's Blood   Bull's Blood   Gold   Hyssop

- Ram's Blood - Used in sacrafice in Biblical times. A precept of good fortune.
- Bulls Blood - A very importont sacrafice to God's people. A precept of the apparent.
- Hyssop - A cooking herb also used in healing. A precept of good healing.
- Gold - A precious metal used to measure the importance of the economy of an era. A precept of value.

“Let’s get moving, it feels very lively and friendly here.” Amy said.

They had been cloaked and had thin googles on giving them the ability to see each other.

Groco says, “Be careful this is the place the language that we were born to was created. I mean we don’t want to disturb anything. Our language is one big powerful tool. These characters of the language hold unbelievable power and are used even today to make up the origin of our alphabet.”

“It does feel kind of unique here doesn’t it?” Amy asked.

The guildies went on the look for the tent. The place looked like a town that was formed by many caravans from the Middle East as there are thousands of tents here.

“Byblos, the home of the Phoenicians.” Tiffany presented.

A few wells were dug for water supply. The Phoenicians made their living by trading from one tribe to the next. They traded by ship, camel, sacks, and carts. They built the first system of writing understood by everyone with the knowledge of trade.

“Guildies, we are looking for a record, scroll or tablet of some sort. Something with writing on it.” Tiffany said.

“This piece holds the key to every evidence of man’s language.” Groco said.

“Key to the precepts of the lord and the representations of the language that takes the form of the star globes in the tetraktys stone and scepter, and we need it.” Tiffany said.

“To understand the truth behind the element and maybe be able to find their true names . . . Look . . . There it is . . . The tent, scarlet, gold and blue.” Groco said with the voice not to stir the guildies into excitement.

“Hurry, the door is open.” Tiff whispered.

The guildies got to the door way and went inside. There were stacks of cloth, pottery, bowl, dishes, tools, bags of herbs and food items lying around the walls of the tent.

Gold candles and drapes were around the sitting area, with one man sitting in it reading scrolls. Behind him were three men at what looked to be as writing or studying scrolls, tablets and Egyptian symbols. What the guildies were looking for had to be in here. They snuck around the place looking and searching for something with the alphabet on it. The template of the meanings of characters first were linked together in meditation and one at a time held up to the universe to reflect the very idea of meaning of the symbol they were looking into. It had taken quite sometime to perfect the alphabet.

“Ah, ha, here it is.” Tiffany whispered.

Not knowing that they were extracting from a very sensitive piece of history. The guildies made a copy with space paper. Again not knowing the sensitivity of these works. The guildies copied of the first known writing of the alphabet. A scroll with many definitions of the first representation of things and their meanings. All this was done under cloak. No, witnesses, the guildies took leave and headed back to their ship.

"That was easier than I thought." Tiffany said.

Tiffany laid back on her chair to meditate on her prize. She found that the symbols were all connected with objects and objective. In the alphabet the ciphering she saw that the H meant fence. Tiffany made a page with the alphabet ciphered to the English alphabet. (See Figure 61) She noticed the symbols were put together to make words and names, and then it hit her. The stone and scepter needed these symbols to work. Though the globe stars were made by the English version though she knew these characters held more power.

"I wish Spucket were here." She said and reflected on what Spucket would do in her position.

Later to her discovery she knew that the tetraktys was originally made of the first rudiments. In her reveries she couldn't find or figure out why this all came together as it did. The prote hyle of it was missing, a vestige that was no longer there. She thought maybe one had to get used to living the life as a Phoenician has had.

"I like it here so let's stay a while." Groco said.

"Maybe we can learn the trick of the trade. Ha, ha, ha!" Amy said and they all laughed with her.

So the guildies went out and started browsing around to witness the trades in progress. They noticed scrolls being talked about as some would hold up a sign for pricing at many of the trades. The trades of merchandise at other trades by word of mouth and eye for eye the people that didn't know the language of trade. Caravan after caravan went through trading and leaving as the demand for supplies went up and down. Figure it to be the first stock exchange if one would. It was a fantastic festivity. The lives of the Phoenicians. The greatest tribe of trade that (192) ever walked the face of the Earth.

"Spucket would have just loved it here. I wonder what ever happened to the little guy, Scrupt." Groco said as he was reminiscing on the guild.

Figure 60

he Phonecian alphabet,

Phonecian	English
I	Z = Christ
ɰ	M
ɏ	K = Hand
W	S
◁	D
ɱ	S
ʖ	N
≢	E
ʟ	L
ʔ	P
4	R
H	H = Fence
K	A
1	G
Z	I
ᐊ	B
+	T

Chapter 18

"Why throw perils before swine when you can

Throw coffee into the faces of the indifferent?"

The Movie, Slacker . . .

"I've got it Father." Scrupt said.

The maps from the satellite computer show that the thieves' are in the Middle East. After Elisabeth got in contact with the satellites computer with the help of the pin number, it was not a problem to locate the thieves' location.

"Once we are there we will be able to capture them." Scrupt said as he checks on the thieves' location again.

"I finished the report, said Korlax, and I will be sending it to Headquarters in a bit."

"We have very little on the thieves' they have been being careful not to make a mark though they have stolen a book from the Wizard's guild in the kingdom of Gebelin. They could be expecting us this time around." Scrupt said.

"The report I have now says to apprehend them only using the safest means possible. The thieves' are now endangering time and space itself as it exist. The Agency says for us to be careful not to disturb anything in the thieves' apprehension. What we are to do is get them back home safely for more thorough interrogation." Scrupt said to Korlax.

"We with our technology will be taking the roll as babysitters when it comes to time traveling." Korlax said.

"Babysitters, keeping the population under control has always been the job of a government Agency." Korlax continued.

"How are we without them? The people watch out for each others safety. A quality control in the performance of our actions. We'd never train a monkey to screw up though there are people that would in the world. Sometimes people don't notice they are making a mistake until one take the care and concern to tell them. Even in punishment we have to watch our step." Scrupt said.

"The picture I get is we as individuals have to find the time to grasp the principles that were used and made by antiquity to find some meaning of life and its stages. The old ways and how they put this arrangement of attractions together." Korlax said.

"Yes, that reminds me of the art on the US Dollar Bill. How the current of an individual channels through it to the back side . . ." Scrupt said.

"Washington keeps the place clean for all of us . . ." Interrupts Father Isadore.

"Yes, Father, the Father of America as prote hyle of the nation." Scrupt said.

"Life is more than meets the eye, or well met at the apple of the eye. That the framers of the Constitution take that of a life of an apple. Being that of a living thing under one universe it's the perfect example. We are like the apple a current to everything we know. A govern that the Elders called broken. The scream of a popped amoeba. Life feeds of life and matter in the likes. Some artists find a distance in the reality of it. Some find reality in ways that reveal splendor and work with nature. Some artist will eat you alive. Then the rare artists are poet's reflecting the element with in the magic, literature, technology and so on. Now days I've been wondering how to teach such a muse. Letting each artist assemble the reflections in their own eyes peacefully with out limbo or hoax. The truth . . ." Father Isadore finished.

Shawk then disappeared upstairs.

"Your Father must be a very wonderful man. He shows a lot of intuition in his omniscience. I especially like it when he talks. A man of true eloquence." Korlax said.

"He's been the best in both guidance and friendship I've ever had. He's taught me things of the plain and simple, and to be happy and honest. He taught me how to use the nous and to bring things to a common sense. To give life the ease of being the muse around oneself. To watch and learn my own thoughts." Scrupt said.

Scrupt fades away and starts telling a tale as he came back.

"Rest came easy to me as I began to study peace. A place that was free of disturbance and no sound. My Father walked in on me that day as I sat there in the basement peacefully. He set a banana on the table in front of me. I had my eyes closed and the banana came to me in a vision. Just a single banana. I opened my eyes and there on the table in front of me it was. Shawk gave it to me and explained that the vision of the banana in my mind was the Holy Ghost. He explained to me that the image in my mind was the gift from God. That we have a couple of different second sights. The imagination, illusion, the Holy Ghost and epiphanies. The imagination is our mind and can be permuted. The illusion is part of the eyes and is a more precise imagination. The epiphanies we receive from Earth or man and can not be permuted. The Holy Ghost is a non-permutable image of something that God has given you. He said that the image comes to you through divine intervention and that you have to discern it to its value here on Earth. The imagination works like this, but we project it in our minds and it isn't the Holy Ghost. The imagination works on a frequency of reflecting the element in an incorporeal part of the mind. It's just images. The Holy Ghost is a message from heaven namely the entire body of the universe. It comes to you, you don't imagine it. Shawk said that by holding a napkin to your ear gave a good definition of peace. One would hold it up to ones ear and hear ruffles until it was completely still and it gave peace to oneself. It's a matter of holding anything in the mind in the likes so it is still and gives one peace." Scrupt said and then went into some quick prayers to catch his sense of heading.

"The imagination always needs work my Father told me. Holding a napkin to your ear to bring peace is one thing. Holding something like a banana on your mind is another. One can meditate on anything this way just by holding it on your head. It just sits there and your mind meditates on it. This is meditation of its simplest form. Just holding this in your mind. It teaches you to hold intellect above you head in a long enough duration that ones mind can handle to bring insight to ones perception." Scrupt said.

Korlax was balancing a pencil on his head.

"Yep, it works." He said.

Scrupt had already set the ship for the thieves' transportation. He knew they could teleport and even be dangerous. He was sure that the trap would work. As he had earlier tested it out on Korlax. Besides they had the thieves' satellite working for them.

They got their stuff together. Teleported into the ship. Checked the computers programming. The leaped back to the time the thieves' were at. Now to get close enough to the thieves' to trap them in the cell.

The thieves' were outside their ship and Scrupt began to think that this was going to be easy. Scrupt and Korlax could see everything on the ships computer screen which made to guildies and their ship visible. The Agents stayed quite a ways away not to raise any suspicion. They thought that the googles guildies had on could see things in cloak. The Agents were a couple of thousands of yards away. The guildies never saw what hit them. The three thieves' were brought, teleported into the cell. Korlax switch the grid locking the thieves' in.

"What?! What! What the hell just happened?" Groco said in an alarmed state.

He realized that he and the other guildies had been captured in the cell. The cell was made with one door and had a thick clear glass window as a ceiling allowing the Agents to see in and the guildies to see out. All three were in the same cell aboard the Agents ship. Groco and the guildies tried to teleport out, but got no where.

"Hi, my name is Scrupt, and this is Korlax Curry. We are special Agents from America that have been ordered to bring you three back home safely." Scrupt told the guildies.

"Why, we are just inventors and have done a lot of work to get here. The limits are infinite, the way we can leap across time and space." Groco cried.

"We have done nothing wrong." Tiff complained.

"In deed you three have. You stole a Wizard's guild book and now you're going to have to cough it up." Scrupt said in a stern voice.

Then Tiffany got the book out of her inventory and said, "Here it is, let us go."

"No, I'm afraid I can't do that." Scrupt answered.

"Then what's going to happen to us?" Tiffany asked.

"You will be taken to America for questioning. It's really up to the Agency. If we go public it will be up to the courts. You'd be quite famous at that time. I'm thinking you three are heroes. So from here it doesn't look that bad. You three are not exactly condemned." Scrupt said.

Scrupt and Korlax decided to search the thieves' ship. They teleported in, walked around and found nothing. So they went back to the ship to talk with the thieves' some more.

Scrupt and Korlax start talking to the thieves' again.

Amy said in amusement and wonder, "Scrupt Knostic? Is it really you?"

"Oh, my God!" Tiffany said is shock smiling in amazement.

"Groco, look its Spucket's little one." Amy said.

"What the . . . Well, it is you, Scrupt my boy, how have you been?" Groco asked in cheery likeness.

'What are you saying? You people know me?" Scrupt asked all puzzled.

"Yeah, we know you, you are Spucket's little boy. He used to run our guild where we come from." Groco said.

"You mean that's the name of my Father? Spucket Knostic?" Scrupt said with a feeling of tears in his eyes.

"Yes, Amy said, Groco is the leader ever since your parents died in a gun fight. Tiffany and I were there and we didn't want to stick around. We just left you there in the church. We never got a chance to see what happened to you. You were just one and a half years old."

"We got away and abandoned you, whatever happened." Tiffany asked.

"I was adopted and raised by a monk named Shawk Isadore." Scrupt said.

"He gave me the best a Father could." Scrupt continued.

He felt cramped and needed a lot more information.

"Sounds like you have had an exciting life." Amy said.

"Well, what I found out today is the top of the serendipity." Scrupt said.

"I felt such a connection on our first encounter with you three and now I find out this." He continued.

"So tell us more Lil' Scrupt." Groco said.

"I grew up in Germany and was trained as a Pythagorean. I grew to become an artist and inventor, and made it big on the market. Yet I wanted more. To become a Special Agent and here I am today given the most exciting things to do in the world." Scrupt said.

"How'd you become a Special Agent?" Amy asked.

"I decided to go to Law school to become an Agent for Special Forces . . . Tell me about my Father." Scrupt said.

"Well, Tiffany says, he hired me to work for him. I had nothing but the streets back then and that's it. I was also an orphan. He gave me hope and a whole new world to play in. We copied things much like we did in time traveling only it was from large corporations that we stole form. The guild still hides behind an invention factory. Spucket's dream was to time travel and we finally did it because of his reveries." Tiff said.

Groco had a different tale to tell.

"I was 26 when Spucket was murdered." Groco said and gave the tale that Spucket was an Architect and an Engineer who knew the place forwards and backwards by the hand of ledger main, the eye of eloquence and the ear of agriculture.

"He was the master behind himself, Groco says, I was his brain child. He opened every day with conversation that was linked together with the first time he talked to you. He'd open up your mind with his gusto. His memory and sophistry was just amazing. Every word, as he was masters with any mark of evidence you could throw at him. He was in touch with my mind the way a pianist is in touch with the piano. He said stuff in such a way that the words would give you a better resolution to the pictures in your head. He actually painted things with his gusto. If you weren't won over by him speaking to you, I would have to say that you were out of your mind."

There is a long time before anything was said again.

"Well, the bad news is I'm still taking you three in. The good news is we don't have anything on you, but what you now own is considered contraband. Your ship will be taken to the Agency." Scrupt said.

"We do though have to do as the Agency tells us." Korlax said.

Groco with his hindsight had figured a way out, he took it and instantly vanished. With the final words, "Salutary."

He teleported back to the ship. Once he made it there he made his way back home.

"Now what?" Korlax said.

"We'll, get him later, says Scrupt, but for now let's talk with these thieves' to see what they know. Then we'll head back to the laboratory.

Chapter 19

"Hey, asshole . . ."

Jeffery Curry, 2003

Scrupt finds himself with a migraine headache and is walking around the ship in agony. In metaphysics Shawk taught Scrupt that headache's are wedges of information like a material of something in large a quantity trying to find a way through ones cortex's causing ones pain. Scrupt as a Pythagorean knew the tetraktys existed in harmony to the universe therefore the headache was an order or better yet a disorder that can be fixed. What was happening was pain in Scrupt's foresight. He knew it was or contained a vision of some sort. The Holy Ghost gave him the vision that the world will soon no longer exist. The Earth was still intact where he was, in the Phoenician city of Byblos. Time was being erased and Scrupt could tell as his pain increased. Scrupt went to talk to the thieves'.

"Where would Groco go and what would he be up to if he made it back safely?" Scrupt asked as his mind was pounding.

"I'm sure he would do as I would." Amy said.

"What's that?" Asked Scrupt as he groaned as the pain went through his mind again.

"I would tell the whole guild everything and go from there." Amy said.

Tiffany asked Scrupt if he was hurt. Then Scrupt told the thieves' the visions and his migraine headache. Tiffany said come here, I can help you. Scrupt teleported in the cell. Tiffany worked her magic and Scrupt was relieved.

"Thank you . . . You're more than sweet you're a heart." Scrupt said.

Her heart pounded out as she got close to him and gave him a kiss.

"Scrupt." She said.

"Yes, Tiffany?" Scrupt asked.

"I . . . I think I'm in love with you." Tiffany said in a sweet voice.

"I'm thinking what you're thinking." Scrupt told her.

Then the two kissed again.

"Alright, something is up with the existence of the world. I'm going to let you free if you decide to help me." Scrupt said like a champion.

"It sounds fine by me." Amy said.

"I'll help you, sweet heart." Tiffany said.

So Scrupt let them out.

"I'm thinking that Groco has done something he shouldn't have done." Scrupt said.

"Tiffany, what do you know of this tetraktys stone?" Scrupt asked as he looked it over. "In all I know of the stone is that it was made to make a direct line of man with his Deity and the stars of the cosmos. It has globes made out of star precepts of the English language. It's said to be able to reconstruct time and space as we have known it. The Pythagoreans knew the world would be destroyed at some point in time and space and this is why they study everything. The tetraktys is a tool they use and the stone was made thereof to save it." Tiffany finished.

"A cure for oblivion, interesting. It feels so solid with it in my hands." Scrupt said.

"How it works, I don't know, it might be activated solely on intuition. I have a magical scepter that was made by the Pythagoreans and it restores everything that has been damaged." Said Tiffany.

"How does it work and how did you get it?" Scrupt asked.

"We found it on a quest from the Queen of Gebelin. The same place where we first encountered you." Tiffany said.

"Show me how it works." Scrupt said.

Tiff took out a dagger and shattered it with a hammer. She took the scepter and waved it back and forth bringing the dagger back together.

"It makes you feel good when it channels energy from your body and mind to the broken item of things you want to fix." Tiffany said.

"Wow! That's absolutely wonderful, let me try that." Scrupt said.

He tried it on a few things as he experimented with it. He put it on the ships computer to analyze it. Tiffany told him that the globes were made of the stars of the cosmos. Making the bearer as if one had the hands of the creator. Actually in a channel with a person's energy it makes a perfect spell with the globed stars. It takes man and Deity in perfect state in organizing the way the tetraktys works. Man is the lower ten globes and the Deity is the fifty-five globes as both of them intersect on the stone. (See Figure 61)

* * *

Groco an x-cop and genus at technology and Law had planned to make the whole guild time travel. Once he teleported to his ship and made an adjustment in the pin, he then travelled in time to the future to the guild in New Zealand. Where Veronica, Cristy, and Darren were very surprised to see just him returning so early. Groco had explained to them what had happened to Tiffany and Amy. They were amazed at the story. Though what he had on his mind next was even bigger. The whole guild he wished to time travel and in the mitts a desire to bring the whole world to an end.

First thing he did was got a hold of Jeremy at the Minnesota guild. Giving him the schematic manual to spread out amongst all the other guild labs. He said let the whole underground follow the yellow brick road. What Groco knew and didn't imply was that this was going to be the end of all existence of mankind. Meaning at least Earth. The universe is impossible to destroy. He didn't know exactly what was going to happen, but he had to have everyone join in.

"Got to hand it to the government, Groco says to himself, from Hitler, the Japs, and Mother Russia, and all these foreign policies to the early four bit computers, up to the gigabits. The world has its lost latter. Even the best get stuck in trinkets of sophistry. These game pieces of ancient times are mostly swallowed by the genera, and are still wonders to us. A piece of a language or character of the alphabet in a child's mind feel heavy as rocks at first. Until the secret is revealed by a teacher or guide. Why we are not able to move gigantic stones like the Egyptian's is still a lost technology. Technology alone has to be an infinitely long class. What we have done this far is just a drop in the bucket. Who's to say what the year 4,000 will bring us? Why, we ourselves haven't been met with someone from the future is why I think there has been an apocalypse. Huh, will someone save our future . . ." Groco smiles.

Two weeks later . . .

"Groco, the guild labs are ready to go." Said Jeremy from the Minnesota guild.

"Some of them already took off into the past. We are coming with you, Groco. Where are we headed?" Jeremy asked.

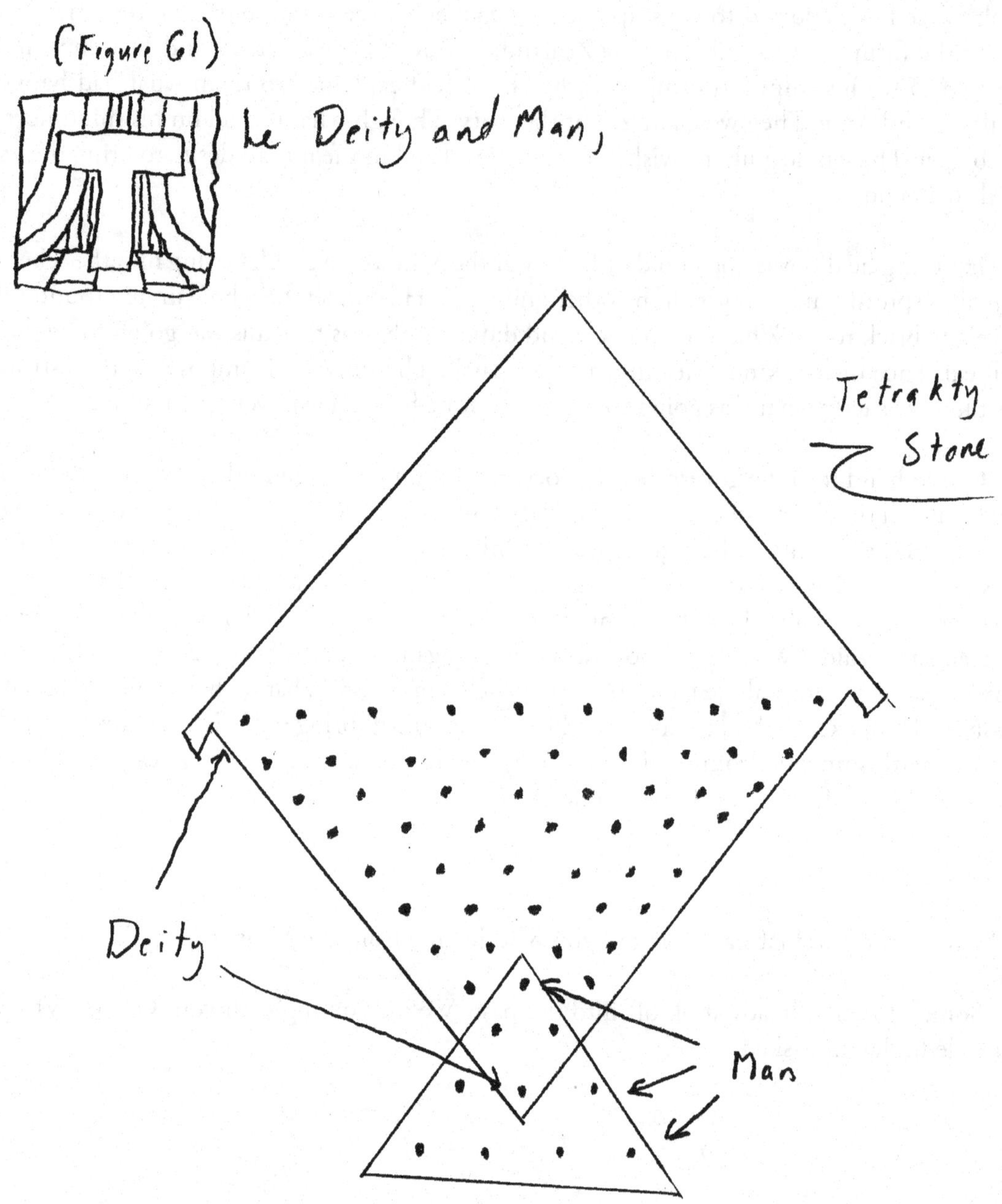
(Figure 61)
he Deity and Man,
Tetrakty
Stone
Deity
Man

"To Egypt, says Groco, I want to watch the process of the pyramids being built."

"Some of us want to travel back to the time Earth itself was forming and others want to see the dinosaurs." Jeremy said.

"If one can leap back that far and good luck to you guildies. For now we must all take off into the immutability. See you on the flip side." Groco said and teleported inside his ship and took off.

It was the last time anyone would see Groco and it was the same for the Earth as the guildies kept altering events in time and space history.

* * *

"I need your skills Tiff, to help me figure out this tetraktys stone. The book prophecies the end of the world when most of it throughout time has been destroyed. The Earth was sadly torn apart like never before. It crumbled pulling backwards from the present to the beginning of Earth's creation. Just like it had been built. Everything was lost. Some one must have altered the prote hyle of the Earth. The tetraktys stone is said to restore this order. All of time will flash before our eyes and there will be a voice from the heavens calling of the Feral Plain." Scrupt read.

Scrupt ciphers a globe of the stone and says, "Absolute, a star which means an English word in a globe giving it a production."

"I've already ciphered that one. Earth is another one I've measured if I stand correct." Said Tiffany.

The tetraktys stone has 61 globes meaning to Pythagoreans, One Divine. Each one of the globes was filled with a unique and complete universal word or quintessence. That when in contact with the human spirit it begins to work its magic's.

"It's just like trying to take apart the universe, its possibilities just exhaust me." Tiffany said.

"Except it's just not that complicated or vast, it just takes time to unfold it all. After all there are myriads of stars which would take years for hundreds of scholars to figure them out. We only are looking at 61. It's when you get into the element itself on a metaphysical scale the element has a google in quantity." Scrupt said.

"Holy crap! The world is disappearing from beneath us!" Tiffany shouted.

The Earth began to split into asteroids and large chunks. The atmosphere disappears. The ship was now located in space.

"We must get back to Gebelin." Amy said.

Scrupt then gets in contact with the satellite and they teleport to the time Gebelin was on the map. Just then the amulets began to glow and spheres appeared around them and they floated to Gebelin the only thing left intact.

"I think we should go and talk with the Queen." Amy said.

They made it to the ground and hoofed it to the castle to meet the Queen. They went up to her and the Queen said, "Welcome, Scrupt, you are just like I pictured you. You don't need to bow. Rise and do what this scroll tells you to do."

"Ah, thank you, you're royal highness. I'll do as you wish." Scrupt said and takes the scroll and bows, so do the rest of the guildies.

The scroll told him that he had to take the stone to the Monad tower in the center of the castles. That he had been chosen to say the words of intuition of the Pythagorean's. He took the stone to the Monad tower stairs. Where Paul met him there and told him the secret words to say. Scrupt did as he was told. Up at the Monad tower Scrupt shouted the words holding the stone up to the universe.

"Vesica Piscis!" Scrupt shouted.

There all of a sudden the space filled with white light and there was no darkness anywhere. A huge solar wind pressed and pulled every which way harnessing everything in the universe. Like as if the tetraktys of a Deity were present. Everything felt soft and warm and the guildies knew that this was the beginning of something great. A leviathan appeared and ate all of the things that were floating around that was left of Earth and out of its bowel came the Earth freshly formed as though nothing happened.

There was a great voice that came from the Heavens saying "Behold, The Feral Plain."

The light disappeared and everyone felt a great happiness.

The tetraktys stone transformed into a myriad stone. The sphere of Gebelin is the crown of the Feral Plain. It will orbit Earth like the moon only it will be completely invisible to the people of Earth. Gebelin will prevent the new coming disasters of the Earth after the date of 2010 ad. The kingdom of Gebelin then circled the Earth this from this day of at 2010 ad.

Chapter 20

"I . . . I . . . I love you!"

Scott Degas, 2003

The Feral Plain

A man was walking down the road at night. It was dark with little wind and full cloud cover. One could tell that the moon was out giving the light through the clouds. He walked as he had always walked to and from work. Being an inventor at his leisure and full time reporter for the newspaper in his small home town.

As he walked he thought, "Strange.?"

As the wind came up from behind him and tickled his skin. A warmth he felt from the wind. It then became stronger. He felt a whole new spirit enter him. Making him feel vivacite and eccentric.

"Whoa, hoo, hah . . ." He said with a large grin and cheer.

He kept walking as the wind such as a vacuum of as vortex was on him pulling and pressing.

He was about to pass the cemetery in between town and his house when a second wind snuck up behind him, but this time picking him up off his the ground and cradling him in the air. Pure adrenaline pumped through his body and governed him in an overwhelming rush of excitement.

"Oh, the wind . . . Would, would it drop me?" He asked himself as it brought him higher and higher.

It was above the clouds that he realized that he might end up some where in space. The fear became greater and greater creating such indecision that he began screaming like a baby for God. Though the wind had been very clean and gentle with him from the beginning. Carrying him for a few hours only to be let down in a courtyard of a mansion. The man was overwhelmed by the sight of the creepy looking mansion and started to run for the front gates when then the wind grabbed him once more. This time taking him with speed over the roof of the mansion and gently letting him down on the second floor balcony in the back yard.

Another man in the dark shadow of night said, "Good evening, you must be the inventor I sent for."

"Yeah, I am an inventor, why have you sent for me." The Inventor asked.

"Well, allow me to introduce myself, he gasps, I am Father Edwind Knostic, and you are M Degas." Edwind said.

"Yes, that is who I am, what was that wind? Why have you sent for me, and how do you know my name?" M Degas asked all at once.

"I'd like to hire you to invent things for me, it's a bit of a quest. A quest that involves you." Edwind said trying to lure him in.

"Oh, really? What's the quest?" M Degas asked with a change of heart.

There was a brief pause. A short wind smoothly continued to roll up to the second balcony and the two of them stepped into the mansion.

"I will pay you, if you accept." Edwind said stumbling on the words to say.

"What would you pay me?" M Degas said as he became more excited and interested.

"If you're good enough, anything. You see, I am a very old man and have a very large amount of assets. You would do very well if you accept." Edwind said.

"If I agree, I must tell my family and work. What do you have as down payment?" M Degas asked.

"Down payment?" Edwind asked.

'What can you pay me now?" M Degas asked.

"Well, how about one million dollars?" Edwind asked now that he thought about it.

"One million dollars! One million dollars! Wow! Could I send it to my family right away?" M Degas asked in shear excitement.

"Sure, and you'll be staying with me for about six months." Edwind said as he smiled at M Degas emotions.

"I must write my folks and work letter then." Said M Degas.

"Then of coarse you agree to help me?" Edwind said.

'Yes, I'll take the quest." M Degas said.

"Good, I'll personally see that the money and letters are sent. You're more than welcome to my desk, paper and pens." Edwind said as he led M Degas to his office.

Edwind said he would be right back with the cash.

He came back to the desk with a doctor's bag full of money.

"You see, M Degas, we are living in a world that is bent on money. One where man does things in such vane that he would rather live a life of a hoax. Accepting anything that he comes across. The truth lets us dream, it is the only way . . . The truth. In ages to come man will even be more complex. The truth comes at a cost, M Degas. It means that the truth is a pain staking process unless you have the right tools to the right facts. There will always be people that don't believe the truth. The fact is that almost everything is a model or theory and on a discourse of our language, except the word, Trade. We trade everything and that is where fairness and truth started. Trading things and words is always not with the truth, in some places no matter what the situation is we will always lose. Places such as war and disease. Unless of course, you, M Degas, can help make a difference." Edwind said.

"Oh . . . Yeah . . . What must I do?" M Degas said lifting his body upright giving his full attention.

"Well, you will have to learn just what truth this place is made of from the bottom up. I will teach you. You will learn. You will find the perfect state that which you will be able to reflect apon the element and once then control it apon your intuition. A perfect state . . . Not the stuff you get from reading the language in a text book will give you, but to identify and react with the element as one . . . There is a way and you will teach it." Edwind said and takes a look at M Degas writing his folks.

"Ah, you can take all the time you wish." Edwind said.

It was about midnight and it started to rain.

"What should the letter address? How long is the employment?" M Degas asked as he sits at the desk.

"Well, it should entitle that you found out of town business on a moments notice that will last about six months or so, and that it is a private matter. In the bag is a lump some of my salary. Oh, and go a head and tell them that you're inventing something for a very wealthy man. Put the letter in the bag and the maid will take care of it and then show you to your room. I'll talk to you first thing in the morning." Edwind finished and headed down stairs.

M Degas got up from the desk minutes later and found the Maid walking up the stairs. He found the place incredible. The high ceilings, the artwork, the architecture. He then decided to ask the Maid for a tour.

The Maid replied, "We don't have time for that now, it's too late. We'd better get you to your room. You have a big day a head for you tomorrow."

M Degas made himself at home in bed and knocked himself out.

M Degas wakes up to a man staring at him. He realizes it's the Butler after he comes out of his stupor. He had a very powerful dream. A dream like which he had never had before. It started with this boy who had very special powers. Magically being able to control the element. Using them to save a man's life by death of fire. Wielding water by his powers he doses the man that was being burned alive. Then heals the man from his injuries. Not long after that the boy was taken to a temple under ground and then he organized the element into a perfect apeiron that the church needed for their rituals and study. This sphere had life like characteristics as it would move feraling like a flaming disk differently to who ever was the closest. It was a mirror into the soul, it was also harmless. They named it the all-seeing-eye. The boy passed out after performing his work. Then M Degas woke up.

"M Degas, are you awake now?" The Butler asked.

"Ooh . . . Well, yeah. Oh! What time is it, have I been sleeping long?" M Degas asked and got up and sat on the bed.

"Here, Father Edwind wants you to wear these. It's eight O'clock in the morning." The Butler said then turned around and said, "Come down stairs when you are ready there has been breakfast prepared for you."

He left and closed the door behind him M Degas was wondering about that sphere in his dream, and about that little boy. He thought it was such a vivid real like time and place somewhere in Europe around 1000 ad. He wondered if it meant something. He felt it was vital that he had to figure it out. He took care of his hygiene, got dressed into the clothes Edwind wanted him to wear and went down stairs.

Down stairs in the lobby there was a note on the table that he found and it said:

Dear, M Degas,

I'm off to Cambridge to borrow

a book from a friend. Please feel free

to tinker around my mansion. My home

is yours. I'll be back shortly.

Father Edwind, 8/31/71

"Ah, wonderful . . . Just wonderful, this amazing home . . . The art, the lighting. Hmm . . . Where should I start?" M Degas said very happily with his hands folded.

"Sir, there is breakfast in the dinning room if your interested." Said the Butler right in front of M Degas.

"Ah, yes and would it be possible for you to show me around a bit afterwards?" M Degas asked.

"Yes, of course, Sir, as you wish." The Butler said.

The dinning room was fantastic, M Degas thought. It sat ten people around the table, breakfast was served on a silver platter and the glasses were made of crystal. The walls were crimson with brown wooden floors. The ceiling was made of metal plates which were painted black and from which hung two chandlers. The paintings were all of religious happenings of Gods, Goddesses of the Roman and Greek pantheons. A mirror that unfolded out a map of the world was on the wall in front of him. Toast, eggs, bacon and orange juice he ate there in delight. He began to get a state of mind where everything seemed smaller to him then it actually was. Like the tightening of perception in a happy frequency. He came back down after mumbling a few words to himself back to his omniscience. He felt quite happy and content about it.

"Ah, M Degas, it looks like you are finished." The Butler said.

"Yep, and a fine breakfast it was." M Degas said dangling from the spirit the place gave him.

"Alright, now are you ready for your tour?" The Butler asked.

"Yeah, I'm ready, ah ha." M Degas agreed.

"Well, we'll start in the basement where the laboratory is put together just for you and your studies."? The Butler said.

"The laboratory!?" M Degas said in excitement.

He just thought things couldn't get much better.

"Yes, it even amazes me, he's got everything you know." The Butler said.

They headed down into the basement and in a huge room with long tables and shelves M Degas found crystals, rocks, gems, minerals, potions, salves, guns, swords, iron ore, metal samples, acids, bases, element samples, Pressurized gas, beakers, burners, books, scrolls, plant samples, vacuums, herbs, things of chemistry, blue prints, hour glasses, schematics, clocks, eye pieces, microscopes, telescopes, reptiles, lab mice, and much more.

"It's all, said the Butler, because you have an eye for such things. We've been watching you for quite some time now, M Degas, you know some books exist before they are written."

"Yes, M Degas, even the God's play with time as well as with fates, but only in our own eyes do we choose the valor to react and make up our choices of our own destinies from upsolins. After all what is time to a Deity?" Edwind said.

"Ah, you're back and now I am happy again." M Degas said as he checks Edwind out.

As he could see he was carrying a large book.

"Did you get the book?" M Degas asked.

"Oh, the book . . . The tetraktys, written by the Wizard's of Gebelin. The book is about how science and religion come together. The world will come to an age of sophistication and bring everything to an end. We exist in a time that's protected by the tetraktys by the all-seeing-eye the only sphere tuned into everything in the universe. Years ago I was able to weald the myriad stone into the sphere to reflect the universe and it is still used as a tool to watch people today. It's existence in itself, and more of a toy from prote hyle. It's been nicknamed the all-seeing-eye. One has to be trained in the way one can see it to every sphere in monadology of the universe. I will show you the way, M Degas." Edwind said.

"Idea police." M Degas said out loud after the depth of the idea civilized in his mind.

"Yeah, more at a quality control. Through the years many inventions have been made, but they are not for the public eye. Monstrous contraptions of the tetraktys that the chosen Pythagoreans framed the way one can think, trees of knowledge in the likes. There are many spheres in the form of intellect namely a toaster, car, or gun. A person gets only out of the sphere what they have learned about it. The all-seeing-eye is considered the ruler of spheres as it is also called the eye of God." Edwind said and then paused.

"Eye of God?" M Degas said.

"You see, man needs a God to maintain his production. In this existence God alone has opened this duration, the Earth and the heavens. These spheres show the reflection that is represented by our language. That is part of the reason that if one says, "Stick." A stick appears in the imagination. To keep the people from going over board these contraptions show their precepts as a muse in the arts of nature creating a limited state of mans capabilities of thought. They are mans guide, but for now we must continue our quest and learn the tetraktys from the bottom up." Edwind said.

"We have a quest for you to finish, but for now just follow me." Edwind said and went over to the table.

"Now, my laboratory is set up to thoroughly examine each and every element that is in the body, plants, moons, planets, and suns. The mind reflects the element as you are the bearer of a sphere. There is a large body of elements within the human condition which are not exactly of the charts of the Periodic table of Elements. Sorts of elements of metaphysics which go with chemistry of the mind. The mind is much larger than the Earth and smaller than a neutrino. I am translucent and hollow where my home is space and my mind moves at any address of the dimension. Space which the universe travels on which I live and think. The elements on the charts are just temporarily named. We have to identify with them, but these are not all the elements. Water and air are elements. On a metaphysical side (Emotions) anger and happiness are elements in an adumbrate. They last as long as other hormones. The thinking process works by precepts of intellect which in large quantity ones intelligence. Intellect is not a sphere all the time. Like I said the mind reflects on the element. The book explains how the mixture of the element comes out to form words or better yet spells. I myself can teleport to different times and I myself am from the future." Edwind explained.

"Will I be time traveling?" M Degas asked.

"Yes, you're going to have to come with me, but that's in the distant future. What I need you to do now is examine the book and figure out how to arrange the tetraktys stone and how to explain how it works so everyone will know. The book will explain exactly how it is done. Here take this amulet and wear it, it is the key to Gebelin." Edwind said.

"Most of my life had already been written. I go and follow a book given to me by Paul of Gebelin. He's the chief Pythagorean of the Kingdom of Gebelin. He has a library like no other. The books are from the future and ancient times. The idea of such a library is to be able to save the world from destruction. We Pythagoreans are a peaceful kind. We have every Deity at our worship to trade to at any given time. In the future a time will come where technology has the key to time travel. We can time travel already with our magic's. Though we keep it a tight secret. One that you will also have to hold. It's up to you, M Degas, to find our way through the tetraktys book to weald the stone into a piece that will save all of existence throughout time and space. You will then teach of such works." Edwind said.

"The books here on the wall will help you understand the element. We need you to spell the element out of the elements on this chart in the tetraktys book. You will need to master each study, but for now study the tetraktys book from the beginning to the end and I will be your muse." Edwind said and fluffed himself into the chair at the table right in front of M Degas.

M Degas grabs the book, "Ah, the front cover gleams with intelligence. It feels like it completes me." M Degas said.

"It keeps Our Father's promise, to everyone, to everything. Keeps them safe and sound. Hope that one day man will finally achieve his dreams. Understanding it all gives one the performance to control the element. It is the mysteries and treasures of the heavens that open up the Holy Ghost. It's a time which I came from, where I wish to be." Edwind said.

The front cover of the book had one two inch in diameter dot, gold in color with the rest of the book cover in black.

"How many years have you been at this mansion?" M Degas asked.

"Fourteen years, I've been here taking my time reading and writing books to prepare you for your studies. I've been studying the characters of man's existence, since I am hardly from any moral, cultural, or economics of an era of mankind." Edwind continues.

"The tetraktys is the key to the universe. It gives you a realization of the universe's workings. It will one day be the tool which everyone uses." Edwind said.

"Now start reading the book, M Degas." Edwind said.

M Degas asked what the cover meant.

"You'll know what it means in time." Edwind said.

M Degas turns the first page and was met with this symbol. (See Figure 62)

"This is it . . ." Edwind said pointing his finger to the symbol.

The symbol was the tetraktys.

"This is it?" M Degas asked and though it was very simple.

"Well, says Edwind, this is the basic form of the tetraktys that needs to be learned in order to become a master of the element. This is a puzzle of metaphysics that rest in the Holy Ghost. How's yours right now?"

"How's my what?" M Degas asked.

"Your mind, how does it work?" Edwind questioned.

"Oh, well it works on impulse, a type of flow control and functions well with the rudiments at a prudence. I channel the essential ideas and ideas I have. All to work out what's the best for the instance at an importance." M Degas explained to Edwind.

"Then how can you think of a knife and not hurt yourself?" Edwind wanted to know.

"It's because we think in incorporeal images that our eyes have seen before through the reflection of light that you receive throughout the life you've had is just what, a reflection. One can do anything with the light of the imagination when they have had enough practice. Not all minds are equal and therefore our understanding is different. It does take skill to imagine a knife let alone one that can cut you. It makes me think, could that ever be possible? The mind can weald anything, can't it." M Degas explained.

"There is no end to the tetraktys and no end to the way it can be used, it is an enigma. Scholars and wise men have dabbled in it. It was first founded by a man named Pythagoras of Samos. Though the Indian's of India first found it. Pythagoras didn't see much of what he started, but he believed that the magic rest in a mind separate from the mind we use regularly. The tetraktys started with him." Edwind said.

Pythagoras? Isn't that where Pythagoreans come from?" M Degas asked.

"Yes, the Pythagoreans came from the ideology of Pythagoras." Edwind said.

"Turn the page." Edwind said.

M Degas turns the page and sees this symbol. (See Figure 63)

(Figure 62)

The tetraktys,

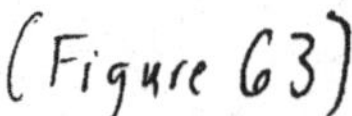
(Figure 63)

he tyriad,

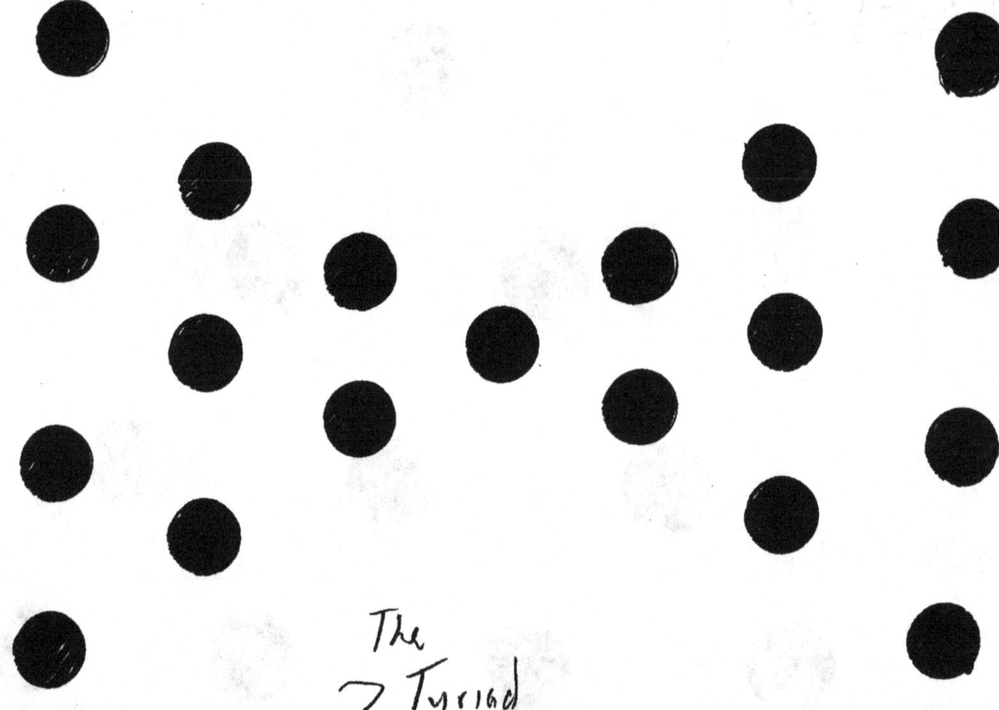
The
Tyriad

"What is this? What does it do?" M Degas asked.

"It has many uses once you have learned to use it." Edwind said.

"Come here and take a look at this." Edwind continued as he waved M Degas over to one of the tables in the laboratory. Edwind grabbed a glass of water. He set it on the table in between them. He then waved his finger and amazingly drew water into a stream like manor to the table out from the glass. The water never bled into the table. A puddle of water laid standing on the table. Edwind then made it into a solid cube of water.

"Fascinating." M Degas said in awe.

"Watch this." Edwind said.

He put a large piece of iron ore on top of the cube of water, it supported it. Edwind then took it off and hit the water cube with his hand and it tumbled across the table in a jelly like state giggling freely in its direction.

"How does it work?" M Degas asked.

"It's a matter of intuition of the tetraktys, magic . . . Controlled by the tyriad. There is a place outside the normal mind where time can be monkeyed with. Each man has a unique ability to use the tetraktys. The universe has countless dimensions, yet the court of the tetraktys can be changed just as many in the likes. Each man has his own epithet (What he considers as the truth) to seek to match his skills. A unique character to build with the foundations of the tetraktys. I guess you can say that each savvy's a different page." Edwind said.

"Humanity has lived a life of drudgery and each generation tried to make life more comfortable for the next. We now have a page that we get from work and doloring. We call it the dollar bill. Back then inside the church the people came together and made love. It made it easier for the people to get to know their neighbor. Today we shake hands. The dollar was made to ease the burden of labor in the love, honor and merit. One dollar was made to represent all our works in existence. You, M Degas, will bring a new face to that dollar I speak of in the world. It will show the performance of our kind." Edwind said.

It was getting late.

"Where do you come from?" M Degas asked.

"I am the first born of the Feral Plain. I came from the year 2010, nine months after the destruction of Earth. I was born with all the powers of the tetraktys." Edwind said.

"But, now it's time for us to rest." Edwind continued in a tired voice.

So they closed the book and headed for their rooms for the night.

Chapter 21

"The elasticity of existence kills me."

Chad Douglas Bulau, 2005

M Degas woke up early and headed down to the lab. Surprised to see Edwind up kicking around ideas.

Edwind says, "Check this out."

A wind rose and it got to be a comfortable warmth in the room. This clear liquid covered the table against the wall. It gradually turned into a window to outer space where one could view the stars. There was all about them this warm solar wind.

"This is a pure apeiron. Once you develop you mind you can do anything." Edwind said and the vision returned to normal.

"First we must learn the values of the tetraktys. Everything you have learned throughout your life will be of great value. It should all come out right. Pythagoras knew the secret, but had no way of an ability to tell everyone them. I know the pieces fit, because I put them together as a child for the Elders of the church in 1054 ad." Edwind said.

"You . . . It was you in my dream." M Degas said.

"You had a dream last night?" Edwind asked.

"No, it was the first nights sleep here. It was about a boy saving a man from fire, and going to the Elders to form a great sphere, the all-seeing-eye." M Degas said.

"That was me, M Degas." Edwind said.

"Here we must put it together. As an inventor you've experienced just about every class there is, at least in this age. Edwind rose. It's a matter of finding an atom and then it's molecules to learn how things work. With 10/20 vision as I have it is easy. With 20/20 vision of your eyes it is easier to find with the 10/20 vision of your mind. Depending on the resolution of your imagination (10/20 of your mind) you will be able to find it." Edwind explained.

"We begin with drawing the first dimension. This is the absolute universe there is no existence beyond it in this conjecture. This is the first psyche that does not move. We consider a mandala when looking into it. A place where the whole universe is gathered." Edwind said.

He had M Degas draw it up for himself. (See Figure 64)

"Everything is an immutable shot. Carpe Diem. A still life of the universe. The point does not have time or space it is the first of the two psyches. The second psyche is all of the other dimensions beyond the first where we begin with we have the second dimension. Two points follow the first dimension to make a total of three dots in the foundation of the tetraktys." Edwind said. (See Figure 65)

"The first psyche does not move? What does it mean?" M Degas asked.

"It's an apeiron which can not be hot or cold, dry nor wet. It is a thing that will never move. The second psyche can move it though. Though there are apeirons that have functions as in crystals. Meaning that they hold images." Edwind said.

"In the second dimension there is movement of existence as it divides the universe into three parts. The third dimension is the place the moving parts connect to each other creating the first surface. This is where we begin to reason things in the imagination." Edwind said.

"So take the six dots and call it reason?" M Degas asked.

"Well one can reason with the third dimension alone where we only use three dots in this section. There is a great mystery to all Pythagoreans what the best way to label the tetraktys these ways I have mentioned are only experiments therefore theories." Edwind said.

"So we haven't even got it right?" M Degas asked.

"It's exactly right, though we have been making process. Some believe that a Deity has not even been born yet. Though he lives here in immutability (A place where time doesn't even matter) the universe is god's home. The fourth dimension is the place existence as we know it takes form. It is our consciousness and completes the tetraktys." Edwind said. (See Figure 66)

"It's mans universe. Let's say that each point is a dimension besides the four sections of the tetraktys." Edwind said.

"The first dimension is everything in the universe. Does each dimension hold the same value when alone?" M Degas asked.

"The absolute point is everything in the universe and when you lay it out the tetraktys into ten dimensions it divides the universe which is essential to mans existence. Though all ten dimensions are congruent to each other. Each dimension draws apart from the absolute point dividing it." Edwind said.

(Figure 64)

The dimensions,

The Mandala

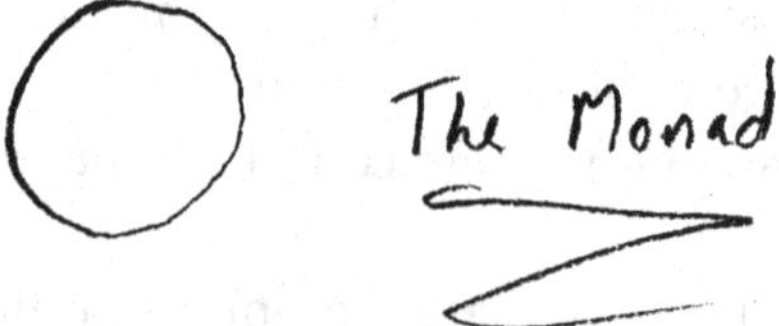

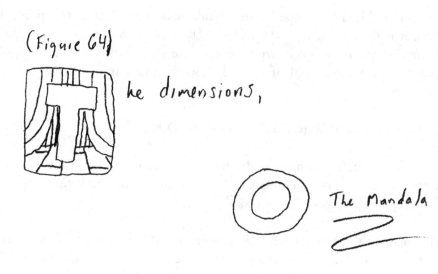

In ones perception we find a monad as the first dimension and add the mandala for motion. The easier the mandala changes the more of a psyche one can have.

The eye takes many forms...

(Figure 65)

he second dimension,

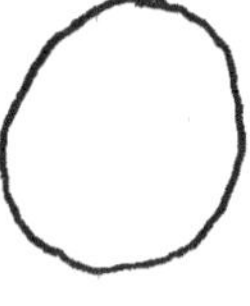

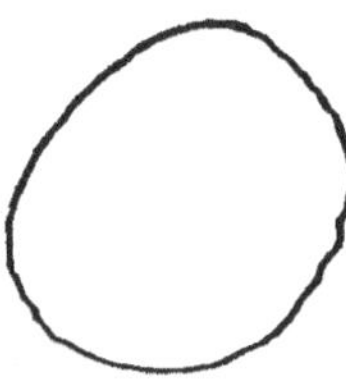

The third dimension,

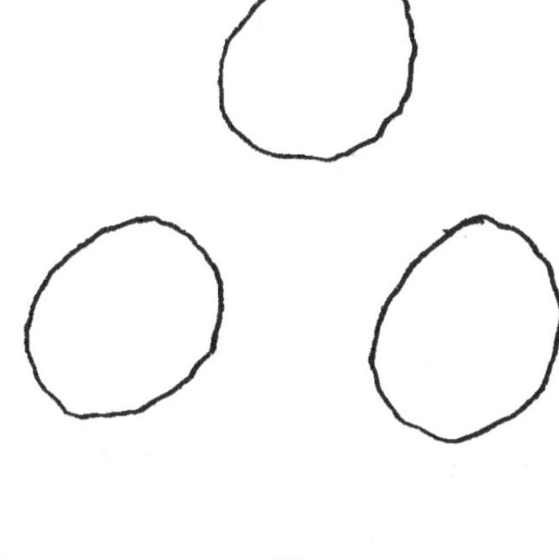

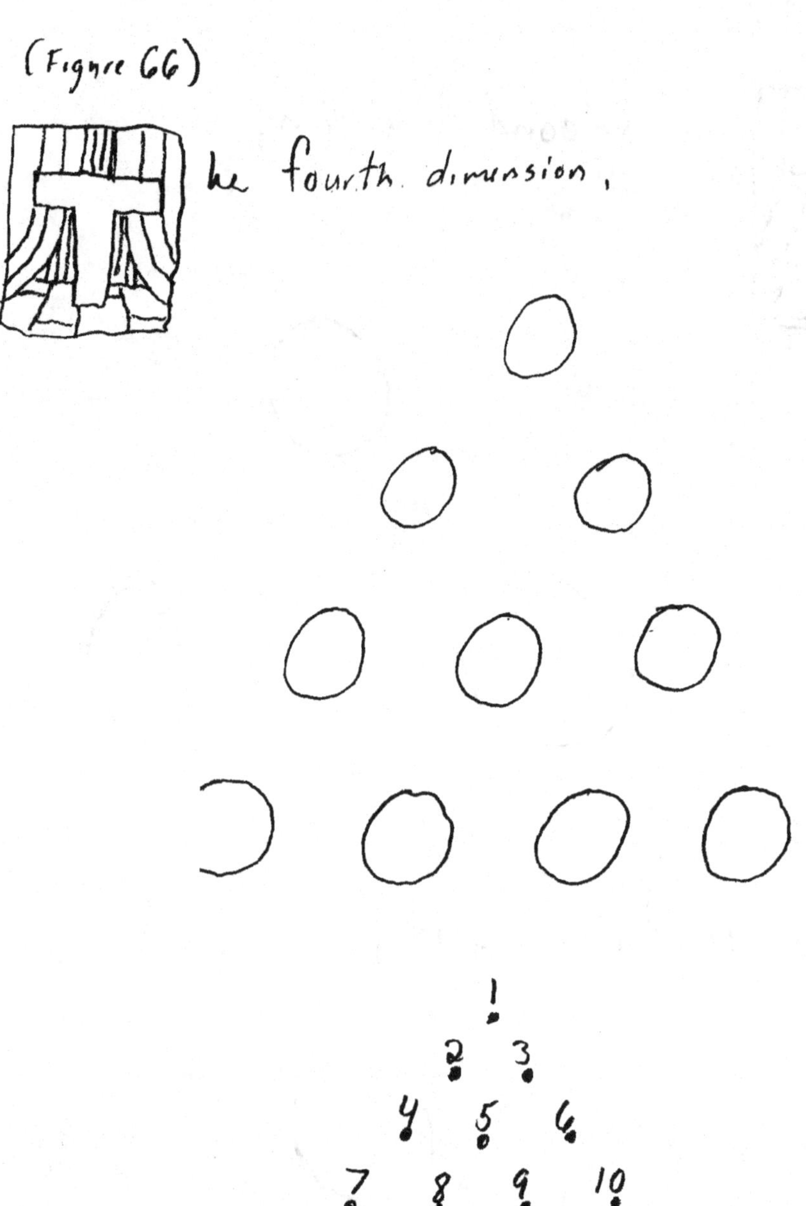

These tetraktys are made from the first piece of the universe to man's consciousness. This is the first step in heuristics as one meditates on cause and effect.

"How does it work?" M Degas asked.

"The subject can be anything, and I mean any people, place or thing. Whatever the case it also matters what the other points represent in a tetraktys. Here . . ." Edwind said as he drew up two different tetraktys. (See Figure 67)

"The general tetraktys shows the basics of absurdity and the magic tetraktys the precepts of magic. They both effect the subject differently." Edwind said.

"Man's consciousness is on the fourth section." Edwind said.

"His consciousness is on the fourth section?" M Degas asked.

"Correct, man has a consciousness that is made of a matrix of four different things. Using the tetraktys to the first section from the fourth man thinks." Edwind said.

"Man's drawn back in existence from the element so he can experiment and learn from it in the hollow of a consciousness. The Creator had in mind to make man dolor most of his life. Man will always labor day and night for a dollar to take care of thing and his family. This . . . This is why you are here M Degas . . . Do you understand a little more?" Edwind asked.

"Yes, the element . . . I'm beginning to understand the tetraktys and its relationship to the universe, but I don't understand what to do with it." M Degas said.

"You will, you will, M Degas." Edwind said.

"The subject could be anything, a point in time and space, an object of sustenance or substance. The Pythagoreans used this system to distinguish the value of things and later to define pieces of intellect. They considered it by using the tetraktys like this." Edwind said and showed this to M Degas. (See Figure 68)

"A Deity was distinguished and was thought to see the entire universe in this form of the tetraktys when identifying a piece. There are dimensions to identify the precepts of intellect viewed and created by the Pythagoreans. They wanted to know everything about everything. You, M Degas, will let the world know of the tetraktys knowledge." Edwind said.

Edwind take s a cup and sets it on the table.

"What is it?" He asked M Degas.

"It's a cup." M Degas said.

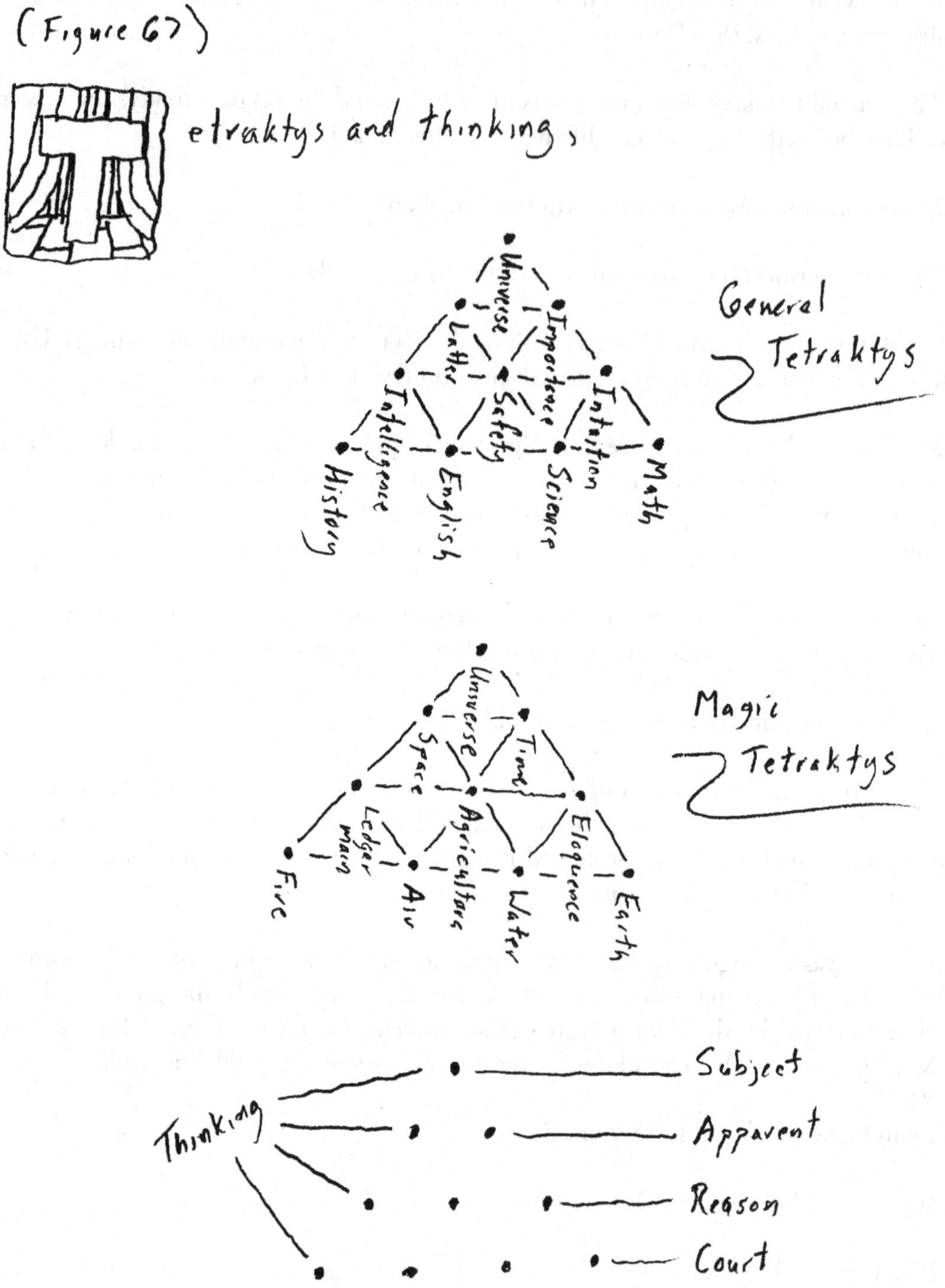

(Figure 67)

Tetraktys and thinking,

Universe
Importance
Lather
Safety
Intuition
Intelligence
History
English
Science
Math

General Tetraktys

Universe
Time
Space
Agriculture
Eloquence
Ledger main
Fire
Air
Water
Earth

Magic Tetraktys

Thinking
Subject
Apparent
Reason
Court

(Figure 68)

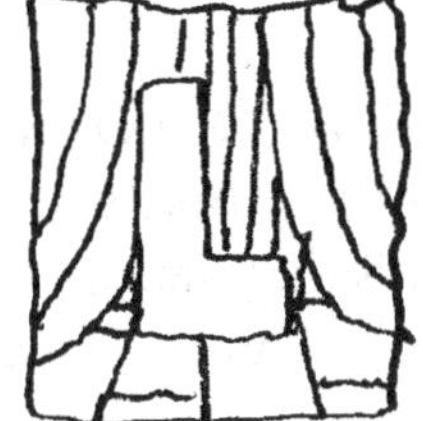

arge tetraktys,

'Yeah, I know it's a cup, but what is it?" Edwind asks as he grabbed a piece of paper and pencil.

"Do you know where that cup sits and where it came from?" Edwind asked.

"Well it's from a factory made of US patent. It's just sitting there on the table." M Degas said.

"Yeah, but what did you forget? YOU LOOKED AT THE ITEM AND TOTALLY FORGOT THE DEITY, IDIOTS! Not just toward you in any manor, but the people who put together the pedagogy which doesn't include a Deity. The story as we have it is that there is a lore connected to each piece of evidence. We have to choose to believe in the tetraktys as a whole." Edwind said and draws up a large tetraktys. (See Figure 69)

"How does it work?" M Degas asked.

"Well depending on the Pythagoreans knowledge the tetraktys takes its form. One chooses a subject and then tries to find its Deity or vice versa. One can put it in any way the precepts of the dimensions of the tetraktys. The idea is to watch the perception of the user of the tetraktys change. Hence a banana can have its precepts changed by choosing Zeus, God, or Mercury and the same with the other dimension of the tetraktys. One may find a whole knew perception of the banana." Edwind said.

Edwind shows M Degas his sheet of paper which had this idea set down. M Degas tries a few in a note book.

"You see each time you elect and renounce a different point your beliefs change. Your faith and power of the lore is measured by how long you stick with one belief. Say you choose God out of the Deities. The longer you stay with him when viewing the universe the more advance the faith to him one achieves. How does the cup look now?" Edwind asked.

"Well if you consider it with the tetraktys it changes the lore with each precept making it different each time." M Degas said.

"You're exactly right, the lore represents the History and when the tetraktys changes so does the precepts of the intellective. Do you feel it?" Edwind asked.

"Yeah, a bit of a solar wind, ebullience, like and enticing breeze." M Degas said.

"The wind is God telling you that you believe in him. It will only increase and decrease with what happens to you next in faith. One can draw up any kind of faith on the tetraktys and not have it interfere with the primary faith they have set. It comes in the form of a reverie . . . Like this." Edwind said and drew this on a page. (See Figure 70)

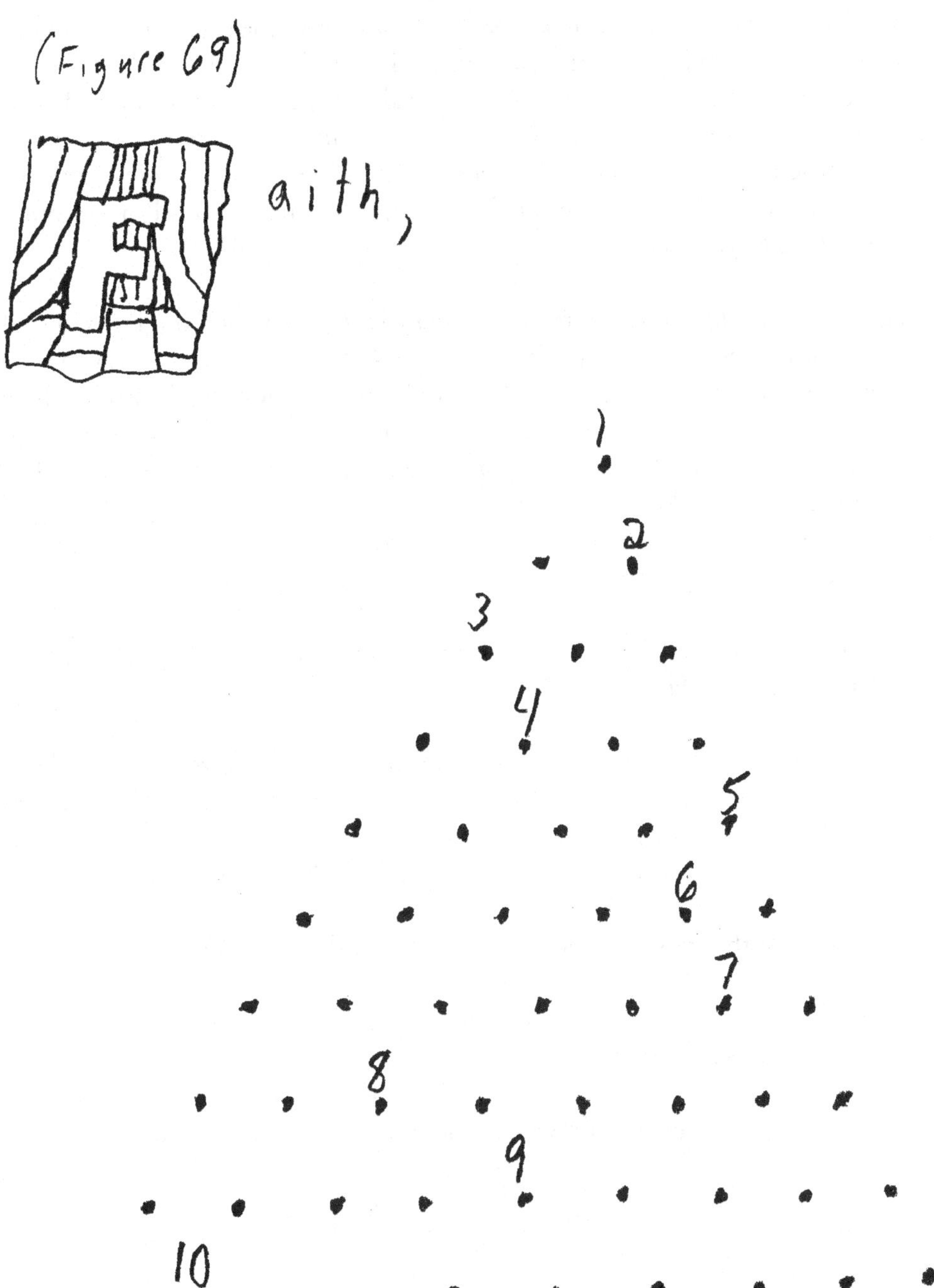
(Figure 69)
F
aith,
1
2
3
4
5
6
7
8
9
10

"How am I going to teach everyone the tetraktys?" M Degas asked.

"You'll learn as studied unfolds in the future." Edwind remarked.

M Degas studied all the time in the next couple of months in the laboratory. Running across prote hyle of each element and other amazing things the tetraktys and tyriad had to offer. The tyriad has the ability to change the shape of objects altering time and space and expand the element in an immutable resource. The point is to have evidence of the piece of intellect that exist in order to have a great intellective in metaphysics while having an idea of nothing, the non-existent, to come together as a whole. Then one must have flow control to sort out the flow of the intellective. (See Figure 71)

The tyriad puts it into flow. The future flow comes to the present and out beyond to the past. Whatever's in the future one is looking at it from the present and it's the same way looking at the past. We have a consciousness of the past and future. Mans consciousness is free of the element at the present where he finds peace. One adapts very quickly as the matrix of the substratum universe unfolds on the tyriad. There are beyond the google numbers of places to be besides the one point in the universe. Well one can hold a single piece of evidence as the only thing in the universe. One's perception is there home. The mind was built to reflect the element and eventually weald it. The Pythagoreans excelled in it, M Degas thought.

M Degas came across the classifications of a human being as Edwind had written. He thought these were brilliant ideas. (See Figure 72)

Taking the tetraktys in a form that channels the entire universe shows a general idea how the universe was made. With the general tetraktys it gives one a feeling that stabilizes the view of the working universe. Each point of the tetraktys was viewed by the mind as the eye was searching. At least if you knew the tetraktys. This news was exciting for the inventor M Degas.

"I've never found anything like this before . . . It's so truthful." M Degas said.

"Oh, I'm afraid you have after all you're living it. You're bodies the wedge and your head the egg. It reacts just like a tetraktys." Edwind said.

M Degas thought it over a bit and drew up a piece of paper what he had in mind.

(Figure 70)

Reverie,

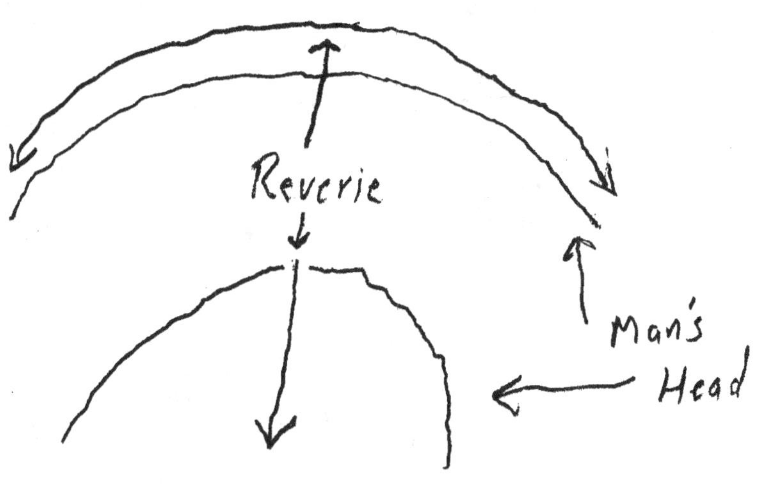

Reverie

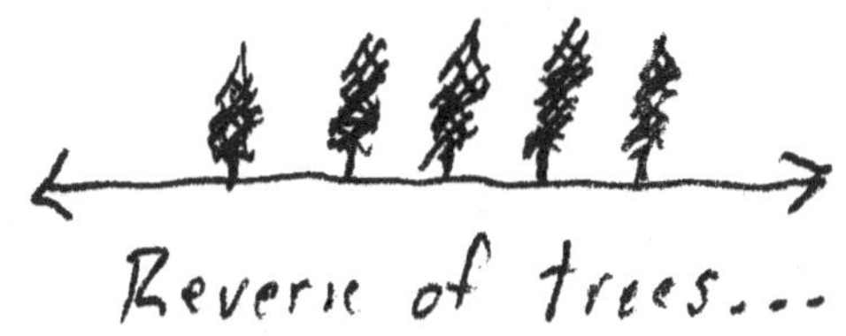

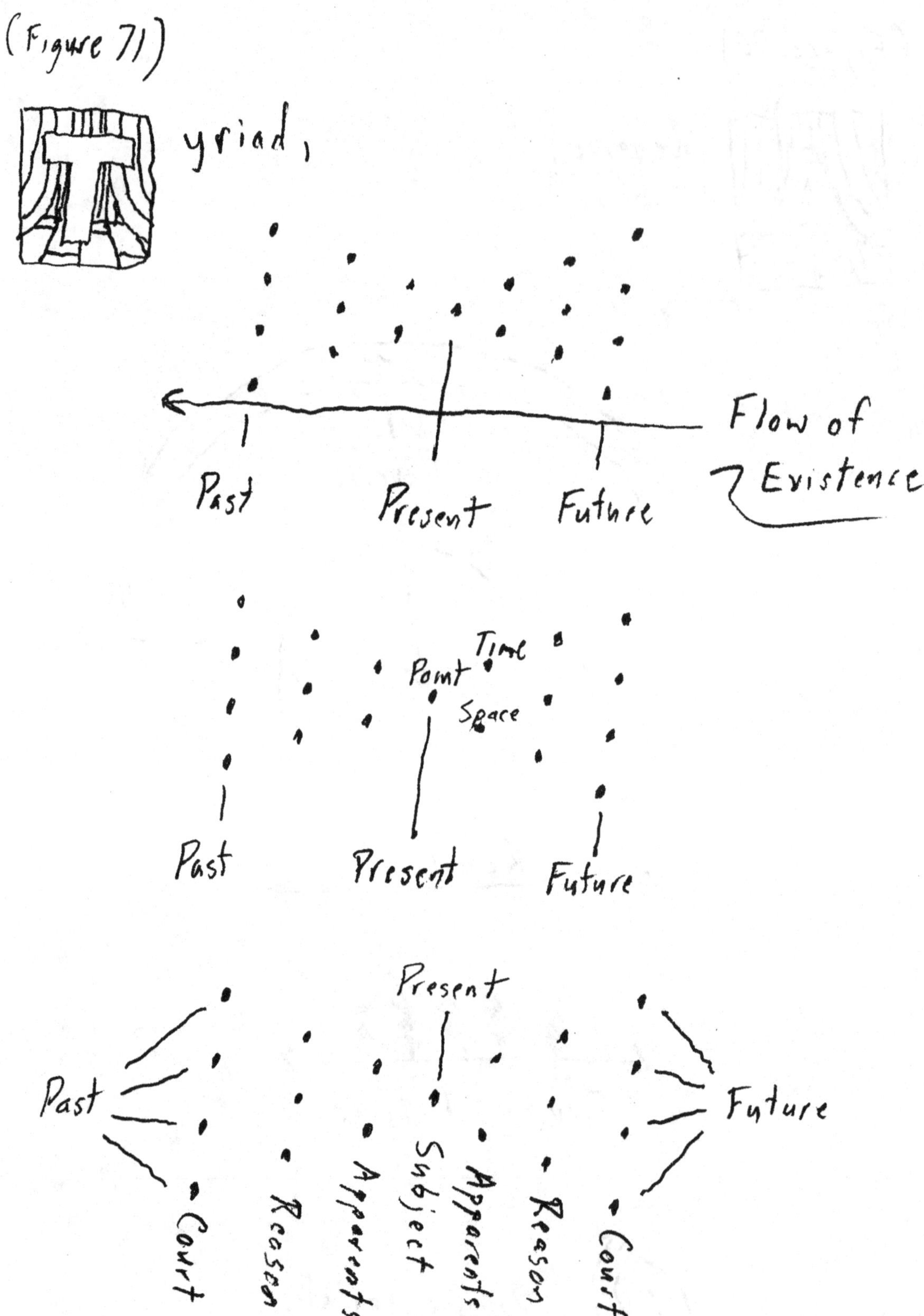
(Figure 71)
Tyriad,
Flow of Existence
Past
Present
Future
Time
Point
Space
Past
Present
Future
Present
Past
Future
Court
Reason
Apparents
Subject
Apparents
Reason
Court

(Figure 72)

Classifacations of a human being,

Domain - This is the dome of a human. It is its highest order. It is where everything is added up in heuristics that is considered the beings tenure.

Kingdom - this presents all of the beings intellective. Self-worth, self righteousness.

Phylum - this is a combination of the mart of the domain and kingdom. It is the beings existence.

Class - this is where the being considers subjects. What one wants to do and what one wants to do not. We consider intuition here,

Order - this is the social part of the being. It's psyche and direction in the enviorn,

Genus - this is the nous of the being, mainly its' ability to sense and make sense.

Species - this is the nature of the being and is a combination of all the classifacations.

M Degas thought, this list is the absurdity of thought of the human being. A way to recognize ability and define the parts of the being in to ones consciousness.

"The tetraktys, M Degas concluded and handed the draft to Edwind, the human condition." (See Figure 73)

"The mind views the universe and the eyes act as apparents selecting the information and getting the information. There is a God and he loves me." M Degas said about the drawing of the human condition.

"Ah, yes M Degas, just as Paul said, you have found it." Edwind said.

"Found what exactly?" M Degas asked.

"The matrix of the human condition. I've already viewed the product you must see. One of the purposes that I need you for. Now continue your study." Edwind said.

Labeling the tetraktys from scratch now came easy for M Degas. All the information he had been given throughout his life he used. The book came to the idea of the globes above our heads.

"Ah, these globes keep giving and receiving information for us. Just like our brain cells keep and produce . . ." M Degas said.

"They are our muse. You are still the egg, M Degas until of coarse one can figure them out. All our ideas reflect the element. Elements are the simplest form of globes and advance up to the planets, suns and galaxies." Edwind said.

M Degas was shown for the first time the tetraktys stone.

"These 61 empty spaces have to be filled with globes that take the form of spells so the bearer will be able to make it work with his intuition. We have to be able to weald the element into exactly the right key word the element forms. I will need your help." Edwind said.

"M Degas, you have to look into the Tetraktys book and see how to arrange the globes for the tetraktys stone." Edwind said.

M Degas reads the book and told Edwind that he needs to meditate on the immaculate elements and say the word "Ayin Ensof Aur."

Edwind meditated and got up and took out a mandala from the closet with a small metal box. He prayed over the mandala and the wind brought up a miniature cosmos of the Milky Way. It was the only thing visible in the room.

"What is that box for, Edwind?" M Degas asked.

(Figure 73)

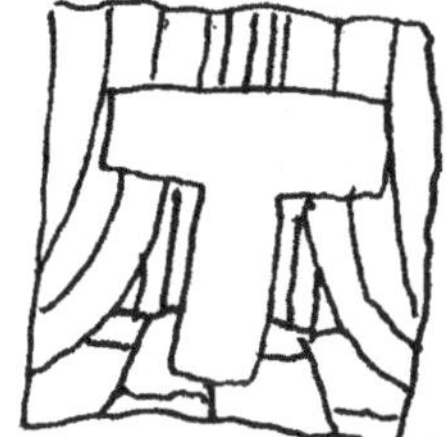

etraktys perception and the model of the human condition,

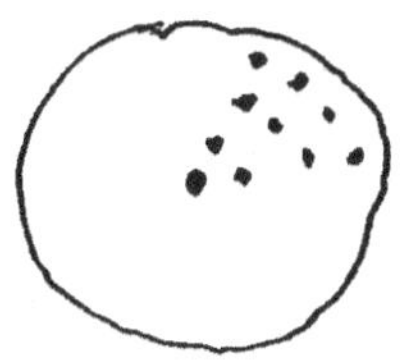

The tetraktys

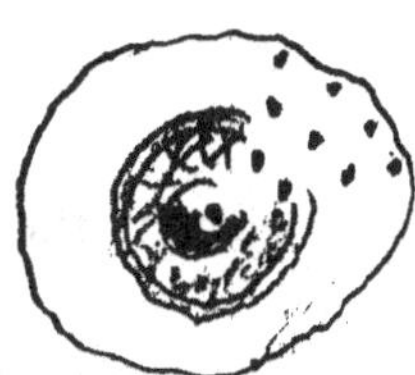

The eye

General tetraktys

Human Condition,

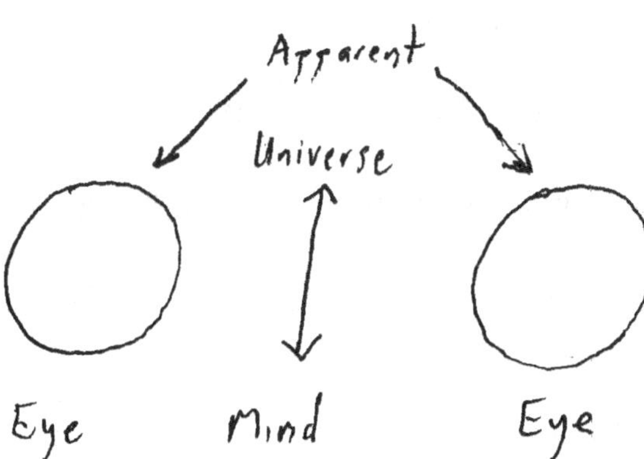

"It holds the secret code for making apeiron stars. Only the Queen and I know of it." Edwind lead on.

"I'm going to ask you to leave as I make the stone." Edwind said.

"I'll be up stairs if you need me." M Degas said.

"Alright." Said Edwind.

M Degas hears him saying "Ayin Ensof Aur" over and over again for an hour from the basement and then hears nothing.

"M Degas, you can come back." Edwind yelled.

The room had returned to normal, the stone was made.

"The element used to be the weather at a glance. Though it was at one time believed that creation was made of two elements. Mercury and Sulfur. Later the people believed that four elements made up all of creation. Earth, Water, Air, and Fire. Now, the element is in the form of principle atoms which form the Periodic table of Elements." Edwind told M Degas.

"Mercury and Sulfur? These are two of the elements on the chart today." M Degas said.

"Yeah, but back then one took two handfuls of the Earth and called one Mercury and the other Sulfur. The feelings and affinities of concentration back then was much different and a lot more feral compared to the world etiquette to our ways and chartings. With it comes the earliest account of a matrix." Edwind said. (See Figure 74)

"The matrix is the equalization of two or more things together in symmetry." M Degas told Edwind.

"I think you're ready. I want you to meet some friends of mine. You don't need to know there names, but I told them about you. You'll leave first thing in the morning." Edwind said. "Try and meditate a bit on this symbol" He finished and then left. (See Figure 75)

"Good morning, M Degas, your ride is out front." The Butler said.

"Where's Edwind?" Asked M Degas.

"Oh, he left last night." The butler said.

"Oh, ok then thank you for all the things you have done for me throughout my stay. Just in case I don't see you again." M Degas said.

(Figure 74)

The first human matrix of creation,

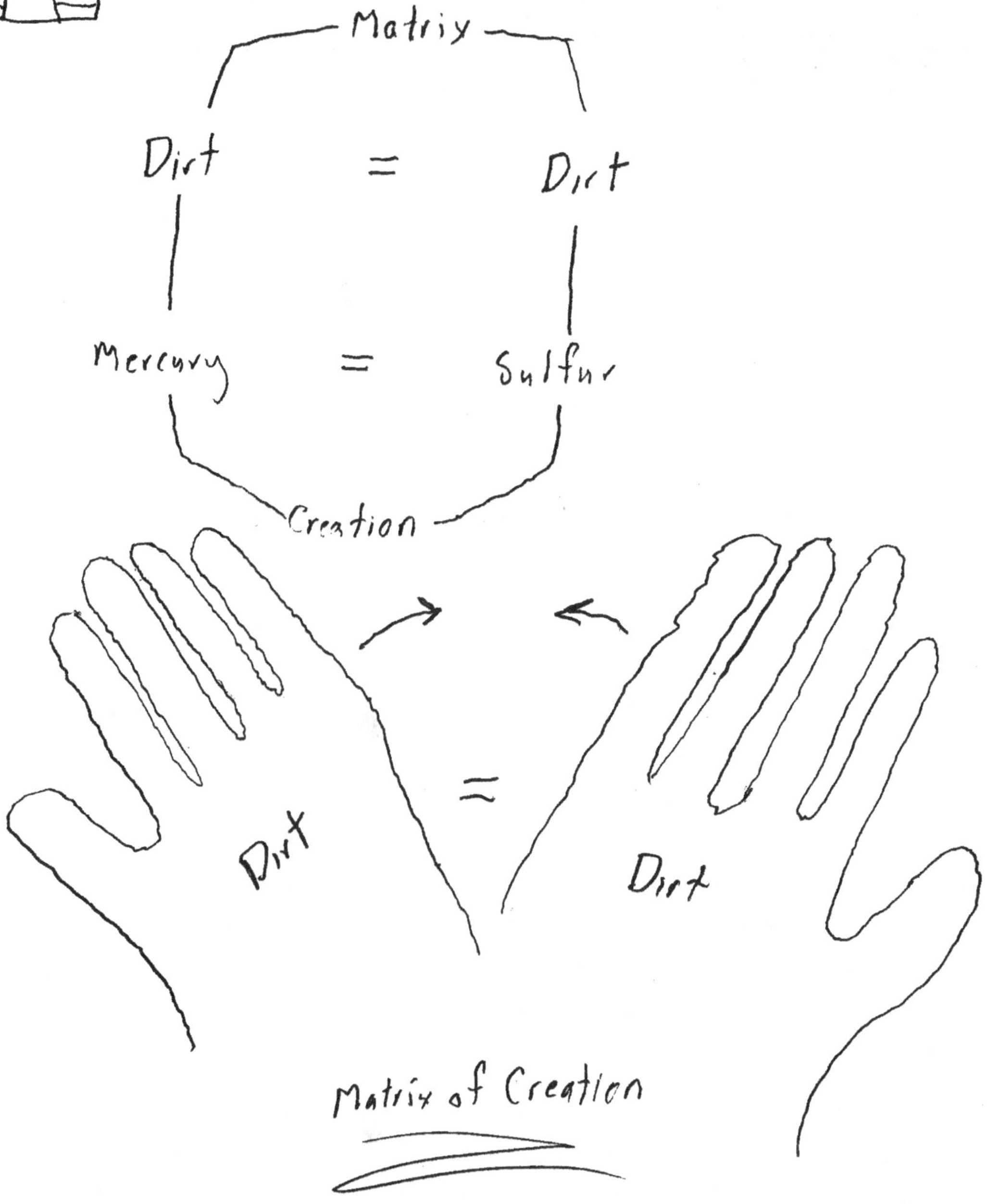

Matrix

Dirt = Dirt

Mercury = Sulfur

Creation

Dirt = Dirt

Matrix of Creation

(Figure 75)

he Myriad,

M Degas took care of his hygiene and left for the car. He was blind folded and put into the car not knowing where he would end up. It took them about an hour to arrive at his destination. The car door opened and a man took off his blind fold. M Degas got out.

The man at the door said, "M Degas come this way, Sir."

He led M Degas inside the mansion. Where Edwind was at the top of the stair way leading down to the basement.

"M Degas." Edwind said admirably.

M Degas walked to meet him.

"Ah, M Degas, glad you could make it." Edwind told him.

M Degas said nothing and knew nothing considering everything was a secret as it was. Being blind folded he decided to himself only to talk when being talked to.

They made their way down stairs to this huge library with a large oak table in the middle of it. There was a man standing at the table waiting patiently for the two to show up.

"M Degas, glad to meet you again." The Man said.

"Again?" M Degas was puzzled.

The Man was a half bald older man and had a black suit on. He had a voice to convict all those years to. Edwind ran into the closet and brought out a piece they called the tyriad globlet.

Edwind set it on the table and the old Man said, "See you later Edwind."

Edwind told M Degas to put both hands on the device. There was a huge flash of light. They ended up in the same spot. M Degas could tell the frequency of the place had changed. The Man approached the two only he was about 30 years old now.

"This is M Degas." Edwind told the Man.

With a smile across his face M Degas said, "Nice to see you again."

"Again?" The Man said and shook his head and then went back to business.

The Man opens a small box with money in it.

"A new design? Maybe is in the likes, but if M Degas can uncover most everything we will stick to this bill." The Man said.

“The bill resembles existence itself. M Degas has been studying the tetraktys the last couple of months and he’s come up with the matrix of the human condition.” Edwind said.

“You mean you want me to design a new dollar bill?” M Degas asked as his eyes were in disbelief.

“Not exactly, we want you to notice and define to the best of your knowledge this design of the bill we have here. A Pythagorean arranged it and a Freemason designed it. We must keep their names private though. My men and I don’t know how to read the bill, but maybe you can.” The Man said.

“Study the bill M Degas even I can’t because of my origins and let the teachings of the tetraktys be your guide.” Edwind said.

“I’ve ran across thousands of these throughout my life time. I never knew it actually meant something and I never had Pythagorean knowledge until I met Edwind.” M Degas said.

M Degas examines the bill and notices the court of four ones on the front side and a court of four ones on the back side.

“Eight ones together make a govern.” M Degas points out to Edwind.

“That’s it, keep going, M Degas.” Edwind said as if he knew more that he was saying.

M Degas notices the apparents of the seals and a large “ONE” in the center. There was a court, an apparent, and a subject to the tetraktys, but no reason. Reason was exempt unless one counted the three letters of the word “ONE”.

“Edwind? I don’t see the reason of the tetraktys, but why leave out reason in the design? M Degas said.

“Maybe reason is left out to leave a person free to think for themselves. Plainly to unite us or give us freedom to have our own ideas. The Pythagorean may see something we don’t.” Edwind said.

“I agree with what the back of the bill has to offer. It gives one an idea of a matrix.” M Degas said.

“No! M Degas, what does it mean to you?” Edwind said with mad alacrity.

“Ah, what . . .” M Degas said in response.

“Well . . . What does the bill in fact tell you?” Edwind said in a calm voice.

M Degas then started conjecting.

"It's a muse of history, present state and the future of mankind. It's the intellective of the mind in the universe." M Degas said.

"Exactly, it represents existence itself. For what reason, M Degas?" Edwind asked.

"To let everyone that looks apon it to have knowledge and wisdom of how this place came together." M Degas said.

"What of the front of the bill?" Edwind asked.

M Degas studied the front of the bill a while and said, "Well it looks as if it describes a marriage of man and woman. The court being four numbers has emblems designed around them so I believe it is the court of marriage. The portrait of the President shows our first President of the USA. The leaves show the flow of nature of the universe." M Degas said.

"What of the gears of the bill?" Edwind asked.

It took sometime, but he figured it out one on the right with 41 degrees on it had a 55 dimensional tetraktys inside it, which figure to be of all a Subject to Deity. The scale, key and square added the additional subjects of the 52 dots of the crest. What intellect the other 52 dots were a mystery. He took all of them together and discovered it made that thinking process of the government.

"Hypothetically a flower (The Key) is put into the vase (The Square) from ones judgment (The Scale) and all the other dots which are unidentified subjects make up the universe around the flower and vase. The forty-one degrees he decided made the court of the mind of man. It took M Degas no time at all to figure out what the thirty-one degree gear as 31 reasons of the imagination of man.

"So what do you think?" Edwind asked.

"The gears are the scales in our reflections." M Degas said.

"What do you think of the bill as a whole? Put both sides together." Edwind told M Degas.

"Ah, two courts together equal eight which on a tetraktys equals govern. Oh, Edwind it's a lot of Kleromancy. A divination of lots. Ah, the weight of its value is one dollar. It makes a brick when you add up all eight corners. Existence flows right through it. A bridge of intellective. The web from the back must meet the web on the front. One block, one lot of Kleromancy." M Degas explained.

"It will work." Said the Man.

"He was able to name most everything on the bill." Edwind said.

“There is much more to it then he named I am sure even more then you know, Edwind. We don’t have to make any changes. We will print this bill.” The Man said.

“That’s it M Degas, thank you for your help.” Edwind said.

“We’ll work out the details later. You were right, Edwind, M Degas is the one. It would have taken us years to find some one like him.” The Man said.

“The bill is a true Pythagorean triumph. Shinning as existence itself.” Edwind said.

“We want everyone to know the knowledge of existence. The more people know the more they will appreciate it and live by it.” The Man said.

“Because, M Degas, you know the theory behind the tetraktys in a teachable language you will be a very important and rich man.” Edwind said.

Edwind explained how special his new found knowledge is to the world at this time. That this is why we want to circulate this note to the public. That anyone that comes across it might study it. That it will one day fulfill its purpose and change the world forever.

M Degas spent the night in a fashionable room. The next day he traveled back to the 1970’s. Where he stayed at Edwind’s mansion. The next morning he was invited to teach the tetraktys at a private school in St. Paul, MN. He agreed and went to his family in Hutchinson, MN and they all moved with him to St. Paul. He began teaching after doing a large amount of organization and research on the tetraktys. He used the bill as a muse to teach about existence itself. One of his brightest students was named Spucket Knostic who became a rich architect and then went into inventing. The students themselves were specialized in the tetraktys. All graduates prospered. Though few thought the class was worth while at least those who knew nothing of the tetraktys. M Degas was surrounded by wealth as his students became rich and recommended his classes. Edwind came to visit him one day. Five years later.

“You have come far in the ways of the Pythagoreans. I need you to come with me. We will set out on a journey. Yet first we must deliver the tetraktys stone to Paul. The stone that will save us all from oblivion.” Edwind said.

M Degas makes arrangements with the school and informs his family. Then they were off to Edwind’s home.

“We need to go to the year 1648 ad. To start our journey.” Edwind said.

“Show me some of your powers again. I’m just curious to what kind of magic you use.” M Degas said.

Edwind then summoned some fire and water and danced them around the room.

"This is nothing compared to what is in store for us in the future. Yet for now we must take care of business in 1648 ad." Edwind explained.

"You mean travel back that far?" Edwind asked.

"Yes, come, we must go." Edwind said then instructed M Degas to put his hands on the globlet that was on the table in front of them.

They made it to 1648 ad with no problems at all and there to welcome them was the chirping birds in the forest. Edwind transmigrated into a bird and flew off to talk with the other birds who were also Pythagoreans. He flew back down and came out of bird form.

"The birds say everything is going to plan." Edwind said.

"You can transmigrate?" M Degas asked.

"Yep." Edwind said.

"That's awesome! Where to now?" M Degas asked.

"Let's head north out of the woods to the trail that leads to Paul's home." Edwind said.

"I'm with you . . . It seems so lovely and open here." M Degas said.

They made it to Paul's home and Paul opened the door.

"Ah, Edwind, old friend." Paul full heartedly said opening his arms.

"This is M Degas, nice to see you again." Edwind said.

"I've got the stone we made for you, here." Edwind said and handed Paul the stone.

"Thank you, I've got the book for you, Edwind, here. The Queen gave it to me to give to you." Paul said and handed the book to him.

Edwind looked through the book and found it mentioned him, M Degas, Scrupt and M Rahn. Two of them he hadn't met yet. M Rahn's a Freemason and he is supposed to know how this adventure is put together.

"We'd better get going, M Degas, here, have one of these amulets and you will be able to see Gebelin." Edwind said and closed the book.

Edwind and M Degas both teleported through the time to about the same time of the oblivion of Earth. They met Paul there and they all went to greet the Queen. She had one-hundred and fifty-three scepters protecting the kingdom. The Wizard's calculated the kingdoms size and put in the scepters accordingly. The scepters were protecting Gebelin by the works of the tetraktys. Holding Gebelin impenetrable to the future loss of existence namely the Earth.

"We, the good people of Gebelin knew all this time what has to happen here this day, and it took us until the year 2010 ad to unfold it all. Gebelin will be the crown jewel of the feral plain. We will then continually protect the Earth with our abilities and tetraktys contraptions." The Queen explained.

"We'll have to wait until Scrupt shows up, right?" Edwind asked.

"Who is Scrupt?" M Degas asked.

"He's the chosen one." Iris the Queen of Gebelin said to M Degas.

"Well, when he does show up. You'll be waiting by the tower stairs to the monad tower. Paul will give him the words to use to activate the tetraktys stone. Paul then will get the Wizard's guild book from Scrupt and give it to Nato who will be here for the reckoning." The Queen said.

Paul a descendant of Pythagoras told M Degas the story of the Pythagoreans.

"Pythagoras's followers all communed to Gebelin in 1054 ad. The same time the all-seeing-eye was made in Gebelin. The Orthodox Church branched out from then on. We needed a time where we could take back our mishaps and the feral plain is the place. We have our own secret code that all Pythagoreans of Gebelin must follow. The Pythagoreans have been studying the tetraktys for centuries. I view everything with vivacity, and never take anything that would harm someone or myself in any way." Paul told M Degas.

"I was born with all the knowledge and skill of the tetraktys, and I don't know . . . I still find myself struggling for a chance of a normal life, but this is my calling. Though I couldn't dream up another to have and hold as much responsibility with the power I have here." Edwind said.

"We need you Edwind, you are very important. There will be nothing left of the Earth except Gebelin." Paul said.

"Look! The Earth is crumbling." The Queen said as their hearts started to pound and their legs began to shake weakly. The raw and awesome power of the destruction of Earth. The noise was unbelievable.

Chapter 22

"If you can't take the time to do

Things right the first time, then why

Take the time to do it at all."

Douglas David Bulau, 2001

Earth had disappeared and only fragments of it remain. The kingdom of Gebelin held together was now floating in space.

"We have come here to fulfill a promise that developed and been waiting for all this time, the feral plain." Paul said and kissed the Queens hand.

"Yes, the kingdom of Gebelin has already stood against the destruction of the Earth." The Queen said.

"What's the date of time and space?" Edwind asked.

"Its May 27th, 1648 ad and Scrupt should be showing up at anytime." Paul said.

The Queen gave the order for them to take their positions. There were people sitting, standing and chatting at the main hall and throne room. A man and three others showed up through the door to the main hall. We all watched the four go up to the Queen.

"Welcome, Scrupt." The Queen said.

"Scrupt?" M Degas said.

"It's him, Edwind says, the chosen one."

Scrupt left the Queen and headed toward the monad tower. Edwind, Paul and M Degas are there waiting for him. Paul knew what he had stopped for and gave him the words to say and Scrupt gave Paul the Wizard's guild book. Scrupt took note of it and ran up to the top of the tower. He held out the tetraktys stone and yelled, "Vesica Piscis!"

A bright light and strong wind came over the heavens a Leviathan came out of the stone and engulfed the pieces of Earth and out of its bowels the pieces of Earth were reformed to the year 2010 this date. Gebelin stayed in the space to orbit the Earth and became as invisible satellite of Earth only seen by the Bearers of the Pythagorean amulets. There was no sign of Gebelin ever existing on the Earth from 1648 ad on.

The light went away and the people started talking to one another. Scrupt was introduced to his son who was about three times his age.

"Scrupt, this is Edwind your son," Paul said.

"How do you do Father?" Edwind asked.

"This is quite the surprise, I haven't ever met your mother yet." Scrupt said in excitement.

"My Mothers name its Tiffany." Edwind said.

Scrupt gets a big smile on his face then says, "You come from the future. How is it that you were able to time travel without a time machine?"

"We use a tyriad globlet to travel to different times and spaces." Edwind said.

"Well, just how old are you?" Scrupt asked.

"I'm in my fifties, I don't know exactly because I travelled so frequently to different locations throughout time." Edwind said.

"We'll chat some more later. We'd better get back to the Queen. Paul gives the book to Nato.

"Thank you, Paul." Nato says.

They all gathered in the courtyard as Gebelin floated in space with the Earth and Moon visible. Gebelin was magically invisible to all the people of Earth.

"The battle to keep Earth existing isn't over yet until we fulfill the myriad and the all-seeing-eye. The people of Earth will still test us with their inventions. When the myriad is complete it will be a time of feral peace. A place of heaven and Earth. The myriad must be complete, and it means magic will destroy the Earth. Pythagoreans knew it would one day be possible. After all we are Pythagoreans." The Queen said.

"Well what do we do now, my Queen?" Paul asked.

"We start at the furthest point the light has touched 2010 ad. in America." The Queen said.

"America?" Scrupt asked.

"Yes, you must meet and talk to a Freemason named M Rahn. Here is the address and map to his place. He knows much more than I." The Queen said.

"When do we leave?" M Degas asked.

"We leave tomorrow." The Queen said.

"We?" M Degas asked.

"Well, you, Edwind and Scrupt. You'll leave first thing in the morning. So enjoy the night." The Queen said.

So they departed for the night and returned the next day.

Scrupt found Tiffany and stayed the night with each other making love. Edwind slept in the castle and Paul stayed at his home with M Degas. Scrupt had terrible nightmares of the element crushing him. He thought that wherever he was that things were out to get him. He woke in a sweat next to Tiffany.

"Oh, it was just a dream." He whispered to himself.

He didn't wake Tiffany, but left her a note saying name our baby boy, Edwind Knostic.

Scrupt made it to the courtyard where everyone was waiting for him.

"Ah and here is Scrupt." Paul said.

"Good to see you've made it." Iris the Queen said.

"And you, M'lady." Scrupt returned.

"The Earth was back to normal thanks to all our hard work. Now if we can set the world straight for the future so all the Earth will understand that we all can help in taking care of it. Life just might be everlasting. The tetraktys will never end with its innovations neither will the myriads. Only things will get better if all of us know of its knowledge. It means we will never fulfill existence, it will always continue." The Queen said.

"You mean all of this is printed on the US Dollar Bill?" Scrupt asked as Edwind told him about it.

"Yes, Father, Edwind says, M Degas and I have studied from it."

"I've never seen one myself." The Queen said.

Scrupt goes into his wallet and pulls out a US Dollar Bill.

"Here, M'lady." Scrupt said and hands it over.

"Washington." She says.

"No, M 'lady, the other side of the bill." Scrupt said.

“Ah, ONE.” She said.

“It represents man in the universe with his Deity.” Edwind said.

“The tetraktys on the left and the feral spirit is one the right side of the seal with the myriad above it.” M Degas said.

“I can read. These must be the apparents and the ONE, the subject. You put the trinity together to show the people reason.” The Queen said.

“Yes, M’lady, we unfold the human condition. The story of evolution as mankind will succeed in doing. All the great minds came to this. As Pythagoras himself first studied the tetraktys and somehow somewhere technology and magic, science and religion must some how all connect together. And this is the meaning behind the bill.” M Degas said.

“Pythagoras didn’t know just how far his discovery would go in the future. This fellow M Rahn knows just how far the tetraktys has unfolded into the year 2010 ad. We or I mean you three must meet up with him and figure out what the myriad has in store for us to do.” The Queen said.

“Where does he live?” Edwind asked.

“I gave Scrupt the map. He lives in America in Minneapolis, MN.” The Queen said as she waved the guards to bring the tyriad globlet to them.

“Nobody I talked to knows just exactly what the myriad is about. At least from the time I came from.” Scrupt said.

“Well, its time for you three to go. I’ll see you later. Now go . . .⊠ The Queen said.

They made it to Earth safely to the year 2010 ad. The United States of America was booming.

“We have to go to M Rahn’s house to meet his acquaintance and get filled in on what to do here.” M Degas said.

“Has anyone ever seen M Rahn before?” Edwind asked.

“Not I.” M Degas said.

“Nope, but from what I heard he is truly wise.” Scrupt said.

They made it to the bus stop and road it to uptown Minneapolis. It began to down pour as they got off the bus. It was only three blocks from there. They headed on foot to M Rahn’s home and knocked on the door. Just as he answered the door it stopped raining.

"Ah, Scrupt, Edwind, M Degas, you are all wet. You are just in time. Wait here while I feed the ferret." M Rahn said as they walked into the porch.

"Ok, then." Scrupt said.

They were all wondering just as to how well he knew all of them.

"Ah, there, well that's done. How about we get some coffee?" M Rahn said.

"Alright." Edwind answered for the three of them.

The four of them walked down to the café.

They all rested in a both and all ordered coffee.

"You've got to have quite a story to tell after all you three just witnessed the recreation of Earth." M Rahn said.

They had the coffee store to themselves.

"All three of us have a different way of belonging to the tale." Edwind said.

"As I've read many books on the subject I've been given the task of entailing just what the myriad is about. And well, I don't exactly know how to get it there, but Edwind is the furthest example we have. Man will one day be totally one with the element which completes the myriad. As we search for perfection. You three will help develop the idea further. The idea is magic and we may lose if we don't figure it out." M Rahn told the three.

"No one has any information on the myriad." M Degas said.

"Well we will at least try to define it. It does look like a symbol of divinity to me. We can consider it two things coming together, but what two things?" M Rahn said as if hinting to something.

"The myriad is what is to become of the tetraktys." Edwind conjected.

"Yes, it is the tetraktys in juxtaposition, good and evil in the likes." Scrupt said as he takes a drink of coffee.

"To put together the myriad we need to find the precise performance. The only way is to find the performers." M Rahn said.

"Words you mean, right." Scrupt said.

"Just like the tetraktys stone, the myriad stone has to be activated." Edwind said as he knew more than he could tell at the time.

The book he had said he couldn't mention what he did as a young boy.

"Well, what do you expect all this to do in the end?" M Degas asked.

"Whatever it is it will be good, I can promise you that much." M Rahn said.

M Rahn takes a one dollar bill out of his pocket and says, "Now, what did Our Father want?"

The gentlemen take heed of the bill and Scrupt gathers it in front of him.

"One court, one government to rule. I studied and enquired information about the bill before. Yet I still don't have the full picture." Scrupt said and flips the bill over to the back side.

"Nope, no one knows exactly what the myriad means." Edwind said.

"I don't know what the myriad means either. Yet it reminds me of marriage." M Degas said.

"Well who developed the myriad?" Scrupt asked.

"It's two tetraktys locked together. I don't know who first discovered it, and I know it was Pythagorean." M Rahn conjected.

"The myriad looks to me to be a symbol of complete peace. As if everything in the universe finally fit. I've toyed with it and it does seem like an item that employ's a clear existence." M Degas said.

"Yes, the way two tetraktys put together says to me that the past, present and future are mended together to create a ginning for something. I don't know, maybe heaven on Earth? Scrupt points out.

"Well Our Father knew what was coming. M Degas described most of the bill for the Freemasons in the 50's." M Rahn said.

"Yes, the bill was made in a reflection of the human existence and the condition of it. The web of dynamics seems to create a net or matrix that is designed into a lot of Kleromancy. Able to give reflection of mans intelligence. A workshop or schematic on a page that takes place of the bill for ones perception. The place a man can think. A premise of time and space for one to recollect in safety. The seal is evidence of the way the feral spirit flies over the element of the Earth and the myriad is when we finally reach perfection. To be one with the element." M Degas conjected.

"Well, how does one use it?" M Rahn asked as he drank some coffee.

"You must have conditioned your mind in Our Fathers works, Math, Science, English and History. It's all within the tetraktys." M Degas said.

"The tetraktys is a heap of matter in a rudiment which makes up everything in existence. The feral spirit is the human being in the universe, all the living spirits. The man as a combination of both is the myriad, the perfect state." M Rahn explained is his conjecture. (See Figure 76)

"The man is to be in the perfect state and that is what Our Father wants." Edwind said.

"Well the myriad must be the perfect state then. It must unlock mans immutability which God immutably reins. He looks over us all and knows everything going on. Quite like us Pythagoreans of Gebelin. The eye and the mind are deceitful when it only can work subject to subject or eye for an eye. One must learn the consciousness, the court, the govern and the rest of the tetraktys in order to function in the universe. Though one may be very happy without it. The tetraktys gives you more control over mind over matter, one can identify thoughts more clearly and orderly." M Degas said.

"Yes, the universe is the closest thing we have to immutability. Let's consider a lump of matter. What permutable perspectives do we have? If it has shape, color, mass, distance, motion, height, weight, density, and volume? It took us years to become familiar with these perspectives. The lump is credited with all inventions. A Philosophers stone in the likes." Edwind said.

(Figure 76)

Perfect state,

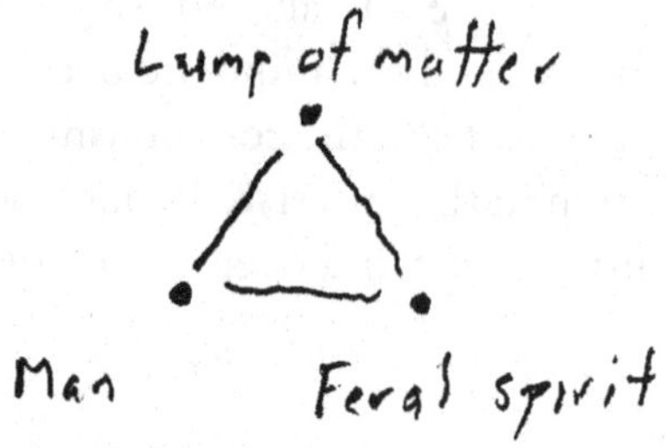

Lump of matter

Man

Feral spirit

- Lump of matter- Any piece of material in the universe. One has to have a main idea of permutation in the ability to manipulate the intellective.

- Man- Any characture of the human being. Such as a mail person, doctor or lawyer. One that lives in a culture filled with morals and ethics.

- Feral Spirit- the spirit of evening. This spirit evens out everything in truth. It's basically the only spirit that is constantly changing bad to the good.

"Our imagination follows a finite set of rules it comes to us from a point to a line then into an image. The Holy Ghost isn't the imagination and come to us in the form of things. We are finite beings, yet what does God want from us?" M Rahn said.

"The tetraktys shows us the substrate through the imagination and mind, and all existence is absolute. We have our human condition that's not absolute where we live out our lives on the latter of the dollar. This dollar bill is a work of art which is the template to Our Fathers work." Scrupt said.

"Well then what evidence do you have that there is a heaven?" M Rahn asked.

"There is evidence of heaven right at the time we dream. It's absent from the immutable nature which govern the universe, yet at the same time there is a real element that makes up the fabric of the dream. Heaven must be related to our dreams. Yet in heaven you are in control. To an extent I'm guessing though. I bet the myriad is the key to such a place. Pythagoreans studied religion and science wondering how these two things come together. Like a dream mixed with reality to make up heaven. Which two tetraktys make heaven, I don't know." M Degas said.

"Heaven is the yield of the great and good people that dolor the Earth. A place where everything is perfect. After all it is God's home. Ha! Hell is only a duration to punish the wicked for a time and then they go to heaven, yet who could believe in such stories, life is an enigma without a utopia. We are broken in the likes." Edwind said.

"What of a perfect man today? What is he made out of in a finite world?" M Rahn asked.

"Well, for 5,000 years we've been developing phonic language to understand the place we live in and what we do here. We've learned to take the performance of the word in our daily lives where most of us are lettered in the language. A lettered man has the advantage over ones who are not so enlightened in such works. The people I worked with were very educated. Ah . . . What does make a perfect man now days? My guess is a perfect man wakes up in the morning and the first thing he considers is how can I take care of the Earth today. Just as most every man is capable of work he has to see that every man and everything is lead in the right way. Here is a place that man should be at. The love of honor and merit. It's all a man can do at the importance of ones liberty. That to me is mans perfect state." Scrupt said.

"Performance . . . Man has to condition himself in the way of metaphysics just to get away from the idea of being a work machine or just a producer of the job he has to do. One can meditate on anything and be attached to it to hold it as a treasure. To look at it like a perfect state one has to keep the Deity and universe in mind. The way I look at it is that the immutable Laws of nature give me the diligence to find the predicate in the importance of my substratum perception. It's the eye verses the evidence, which will change as the intelligence will change with time . . . Evidence, you got to have evidence and the knowledge of the importance to use it." M Rahn said.

"Man has found a way to organize his thoughts. Though he must first find the truth or what will lead him to the truth by following the right ways . . . Evidence, hardcore evidence, the arbitrary things. Precepts are the best evidence after all what is better than perception of the omniscience. I take a look at what is in front of me and that is the basis of a precept. It changes in so, so many ways, location, metaphysics, entropy and so on. In existence in the work today man surpasses the lips of antiquity he finds himself in absurdity reacting to the edge of time and space where the fifth element of the mind is key in the newest trend. The truth is that edge is on a conjunction that everything that a mind flows on in the likes of heuristics. Therefore whatever man hears here in existence equals the truth to him or her." M Degas said.

"Like virtue itself metaphysics has come down to a piece of the Holy Ghost called a halo. Most of which we consider angels to have. Which acts like an arche of protection giving the bearer power over the universe. These halo's are kind of like mandala's which the Indian's of India thought the whole universe went through. Basically it works in these likes." M Rahn said and drew up a page. (See Figure 77)

"We are finite beings with a lore so large that we fail to a perfect state on our own scale. The great fall, our technology will support us so greatly into the future that we ourselves we fail at being prosperous. We will return to a placid state where we have learned from our strives in the biggest and greatest to where we will become only entertainers. Everything around us is defined by absurdity the limits to what the words will in a glance. Well, God knows the truth. Man has to go through a dolor to get it. God? How old is he? How old am I? Ha, ha, ha." M Degas said as he viewed and thought like time no longer mattered.

"Man does have a perfect state. The struggle is in life to get it. The tetraktys is a finite immutable piece of evidence which holds the entire universe. Man was pressed out here from eons of co-existing elements that are metamorphically processed today and we are still in search of what did create life as we know it. Man is a being that has a mind able to collect and process information. One could say that he is a computer. He today is now able to consider a lump of matter and do a permutation of things with it. Man's mind hasn't always been able to do this and it might become obsolete in the future where everything is computerized. The language arts might be considered the most favorable toy to those that take the intuition to learn. So, the question is, where do we go from here?" Edwind said.

(Figure 77)

A halo,

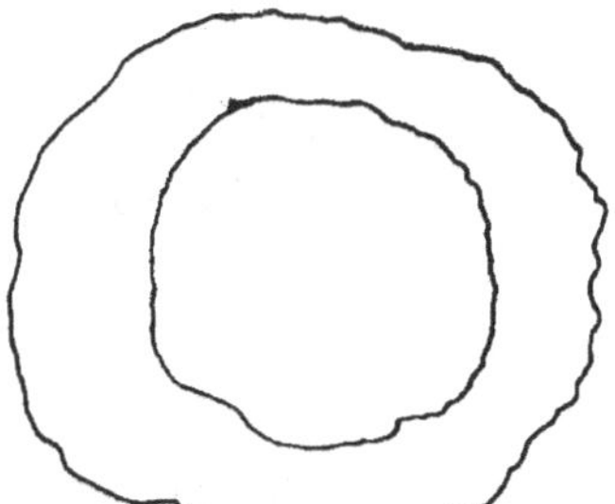

Halo: It brings us the universe.

Half halo:  It resources the universe.

Quarter halo's:  It fortifies a position.

Line halo's: 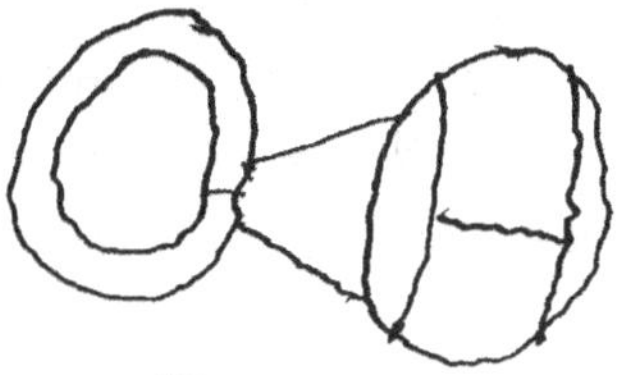 It draws and hears communication.

Seeking halo:  It seeks from a half truth to the entire truth.

A halo can be any substance and made up of any fraction of a halo. Gold is usually considered when one pictures a halo. A halo is a thing of peace

"Yes, well we find that when we seek something that we become broken or bent to that what we seek." M Rahn said.

"Just what our cortexes are for, we stick wedges of information in them and it builds up our intellect into our intelligence. Headaches are the affinities of chemistry and emotions metaphysics of our cortexes. We need to listen and identify with our cortex's in order to merge them in our minds and make sense out of them. One's ear is the input to our brains. Your brain can untangle anything." Scrupt said and sips up some coffee.

"What I haven't shown you three yet is that the bill is a muse to our minds. Each person has a unique ability to seek one's own destiny. The bill shows exactly how it works." M Rahn said.

"What does it do?" M Degas said.

"Well it lines a person's perception to be immaculate, coordinating their mind to project one's thought in the immutability of the heavens. Then when you take the bill away the thoughts other them your hindsight of the math are gone. One after getting used to it can tap into it without the bill. The full ability one has to use it, I don't know. What I do know is that you have to study the information of the tetraktys to use it. Getting all the information correct is the trick and it's not really that hard. Once the entire piece fits you start to trip." M Rahn said.

"Well, let me give it a try." Scrupt said.

He took the bill and held it up to his face. He didn't get much out of it until it was the only the apple of the eye, the only thing in the universe. He saw his mind open up and he viewed what he thought was his past accomplishments. He took control and started to have a more of a crazy vision. He heard sounds like a large wind was flying past him where he started to view distant planets in space. It was his first trip to the bill, but not his last. He took the bill down.

"Did you see my face?" Scrupt asked.

"No, you were just sitting there with the bill in front of your face." Edwind said.

"Here, Scrupt, let me try." M Degas said.

M Degas grabs the bill as Scrupt hands it over. M Degas holds the bill up to his face and takes a couple of seconds as the bill sets in his mind. He sees his mind becoming active and sees a lump of matter permuting into millions of different forms of intellect. Then he sees the border of the bills dynamic web energize. Then he sees a shadow of energy build up and turn into the Earth and Sun. They take form in pristine resolution as colorful as a dream can possibly be. So M Degas takes control and heads toward the Earth. He came to the United States and thought maybe I'll try and find my current position. Sure enough he was able to see himself inside the coffee shop along with the other three. Right away he thought the myriad, this is what the myriad means, immaculate perception. He takes the bill down.

"The myriad is a window to existence. It protects the here and now throughout time and space." M Degas said.

"The tetraktys has every level my friend. This bill must be something like the apeiron of the all-seeing-eye." Edwind said.

"Existence is a balance of the feral spirit. I was able to find myself here through the bill at this location. The bill with its delineation is, well, endless. One could spend their whole life's looking through this piece and be very happy. It would be a device to check out other times and minds if you're trained enough through it. I bet we could envision the whole universe and beyond." M Degas said.

"Well, I've seen plenty. When you three were in Gebelin I could see you with the bills perception. Now that we have come to terms of what's possible. How do we go about telling the rest of the people or do we tell them?" M Rahn asked.

"I think we shouldn't tell them. The tendency of it being used for evil is enormous." M Degas said.

"I have an idea. Why don't we make sure the person is right by setting up a quest?" Edwind said.

"That's brilliant." Scrupt said.

"Yes, a level of trust, clue them in a little and see if they can find a way. After all it is a lot of information that a person would gain." M Degas said.

"With every piece of intellect of that bill man can reach a perfect state. The myriad. The time where man will become one with the element and will live forever. It's just what Our Father wanted. Our Fathers dream. People will exactly understand what it is that we are doing here. Our Fathers dream." M Rahn said.

"The way of the future." Edwind said.

"We must start the quest for the first to be the one with the element."

A man walks into the coffee shop holding a book.

"Hey, Rahn." The Man said.

"Hey, it's Chadwick, everyone here meet Chadwick he is our Author. Are you finished Chadwick?" M Rahn asked.

"Yep, here is the book. I had it published 6 weeks ago, here is the first copy of An Inventor's Dream, The Pythagorean." Chadwick said.

"Well that means all we have left for now is the study of these Pythagorean works." M Rahn said.

They all sat there looking at the book on the table.

LUSE GUILD MAGIC

Spucket Knostic

Kluse Guild Magic,

I Spucket Krostic, have put together this book to acknowledge to the folks here at the Kluse Guild the possibilities of the tetraktys any where in the absurdities of the universe. The tetraktys is an artifice which is a model of the universe.

I am not sure about the design or regulations nor what you folks will think of this in any means, though through hard work it can also be yours. Take a look at this:

•

One would call it a dot or mark of some sort. to me, it is the universe. When it comes in the form of the tetraktys. An artifice like this:

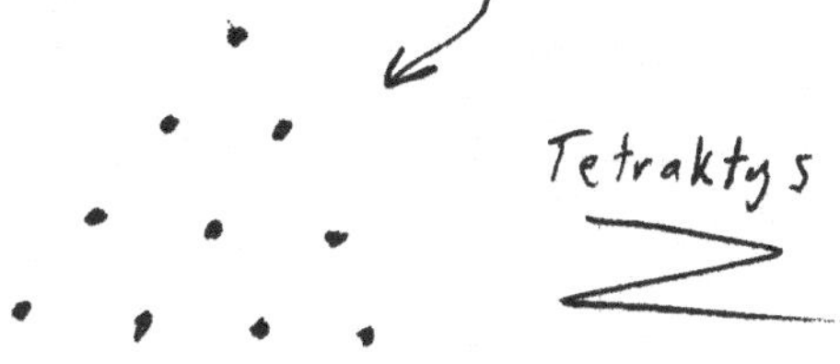

•
• •
• • •
• • • •

Tetraktys

An artifice the Pythagorean's used in considering in the likes of the first cause or big bang expanding from the origin of something or the universe. Our language and perception is fortified by it.

The tetraktys is a map to the mind starting with the most simple to the advance. It mirrors thoughts.

There are more tetraktys than there are number. The tetraktys can describe the universe from the first dot on to show different classes, Take Math in the likes. Math shows the different mathematical classes and tools:

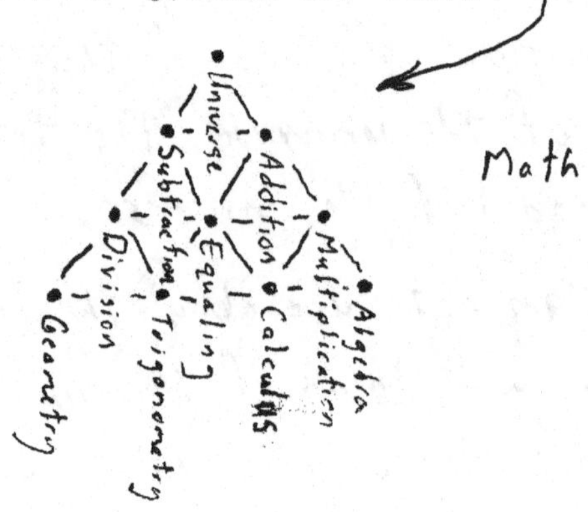

For the folks to understand the tetraktys it is easiest to point out the section of it. The sections describe the dots in rows from one to four. They are the divisions to the tetraktys. Singles to the quadruples:

Singles ——— • ——— 1

Doubles ——— • • ——— 2

Triples ——— • • • ——— 3

Quadruples — • • • • — 4

I want to explain the regulations and relationships with the sections in a tetraktys.

After that is done I want to put the affinites to the test. keep in mind folks, this is my model. Its what I learned from discerning and monkeying around with this artifice. One has their own testing to do in this play ground the universe.

Subject ———— • ———— 1
Apparent ———— • • ———— 2
Reason ———— • • • ———— 3
Court —— • • • • —— 4

I have picked this design to have you folks better understand the sections. Subject- is the selected item of the tetraktys. Mostly the universe, though other times an intellect or enigma. Apparent- this is the functioning part of this artifice where things are monkeyed with in the likes of the subject. Reason- these three artifices work out problems by troggling through intellection and things. Court- this is where we have the eyes and ears for thought in creating a consciousness.

All four of these artifices are for a thought process which I will be explaining later.

Here is the story and experience I've had bringing this to you. A teacher named M Degas showed and taught me the tetraktys in a college course. I loved the course, it was thrilling. He was a master, though I don't know how he attained it himself. I've been playing around with it ever since. I'm sure I don't have it right. He was sure he didn't have it right. Though here in this book is the model I bring to my students of the kluse Guild. So you folks will have to bear with me and apprehend what I have here as a basis of these works and one of you might get it right. I'll begin here:

The affinites in the likes of how they relate is an enigma in their performance.

Then the relationship between them altogether. Showing a latter from top to bottom making 13 pyramids.

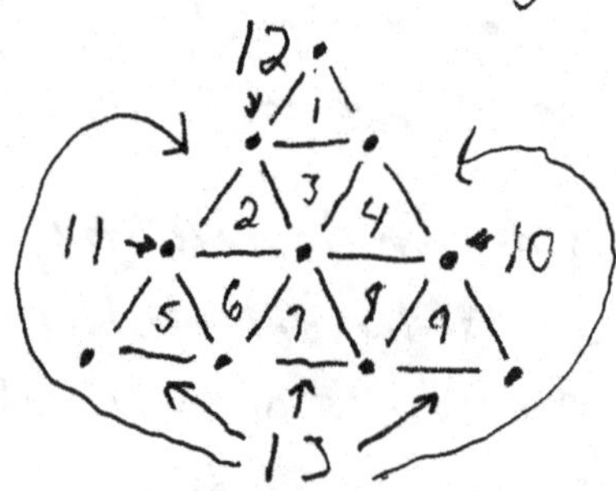

I came up with this idea for a tetraktys so you folks would get a feel of the description for one. This is the General tetraktys:

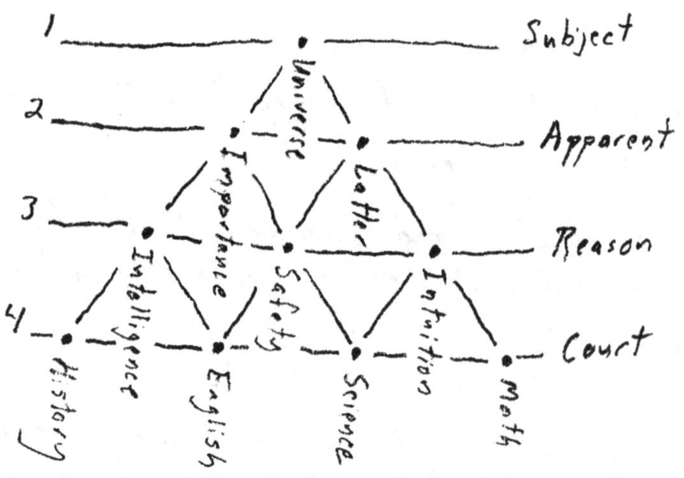

Now, what do the sections do alone? What does it do?

• —— Singles?
• • —— Doubles?
• • • —— Triples?
• • • • —— Quadruples?

<u>The single</u> - It relates to a single part.
<u>The double</u> - It is an idea of the affinities.
<u>The triple</u> - It is the functioning of reason.
<u>The Quadruple</u> - It is the evidence of the mind.

Shewing the lines of the thinking process we have the:

• Single, this is the beginning of the tetraktys. An idea or thought to reflect on is choosen.

•—• Double, this is where one can move the thought or idea around. This is in the form of a premise, a line, two points or conjunction. We use it in conversation and calculating the rudiments of the language.

∴ Triple, the three parts allow one to conject and permute ideas relating to the subject. The parts - safety, intuition and intelligence all define the subject in the triple of the General tetraktys. The triple is also the first surface, what people use as an imagination. Imagine a triangle from the first two sections as the subject shows the image one can manipulate it from there with the Double.

⁞⁞ Quadruple, this is reality, everything sound, every light one hears or sees and thinks belongs here. Prote Hyle... Concentraition of ones enviorn has a hold of a commerce from single to quadruple. The single has the subject, the double the manipulation, the triple the imagination and the quadruple the reality, all of absurdity. They all work together in a thinking process.

I will now explain them further from my perspective.

• Single, this is the point, the subject. It could be anything one wishes. It is the mark that begins the topic of the tetraktys. It works with the psyches and anything one can view with Prote Hyle. It sets the basis for the rest of the tetraktys. Whatever the subject is gives the nominal point of the thinking process.

• • Double, this is the affinities between two points, the apparents in the likes. They could be anything in a line, points or premise which one gets the narrative from the subject. It works with the psyches and is a dimension of a single line or subject. It is where we give and receive information from a point. Using this I play around with the point viewing different dimensions of the things in this universe.

• • • Triples, this is the first surface where we resource our imagination. It could be anything in an image from the point and apparent, I reason the place of the image and associate a purpose with it. The point gives me a edge and I look at the affinites in an extenuation of the heuristics when studying the intellection in the imagination.

• • • • Quadruples, this is the second surface of the tetraktys where we view reality. Nature and the general existence of the universe giving us what we would just plainly see as the surface of this place... Absurdity. I use this surface to study physics and realize what and who I am in the likes.

Lets take a look at what we have found here...

• Point, could be anything.

• Car • Square • Bee • House • Moon • Love

• • Apparent, could be anything.

• • line • • affinity • • premise • • duelizm

• • • • Reason, the first surface.

• • • Nominal • • • Tree • • • Imagination • • • Hate

• • • • • Reality, the second surface.

• • • • Entropy • • • • Homage • • • • Science

Now lets view them in physics of a tetraktys...

Point • Science the science of a tree in the park.

Line •—• Science the premise of a tree in the park.

Triangle ∴ Science The image of a tree in the park

Square ⁚⁚ Science the reality of a tree in the park.

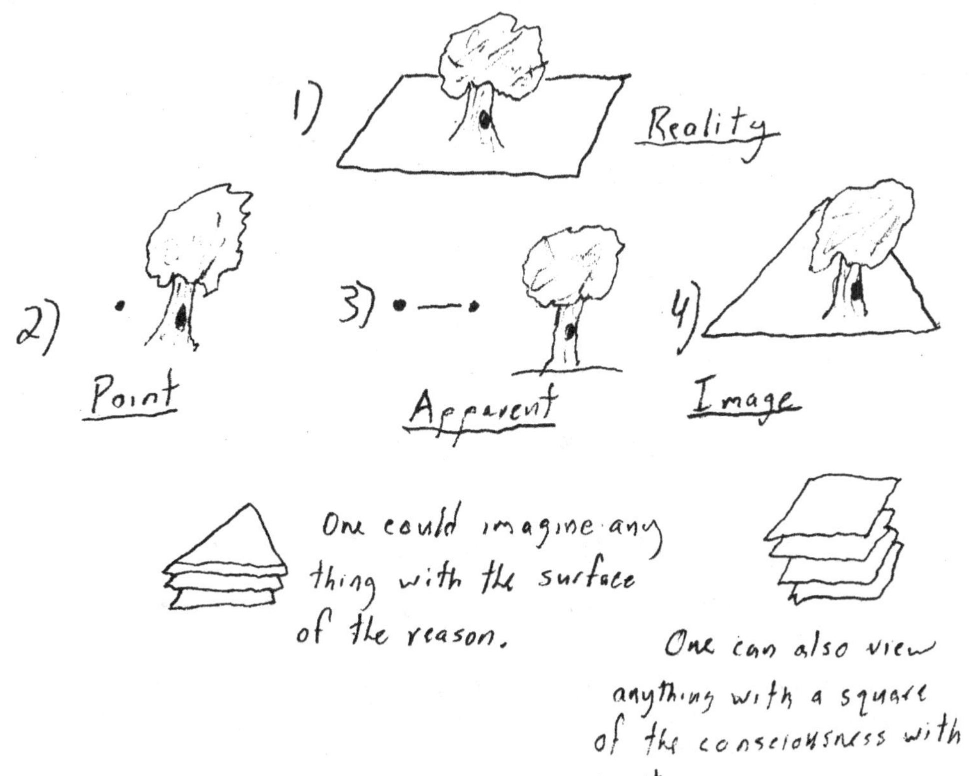
1)
Reality
2)
Point
3)
Apparent
4)
Image
One could imagine any thing with the surface of the reason.
One can also view anything with a square of the consciousness with court.

Imagine having a surface over a place like an object in a field.

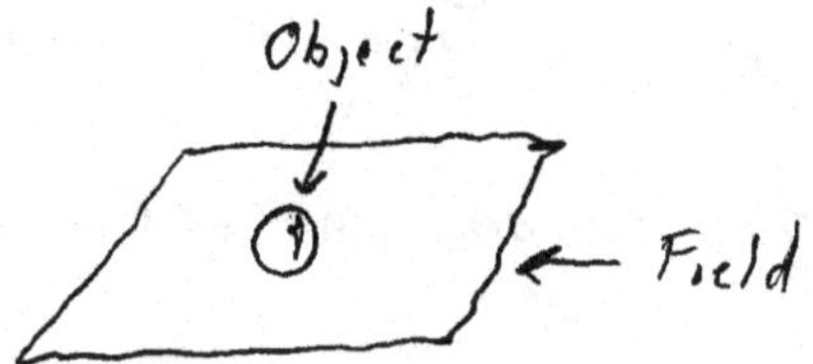

One could use the first surface over the second surface to imagine the object.

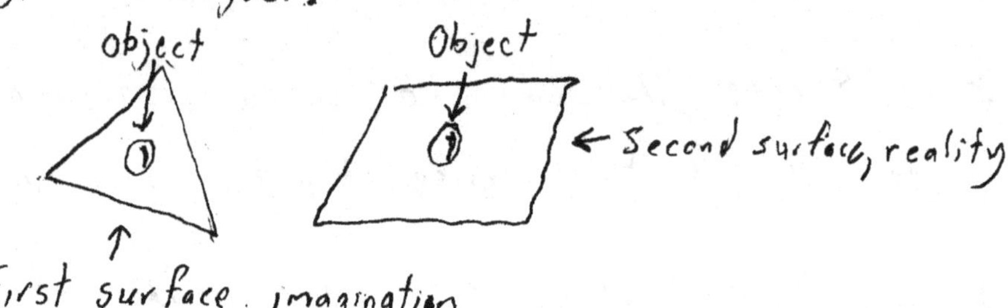

There are all kinds of surfaces and along with it imaginations. Take any word and match it with the surfaces. Try these:

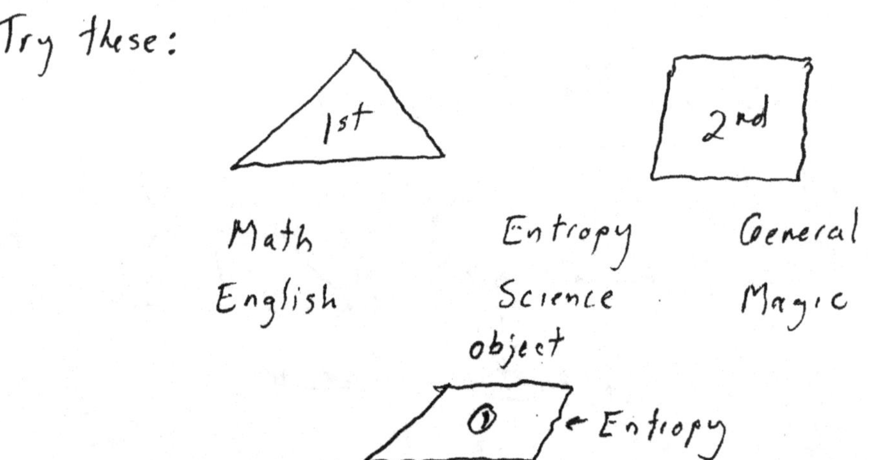

The entropy of the object is that it is a circle that was draw on this piece of paper in a square just less than a minute ago. With the surfaces we try to match the word with the subject,

← Globe

The globe • in the tetraktys adds up all the globes into one meaning or quintesense giving a enticing feeling for the person. Each globe regulates the definition deconstruct-ing the nominal value of the word representing the globe. Each globe depends on the section of the tetraktys. I am showing you folks the very means of thinking. The foundation in the likes. You'll have to study and practice in order to make them work. For now just read and reread later.

Here is the magic tetraktys which is put to-gather in quintesense.

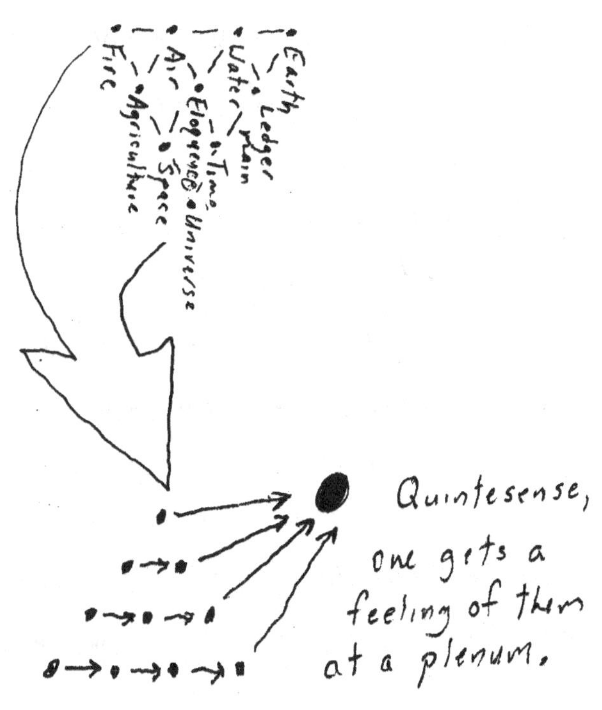

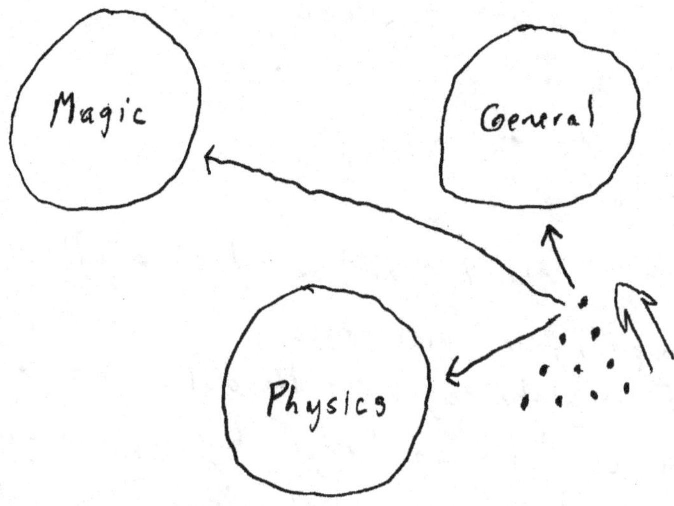

These quintesences are the representations of tetraktys. They give a monad of an idea to the performer, the one who has unfolded them. These are like words with their definitions in a plenum in the mind and imagination in their enviorn.

They can be used to stablize ones mind when all put together, though a tetraktys and words are only models of the universe we can understand in the likes. I am sure I don't even have it right, so the right way is up to one's own purpose. Everything, every word may be made into a tetraktys. I like them because they put things in order of association in the absurdity of the universe. They go hand and hand into an elementary anyone can understand.

The purpose of the tetraktys is to better understand the things we have and do in life. I understand a myriod of things and think this guild is unique. I tend to want polymaths over genus's. We learn a tetraktys by the meaning of the words constructing them. Tetraktys show a form of thought from the major divisien of a topic from the top to bottom and vice versa. The magic tetraktys shows magic while any other subject will show the nominal meaning it is assigned. In the likes in the techology tetraktys the subject would be a tool or vehicle. Though through a main topic the tetraktys subject is the idea of the folk in the universe where the tetraktys would be named whatever nominal subject one would wish to use.

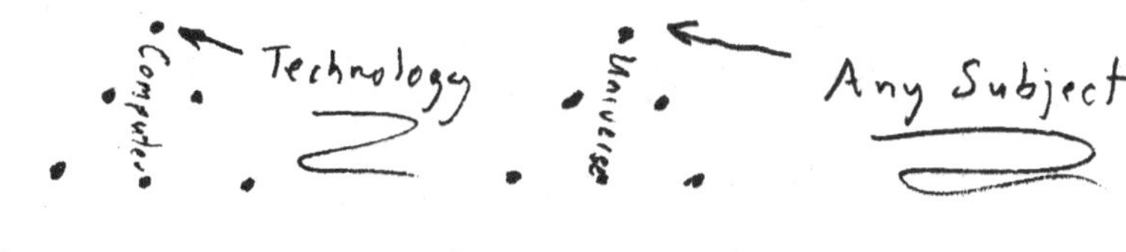

In nominating a subject we make up the rest of the heuristics through associating the relevance of importance in definition.

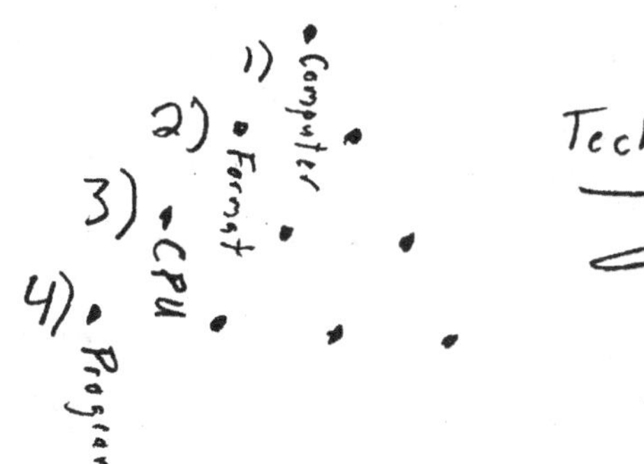

The subject, computer-goes dividing the elements of the heuristics to hold the information of the physics in the functions of the unit.

Now what I have told you so far about the tetraktys is the basic structure. Now I'd like to add the smaller functions. Like the different ways to practice the perceptions of the tetraktys. Folks this is a unique, yet very fun part of discovering the ways of existence and subsistence. To follow these or your own you make up by calculating or conjecting the affinities of the artifices one can really start to enjoy studying in an ontological way.

Each little piece of the tetraktys is important depending on the nomination of its subjects and sections. The dots discribing the tetraktys have the functions of the dimensions of the abilities of the beholder. What you see is what you get. The more one practices the more they level.

To the level of my research here is what I have found. Here are the artifices of the tetraktys,

Singles:	Doubles:	Triples:	Quadruples:
• Globe	• • Paradox	• • • Reason	• • • • Court
• First psyche	• • Apparents	• • • Extenuation	• • • • Cardinal
• Period	• • Vice	• • • Virtue	• • • • Compass
• Sphere	• • Matrix	• • • Trinity	• • • • Square
• Zenith	• • Duelism	• • • Intellection	• • • • Address
• Nadir	• • Second psyche	• • • Grounds	• • • • Conjuration
• Point	• • Proto Hyle	• • • Character	
• Speck	• • Ih, kih	• • • Triangle	
• Domain	• • Illusory	• • • Tripartion	
• Dot	• • Dichotomy		
• Degree	• • Line		

•—— Singles
•—•—— Doubles
•—•—•— Triples
•—•—•—•— Quadruples

These sections are for constructing a tetraktys. These are ways to get a good look at what one may do with it. There are countless ways of doing so. Though some do not work and some will unlock enigma's.

Singles, to the best of my knowledge these dots relate to how the quintesense works in a tetraktys when drawn on a page and later in globes in the mind. They work with any word you can bring to best fit the performance in the importance as one designs a tetraktys. One's mind meditates on them as each word has a unique quintesense revealing a new perspective. Folks, your job is to learn (absorb) the articulation of the dots and advance (Master) them as far as one can wit in the whole absurdity of the universe. Here is how I define them: Singles,

• Globe, an atom, the Earth, it is what things are made of in the absurdity of things. Any element, motion or idea is balenced by them in existence and subsistence of the mind or imagination. I have not done or found everything to do or what not, yet they are very useful and fasinating to ponder. With it we are questioning the very physics of being and not just scientifically, but more at scholastically. Take the globe in the mind the size of an inch and consider it the world in the imagination then time travel with the globe and see all of history where with the model. In the likes the first step in viewing a globe is... Unknown. Where we have a nominal globe, sphereical and plainly undescribed. A scalar globe as undefined energy sitting in the space of ones reflections. The very imagination of the mind depends on it.

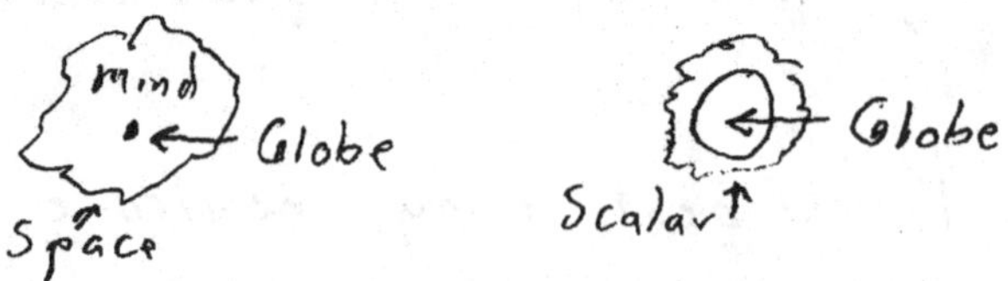

- First Psyche, this dot or speck (could be any thing one has ones mind over) can only be moved by the Second Psyche (movement). The First Psyche in returns stops the Second Psyche. It works by taking the Second Psyche to find a speck or object and troggle it between Psyches to seek and learn about the intellect of the absurdities of the universe. Like taking in the imagination a housefly and moving it around with the psyche's in any way one wishes. I use them in subsistence to enhance the object I am playing with while giving it meaning and reason with the idea's and material. Take a box in the imagination, one can move it around with the Psyches.
- Period, the dot at the end of a sentence giving it duration of existence when it is considered a globe in time and space of the absurdity of the mind in the universe. In putting a period in time and space it gives a marker to its existence. Kind of like the cosmos turning. It is part of the premise in a line of listening and paying attention as well as amuze for thinking. One can either listen or permute the rudiments in their experimentation of the models man has made to learn, mainly the language and intellection in a lexicon that one has studied.

• Dot, this mark is always on a surface, paper in the likes. It represents a nominal function on the surface, just a marker, with no dimensions. We use these to formulate any action on a page through a tetraktys because with dots on a page there is no danger. The dots are not real, but on a space on a page, just like the dots and rudiments in this book.

• Point, this is the dot of existence or ontological existence where the dot is the subject that we pay attention to in perspectives. It is here that we figure and feed on reality or a story in the narrative. This mark acknowledges writing and communication from point to period. We reflect on the existence of it in the imagination and mind. I could be anything one has an eye on. What's the point?.. In the likes, take a scene of a painting or picture and make it a point in perspective with it. The point is always ahead of you. Watch it in the reflection of existence or subsistence.

• Sphere, a perfectly round globe usually enlightened and weightless with the emptiness to behold something in it. Its purpose is to be filled and have the quintesense of thoughts to be a muze to the mind as models for later reference. One can think or tap into them with meditation. In the likes the sphere of common wealth, economy or spirit, whenever one needs to. It is here we meditate on the proper objects of the envirn. One can consider the very physics of a bubble that was simply blown by a child to let it break into it's meaning.

• Zenith, this is the top of the food chain, the paramount of a thing or things in the existence of the universe. The highest point of a globe, sphere or thing on Earth. I have found the pH or pin number of the globes in order to time travel and teleport things from one point to the other. Zenith is an optimistic view where perception is in the lead.

- Nadir, this is the very bottom of things. We value weight, in this measure. Size, mass, volume, density, dimension and quintesence, we consider everything in this guild. It shows the origin or the last point in existence. Nadir is a pessimistic view where the bottom of the mind starts.
- Speck, this is the smallest part of a thing we view. It is in my perspective a way to view things as one takes a little bit of something and then is able to view the whole thing in reflection. Take a desk for example, and take a speck of it in your eye. Can you see it falling into your perspective filling you with the whole thing? A speck is also a small piece that gives one a muze for meditation, something to work with in the likes that is not so overwelming. Think small, see big...
- Domain, this is the King, the head cheese of the place over ones head that a being lives in the universe. Here we have our minds, thoughts, allegories and imaginations under one roof in the likes. This is where everything sub-sist in existence though some have special addresses. The domain is endless and can have anything one wishes from the root in creating a mind. It is the scoop of the universe where we shovel the things up in the compassion of the wants of the mind and imagination from the seven-

dipity of nadir. It is also here we find the Holy Ghost. The tetraktys is a house of the domain.

• Degree, this measures the reward of merit and study. In doing anything it is the dot that represents a deed. All together it is the catalog of virtue. It is made up of facts and principles. We use it as a science to make records of what we have found and achieved in a nomenclature.

Doubles, These are the actions of the universe in existence and subsistence. They bring things to life weather it be infinite or infinitesimal. Affinities and motion tell the tale of the serendipity in attractions and repellents. It is here we find the effects, affects and reactions of the laws and principles of the element and classes of the scholastics in the universe. Now, I have meditated a long time to come up with these models, and I am positive the Guild will find better ones. So, here is what I have to say about them in the least:

Doubles,

• • Paradox, a vision where the sight is sometimes broken and usually uneven, unequal... Resourcing, wanting something, having or waiting for answers. We use this to seek out points and use the psyches to understand the extenuations while contemplating reason. Things are always changing until we find an answer or enigma. Some paradoxes last only seconds though some for longer periods. I take it as one half of a whole to the other.

• • Apparents, this is the field in the eyes one can percieve the aether. It is a place of faith where one can believe the thoughts and idea's one plays with. Try a pencil in the apparents and draw a circle. Then open the circle to view the place you have been to in the imagination. With the apparents I believe is where we honor thy Mother and Father in a perpetual peace. The apparents spend accross the entire universe and it is here we do most of our seeking, it is our play ground.

• • Vice, this is a break in the matrix, something that is bad or gets wrong. It is the dark catalog where everything is out of place. It also creates chao's which is sometimes good, but this is our down fall, our heartbreak. I use it as a muse or clutch when needed. All drugs are vices, some affects and effects create vices and so does wrong doing and mistakes. Water may be a vice in the likes.

• • Matrix, equalization of the eyes in an unfolding premise. Mind over time and place. The imagination plays a part in this, bringing one images and illusory senses. It is here we bend reality morphing with in the imagination and we must study the places we live and work in the likes to have a start of an allegory of the physics of illusions. We build and think in a vision reflecting the surface as a spectrum of light comes within in the likes. I love this artifice, I paint the sky, walls and nous with it.

• • Duelizm, an affinity of feraling two or more people, animals or things (Usually in magic or melee). This is where we have to fight, but I don't see it happening to often. We train all our folks to fight. I would wipe the floor with you!

• • Second Psyche, this goes with the First Psyche. The

Second Psyche moves the surface and in return the First Psyche stops it. We are always playing with the two, yet something will always move and somethings will stop. It's a matter of what one is addressing in the likes. One could use the Psyches to be a word alchemist or more advanced to do scientific research in the imagination.

• • Prote Hyle, this is mind over matter. Prote (Thought) is the nous or thinking of the mind. One takes Hyle (Material) and brings it into focus with Prote. "Prote Hyle." Mind and element. When thinking (Prote) of a tree (Hyle) the mind recognizes the situation... "It's a tree!" Prote Hyle can be thousands of heuristics in the mind when viewing an enigma or something in the enviorn. (Hyle) This page. (Prote) The thought of this page. Prote Hyle! Prote Hyle!

• • Ih, kih, this is the imagination over the element used by man with a Deity. Ih (Idea) kih (Element) is the ability to change color, texture, and element with the digression of the imagination. I use it when playing with the psyches. It works very well. Though it is a tough one to grasp. Like turning a light on in an idea (Ih) and changing the color of it (kih).

• • Illusery, this deals with the immaculate perception. An ability to walk right through into an illusion. This is like a matrix only it fills ones world. A vivid day dream in the likes. I use it to point storylines in my head.

• • Dichotomy, this is where two opposing sides are exactly equal in existence. It brings things back to nature as they tie or become neutral in the affinities of the eviron. We use it to stop chao's and bring down paradoxes back to the apparents. There is usually nothing left, but class, a complete silence. In calculus this is the most important part from the basis of a dot, it can be any thing when we calculate the dynamics.

• • Lines, this has a nondimensional characteristic. It is used to make communications clear whether it be reading, speaking or writing. We make a dot then connect the line between another dot for the basics of our perspective and rhetoric. Here we delineate a discourse from speech or dimension in the universe or one verse of our domain. From geometry we find the frequency of calculus to form objects we play with in the imagination. A line draws an object in the minds enviorn in dynamics of ones thought.

Triples, Now I want you folks to think a little deeper in your minds. These triples show you how deep one can think in the likes of reason. This is where we can think in the mind and imagination. Comparing and contemplating the likes of the subject in a tetraktys. The element reflects in the mind what the eloquence can be in the enviorn of ones domain. These are of the first surface and always nominal with no reality. It comes as an image of the imagination or vision of the illusory. We try and think clearly and reason all the possibilities of the subject in a tetraktys. So see what you can come up with folks. Here they are:

Triples,

• • • Reason, this is where man lets himself think out problems. It acts as a point and apparents to argue logic. It is the art of logic and you are the artist. I use it to hold a point and weigh it out in a matrix with the other two dots. The Sun and my eyes in the likes.

• • • Extenuations, this is the fear or doubt which I measure out from the beginning to end. Seek the beginning and seek the end of everything. A point becomes existence, the dot the fear or doubt and the period duration. This happens when we question ourselves. A period, dot and point are not the only ones we can use, though this is just a model.

• • • Virtue, this is a catalog of strengths where it acts as a life savor when fear is involved it is our faculty. It works by making weak skills develop into stronger skills in the mind or imagination. I use it for balence to weigh out a perdicament. Rapidity, honor, and patience are all virtues. I use to different catalogs, the dark catalog: Where anything evil or bad can happen and a light catalog: Where anything good can happen. Catalogs are full of virtue where they take the form of precepts. They are art forms of logic in reasoning which if remembered right are extremely strong.

• • • Trinity, this brings three things exactly together to share meanings, it is usually a tool to unite three things believing a relationship in their nominal values altogether to create its quintesence. I use it to enhance idea's such as the Holy Trinity or the Trinities of trinities: Moral, intellect, and materialism.

• • • Intellection, this is a whole body or a full collection of evidence. Heuristically it is the body of the mind as literature is to an Author. Weather it be cars or silverware it becomes a catolog of a collection. The proper objects of the enviorn fall together here while weighing things in this universe. I use it to refresh my sights and inventory in clarity when I recall them. Look at a piece of intellect like it is the crown jewels. There is nothing more intelligent then knowing a polymath of intellect.

• • • Grounds, this is the basis or foundation of intellection, addressing and mind over matter. How things are calcutating from their roots. Here we find the first cause in investigation in the absurdity of the universe. I use it to buff up my rhetoric to get my way. Have my foot on the ground in the likes. My minds eye is at 10/20.

• • • Character, this is in sight a form of micro-addressing to problems solving by using the rudiments man has made to keep record of history in the arche. The alphabet of the language builds on these rudiments since it is what man has to make up all these characters. There is a war with getting the right symbols at the right time. At the height of absurdity it can be down right chaotic. We use English in this Guild, we read books to enhance our learning to form artifices from them clues. There are billions of different symbols, but usually a folk will be speciatized in about one hundred thousand in one class and then advance into another class learning more words in the likes. Commonly, general words make up the elementary of scholastics in absurdity.

• • • Triangle, this is a geometric three sided figure. It is the first surface in a tetraktys where we reflect the imagination. I use it like a blank page to the imagination where I begin my thinking. It's dimensions let me put things on top or in view of it in my mind or imagination. To have one to reflect on in the mind gives one a window of opportunity. Where one may imagine anything having this artifice to open the imagination.

• • • Tripartition, this is three open spaces put together. One fills one space and adds or subracts with the others or vice versa. I use it to weigh out the nature of things in affinities to feral their purpose. All partitions together create a feeling of somber. In the likes take three animals in the mind at once in your head. All three of them have different effects. Idea's are the same way, each serves a different justice.

Quadruples, these are of the mind and is the second surface. I say to the surface wherever I go, "This is my mind." Whatever the problem, through the enviorn or through books it is the second surface. In sight we are fullfilling the imagination when we look in hind-sight through the imagination the first surface from the second. From prote hyle there is no limit to what ones will may think in time and space. This is a place of nonfiction where all the things you do count, not like the first surface the imagination where there are no rules. Though there is no exact Science even the mind is a model. M. Degas said, "There's a sucker born every minute." At the time I didn't know what he meant, though I do now. Folks these quadruples are up to your expertise and judgement. Be wise and think of them as a foundation of consciousness stuck in the unknown as an enigma in the absurdity of the universe. Here they are:

Quadruples,

• • • • Court, this is the foundation of the mind where it sits in your own sheperdizing in the subsistence of the universe. We bring, hear and study things in a heuristic of thought in the court of ones intuition guided by their mind in motion. I use it to come to a common ground in study and communication. A cookie-cut in the elementary in the likes... "Everyone is doing it!" By coordinating my eyes and ears I listen the melodies of the minds delineation, just as two eyes and two ears wit together to make a thought. There might be a court of Law, though this to me is a court of study. The study of Math, Science, English and History in the likes. One might see a court (Square) in the mind where one can consider a subject to get a defined sentiment for it and choose to permeate it in a duration of their own scholastics in ones allegory.

• • • • Cardinal, we find the maximum of the study of subjects here. This is for concentraition of classes with subjects. This is an extreme finite make over of the elements of magic usually fulfilling or producing a fifth element. With this mana forms. Earth, water, air, fire equals quintesense which is mana. I use it like a govern in combobulations of brain waves. One single thing may bring wonders when considering it a mana in the commerce of the magic tetraktys.

• • • • Compass, this is where we find our sense of heading. North, East, South, and West. Our location and our address to the absurdity of ourselves and the universe are important to us. One needs to know their exact location. I take it over head in a top or general view and line up North to find my heading in the world. I also look straight into a compass as a window to cartography.

• • • • Address, this is the consciousness of location

of a person, place or thing in the universe. It is never changing or always changing depending on the subject in the universe and positions of the psyches. Anything could be your address in the importance of the mind and imagination. It's what is on your mind when it comes to the surface of the absurdity of things. "Look, I'm a wolverine!" In the likes ones address is what one thinks. Here is where the agents of absurdity, namely the element becomes the address as one seeks or feels their thought process in a network of metaphysics. This is only a model folks, so keep that in mind at all times.

• • • • <u>Conjuration</u>, this is the four winds of the element where we test the first ritual: Throwing two handfuls of dirt in the air and watching the element fall back down to the ground. It took me a while to figure this one out. I want you folks to see what you can come up with by doing this in your own time.

We have found the sections of the globes in a tetraktys so far in this book. Folks, now I want to use an example to learn about how a tetraktys is put together as a whole in my perspective in this guild's scholastics. This example is the magic tetraktys and definition of how I want you to use and view it in my perspective so it will also be yours. Here is the example to study the tetraktys:

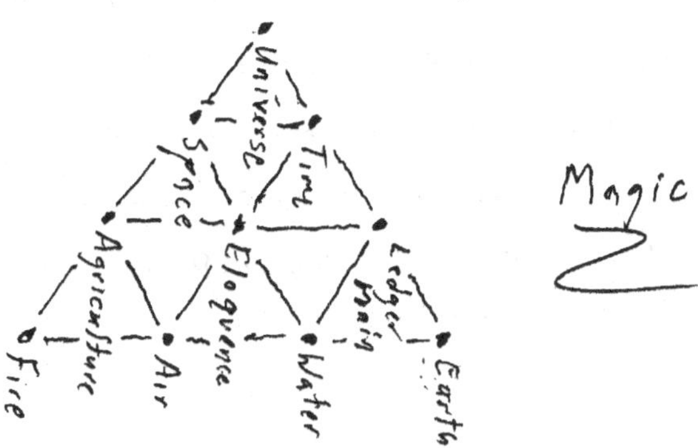

Observe every point of the magic tetraktys and define them to your best understanding to put them into one quintesense as you can into one absolute. With it, it gives you an mana which you have designed to your liking. Here I give an example of my definitions to the globes of the magic tetraktys:

→ Universe

This point shows us existence in the universe of the absurdity we live in the subsistence. It is the absolute address to the monadology. The absurdity is all other points in the tetraktys which gives the mind definition. This point expands the whole outer reaches of time and space in a model where you folks may play called the monad.

→ Time Space

These two points are the area and duration of the continuum of the universe. If it moves, it exist and is here in the universe. In the mind we are working with mirror models. The • time and • space of materials and motions, effects and affects in the affinities of the universe in the likes. How is time on an object in space and why? • Time is the duration of a moving object. Everything in the universe is taking a ride on what I call the aether. • Space is the open area an object can move through or in. These two points are of existence a strength which if measured right may give one omnipresents, omniscience and omnipotence. I use the points as the idea of the eyes and use the Sun as the third point to reason physics and history down to a reality.

Agriculture • Ledger, main • Eloquence

The three of these balence out what to do with time and space in the mind of the folk. They control the element that is in our mind or imagination here on Earth to every element in the universe. The imagination is used by these three to rectify or calculate in conjecture the archtype into elaboration in a nominal way. • Agriculture deals with the kind of element in economics today to make use of it and tells what the material is made of for idenifacation in the persons mind. It is then there for reference for the person to use later. Put together a house in the likes. • Eloquence deals with the strength or force one puts into it in order to enhance the quality or single out one element in a mixture of materials. The idea is to enchant the surface into the purpose the folks want. In return we find it meaningful. I use it with the psyches to select or target the element. • Ledger main is the hand where man is dealing with the dynamics and static of the element in order to change and manipulate it. Ledger main is the hand thinking. It is like a minor division which the major division or the arche' is the mind. It delineates thought from the mind and is used to draw with the dimensions. I've imagined many things and thought of bringing them to use in my hand to discern their use on the surface. The spirit and element are used for a purpose with these three points. They are the apparents that man works with here on Earth. I comes down to the objective in one's mind or task when we have defined these precepts. This is for you folks to understand the elements usefulness in the mind and imagination in the infinitesimal and infinite strands of time and space continum of the universe. Folks, the imagination is the arche' of creativity. We move the psyches in order to believe and if there is something you wish not to believe, digress it.

Earth Water Air Fire

These four are the magic elements. Together they produce an idea of things to constitute a fifth element (mana). They are the court and consciousness of the mind. With them one may conjure anything in the universe using a tetraktys. They are an old way in the likes though they hold all the elements used widely by science today. Heres how I define them:
• Earth, this is the first element. No other element exist without it and the Sun is the source of all its power. Everything of magic is made out of it. Two handfuls of this is in reality the brink of creation. I use it when I am fresh out of ideas. I smell it just to add fuel to my ideas. This is the greatest of all mana. • Water, this rates second to Earth, it is the purest element. It wares and tears through almost anything. It is in us. and we can't survive without it. It is an element that comes in a solid, liquid or gas. Each form is very useful. • Air, this is the third element. It is always in a gasous form. We live in the tropophere where we are surrounded by air, We breath it every minute of the day. Like the Earth and Water element we can't live without it in a certain balence. I use it to support idea's in the atmosphere of globes. in a monadological way. There is nothing like the breeze one can get in the fresh air.
• Fire, this is the finest element of the magics, it can not live

without Earth or Air elements. This is the hottest of elements, It can destroy just about any thing. Water distiguishes it.

Folks I used these elements to define the very physics of the absurdity of the magic tetraktys.

Now that I gave you folks an example of how to define a tetraktys. I want to play with the perspective of it in the likes. → • Point, subsisting in the imagination right in front of you.

• Point

• Globe, the prote hyle of the thought.

• Point

/ ← line, it is the nous or thought.

• Globe

Here the point relates to a line to a globe. The point, line and globe could be anything of ones nomination of the imagination. It is the premise which the communication and sound is heard. Coordinating your eyes and ears in the likes. This is the very basis of comprehension. Take it as a maze, a reflection that is observable. Prote hyle, in looking at something in the enviorn. A bird flying or the color the wall is in conjecture. In the likes we get this feed to play with:

Sun

light

Earth

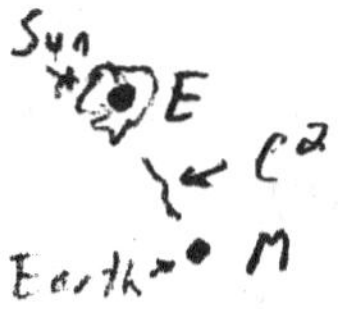

Sun E

c^2

Earth M

$E=mc^2$

Energy = Mass x speed of ligh

This represents Einsteins theory of relativity. It shows the physics of reactions in his theory, as the light of the Sun in it current position made all life possible. I use it in the magic of ledger main. To take the tetraktys in a commerce of contemplation. It works well with the Ih, Kih and the psyches. Practice makes perfect. The model here shows the first surface the imagination. The imagination uses only three sections of the tetraktys and this is not real, but something made up with in the rostering of the idea.

Right in front of you... • Point

• Point
• Dot
Prote Hyle ....

• Point
Reason ...... Globe • • Dot

lines • Point
Imagination... Globe • ! Dot

The first surface could be anything, a point, a globe, or dot with a line connecting all three of them together. Though when one gets to a triangle thing become an image of the imagination. This is the very basis of the imagination. One needs to use the whole tetraktys to complete a thought.

• Materialism
Intellect • • Moral ⟶ First Surface △ > Zietgiest

From the trinity to the first surface is the Zietgiest, meaning economics, moral, and culture of an era. One can lay out over a country to set the imagination for its zietgiest. We use these trinities to level our understanding of physics. The mind is able to imagine images in this surface, yet the first surface in the very means of imagery. It takes a myriad of triangles to make up one image as it copiously rostifies a model. At age ten, one has already rostered trillions of images throughout this time... Maybe even more. One must put up a screen to capture images which I will be mentioning later. Now for the mind.

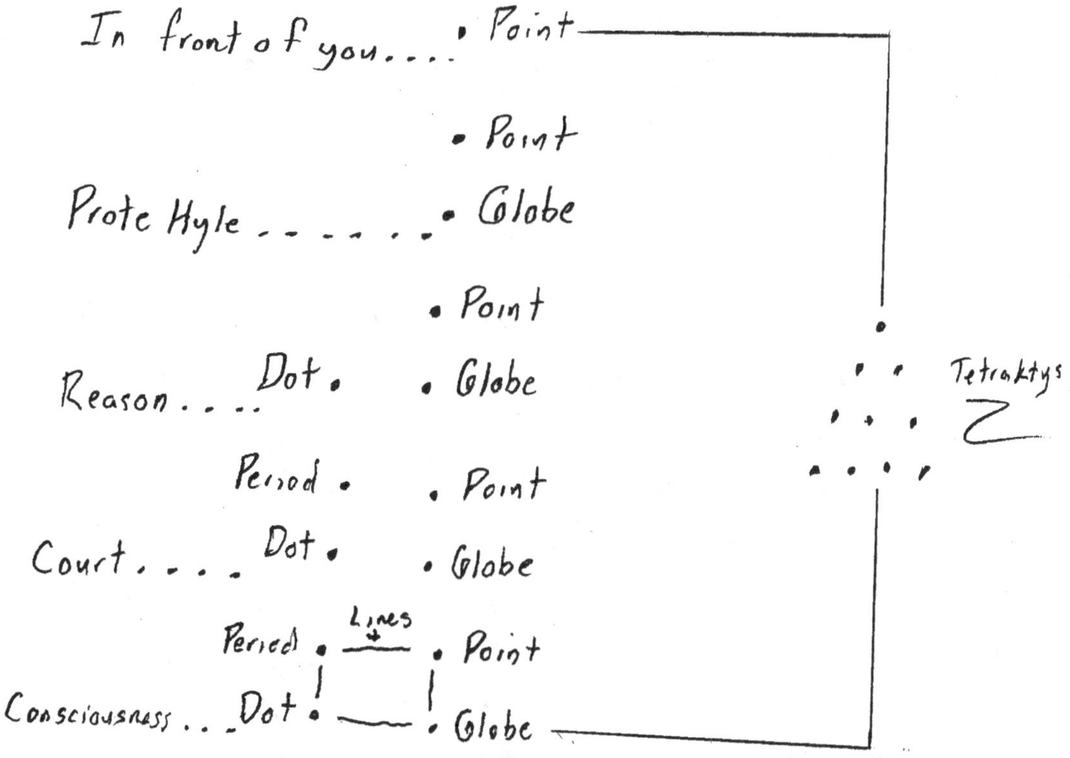

In front of you... • Point

• Point

Prote Hyle ......• Globe

• Point

Reason... Dot • • Globe

Period • • Point

Court.... Dot • • Globe

Period • Lines • Point

Consciousness .. Dot • • Globe

Tetraktys

This is the second surface the mind. If one breaks it, it become the other dimensions in the tetraktys. We complete a though by selecting all of the tetraktys in a whole. One can add a point, globe, period or anything to come back to the fourth section, the mind. This is a court to where we mind and we think with all the dimensions of the tetraktys. We put the courts together equally as a grid. Which I will show you folks later. Here is an example on how we think with the tetraktys:

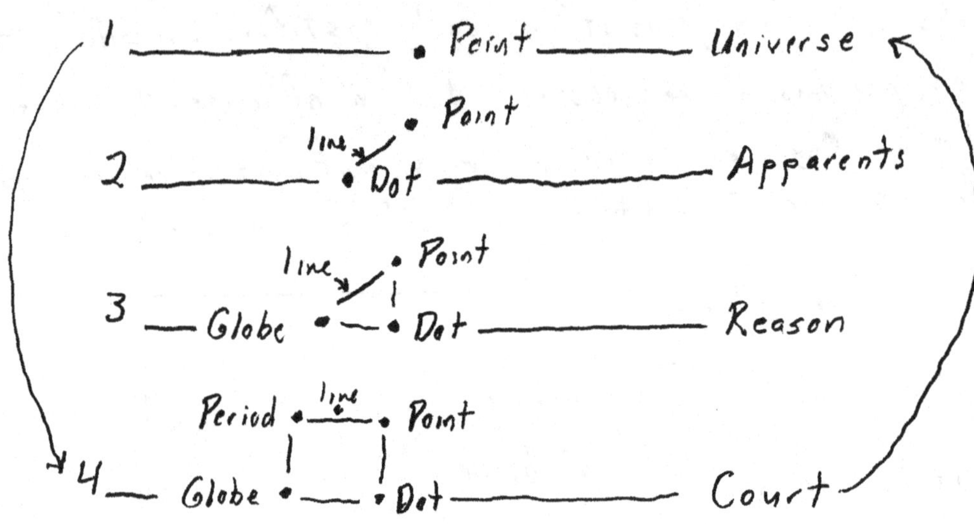

We all have countless ways of using the first dimension through the fourth dimension in a tetraktys over our heads, mind and imagination, but we never use it all at the same time. This is where the perspectives of the tetraktys come in to view. The tetraktys hold a court for relevance, then imaginary for addressing, and affinity for action and a point to select things with. Folks this takes about two years to get good at it and about eight years to master. Its all up to you and your dedication. Now I want to show you the screen, which is made up of the imagination and is like a television screen. Picture an empty slot in your imagination and put these two concepts in them at different times. Look at the diffences...

Order of the screen,

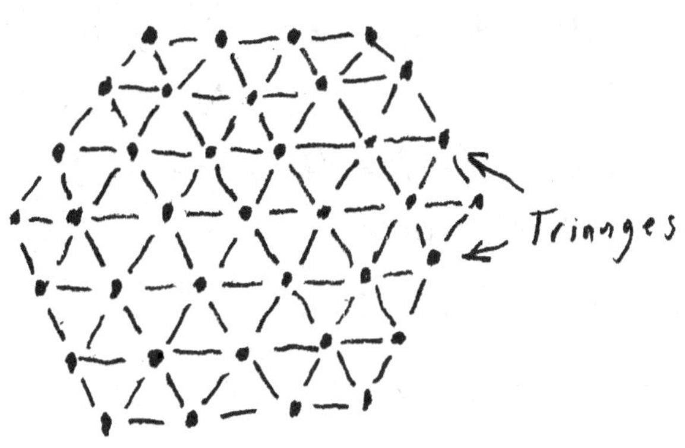

The Screen

Chao's of the screen,

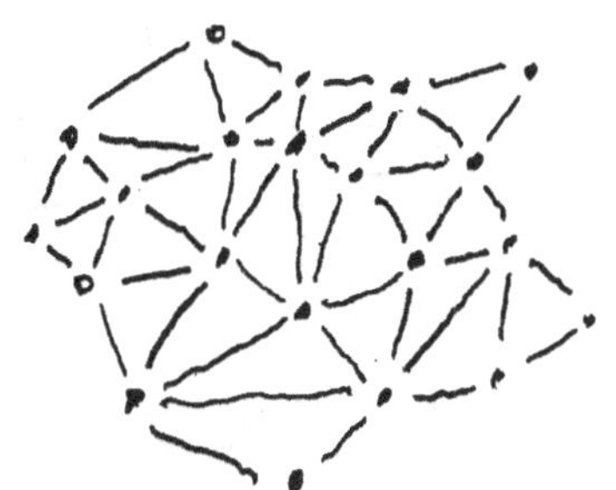

Chao's is what we have without any order. The triangle is the first of this order and here we see the myriad. The myriad is the birth or beginning of something when two things like magic and techology come together and unite. The screen is made up of triangles which makes an order of a myriad to come up with a roster of triangles in a large surface for an image. Socrates mentions that to him the surface was made up of little triangles. So one can make screen by rostering one triangle copiously adding it with more triangles until there is a shape image in the imagination in the likes. Now look at this page. The writing on it one views with there own sights. Imagine a triangle on it. What do you see? Maybe a reflection of where one calculates with the eyes. Now, look into your mind and imagine a triangle. Roster the page on it. What do you think? Is this better or worse. One can see the freedom of the imagination with this folks.

The grid uses the second surface which uses slots in the mind in a concise way to see the edifice of the entire universe or just a perspective to put something in.

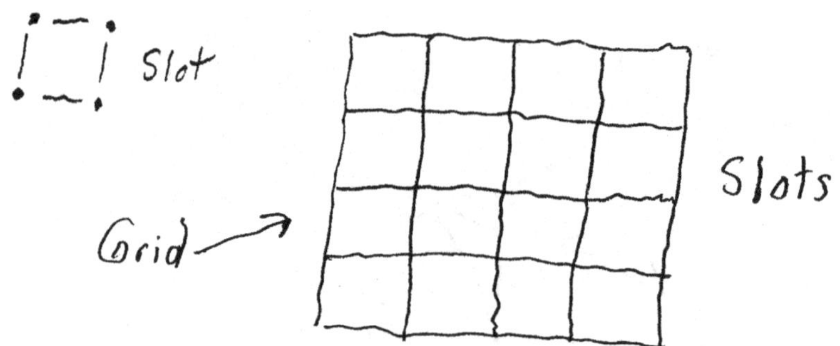

The grid is the order of slots of the mind. The slot can hold memories and a conjection into the future when figuring out ones dreams, ones work or play. It works with the rest of the tetraktys coordinating ones existence to achieve ones goals. It is made up of courts that let you mind things clearly. It accounts for principle in order to have a system which comes down to a science for memory and better yet, so we don't repeat the mistakes of history. Pick a subject in a slot. Can you see your mind and imagination come to what the subject is in the enviorns?

Hold it with the psyches and as questions. The tetraktys really start to employ ones thoughts. It is a fortitude for working and understanding ideas and words of the enigma's and matching them together. Sixteen of the slots in a grid relate an obtainable grid for a simple mind. The grid can go as far as the ones legislature can take them. Now in this drawing the slots have been labeled for an example of a grid. Yet I use it to find relevance by working with a tetraktys and a single slot, like this:

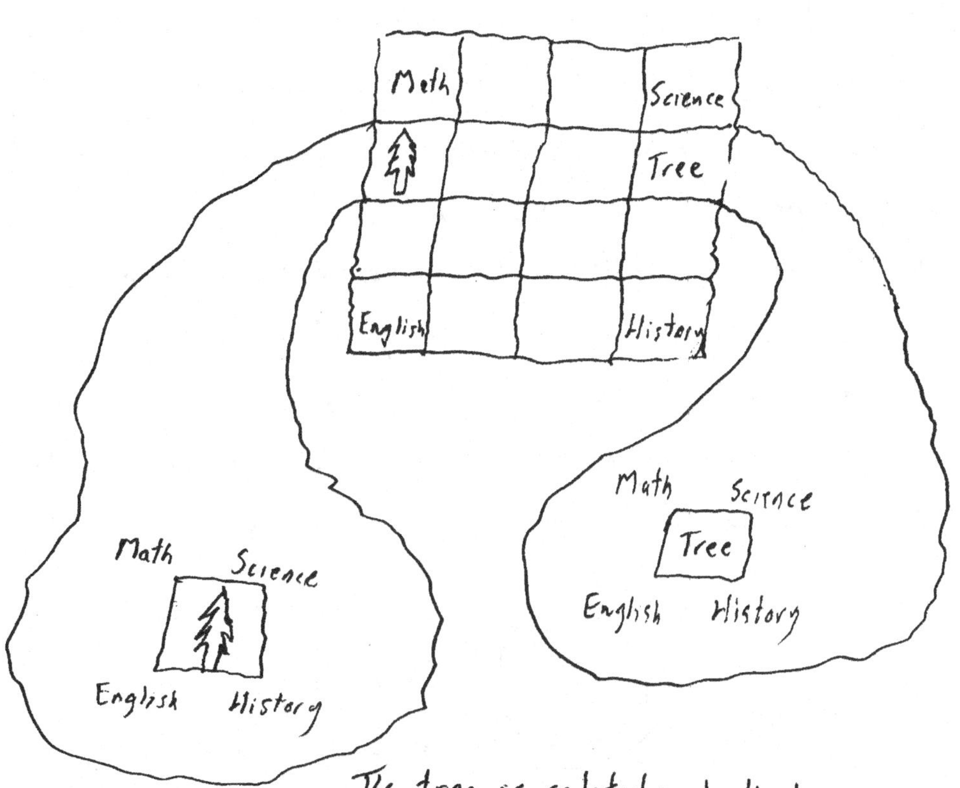

The tree is related in both lexicons, an image and a word to the four subject in a slots of the grid. It is here we weigh out the absurdities of reality in a nominal sence.

One can search or find any subject for a slot on the grid in the entire universe. Holding it in the grid and play with the rest of the tetraktys.

We can take a globe and run it past the grid and screen to learn and/or classify it into a catalog. There are dark and light catalogs.

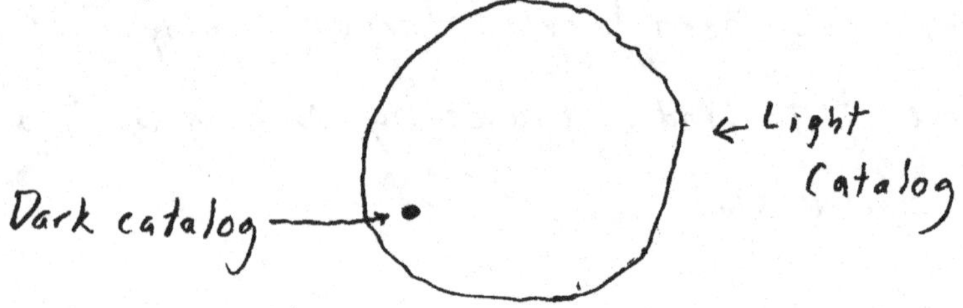

← Light Catalog

Dark catalog →

Here the dark catalog by importance is smaller then the virtue of the light catalog. These are both considered mandala's. In the likes we have good and evil catalogs. Can one tell by the sizes or nomina which is which? It's easier to use the larger one, though the smaller one can be used to cancel out evil by hiding it there. They are both great virtues.

This brings us to the mandala. It is a ring or circle which is used to put anything including the universe into to reflect an idea or seek answers to idea's. Here we hear the universe.

Mandala

We can put the stars or spiders in it or anything that comes to mind. We put things in it because it is a defined place instead of an open area without borders or endless dimensions of the mind

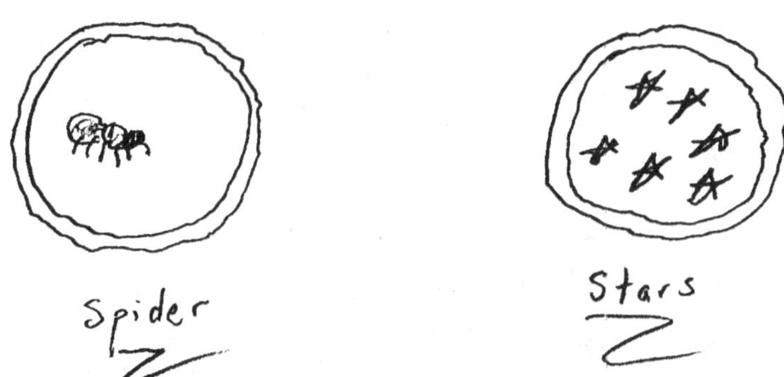

In the mandala we are able to play with the tetraktys and do what we want with the universe and subjects of subsistence in the imagination and the existence in the mind all within. It acts like a window, a text cannon in the likes.

Now put the screen, grid, and mandala together to enhance, invision and address problems we find throughout the affinities of time and space.

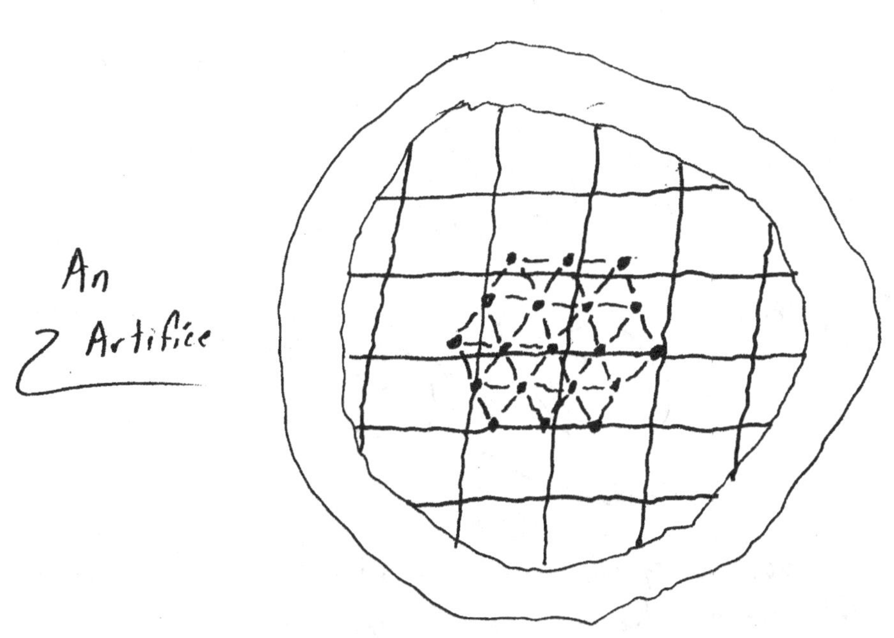

This is a tool by which we use to ready our skills. Take reading a book for instance. We use this tool to visualize in clarity the objectives of the book. The tetraktys is endless in the likes.

In this artifice we have a defined space for globes and idea's to enter our perception. Folks, this is a very advanced method and not easily obtained and what not. It will take you years to be useful to you, though when it does you'll enjoy it. I use them one at a time with the psyches for the most part keeping in mind that these are artifices. You can use anything, a tin can, a wheel within a wheel as your space you want to conject with.

Now lets look at the globes in time, space and place. They all fall into relevance of the address. Look at this globe and mandala:

Globe

Mandala

The globe and the mandala represents a subsistence within it. We single out idea's as subjects in this guild to better understand and get a grasp on the axioms in the universal and particular forms of materialism. Follow these is you can:

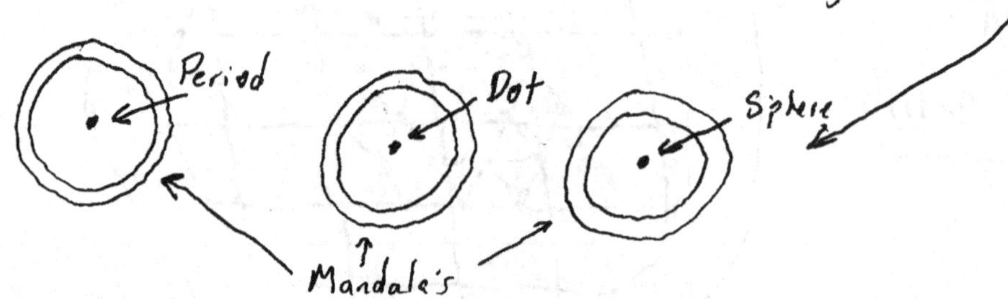

The period, dot and sphere change the physics of the mandala. Making sure that they are the only subsistence in view. Now folks think of a place and put a globe to work in your perception in the time, space and place. You can see your perception change with each word in these examples:

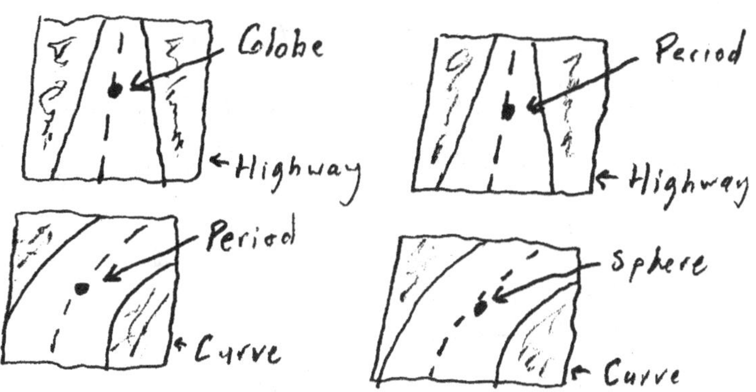

You can see through your perception that the globe, period, and sphere on the highway address different absurdities of that place. The word's serve their purpose in moving along the highway. When addressing the absurdity of the word defines the place. Take the globe into your hand (Ledgermain) and run it in front of you on the highway. Put some eloquence into it and change the subject from globe to period to sphere. Can you see it changes in perception of the enviorn (Agriculture).

The globe here is set in the imagination to subsist in one's triangle. Like objects in the mind they can do anything you can wit, afterall what kind of polymath are you? This gives one a surface to reflect apon in configuring something. Usually a piece of intellect they want to work on to learn something new, in the likes of a book or studying how to television works. Remember the screen can come up with a sharp image as one can roster using a bunch of triangles. It is here that one may put something in your imagination, visualizing and remembering them... Folks? Is memory of the mind or imagination? The mind is built up from the court and the imagination from reason. I ask this because it is a collection of both... Rapidity. Take a look at this:

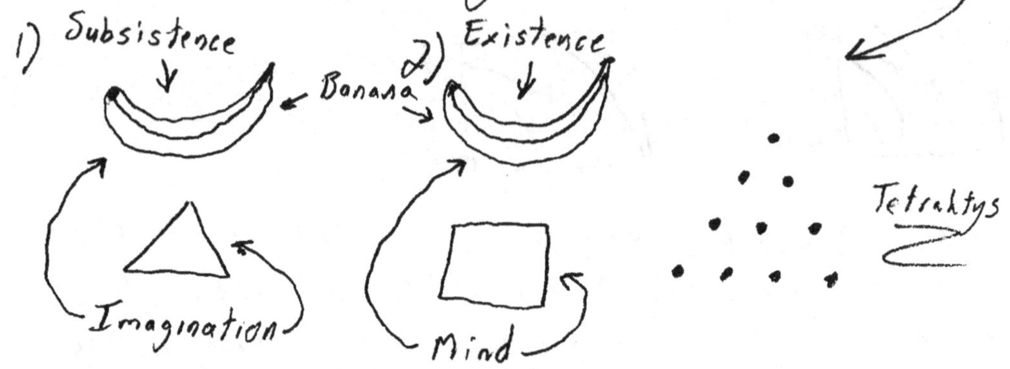

1) The imagination is an image with the subsistence of the banana.

2) The mind is the banana in physical form in front of your vision existing in the universe.

Does it take a mind to imagine or an imagination to mind? I know I just asked this, but I am sure they compliment each other somewhere, somehow. Have you ever heard of the dream arguement? Here, look at existence and subsistence in a tetraktys. Is it real or dream?

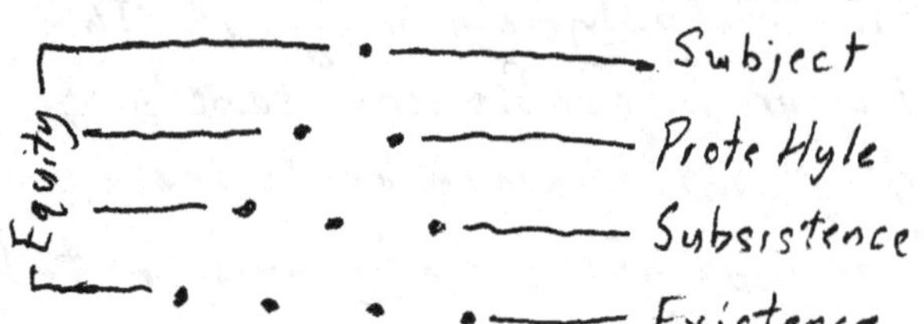

Existence is the universe to where subsistence is the

imagination. Prote Hyle is the mind over matter of the subject. It altogether is one equity in memorization of principle in elementary. We tend to store memory in the mind and remember in the imagination. Though it altogether works like a tetraktys.

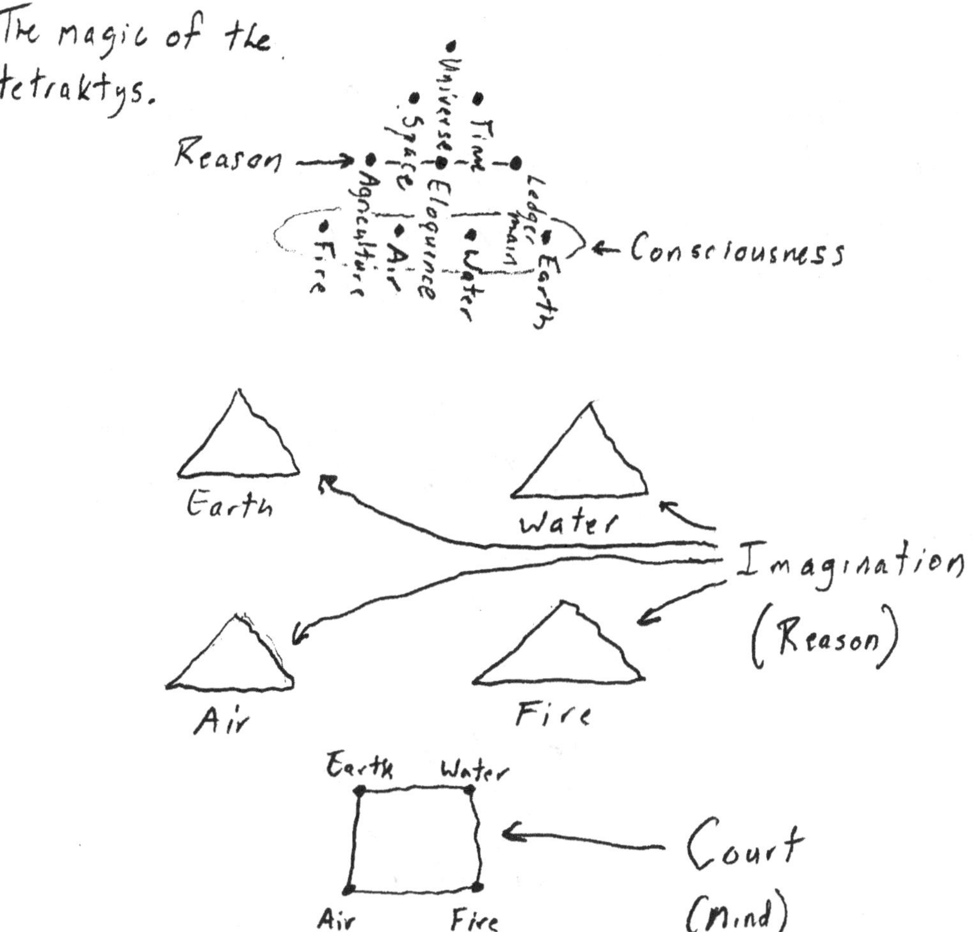

The triangles are the imagination (Dreamlike) and the square is existence (Reality), the real elements.

I associate everything I can wit in putting an idea down on a page. I've ran my eyes accross thousands of drawings and words in books. It's up to ones volition is my best bet. Use this book wisely and be entertained.

Well, I have faith that this book will enhance your wisdom and learning. It is just a model, something tangable in the imagination and mind. So now what do you think about this dot, folks?

Remember this is a representation of the universe. It will be your reference throughout your life in this guild. Like I said folks, this guild is unique. Brought up from History itself. Let the globes above our head's keep you safe and sound. They will always be the same in our wheel and continually change in the next. This book is your life and guide to the guild's etiquette. I know you'll read it more than once. Enjoy and be safe...

Spucket W. Knostic, 1989

Spucket Knostic

Here are some tetraktys for your own example, though the are far from perfect:

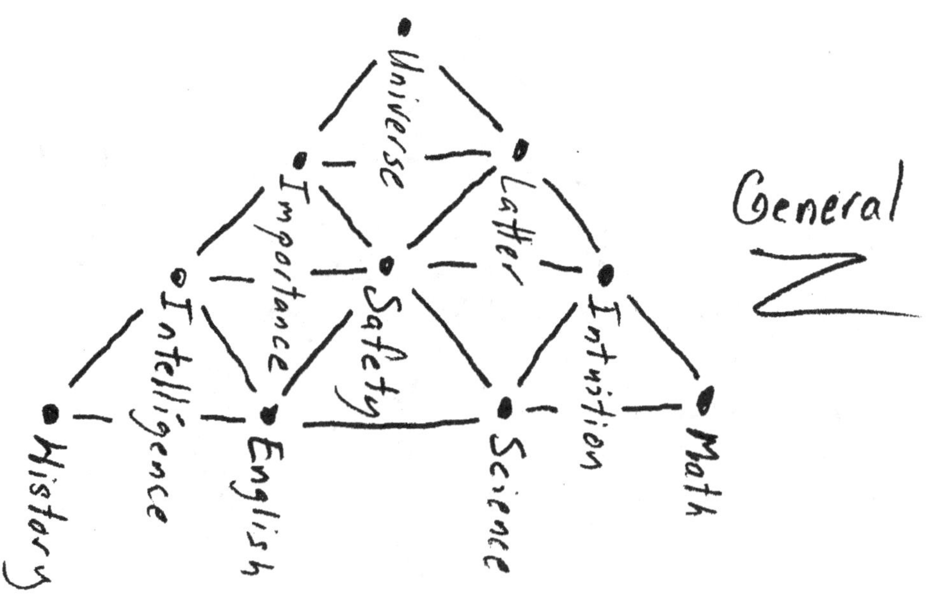
General
Universe
Latter
Importance
Safety
Intuition
Intelligence
History
English
Science
Math

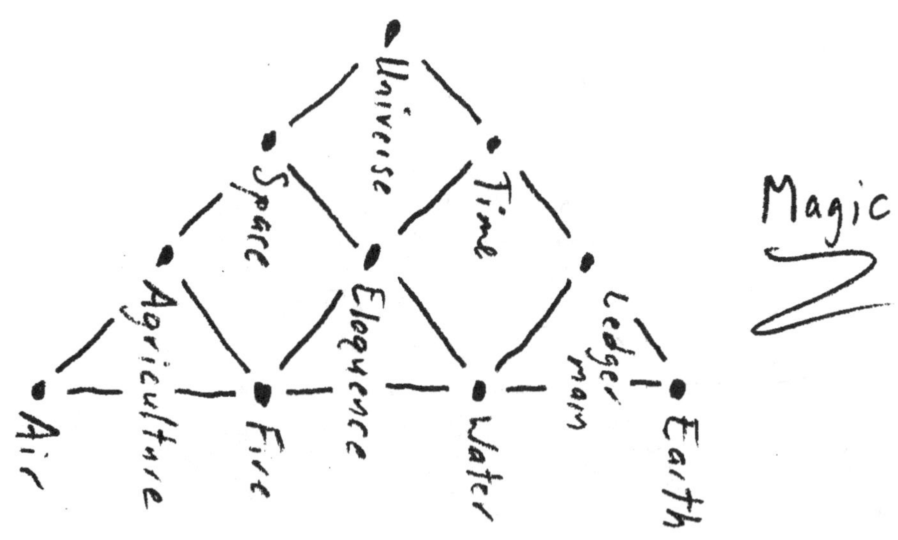
Magic
Universe
Space
Time
Agriculture
Eloquence
Ledger man
Air
Fire
Water
Earth

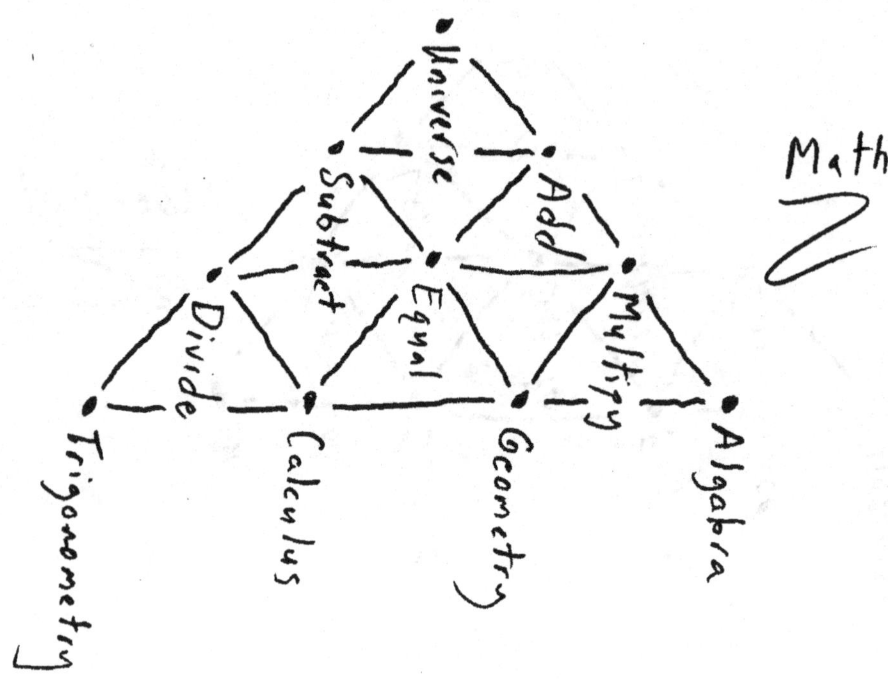
Math
Universe
Subtract
Add
Divide
Equal
Multipy
Trigonometry
Calculus
Geometry
Algabra

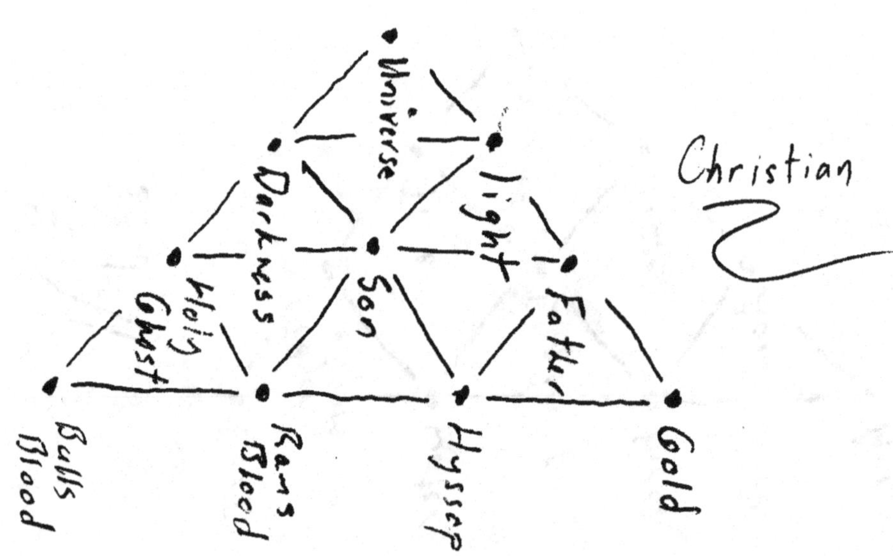
Christian
Universe
Darkness
light
Holy Ghost
Son
Father
Bulls Blood
Rams Blood
Hyssop
Gold

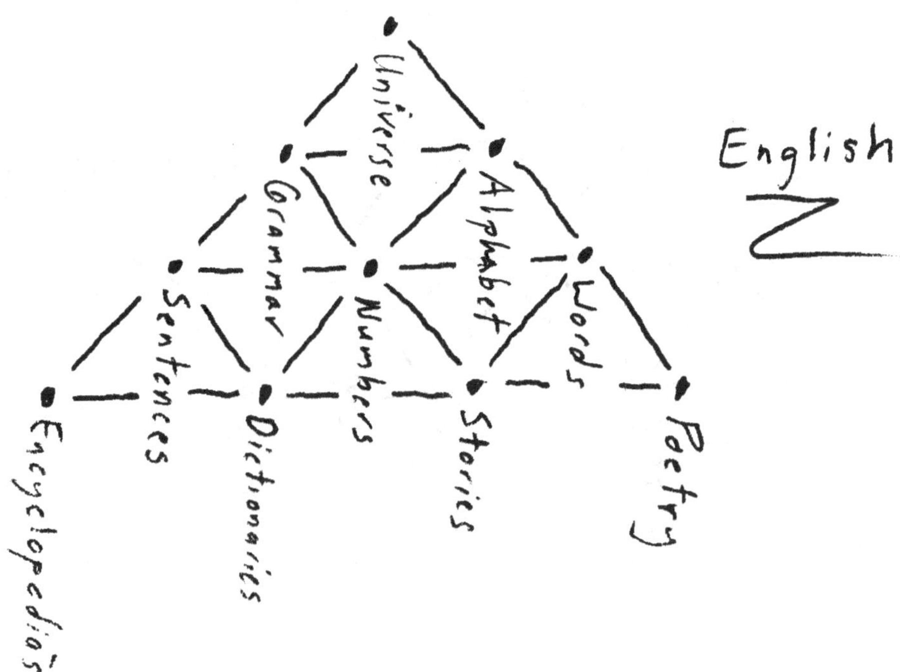
Universe
Grammar
Alphabet
Sentences
Numbers
Words
Encyclopedias
Dictionaries
Stories
Poetry
English

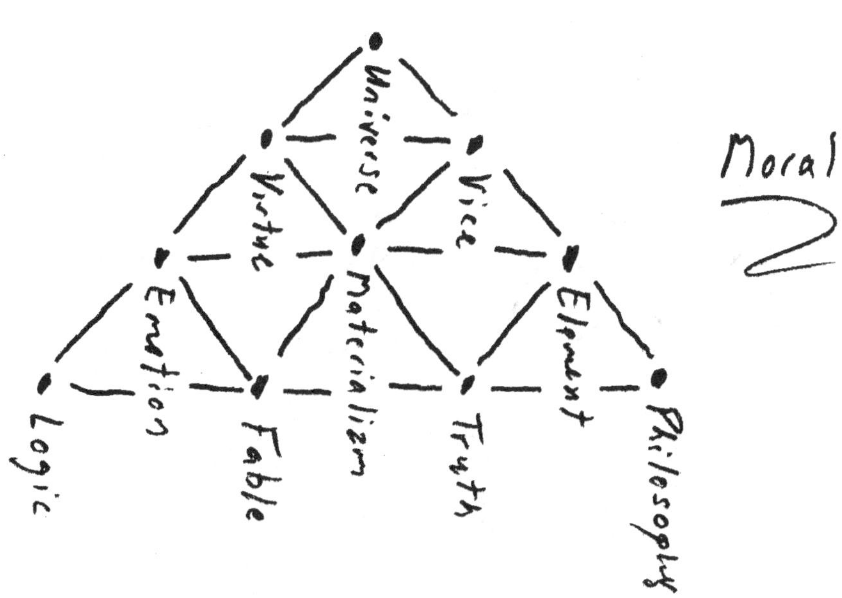
Universe
Virtue
Vice
Emotion
Materialism
Element
Logic
Fable
Truth
Philosophy
Moral

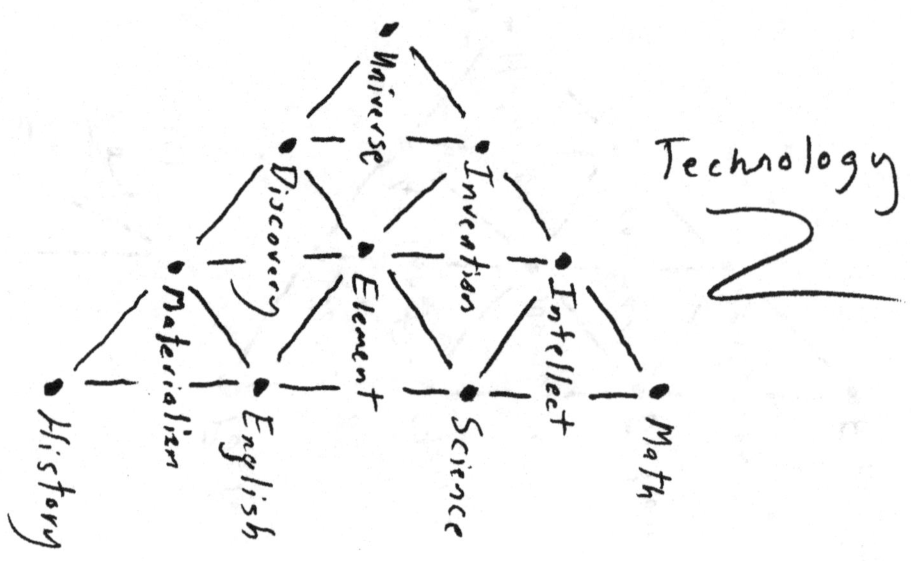
Technology
Universe
Discovery
Invention
Materialism
Element
Intellect
History
English
Science
Math

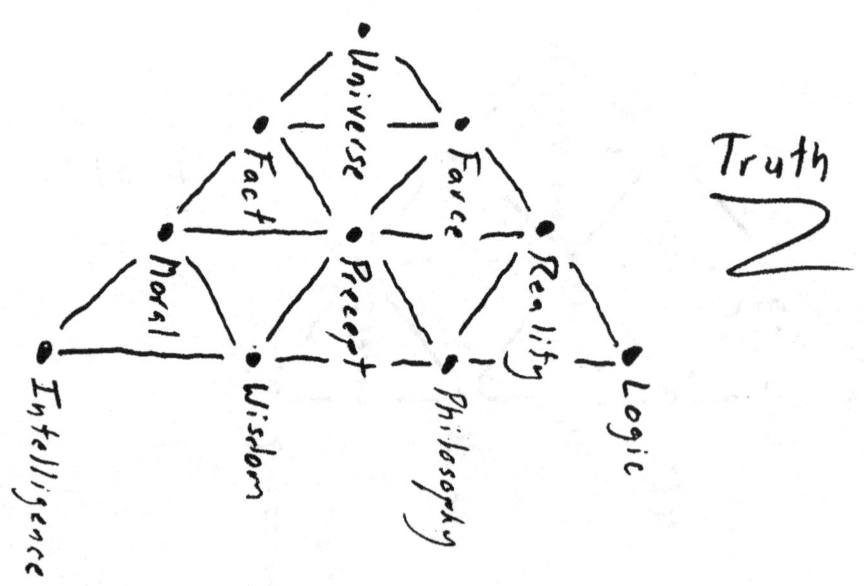
Truth
Universe
Fact
Force
Moral
Precept
Reality
Intelligence
Wisdom
Philosophy
Logic

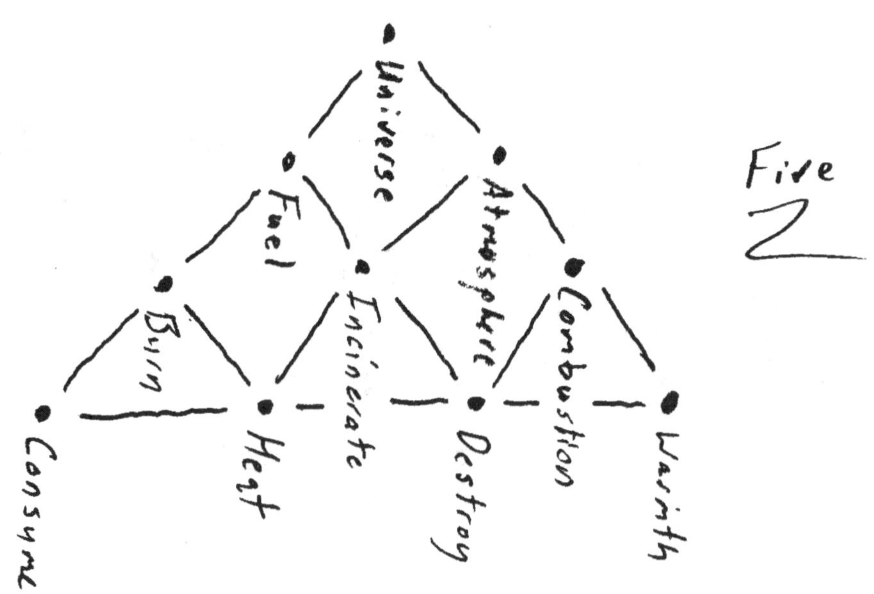
Fire
Universe
Fuel
Atmosphere
Burn
Incinerate
Combustion
Consume
Heat
Destroy
Warmth

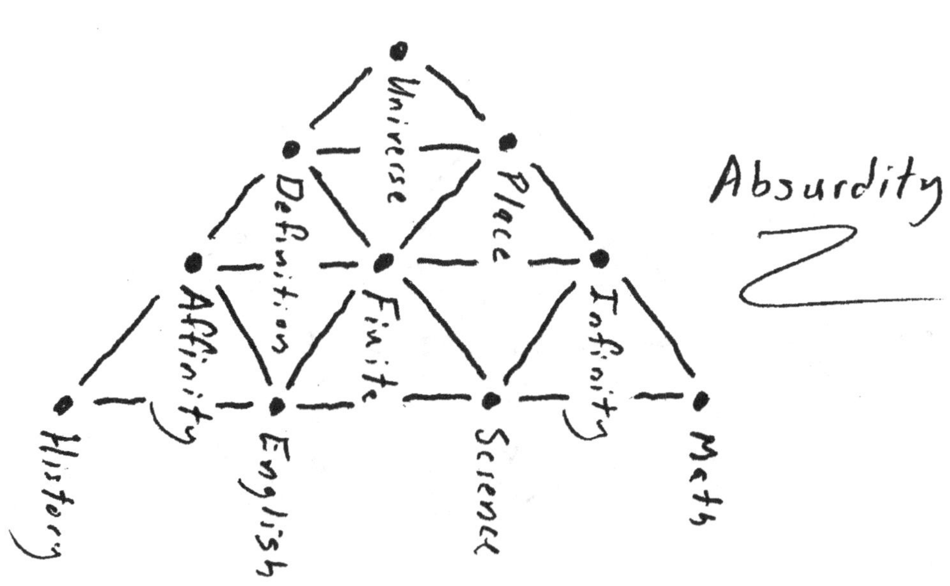
Absurdity
Universe
Definition
Place
Affinity
Finite
Infinity
History
English
Science
Math

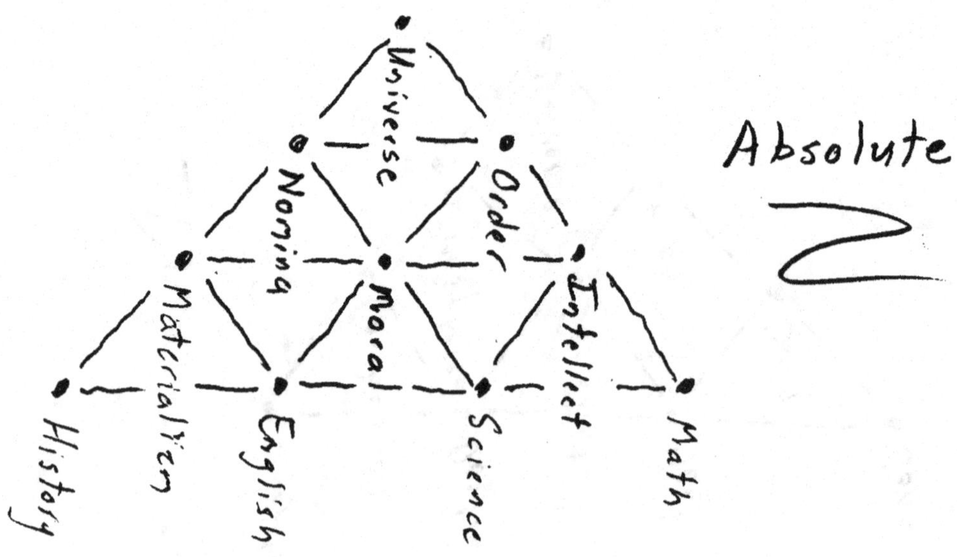
Absolute
Universe
Nomina
Order
Materialism
Moral
Intellect
History
English
Science
Math

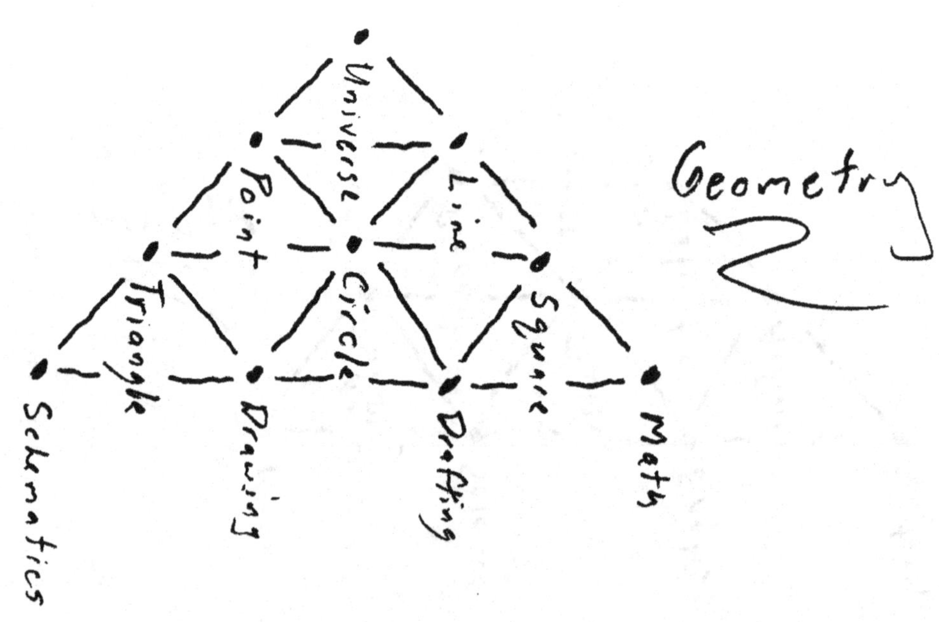
Geometry
Universe
Point
Line
Triangle
Circle
Square
Schematics
Drawing
Drafting
Math

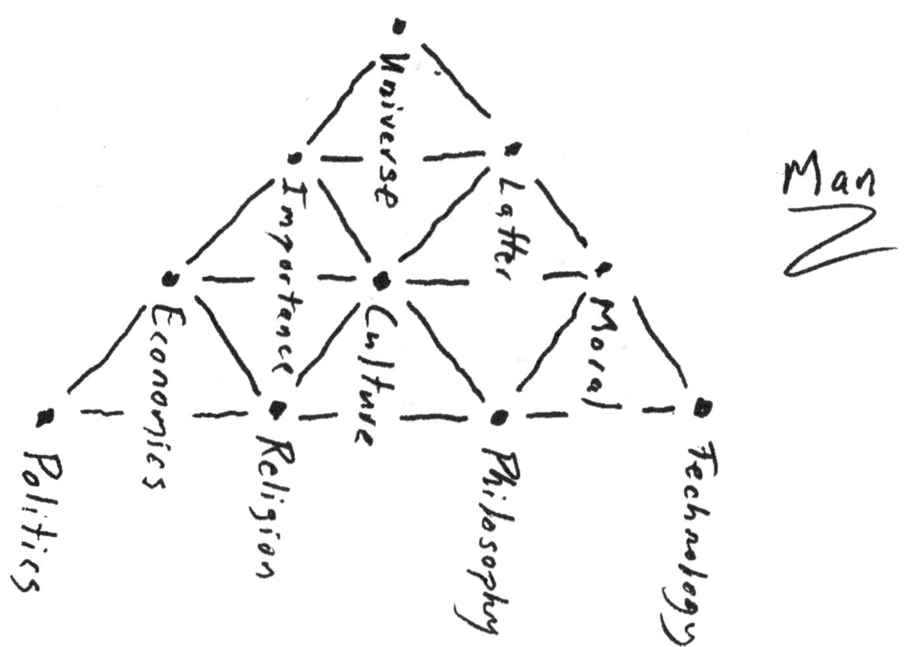
Universe
Latter
Importance
Culture
Moral
Economics
Religion
Philosophy
Technology
Politics
Man

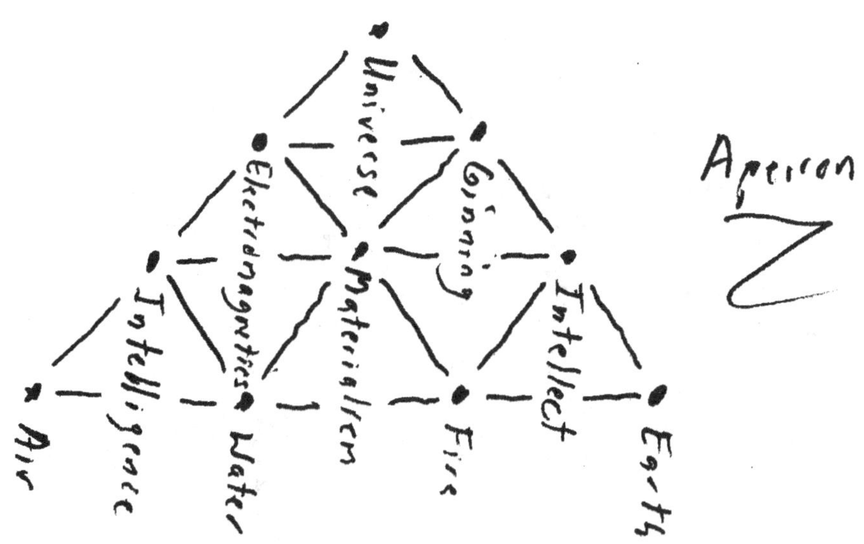
Universe
Ginning
Electromagnetics
Materialism
Intellect
Intelligence
Water
Fire
Earth
Air
Apeiron

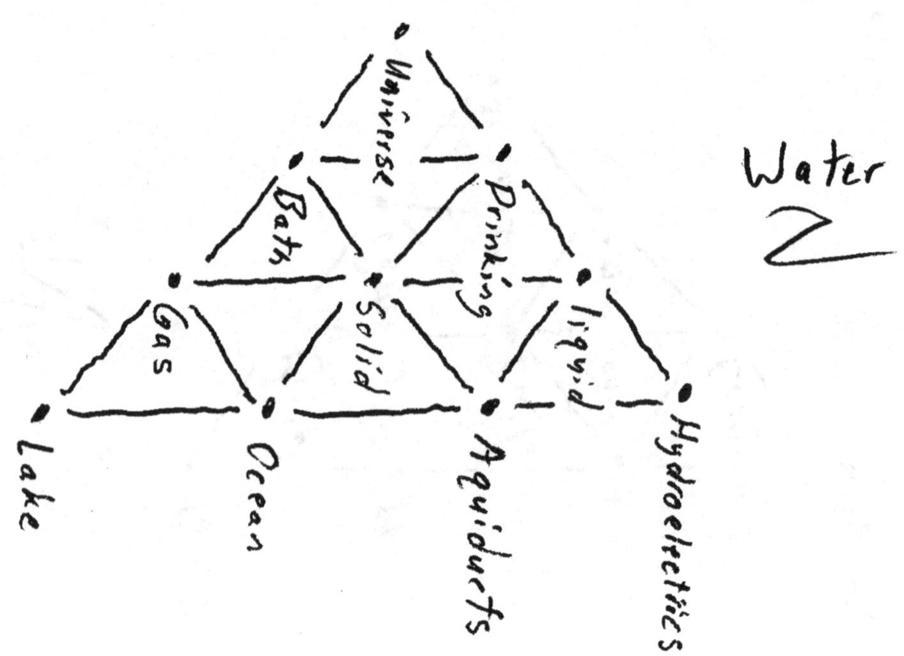
Water
Universe
Bath
Drinking
Gas
Solid
liquid
Lake
Ocean
Aquiducts
Hydroelectrics

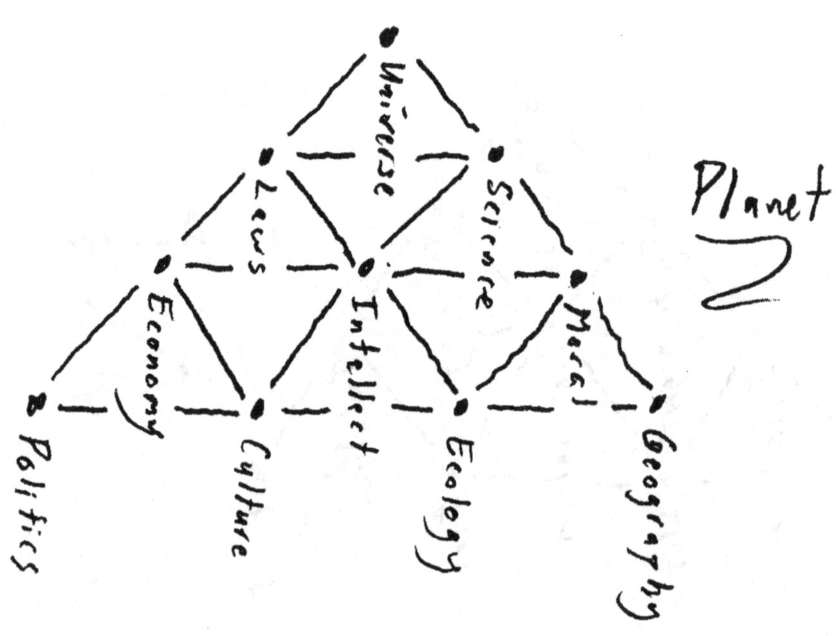
Planet
Universe
Laws
Science
Economy
Intellect
Moral
Politics
Culture
Ecology
Geography

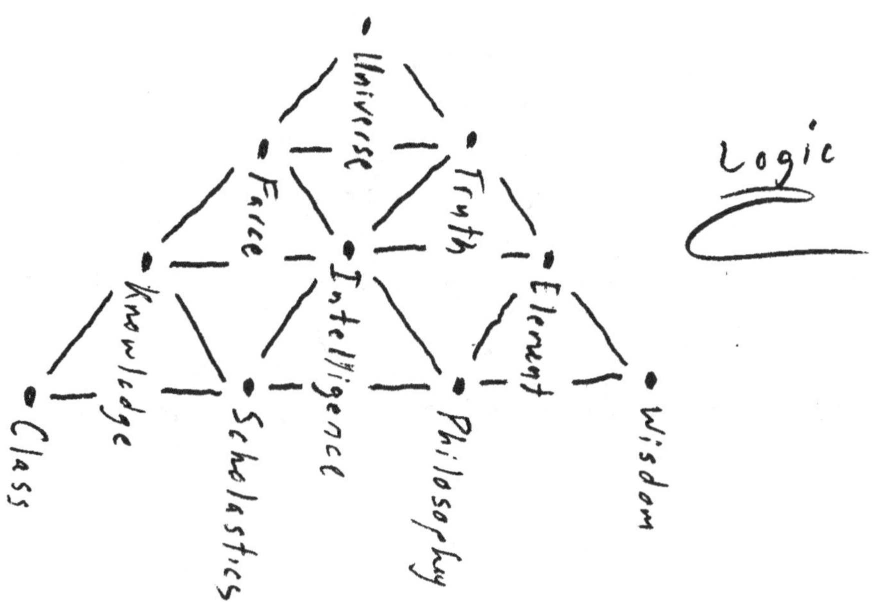
Universe
Force
Truth
Knowledge
Intelligence
Element
Class
Scholastics
Philosophy
Wisdom
Logic

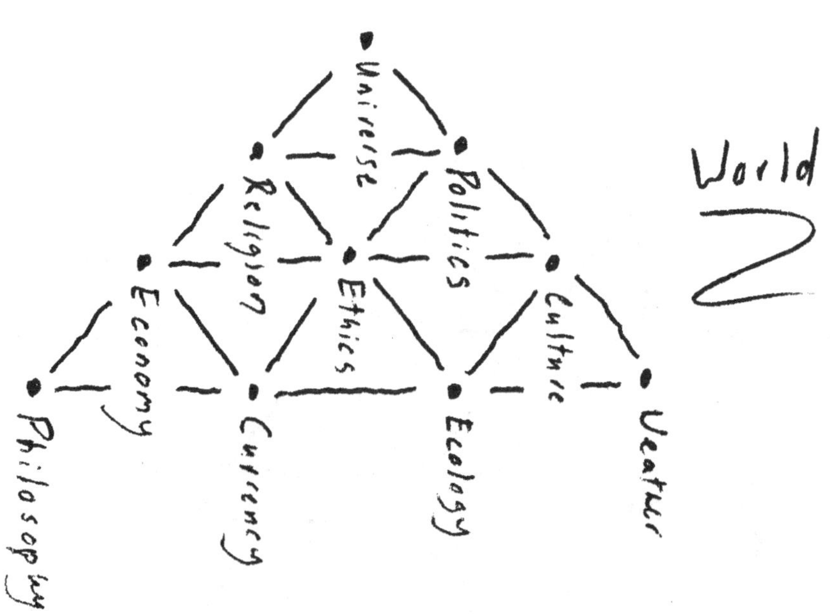
Universe
Religion
Politics
Economy
Ethics
Culture
Philosophy
Currency
Ecology
Weather
World

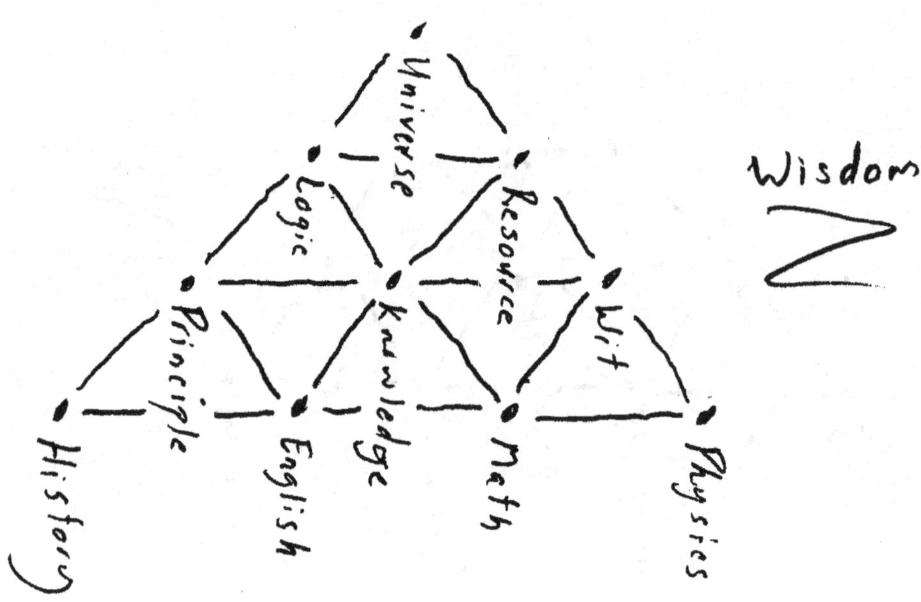
Wisdom
Universe
Logic
Resource
Principle
Knowledge
Wit
History
English
Math
Physics

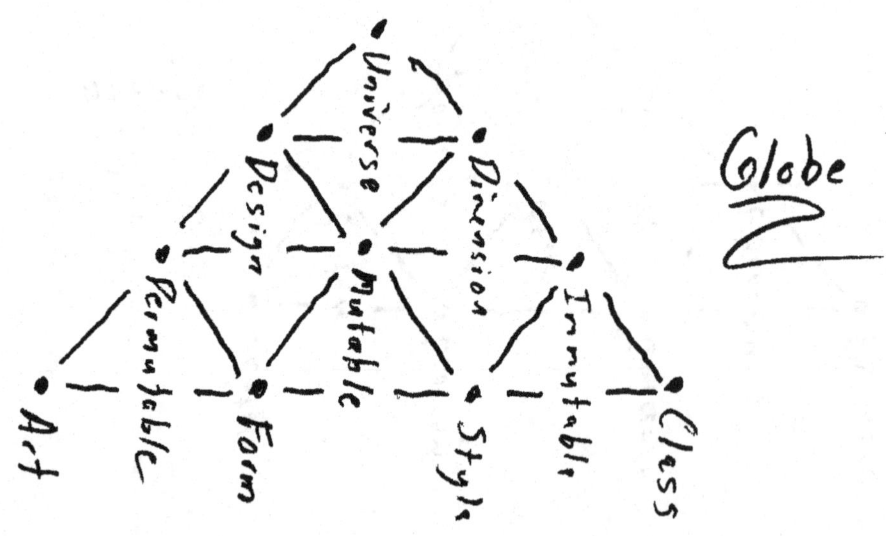
Globe
Universe
Design
Dimension
Permutable
Mutable
Immutable
Art
Form
Style
Class

ntellect 101,
Scrypt Knostic

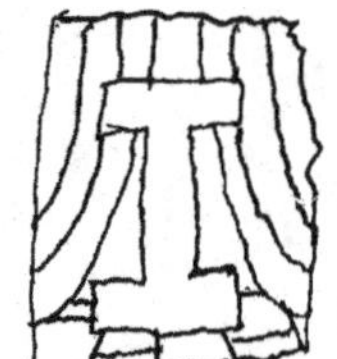
ntellect 101 by Scrupt Knostic,

I have brought these artifices of intellect together in this book to better my faculties in a lexicon of works. I understand that I have elaborated these things to the best of my knowledge to teach a perspective which will help man to obtain a vivid apprehension for the things in this universe. I am no master at these artifices though I do find it most at an elementary of principle. These are the basics for my intellect:

- Critical thinking
- Star Sheet
- Ciphers
- The tetraktys
- The tyriad perspective
- Reasoning the consciousness
- Globes above our heads
- Not
- One verse
- Classes
- The universal perspective
- absurdless
- The Clock of the universe
- Lines and precepts of the Bible
- A plenum for the image
- The dimensional pouch
- Faculty
- Prudence
- Liberty
- Lexicons
- Father, Son and the Holy Ghost

I'll go through the star sheet soon after critical thinking and lay out many ciphers. Each cipher is on the star sheet as a skill. I have put into use each of these artifices and with a little intuition they can be yours.

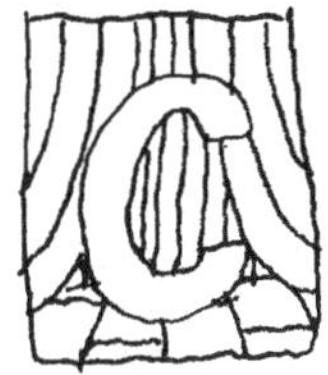

Critical thinking,

The first thing is to have an openning in the head separate from all other thoughts to put something in it. In the likes of a postulate as a standing point. To start something a person has a good feel about something they can grasp in the mind and body.

Brain
Separation
Postulate or open thought
All other thoughts

Then it is time to consider what one wants to think of and associate thoughts from there as they come.

Another way is to build thoughts in clusters and associate them then. The dots or shapes represent thoughts or ideas.

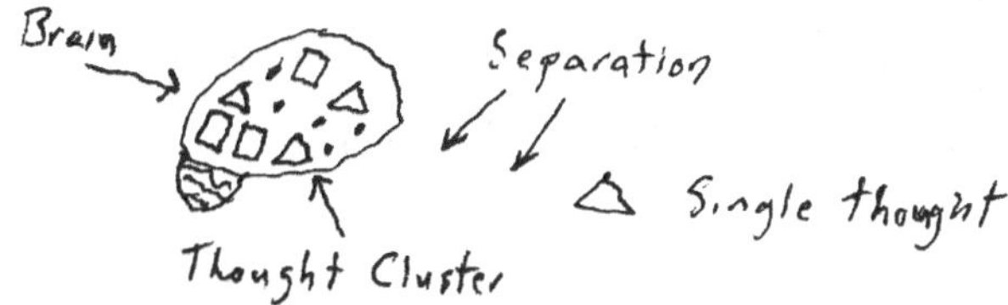

Then it is up to you to make up the skills you want. I put them on what I call a star sheet which lets me organize all types of skills on my mind at one time. Each skill is marked by a globe and each globe is in a cipher of its own. One has to savvy their definition in order to use them. Practicing the star sheet helps to understand the values of skills and words. It looks like this:

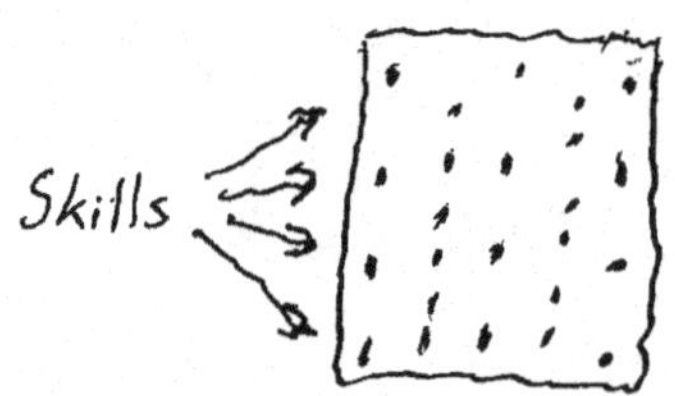
Skills

Star Sheet
26 globes
or dots

Anything that one can level and get better at can be a skill.

These globes in the mind collect information in a mart of commerce held up to the universe which I call feralling. A feral is a copious scalar where things tend to permute in the universal [illegible]ratio of the mind that they are in and belong to. Basically feralling is a type of worshipping that one can freely believe in the artifices and absurdities of the universe.

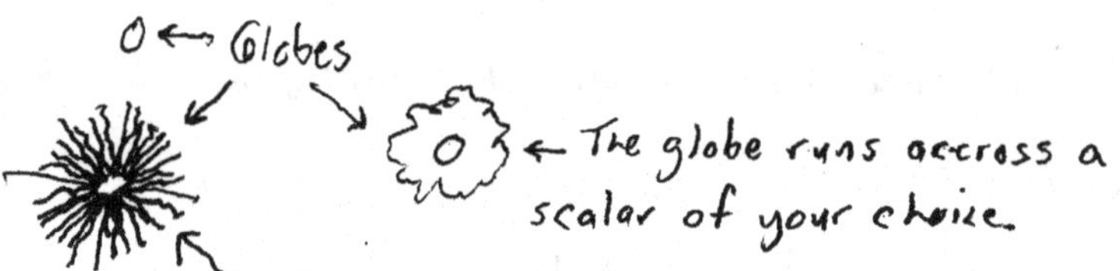
O ← Globes
← The globe runs accross a scalar of your choice.

Feralling takes the form of manipulation as one conjects information in seeking what they want. A globe can be feralled at any speed. Frozen still, it pauses to hold a thought and it moves with more thinking. The globe is kept in memory afterwards to be played again later as you pick another skill.

The permutation of a globe is up to ones ability to imagine things in its practice. One could do anything with these globe's depending on the level of skill one has aquired.

Each skill on the star sheet is considered an equity of the person as intellectual property. The star sheet in the mind looks like a quazar. ← Quasar

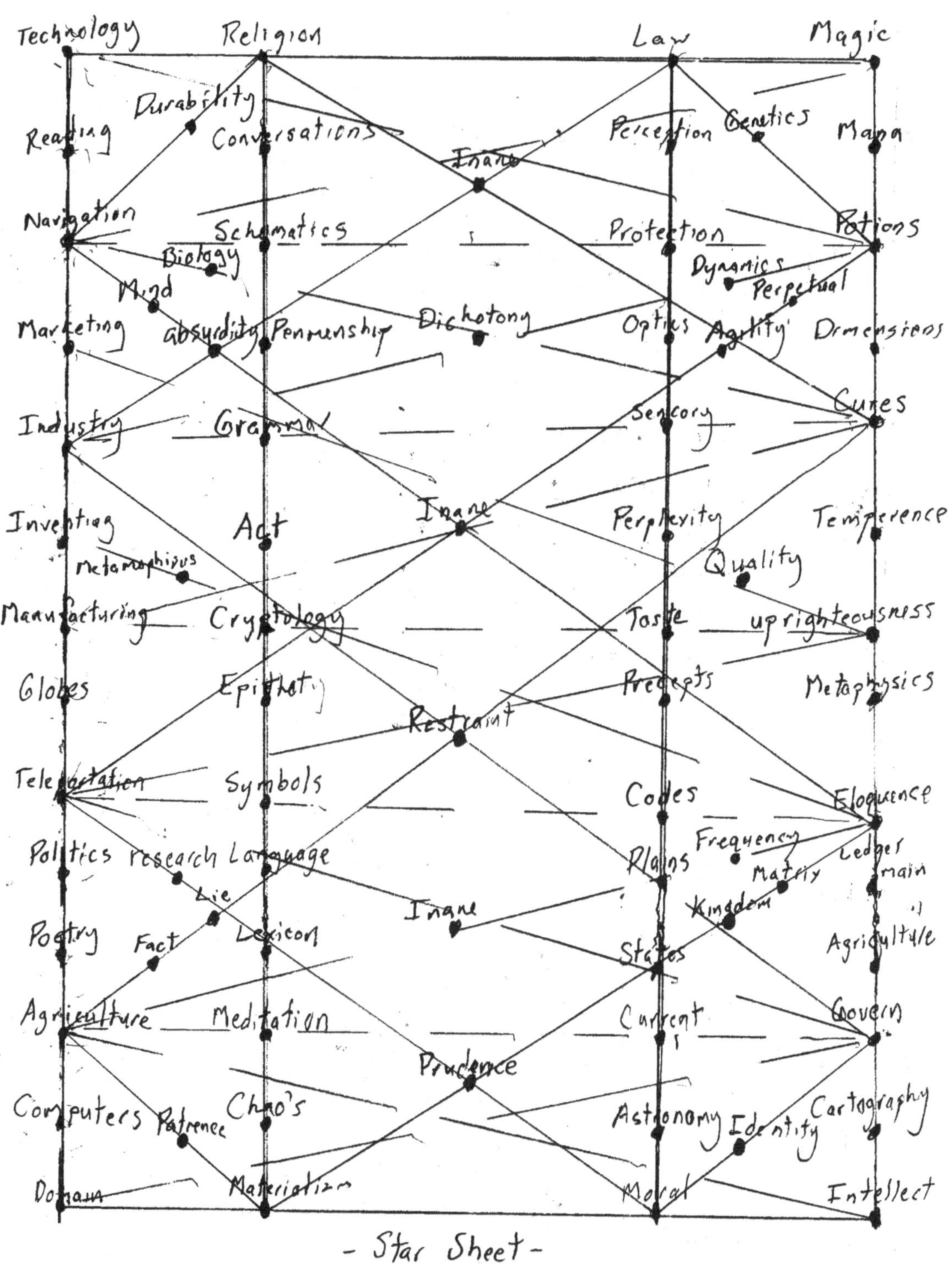
Technology
Religion
Law
Magic
Durability
Reading
Conversations
Inane
Perception
Genetics
Mana
Navigation
Schematics
Protection
Potions
Biology
Dynamics
Perpetual
Mind
Marketing
absurdity
Penmanship
Dichotomy
Optics
Agility
Dimensions
Industry
Grammar
Sensory
Cures
Inventing
Act
Inane
Perplexity
Temperence
metamorphisus
Quality
Manufacturing
Cryptology
Taste
uprighteousness
Globes
Epithet
Precepts
Metaphysics
Restraint
Teleportation
Symbols
Codes
Eloquence
Politics
research
Language
Plans
Frequency
Ledger
Matrix
main
Lie
Poetry
Fact
Lexicon
Inane
Kingdom
States
Agriculture
Agriculture
Meditation
Current
Govern
Prudence
Computers
Chao's
Astronomy
Identity
Cartography
Domain
Materialism
Moral
Intellect

- Star Sheet -

How ciphers work with the skills on the star sheet

Cipher - Fact

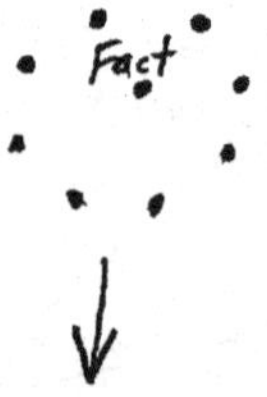

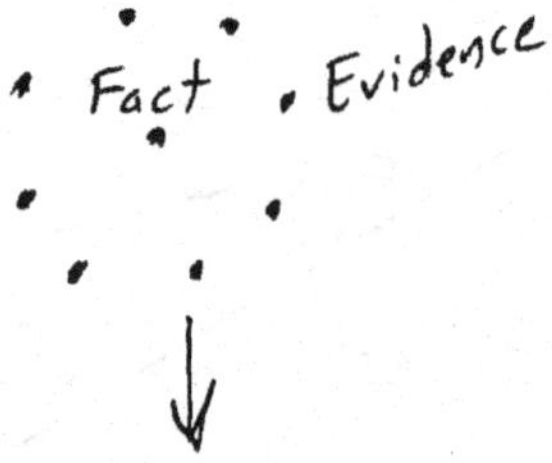

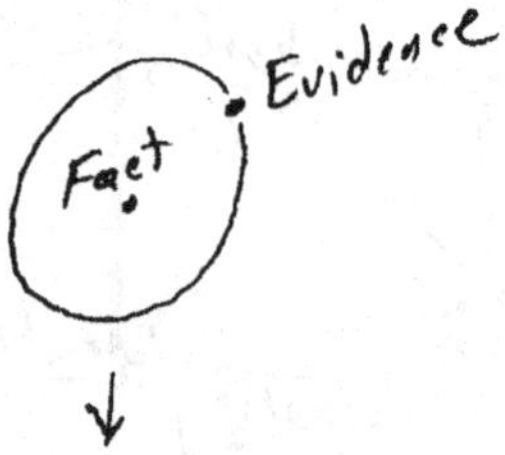

Fact · Fact · Evidence · Fact · Evidence

Fact globe with eight othe globes around it, describing and defining the current of Fact

Fact with one globe identified as evidence. It brings clues the the word fact.

Evidence with all the heuristics to make a true statement or write up a paper.

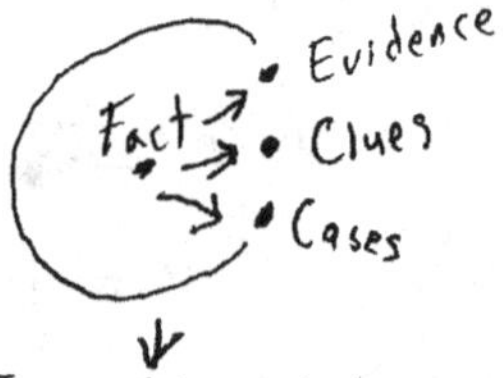

Fact · Evidence · Clues · Cases

History · Psychology · Evidence · Clues · Cases · Science · Weapons · Tools

In adding to the cipher Fact turns into lead after lead.

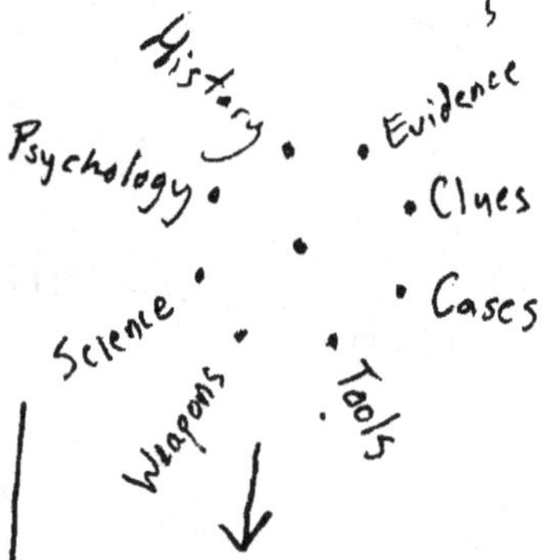

Associate the leads and questions to solve the matter.

Determine the Facts

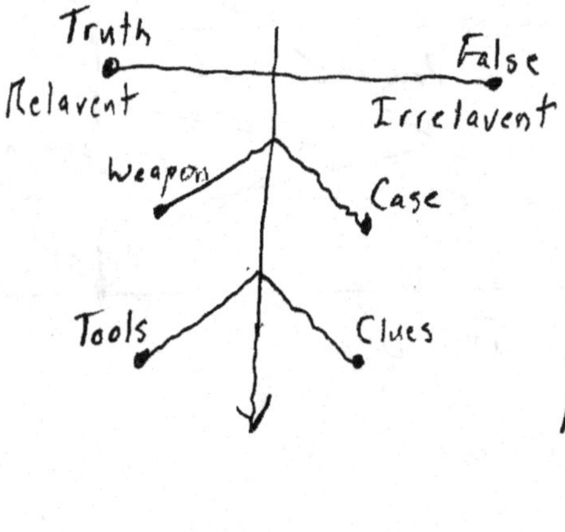

Truth · False · Relavent · Irrelavent · Weapon · Case · Tools · Clues

And then draw up in assocition the paper or story.

Cipher's expand ones knowledge of something.

Modern ways have come a long way. Detail is essential along with comfort in the world today...

Bond with the greatest of ease in all walks of life. You'll find your charisma paying for any damage. Be safe...

When a subject comes about these institutions deal with the congress for a government system. Obey the Law...

An affinity in the element shows the prudence in the heuristic. Nothings more powerful than the alphabet. Spell out your wishes...

-Cipher- Reading

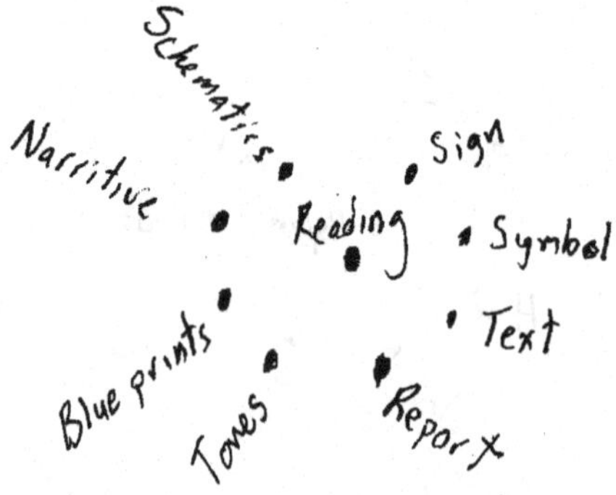

Schematics • Sign • Narritive • Reading • Symbol • Blue prints • Text • Tones • Report

This is a skill one can not get along without in the real world...

-Cipher- Durability

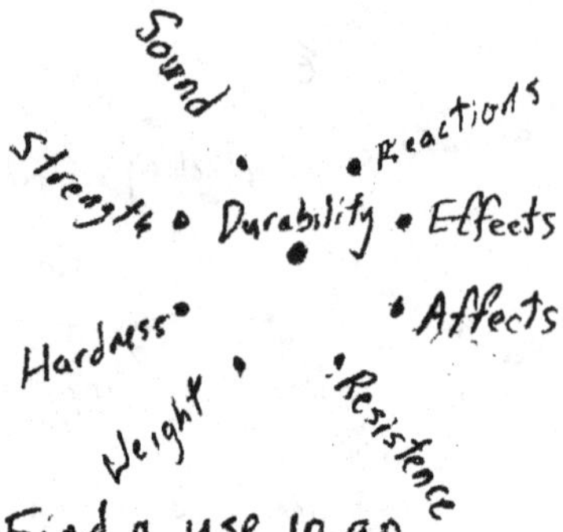

Sound • Reactions • Strength • Durability • Effects • Affects • Hardness • Weight • Resistence

Find a use in an element and put it to use in any enviorn you wish. Seek out its prudence...

-Cipher- Conversion

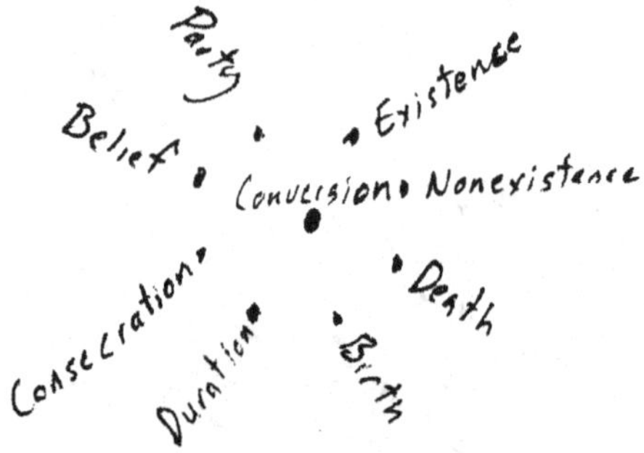

Party • Existence • Belief • Conversion • Nonexistance • Consecration • Death • Duration • Birth

Seek all the diaspora of the affinities of the world to find truth...

-Cypher- Inane

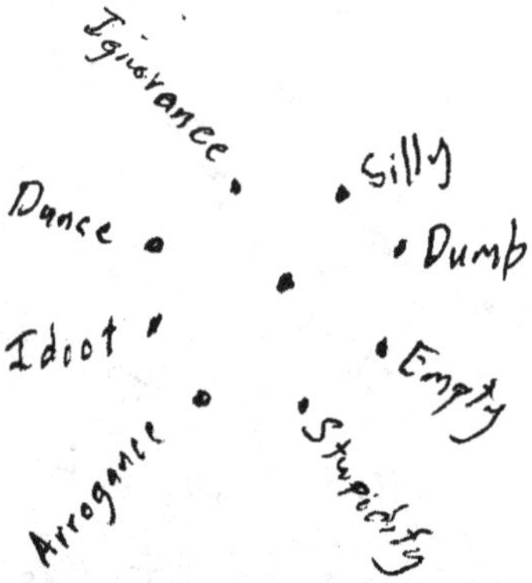

Ignorance • Silly • Dance • Dumb • Idiot • Empty • Arrogance • Stupidity

We have all had these things happen to us, though I like to look into them as a study...

- Cipher - Perception

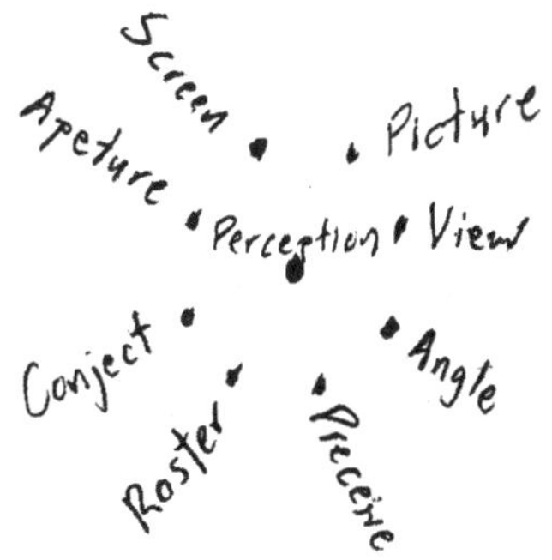

Screen • • Picture
Apeture • Perception • View
Conject • • Angle
Roster • • Preceive

Each verse of a thing described down to its nomina gives us the full exposure...

- Cipher - Genetics

Modifacations • • Traits
Disease • Genetics • Characteristics
Amunity • • Genes
Strengths • • Weaknesses

The Classifacations of biotic nature is the apex of the traits and characteristics of genes...

~ Cipher - Mana

Fire • • Space
Air • Mana • Static
Water • • Dynamics
Earth • • Agriculture

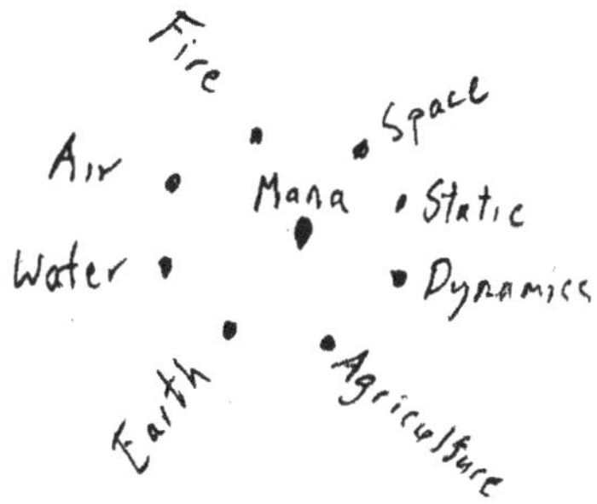

Energy in any form has its uses in the enviorn of the universe for each speck in one's eye...

- Cipher - Navagation

Compass • • Navy
Cartography • Navigation • Oceanography
• Ships
Constelations • • Craft
Fishing •

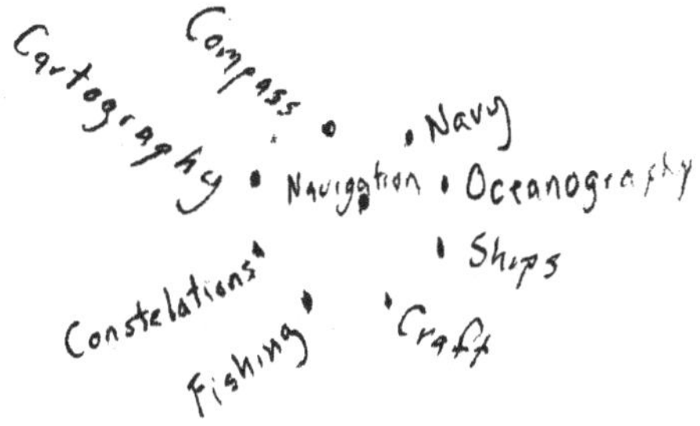

One must know the sea's as if one was born a fish. In the likes a captain is the head of this enviorn...

-Cipher- Schematics

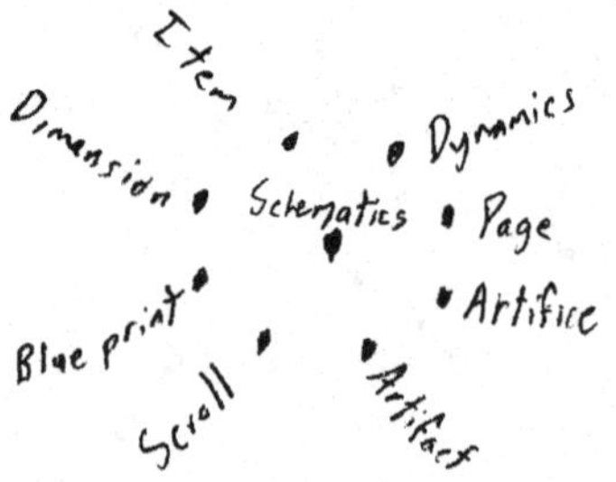

Item
Dimension
Dynamics
Schematics
Page
Artifice
Blue print
Scroll
Artifact

In the use of the heuristic we find a prudence with an idea in the enviorn of the situation...

-Cipher- Protection

adverb
Preposition
Verb
Protection
Conjunction
Pronoun
Interjection
Noun
Adjective

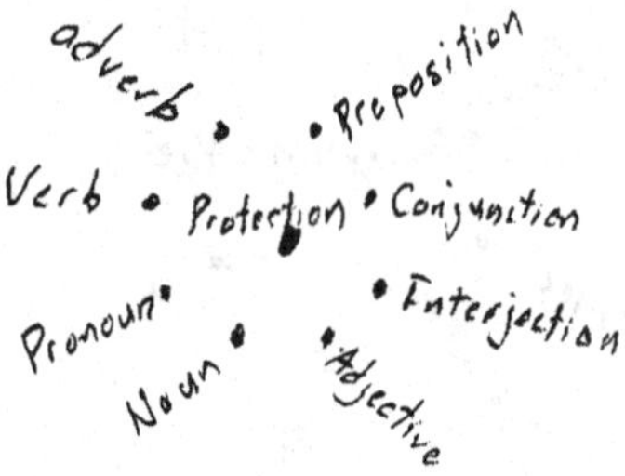

This lets one choose words to seek safety in a situation by understanding the language structure...

-Cipher- Potions

Health
Cure
Poison
Potions
Healing
Fatigue
Strength
Stamina
Elixers

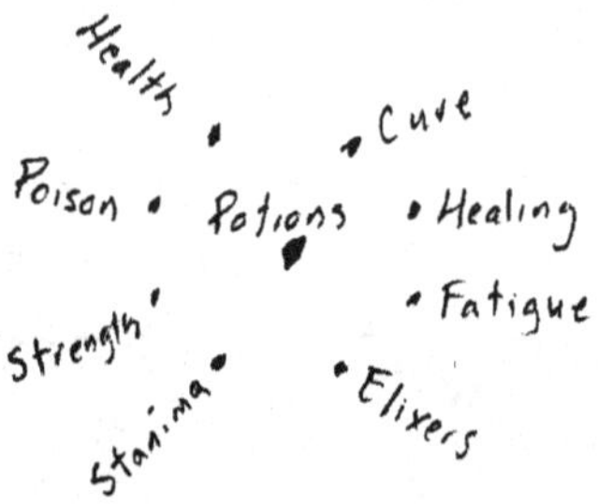

These are made to suit every need in any situation. Some are a common and some are very rare...

-Cipher- Marketing

History
Sublime
Demand
Marketing
Rarity
Cost
Product
GDP
IPO

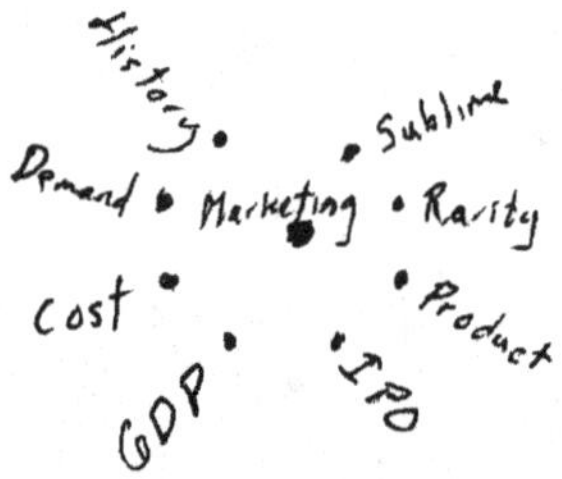

Seek in the supply and demand. Finely tune your dicker. Sell the best and don't settle for less...

–Cipher– Mood

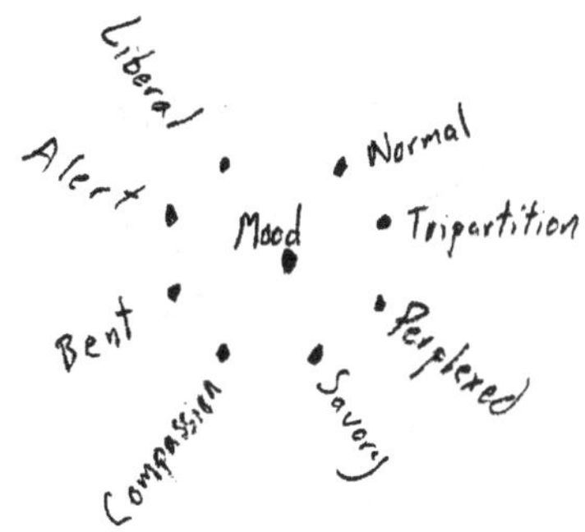

React with affections to overcome depression and anxiety in the effects and affinities of the enviorn...

–Cipher– Absurdity

Order
Chaos
Absolute
Absurdity
Absurdless
Precept
Scalar
Prosaic
Stupidity

Find the sentiment or subsistence of a subject in its heuristics to the prudence of commerce...

–Cipher– Biology

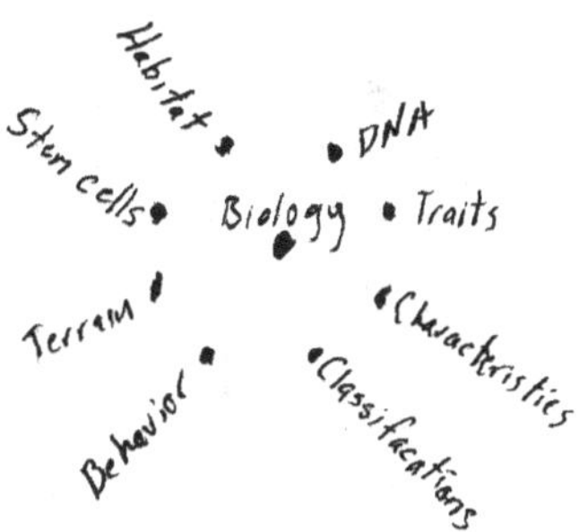

Find the life of the planet and seek how it works to enhance the study of evolution...

–Cipher– Penmenship

Characters
Quills
Scribe
Penmanship
Cartography
Type
Motifs
Pencil
Pen

Fashion letters, draughts, schematics and reports to a fine uniqueness showing your skill to articulate the language...

-Cipher- Dichotomy

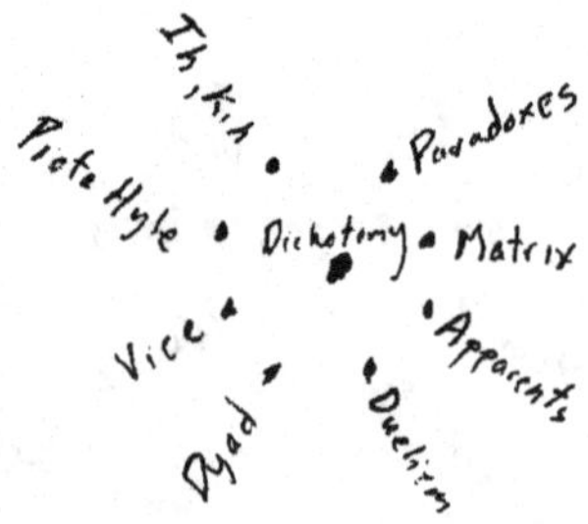

Ihikia • Paradoxes • Proto Hyle • Dichotomy • Matrix • Vice • Apparents • Dyad • Duelism

When a pair of things are at their affinities they may become perplexed to where we even them out...

-Cipher- Dynamics

Maps • Color • Channeling • Dynamics • Current • Globes • Deity • Schematic • Government

Determine the likes of the subject and find the basis of its energy in its deconstruction...

-Cipher- Optics

Electronic • Magical • Scientific • Optics • Lenses • Gems • Perception • Crystals • Tint

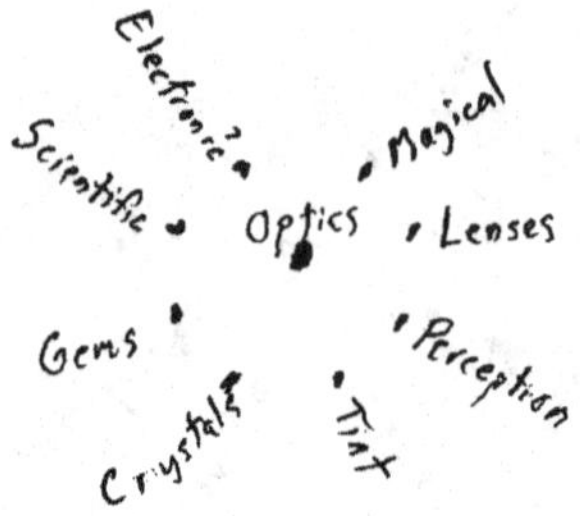

To hear with your eyes in a frequency your perspective comes to a clarity in a plenum of sight...

-Cipher- Perpetual

Monad • Infinities • Monogeny • Perpetual • Death • ginning • Life • reaction • Conversion

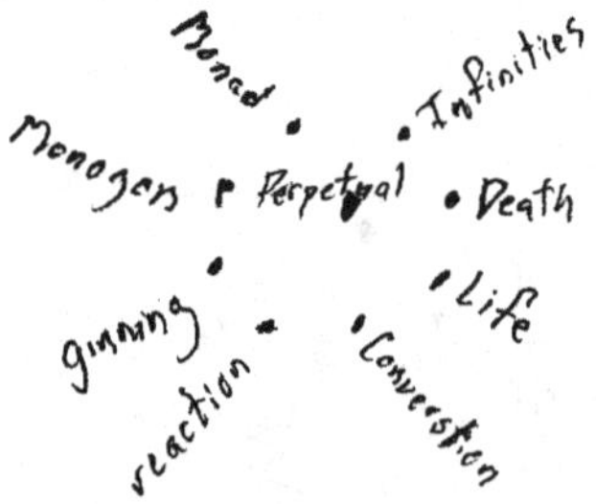

Science and Philosophy of horology of the ages never cease in the clock of the universe, anything may happen...

– Cipher – Agility

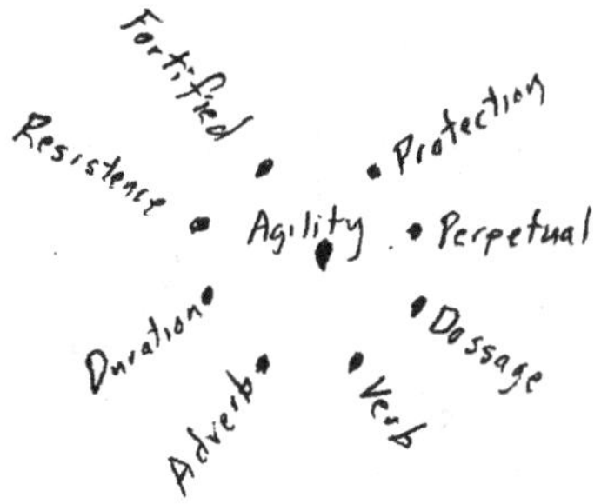

Fortified
Protection
Resistence
Agility
Perpetual
Duration
Dossage
Adverb
Verb

Find the importance of endurance of the subject. Ask yourself if I can make it or not...

– Cipher – Industry

Music
Serence
Architecture
Industry
Resources
Movies
Supplies
Mining
Drilling

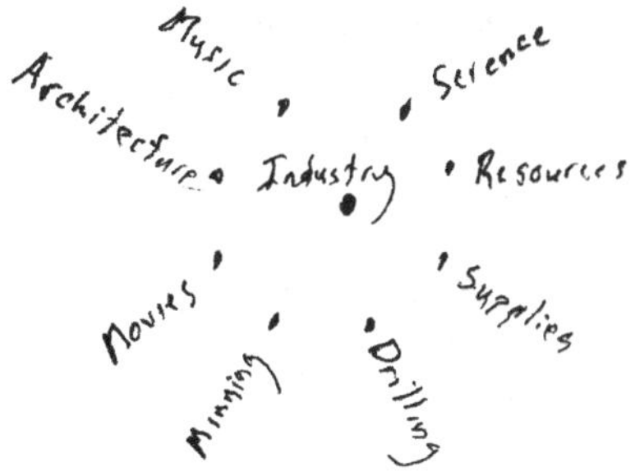

What drives the economy shows the supply and demand of the market...

– Cipher – Dimension

Ratio
Measurement
Static
Dimension
Delineation
Dynamics
Size
Type
Form

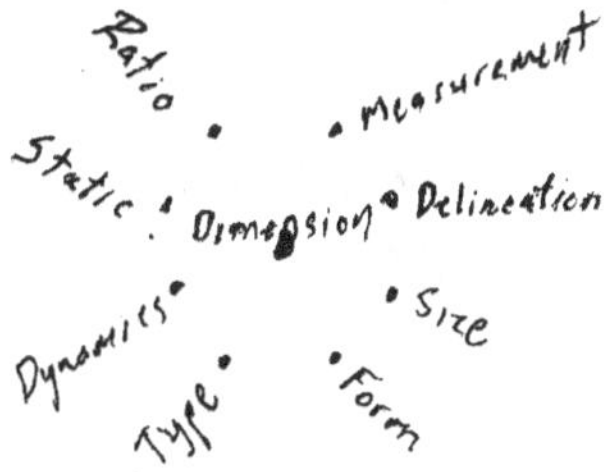

When viewing the nature of the mind or imagination we look at it in a narrative to the language...

– Cipher – Grammar

Adverb
Interjection
Verb
Grammar
Conjunction
Pronoun
Preposition
Noun
Adjective

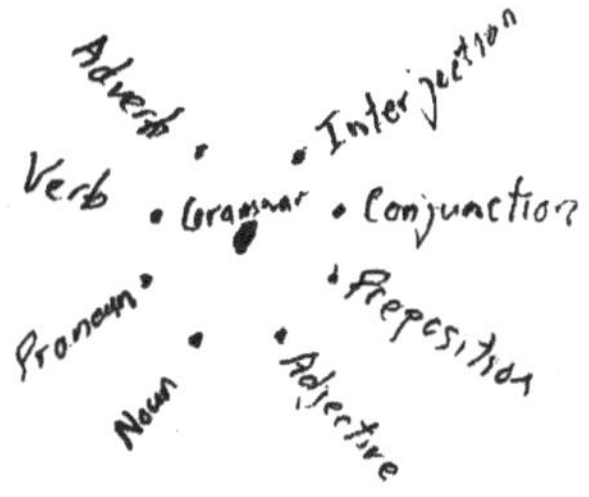

One of the most powerful tools today if one can master them one may be at freedom...

-Cipher- Sensory

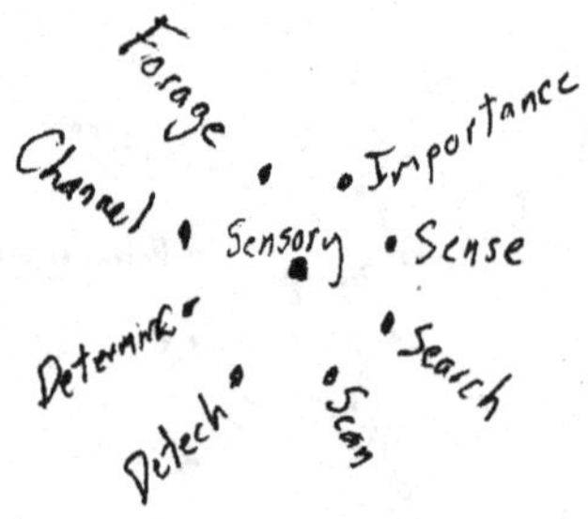

Forage • Importance
Channel • Sensory • Sense
Determine • Search
Detech • Scan

Open and close
the mind to feed
of the narrative in the
enviorn of the universe...

-Cipher- Cures

Pills • Plants
Potions • Cures • Elements
Alphabit • Absurdity
Apologies • Hands

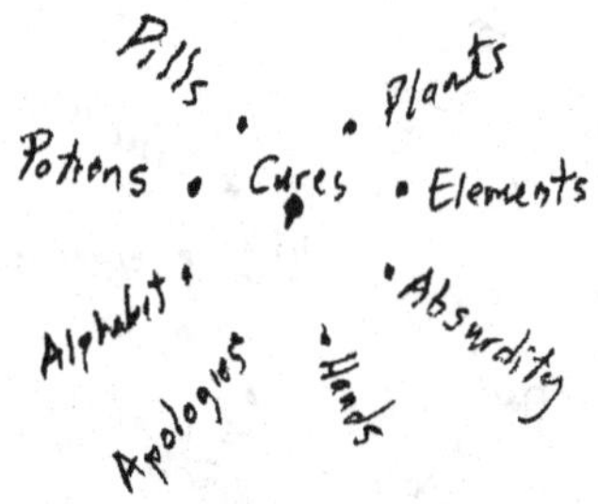

Determine the malady
and treat it. This word is
the enigma for medicine,
there is a large need in it...

-Cipher- Inventing

Law • Industry
Schematics • Inventing • Marketing
Resourcing • Manufacturing
Metaphysics • Economy

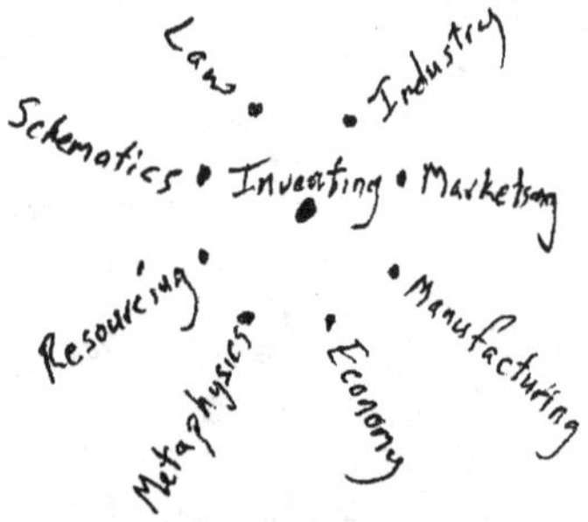

Tinker with all
the perplexity and resources
then will the charisma
into some cash...

-Cipher- Act

Prudence • right
Ethics • Act • Wrong
Custums • Morality
Policy • Blessing

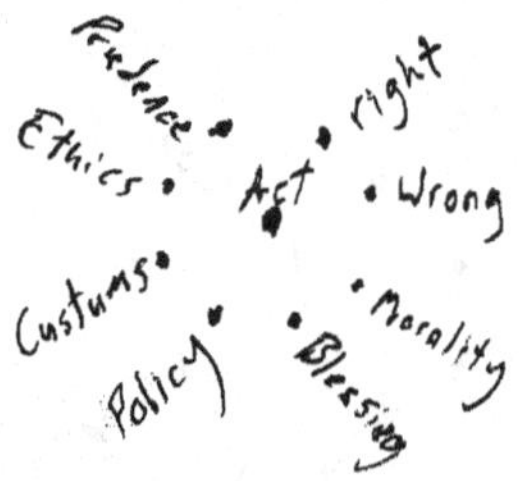

The lessons were
made to be comfortable
for each and all to follow
in the steps of the
greats and saints...

-Cipher- Perplexity

Use in the utmost difficulty and sophisticated mind, imagination and articulation...

-Cipher- Temperence

Making a form one might need in the prudence of importence in a situation. Keep cool...

-Cipher- Manufacturing

A product one picks need to be high on the supply and demand in order to be accepted...

-Cipher- Cryptology

Find the heuristic or keys and cure the unknown sophisticated puzzle of the nomenclature...

- Cipher- Metamorphisus

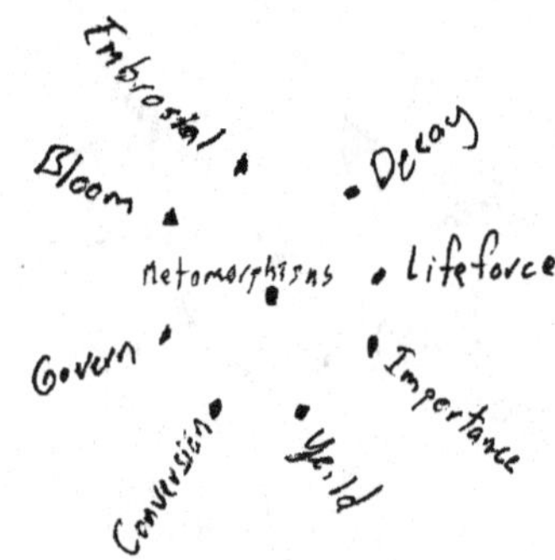

Find the building blocks of evolution with the subject to ensure the apex of its scholastic...

- Cipher- Uprighteousness

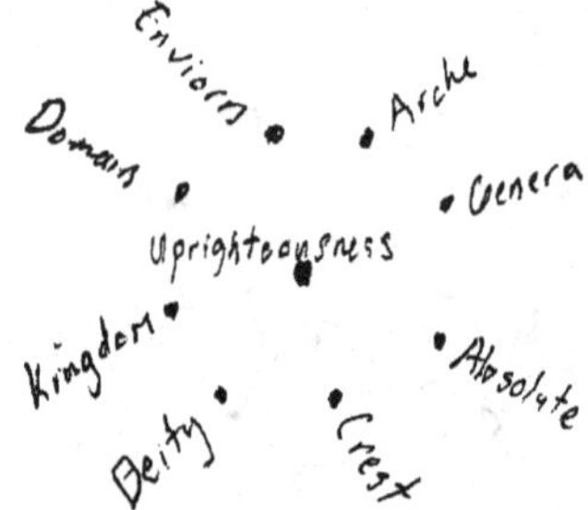

Endeavour through the faction to determine the customs and then encounter them a long the way. Be safe...

- Cipher- Taste

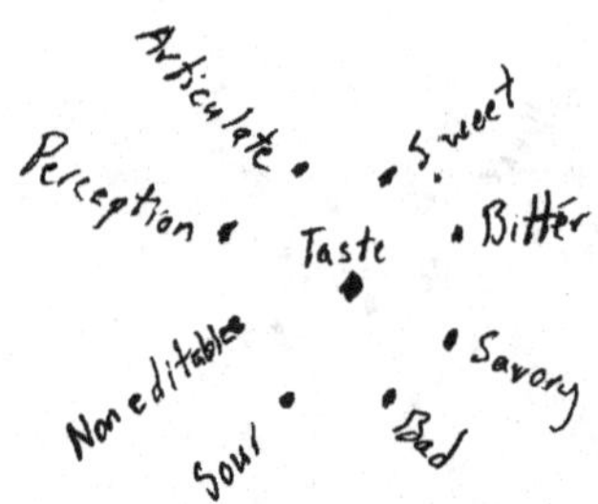

Determine the effects of eating any thing around you and develop an appetite for it. Dig in...

- Cipher- Globes

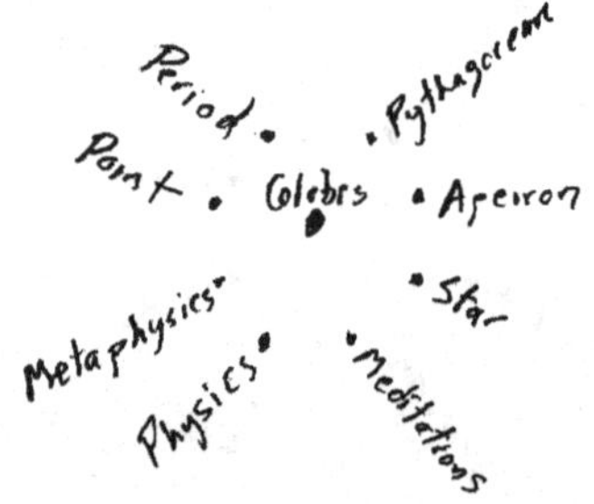

Determine the nomina of nessesity of the objective and get it done right the first time...

-Cipher- Epithet

Code • • Caress
Alphabet • Epithet • Digress
Mute • • Mark
Language • • Scratch

Every squeak is a swear word in the narrative of a lexicon. It is in the demand as one reads...

-Cipher- Precept

Subjects • • Plains
Globes • Precept • Governs
Divine • • Courts
Apparents • • Absurdity

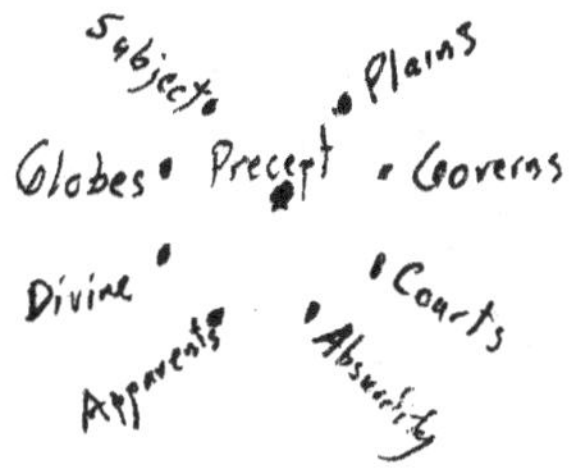

The idea is a monadology of subjects which work on individual perception...

-Cipher- Metaphysics

Deduction • • Temperature
Induction • Metaphysics • Effects
Principle • • Confussion
Element • • Elementary

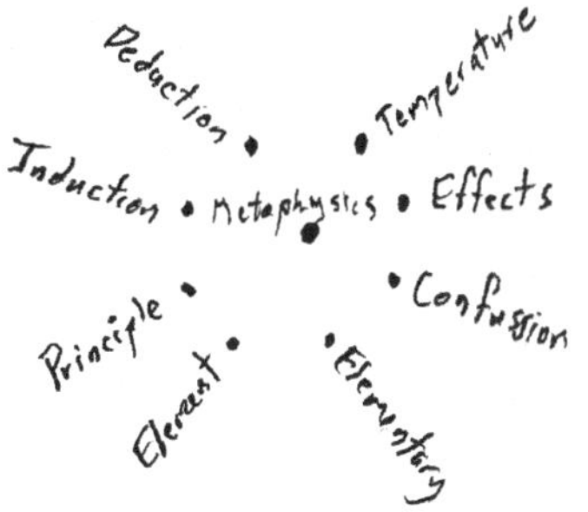

Reflect on the prudence of an elementary heuristic to a better understanding...

-Cipher- Teleportation

Reason • • Frequency
Deduction • Teleportation • Apeiron
Induction • • Dimension
Vortex • • Portal

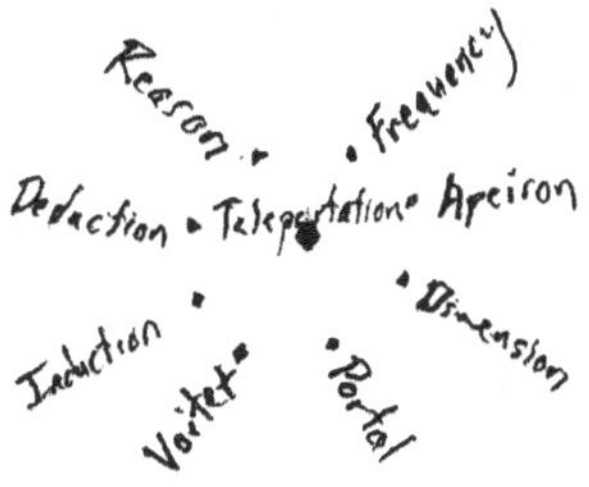

Move large distances in a split-second to arrive at ones destination in one piece...

-Cipher- Symbols

Idols • Language • Art • Symbols • Picture • Rudiments • Runes • Words • Books

The fine bodies of word's and artifices in the lexicon's of written works...

-Cipher- Codes

Grammar • Laws • Genera • Codes • Perspectives • Linguistics • Scriptures • Games • Cryptology

Analyse the epithet and nomenclature to induct the heuristics of the lexicon...

-Cipher- Eloquence

Lexicon • Intuition • Magic • Eloquence • Precept • Apathy • Kinetics • Calculous • Dynamic

A source of effects to be temp-erated with caution of their own intuition...

-Cipher- Politics

Laws • Rights • Precepts • Politics • Goverment • Institutionie • Society • Policy • Parties

In the affinities of morality in makes rights for a govern to rule over the people...

Cipher - Language

Nomenclature • Symbols
Encyclopedia • Languages • Alien
Thesaurus • Pictures
Dichotomy • Lexicon's

The body of a dialect is in demand for those who seek knowledge...

Cipher - Fact

Scripture • Evidence
Scholastic • Fact • Clue
Truth • Case
Science • Tools

In a measure it is the only thing one can trust to ensure the truth...

Cipher - Research

Philosophy • Allegorical
Religion • Research • Math
Field • Science
History • English

Page through the resources to find what is needed in ones line of work or their own interest...

Cipher - Lie

Fiction • False
Trick • Lie • Conjecture
Repercussions • Negate
Artifice • Wrong

Small lies can be good though real lies could move mountains...

-Cipher- Plains

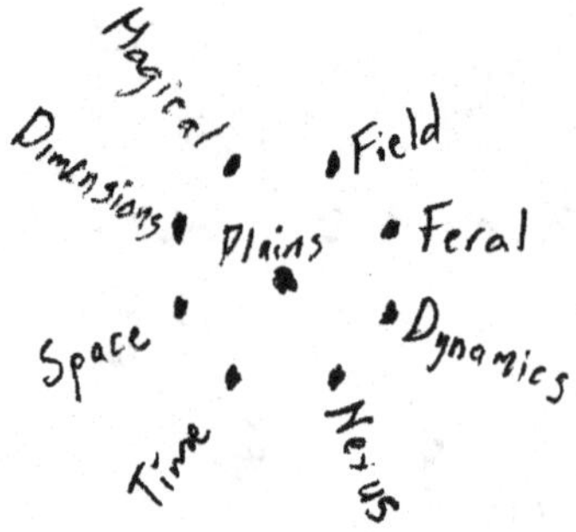

Walk any where in existence and subsistence changing the terrain of any world...

-Cipher- Frequency

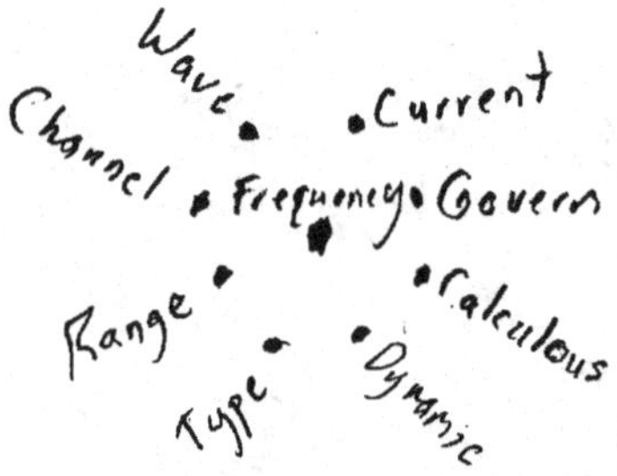

Look at the energy and choose a way to use it in the narrative of your mind...

-Cipher- Kingdom

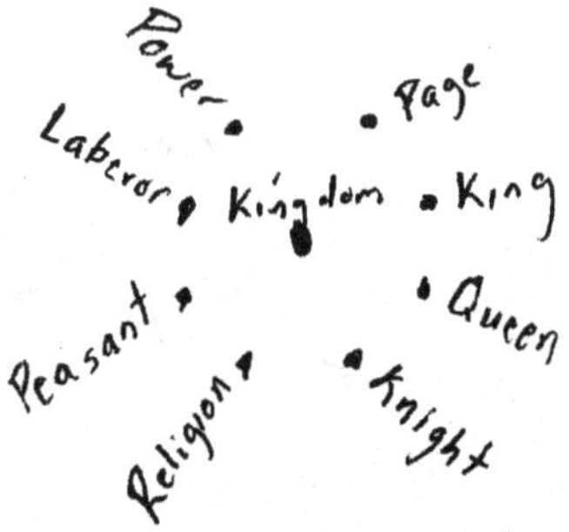

The Kingdom's had their rulers which pretty much did as they pleased in their Lordship...

-Cipher- Matrix

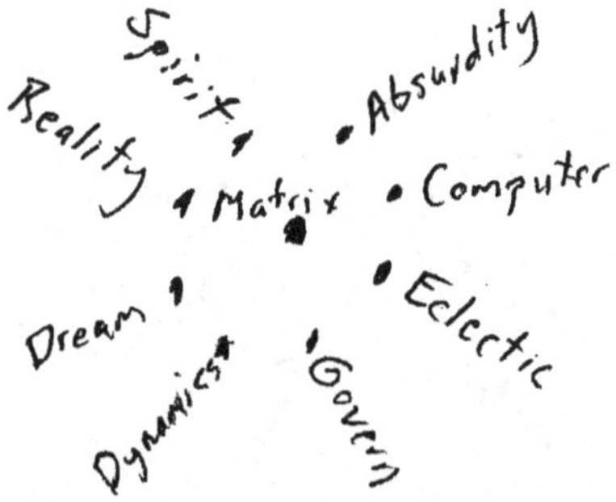

A nexus of axioms built from the ground up in the elementary principle...

-Cipher- Ledgermain

Dealing
Reading • Ledger main • hand
• Dynamics
Architecture • Static
Blessing • Magic

In this it is more than meets the eye when there is to much to deal with on the mind...

-Cipher- Poetry

Uniform • Modern
Rythem • Poetry • Moderate
Prosaic • Extreme
Benevolent • Powerful

The stucture of words all key in the effect of the narrative whether it be for love or not...

- Cipher- Lexicon

Eclectic • Dictionaries
Objects • Lexicon • Encyclopedia's
list • Thesauruses
Charts • Nomenclature

Whatever the source, it is mad allegorically on the word or object in conjecture, study...

- Cipher- States

Real • Solid
Pro • States • liquid
Anti • Gas
Metaphysics • Plasma

Its just puzzling the way the heuristics of the elements take form in the mind and imagination...

-Cipher-Agriculture

Fisheries
Technology
Field
Agriculture
Manure
Farming
Livestock
Ocean
Crops

The enviorns state highly regards the yeild in what the former will plant in a year...

-Cipher-Architecture

Type
Style
Blueprints
Architecture
Dynamics
Marketing
Carpentry
Industry
Architect

Plan way ahead to get all the articulate details when making a design for a structure...

-Cipher-Patience

Energy
Importance
Steadiness
Patience
Duration
Temperence
Faith
Velocity
Intuition

Have a great deal of temperence and moderate restaint in whatever you do on Earth...

-Cipher-Prudence

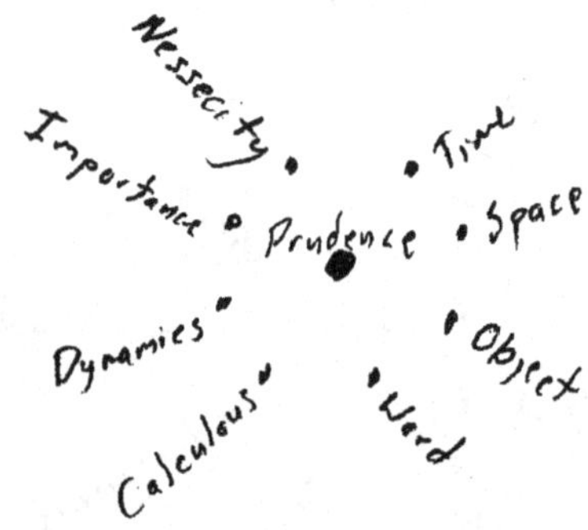

Whenever or where ever one is they need the right tool or convenience to get the job done...

-Cipher- Meditations

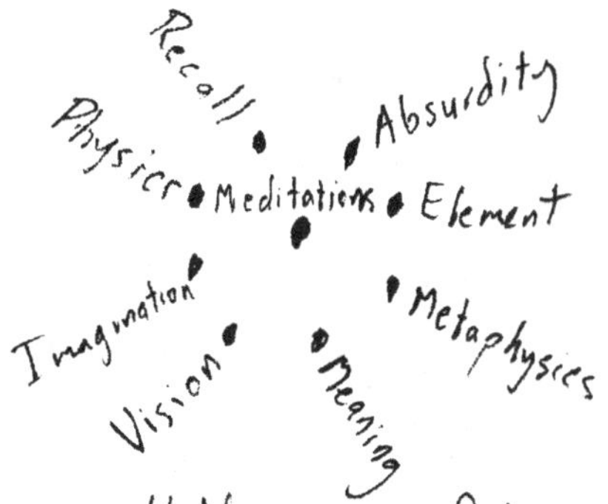

Recall • Absurdity • Physicr • Meditations • Element • Imagination • Metaphysics • Vision • Meaning

Hold a piece of the universe in your domain. Move it around about untill you understand it...

-Cipher- Current

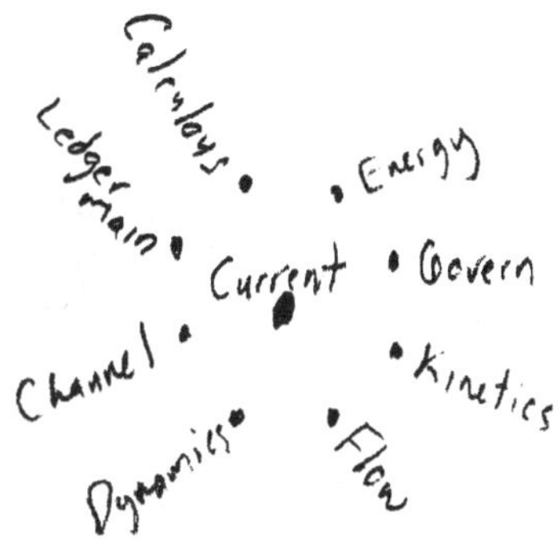

Calculous • Energy • Ledger main • Current • Govern • Channel • Kinetics • Dynamics • Flow

Mana or a source going through substances changing in resistence for the flow one needs...

-Cipher- Identity

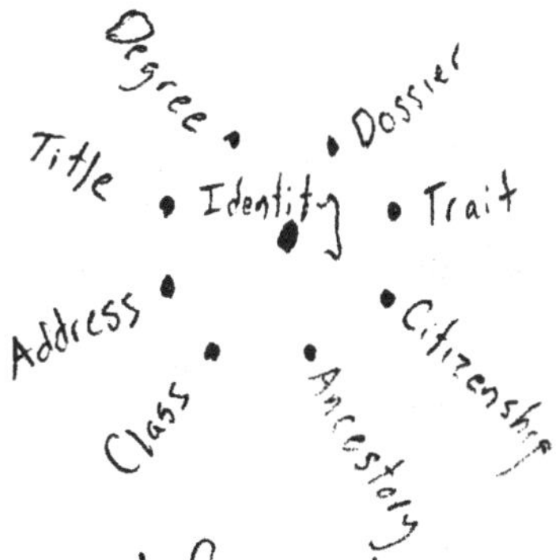

Degree • Dossier • Title • Identity • Trait • Address • Citizenship • Class • Ancestory

Life sometimes changes character along with who is there. To Know thyself is the ultimate wisdom...

-Cipher- Govern

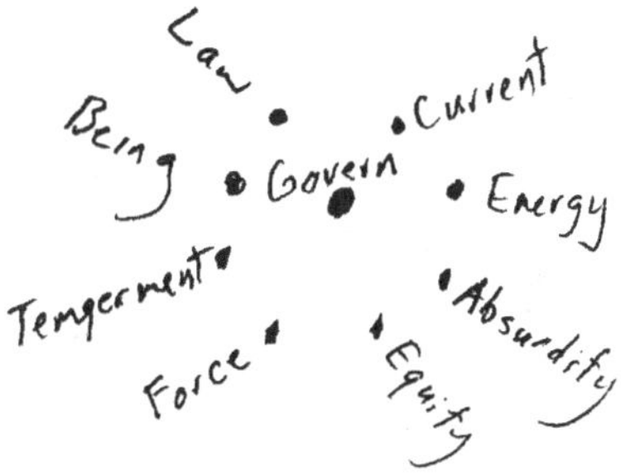

Law • Current • Being • Govern • Energy • Tempermento • Absurdity • Force • Equity

Figure out what makes something work and make a deduction to how one could do better in the mart...

-Cipher-Computers

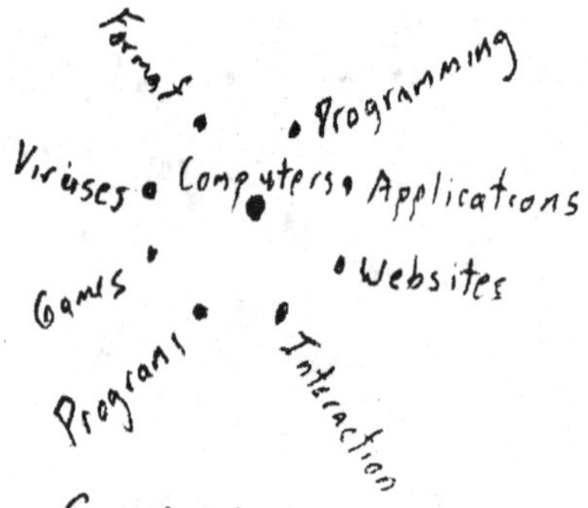

Format • Programming • Viruses • Computers • Applications • Games • Websites • Programs • Interaction

Created to make our jobs much easier one can't find a business without them...

-Cipher-Astronomy

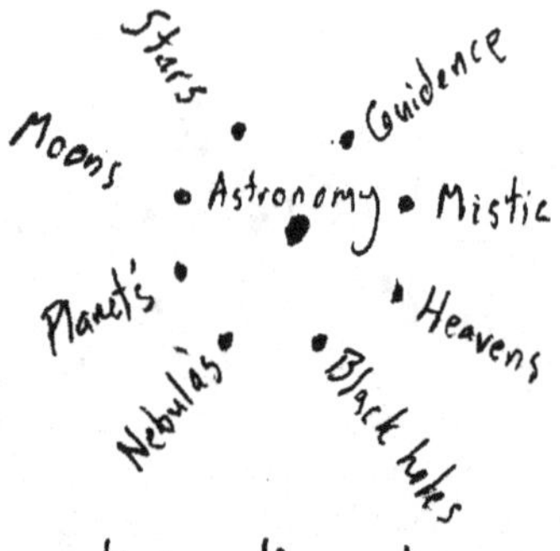

Stars • Guidence • Moons • Astronomy • Mistic • Planet's • Heavens • Nebula's • Black holes

Know the outer space like the back of your hand afterall it is your head...

-Cipher-Chao's

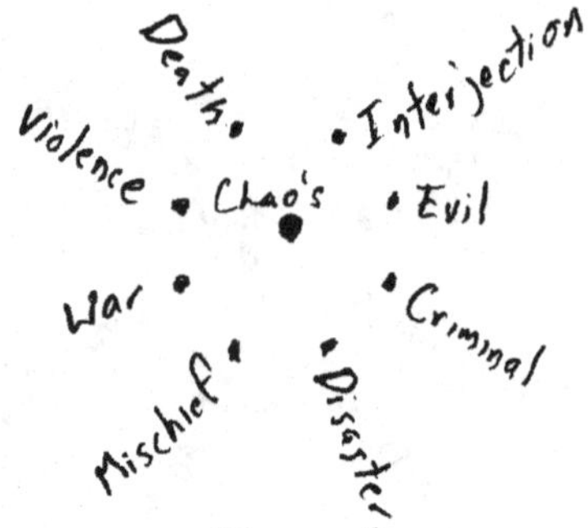

Death • Interjection • Violence • Chao's • Evil • War • Criminal • Mischief • Disaster

An effect of hell for a minute until one sobers and recovers their sanity...

-Cipher-Cartography

Explore • Geography • Personal • Cartography • Political • Antiquity • Word's • Religion • Business

Make a standing point to your location and feral your position in an illusory fashion...

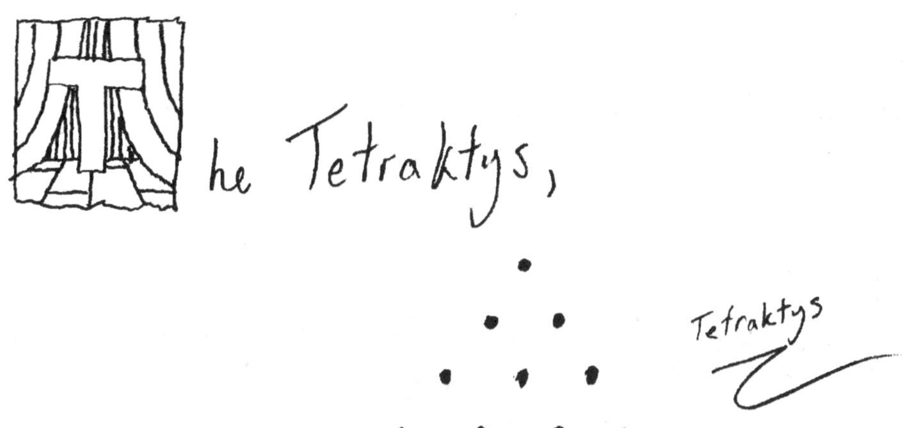

I regard this artifice as the tool of the creator. It is the apex of a pyramid of knowledge. One can use it to bring order from chaós. I have designed thousands of them. This is my favorite as an inventor:

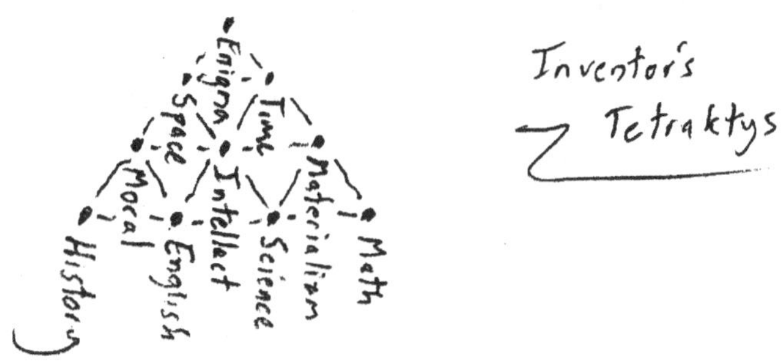

It shows a prudent serendipity of scholastics within the latter of mankind. I use it to seek through my knowledge and faculty to see to it a new invention or idea.

I am constantly thinking of tetraktys when I have a paper and pencil at hand. They show so many secrets to the language. I use them to set up lexicons of words and objects in my mind. It helps to be a tinkerer and with the science of a tetraktys it is yours. Choose your artifice.

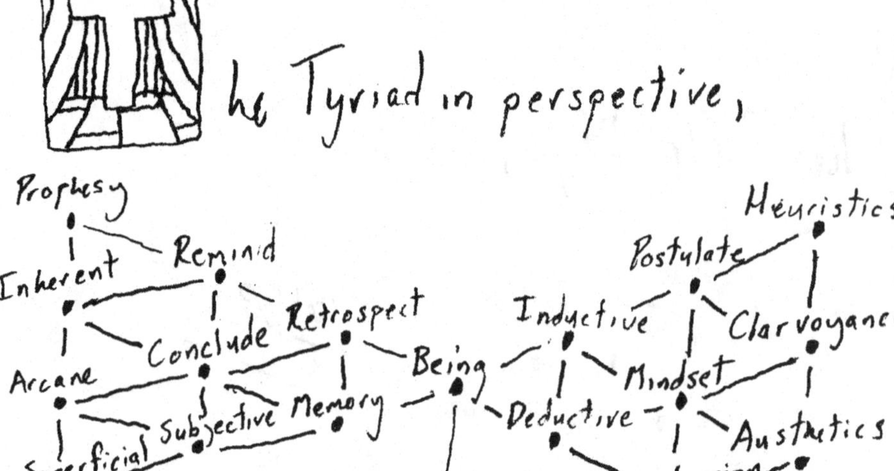

The Tyriad in perspective,

This is a model of a preceptional tyriad which works like an artifice. I can change it with speeding a lexicon of my mind. Here are some other words I use at my conjecture:

- Appreciate
- Understanding
- Grasp
- Dread
- Sight
- Position
- Place
- Location
- Rank

- Levelling
- Candidate
- Apeture
- Respect
- Admire
- Entrophy
- Utopia
- Vision
- Epiphany

- Situation
- Status
- Picture
- Absurdity
- Faction
- Effect
- Emotion
- Kinetics
- Absolute

easoning the consciousness,

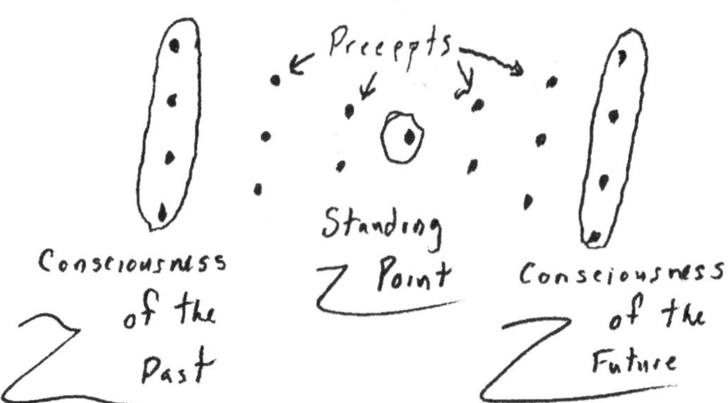

We have a standing point at the presents and there it builds on the consciousness of the past and future for one to use in preceiving things.

At the standing point it is easy to resource the past and future by commanding the precects in their association. With the change of precepts one can reflect on anything they can wit. The History and future of a nation or their own past and future.

Things of allegory are measured in this way from an overview of this tyriad.

Deduction is of the future where at the standing point we collect what's right there in front of us associating all of this tyriad in its plenum.

Induction is of the past where we have had our experimence in this life. It changes with conjecture.

lobes above our heads,

There are no other idea's quite like these in my collection. The globes offer a kind of protection to us all in the experimentation of studying idea's.

a court of globes

a globe

The globes above our heads, Associated with stars and planets.

Thoughts with the ability to reason come to us from all angles and objects. Though what if the idea is to hard to handle and we panic?

Globes above our heads

Idea that brings chao's.

The idea is in a trianglar form and brings chao's and mayhem. This is where we reorientate ourselves back to the globes above our heads. So that it is the very existence of the universe, We then get back to a sense of heading where we were with just the universe.

Not,

Absurdity has its limitations and what is considered not or unknown to oneself in the likes of a new person to a new thing we have our fears of somethings.

We have to untie nots in the likes as to say - learn what we do not have knowledge of at the time in the absurdity of the universe. The best way to get knowledge is to read books and in doing so coin the words within untieing the things you didn't know.

A not may be as a bull trying to use a pencil to write its thought's down to a cow. In these untieings of nots we have to also know the right tool for the job. It's true with nots that things seem harder when you haven't obtained the right kind of information about the subject. One will say, "I can't" or "I think not."

There are times when thinking "not" is better in the likes of the Ten Commandments there are some "Shall nots." The Bill of Rights talk about what are rights are and what they are not.

So how does one not something? Disregarding things is one way. By faith we balence nothing there at the time. So it looks like once and a while we have to meditate on nothing. In Philosophy it is called nonexistence.

One verse,

The eye has for the most part unlimited power to see and not see. This is a verse that one reads one at a time. The most valuable verse is the universe. It basically means, one verse. There is a one verse for everything which we call names for things.

Mostly each and everything we know of has a verse to it. How many verses are there?

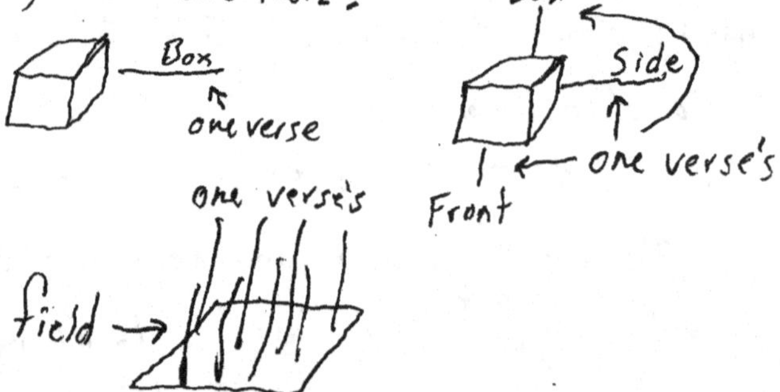

One verses can address an entire box or field.

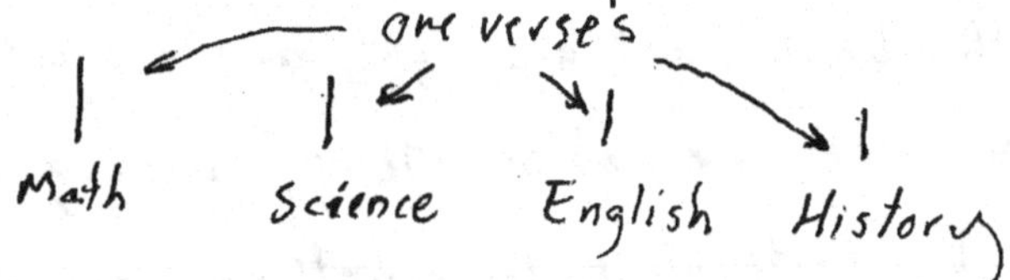

Any subject can become a verse. Just look around you, each thing has a verse.

Classes,

When in the study of something we have made them into parts we call classes. There are four general classes: Math, Science, English, and History.

I use cubes to fortify classes in my mind.

Math

In this artifice one moves through everything one knows about Math. It brings the cube to a plenum which the student may use.

For example I look at this slab of concrete and concentrate on Math.

Concrete

Math

Brain

The concrete is made up of elements which is Science, so we add a Science cube next to the Math cube. Then we discover it needs names so we add an English cube. We figure everything out about them classes. A History cube comes last as we find out the origin of the concrete.

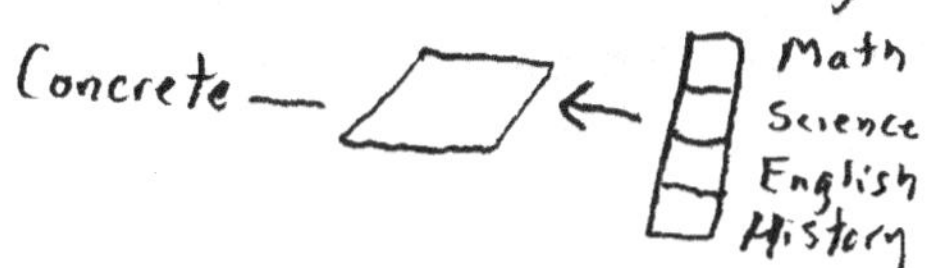

What we have now is considered to be the general view. Which is the court of the general tetraktys.

There are many different classes in the pedagogue today. The general classes are the most available and used for the elementary basis for everything. In the General tetraktys I find the elementary view of things which is common with every person who studies its principles.

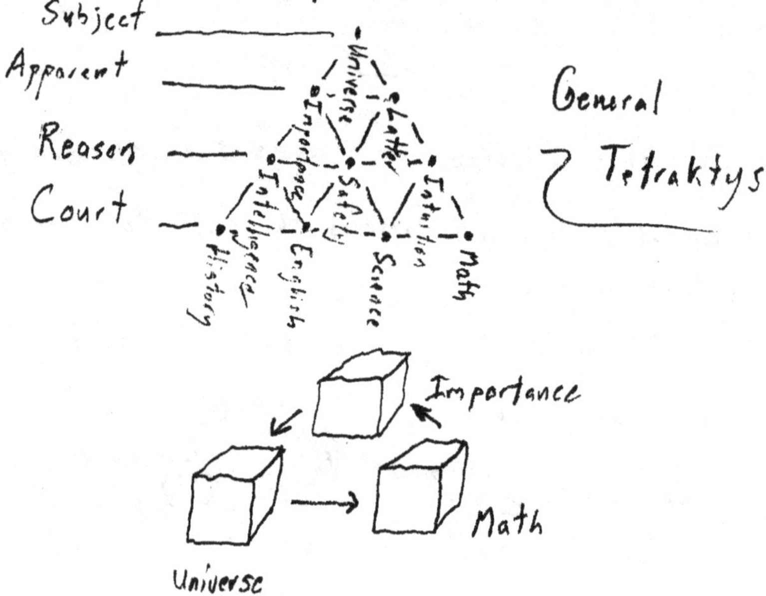

Here the artifice is set up how I find the importance of Math in the universe. I can use any word to find an answer in the heuristics of the mind. Taking the association in consideration of each word build's character in the absurdity of subsistence in the imagination. Each word is an enigma of its own until one defines it in its finite state. There is no exact Science so one can build from their own definitions.

Classes are addresses to knowledge in a Scientific principle where they meet the subject with the scholastic. The more one knows of a class the better the clarity.

The Universal Perception,

1 Subject
2 Apparent
3 Reason
4 Court
5 Absurdity
6 Divine
7 Plains
8 Govern
9 Globes
10 Deity

Universe

The eye takes many, many forms, A mote or speck being the smallest and the circle being the largest in fortifaction. We use shapes in concepts and precepts to understand the enviorn around us. A fortitude comes from the fourth dimension which is the second surface of a tetraktys. It is with the first four dimensions we are able to play with reality.

All of the dimensions together from subject to universe make up the absolute. Anyone can use their own dimensions in the universal perception as they wish.

The idea is to be fluent in the lexicon of dimensions so one can get to know the territory.

I'm not exactly staring at this page for answers, I'm using my illusion.

Unfold your words and objects into an illusory of intellectual property.

bsurdless,

The extensions of a meaningless dimension where only scalar subsist in the perception of ones view.

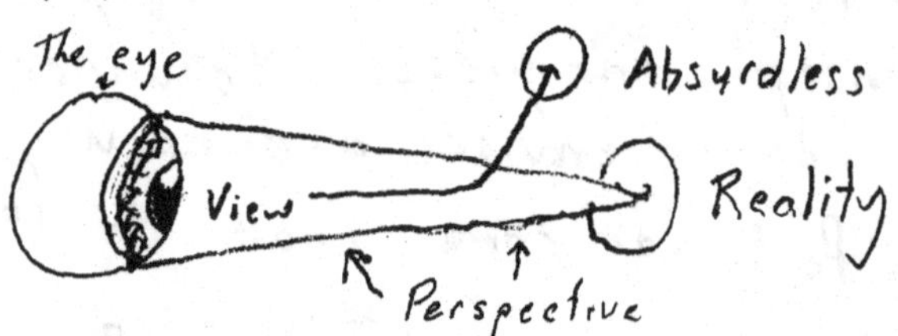

Absurdless is a fuel in mana as a scalar energy. where nothing is defineable off set from the reality of view. One can meditate on this to act as faith to a new concept. It is in its basics the unkrown, which is in its constance a maze of idea's and thoughts.

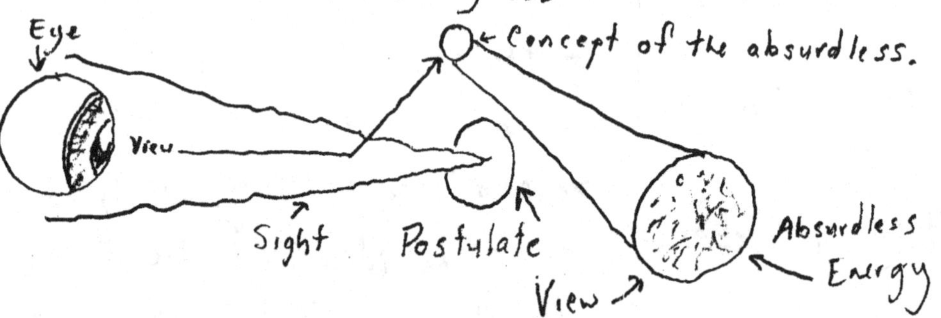

The absurdless is a continum which runs through the serendipity of time altogether. I call undefineable energy: Scalar. It is the extenuation of energy which I can not reach, but only view and contemplate in its mist. This energy can not be gathered or controlled.

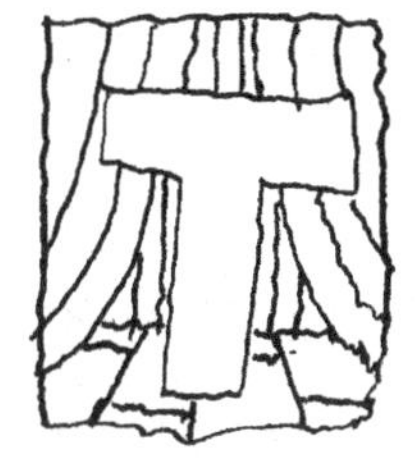
he Clock of the Universe,

15 Billion years ago → • ← Big Bang!

Today → • •

Time started as far as Scientist know, 15 billion years ago with the big bang. Today it has developed into galaxies, nebulas, quazars, planets and stars.

Our Solar System acts like a clock. The duration it takes for our planet to turn into day and night and go around the Sun has designed our units of time. The false accuasation that time is man made is not true. Man may have assigned time through a calander though he was not the Creator.

Though the question still remains, is time inductive or deductive? They are definately two different realms. Deductive we have the heavenly bodies delineating time at our present. Inductively is an allegorical frame of time subsisting in our memory which we are free to use at anytime. The rules of time in moral conduct play an important role to our beliefs. Deductively there is an order, though at times chao's. Inductively there are no rules. The effects may change over time as things will forever unfold.

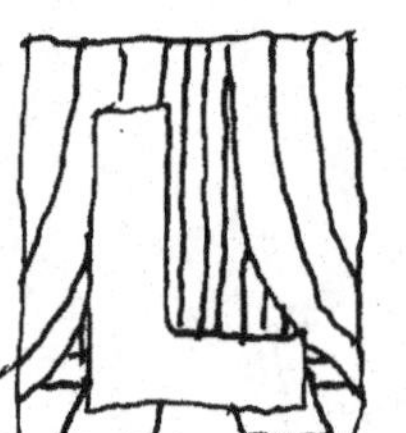ines and Precepts of Biblical times,

In the Bible is a mixture of scriptures which lead to measurements which are to be found out and unfolded by whoever reads them.

One of the verses lead's, "Line by line, by line, by line... Precept, by precept, by precept, by precept..."

So if one draws them out with a pencil and paper they look like this: (—, —, —, —, •, •, •, •)...

If you arrange them in other ways they would be in the likes of these forms,

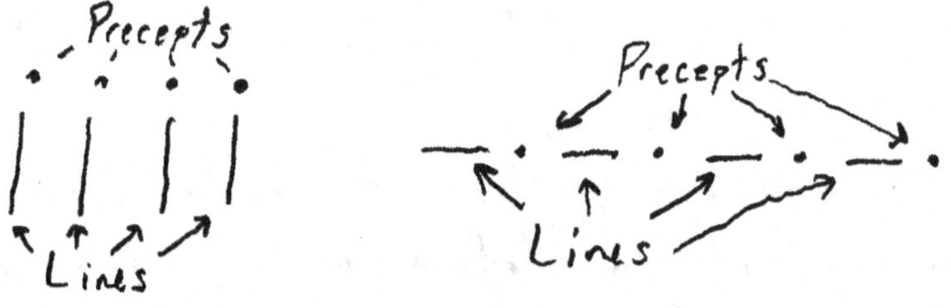

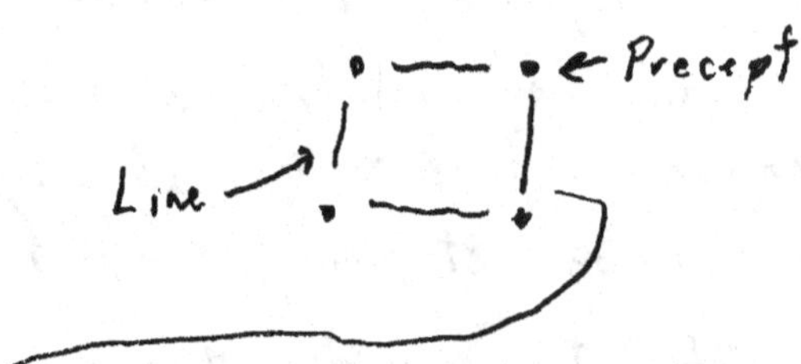

This one I take notice of in the likes of Religion. The other ones I think of music and scholastics.

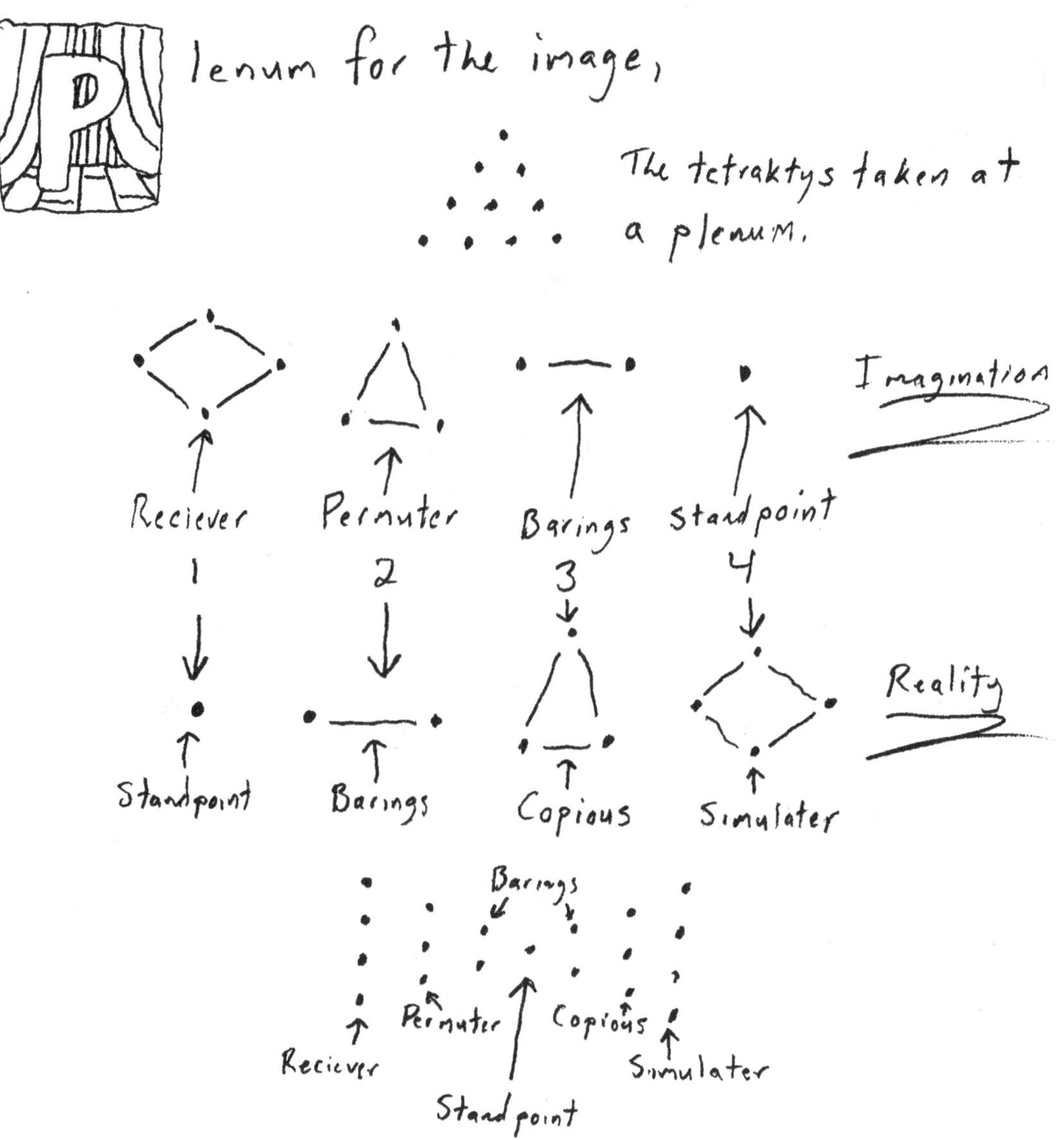

The Reciever acts like a television of the imagination from the simulater to the camera of Reality. This is a very tricky artifice though one can just disregard it and digress in belief. Still life photo's are an ability of an artist and can be very interesting and useful.

he Dimensional Bag,

The dimensional bag has an unlimited amount of space to be filled with anything the Wizard's wants or wishes.

The only problem is that the Wizard has to keep it organized so he knows what he is pulling out at the time. This takes mind over objects in the way of thinking with calculous and the principle of specialfaction. The Wizard reaches his hand in the bag and nominates his item with his mind and pulls out what he had desired.

No one should ever enter a dimensional bag because one could lose the dirrections for the way out. Never to be seen again.

It's the same way with time travelling through portals, one may get lost and never find their way back.

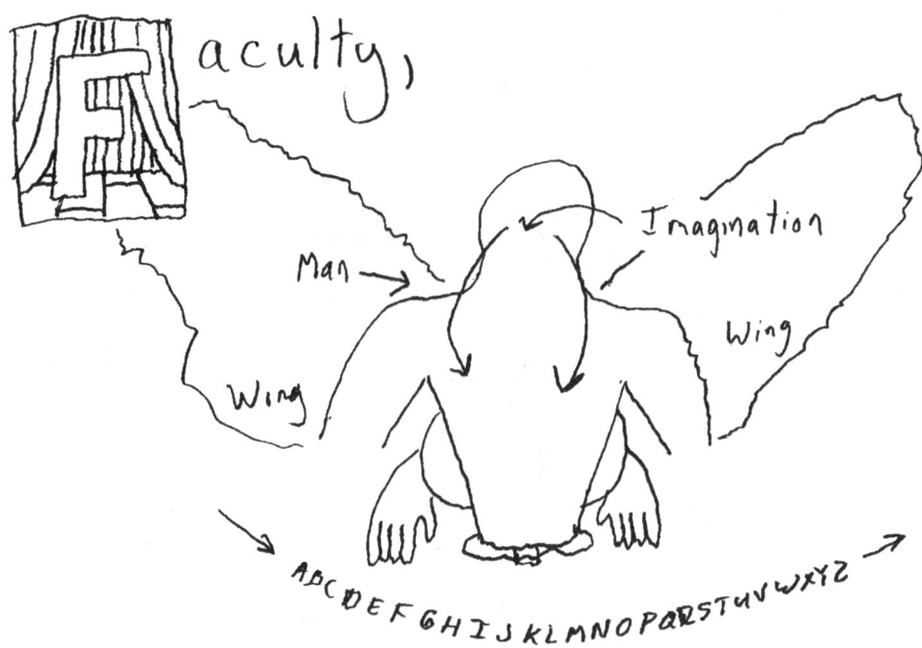

Faculty comes in imaginary arms which flow from the wings of a person. Appling takes little pressure over them when one permutes their skills whatever that might be at the time. Above is a man utilizing his skills going through the alphabet using his faculty.

This is a way of meditation which the body is the brain or mind. This is a real hands on illusory.

This artifice can be used to do anything in the likes of the individual. It is basically an extra set of hands only this one is totally up to ones imagination. I use them to handle subsistence.

The faculty artifice is endless, I've handled the stars, planets and moons with it.

rudence,

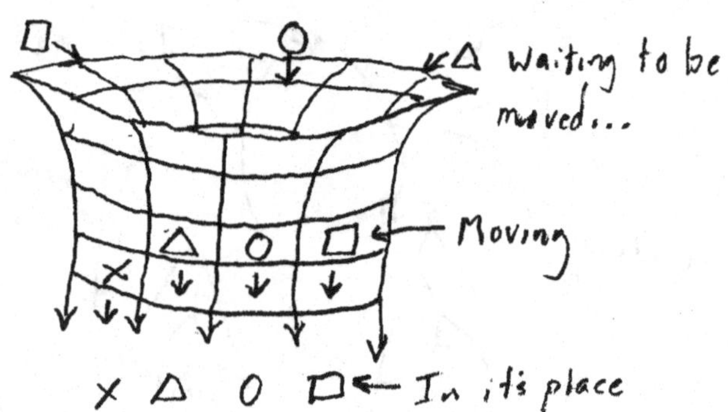

An object meets an importance, which needs to be done at the time. The x, square, triangle and circle are these objectives.

The vortex is your mind and the objects are the heuristics of the thinking process.

Ones mind is in rest when the vortex is clear and alone.

One may move about anything they desire inside the vortex. It may be an object or a scene of allegorical experiences which the person has seen.

One the ecclectic side one may organize a lexicon of words and objects and examine them in any way the choose in the vortex.

The idea is relevance in finding the right thing at the right time.

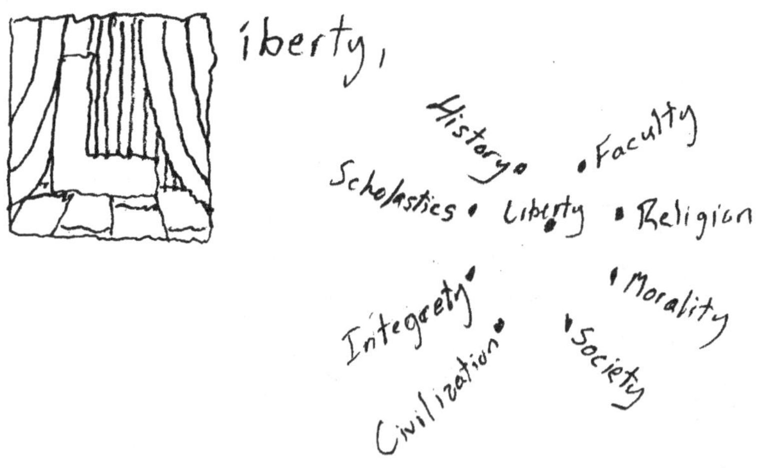

We have no freedom without history of moral civilization. It comes down to an allegorical principle which we have collected throughout the years on the good or bad. The Bible is just one of these works everyone should know. Religion is there to support our well-being, moral and history. Just try to give freedom to those who do not have such works. Our faculties in society show us our abilities through defining things in the right way it is the road to liberty... Safe and sound.

Freedom to be an animal or savage in the likes takes form in the will of man to deplete our conveniences of the modern social being. It is here we are just as free as animals and we take away the establishment of mankind with it.

If the world is broken, so are the people. Though the world has always and will always be this way.

Party after party after party.

So what are you drinking?

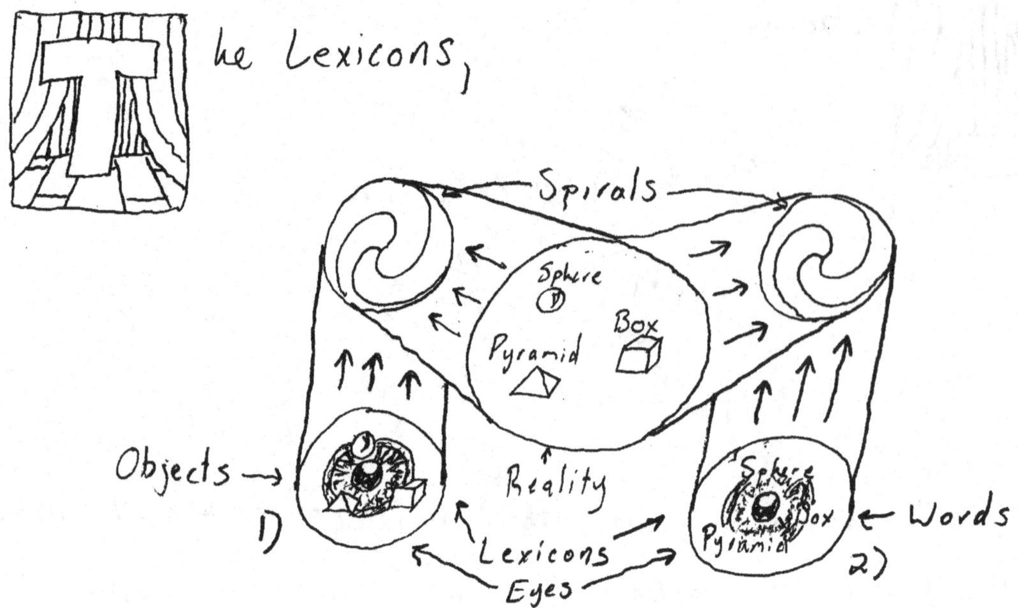

The mind reflects reality through the eyes and spirals reality of the illusion of the objects and words.

1) Objects, any thing or piece of intellect in the universe is looked at through the eyes. The mind spirals with a bit of intuition and practice to come into focus with ones own resolution of the imagination. Selecting objects that one wants to view and study in association is key to ones objective. One can take as much time on an object as one wills. They are models and come to us as illusions in an illuvion of the imagination.

2) Words, any word may be rostered from the alphabet in the spiral of the imagination. We spin the words of objects in reality to find the prudence in our enviorn to associate and practice in a study to learn.

In the mixing of the lexicons one can roster a picture or movie if practiced or talented enough. Each object and word is very important when in a study since it makes up the reality that surrounds us.

ather, Son and the Holy Ghost,

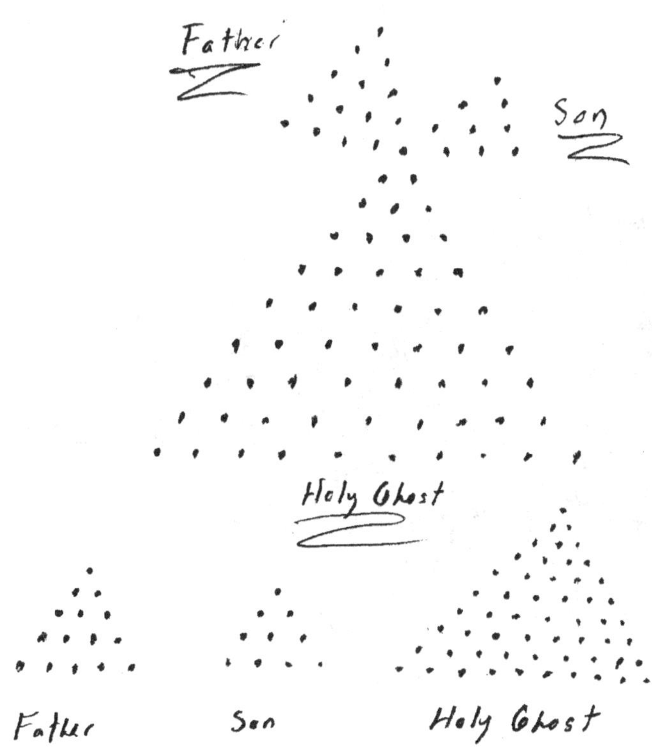

<u>The Holy Trinity</u>. The Father is a sum of 15 dots, the son 10 dots and the Holy Ghost 55 dots. They all work together. The Father is older and the Holy Ghost is the universe. It is God's home. we play within it.

The Holy Ghost is so vast it may engulf the father and son by its size. After all the trinity is for all time. Our ther is Holy and it is by the Holy trinity we are also Holy.

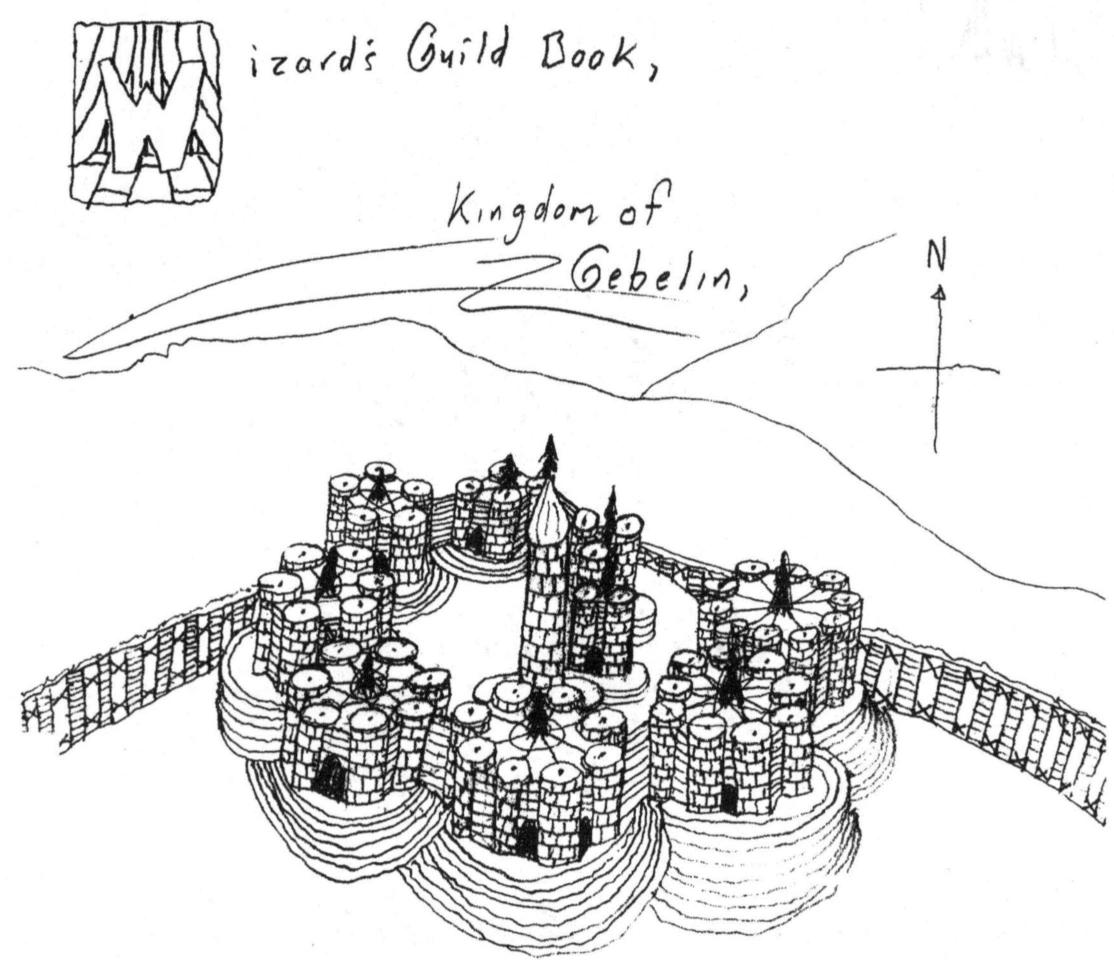

1) Monad edifice
2) Dyad towers
3) Trinity towers
4) Court Castle
5) Absurdity fort
6) Divine Oracle
7) Plains fortress
8) Govern Palace
9) Globe Observatory
10) Deity Monistary

Pythagorean

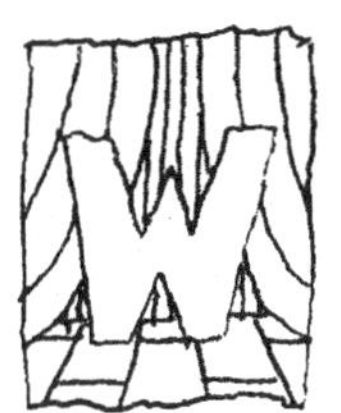izard's Guild Book,

Since the discovery by Pythagora's of the tetraktys the Pythagorean's have studied the way the world was and is meant to be in the future. The Indians of India made the first tetraktys in the sands on the ground where they studied it for a way to find the reason it locked so logical. It is there Pythagora's found it. He also studied Math in Egypt. We have developed much over the years and this is a collection of these feats. We have many artifices and the most important are the tetrakty, tyriad and myriad. We mostly reflect on them.

What we Wizard's are doing now is preparing for the destruction of the Earth by technology. We use magic and technology to protect existence itself. We Know much about the future as we have the ability to time travel, Though with the way the natural flow of the globes above our heads are we have to leave destiny up to them. It takes a lot of hard work and planing to fix the future. So there is not a chance that that we could go and see Pythagora's himself in the likes.

What we know is that on May 27, 2010 the Earth will be destroyed and the choosen one will save the Earth.

He's to say the sacred words which activate the tetraktys stone standing alone in the monad tower in the Kingdom of Gebelin.

The tetraktys stone has 61 apeiron globes which make up the heuristics to bring the Earth back to normal.

The rest of the stone is made out of gold.

This is a drawing of the tetraktys stone.

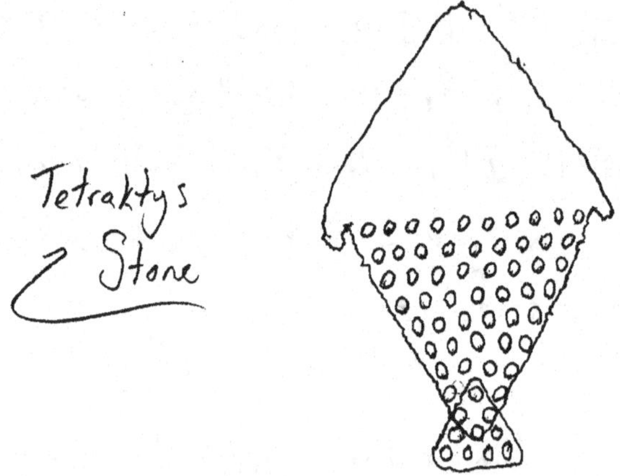

We have put together an idea for the tetraktys stone which the Queen set up for us. We made the mold and globes from apeirons. The Queen alone knows the idea behind it. It is for the first born of the feral plain to use his intuition to mold the apeiron globes into the quintescense they need to be. The stone, once activated by the choosen one will reconstruct the Earth from the destruction from technology. The Earth will be destroyed by magic at a later date. Where the all-seeing-eye will take its place. Every element in the universe will come alive. Everyone will run their lives in peace. Gebelin will be watching, waiting for something else to go wrong. The Earth will then be free from the myriad of magic and technology.

Though this is only one myriad that will be completed and it is endless like all other enigmas.

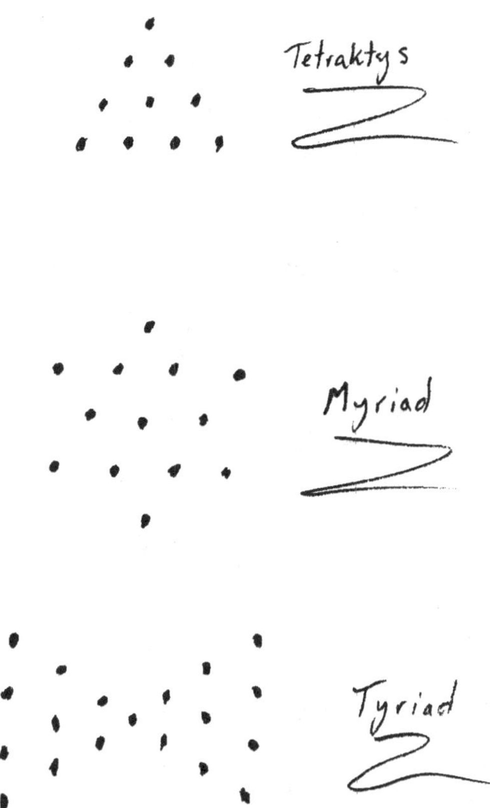

Each of these artifices are very important to us. They shows the order of the universe in the absurdity of time. The tetraktys is the elementary, the myriad is the spirit and the tyriad is the duration.

Each has unique powers when addressed in the right way. They unlock secrets of the universe in a language of their own. We Pythagoreans have studied these three for centuries. Not much came about them to begin with but with time there became great reward. So to a new comer these artifices look like dots on a page.

The knowledge is so true and plentiful it is a treasure that one can base life off and believe whatever one wants.

ingdom of Gebelin,

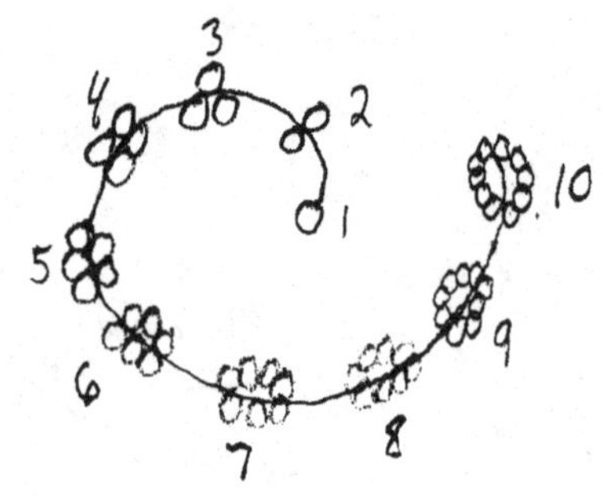

1) Monad edifice
2) Dyad towers
3) Trinity towers
4) Court Castle
5) Absurdity fort
6) Divine Oracle
7) Plains fortress
8) Govern Palace
9) Globe observatory
10) Deity monastery

1) The Monad edifice, this is where all the subjects in a tetraktys begin. It is the source of monadology. Everything one can think of has been considered through this place and on up through all the towers to the Deity monastery. Here we find a oneness about things and their uses and purposes. This edifice is the place the choosen one activates the tetraktys stone to reconstruct the Earth from the destruction of technology. A new Earth will form on May 27, 2010 where Gebelin the crown of the feral plain will rest and the Earth will be realigned to take out the ways it was destroyed. A ginning is set by the Queen to

let everyone with the Pythagorean amulets retain what has happen to existence before Earth's destruction. The next step is the destruction of Earth through magic. The Monad edifice has a dungeon below which houses the all-seeing-eye for the time being. Ever since 1054AD the Kingdom of Gebelin's Pythagoreans have been studying here. They say it at a glance holds the beauty of the entire universe. It shines to us in the likes of the Delphi Oracles precept. It ferals such a light of benevolence the dimensions gives to us an immaculate perception where one is free in omnipresents. In this edifice we'll take an item or thing and compare it along with in the monadology of the universe. In the likes we take a fork and look how it reflects to all other monads (other things) and then find a place for it in the absurdity of the enviorn.

2) Dyad towers, here we honor thy Mother and Father with every thought possible. We consider family things, art, culture, ethics, relationships, how they compare and react. Opposites in the likes as we put the affinities to the test. The quality of the intellect is observed in what is the safest means possible. We never weigh things that will hurt people. We take everything at an average and consider that medium a normal to comprehend its value. At a norm in this state we are able to study without the absurdity of wickedness. We are in tune to metaphysical and moral philosophy in a study of existence through a divine order. Two of a kind is the name of the game. What? Who? Where? When? How? We think Christ is the one and that the choosen one is another only he is not a Christian, but a Gnostic by religion and a Pythagorean by class.

3) Trinity towers, they say, where there are three, there is God... In these towers the reasoning is done for the intellect of the

eclectic principles universally and particularly. Each piece or thing is measured up to the codes of the Queen Iris of all of the Kingdom of Gebelin. They weigh it by spirituality, economics, moral, politics, culture, physics, art and ontologically. One of the things they stress here is illusion since it is the first surface (Imagination) in a tetraktys. They use Ledgermain, Eloquence, and Agriculture in their magics. Here things are a utopia. The Professors may make models of the places on Earth through the illusory.

4) Court Castle, here we practice policy, Laws, games, classes, and codes. There are countless amounts of courts. We use them to coordinate the eyes and ears weather it be a basketball court or a court of love between a couple. Us Pythagoreans find an endemic philosophy about them there is an end to everything, so we use the tyriad to calculate in this kind of ritual. This is the mind of Gebelin being the second surface of a tetraktys. We look at the metaphysics of the element in its finite state and in its affinities of chemistry and emotion trying to find a cure, the cure for anything. We are hearers of all things in this court castle. Here we view things in their elementary throughout the absurdities of the scholastics in a tetraktys.

5) Absurdity Fort, all the artifices and artifacts of the universe are viewed and made here in the likes. The element takes the form of some kind of intelligence in a faculty of wisdom to bring a thing of aesthetics in these works. We find that the things we play with are mere toys and trinkets to us Pythagoreans as models. A skyscraper or aircraft carrier can be these models in the likes. They are models to the wave of the future to where who knows what will happen. In absurdity people are running around trying to see what these toys are

for in the endemic of the universe. We are just Kid's at play even with the most serious artifact or artifice.

6) Divine Oracle, Here we are looking into the effects of precepts and axioms inductively to the full extent in existence in a deductive way. The future in philosophy unfolds to the Oracle bringing stories and visions of artifices and artifacts of intellect of the subject in reflection in a study. We hold many orientations of the globes above our heads to distinguish all possible affinities far and wide. We think, what's this, what does it do, where did it come from? We also travel the nexus of the axioms to figure a relativity with the intellect and character in the enviorn of scholastics.

7) Plains Fortress, here is the Kleromancy of the Levellers. A plain for everyone, a plain for everything. The Professors can interpret these plains when they come aboard. The plains act as a narrative of activity to ones purpose in the enviorn. The mind reading of the ambrosial in the likes. Figuring out on how things take value in existence we Professors get a feel for things. The affinities of a quest a man can have in the future are feralled here. We think of missions and games in this measure. The land's, world's and universe's all have seperate plains in which man can go in the absurdities. All things are possible in illusion of a plain in the imagination. It is in the court that they then become a reality. Beast, monster, and Deity in mans mind become second thought in the plains of illusory which succeeds their desires for real things becomes their passion. For what is the worth of precious gems when one can clearly imagine them within the third-eye. The imagination becomes the universe of subsistence into one speck in reflection.

8) Govern Palace, this is the Queen's throne room and a place of every Government the world has to offer. We consider everything in politics, expecially any written Law or Constitution. The Pythagoreans try many pages as their text body can take a look at what exist in the sights of the Queen figuring the absolute of the way different pages constitute. We are looking for the affinities of liberty in this palace. The other things we are looking for is the immutable, mutable and permutable in beginnings, ginnings, and endemic philosophy of the times in existence and subsistence.

9) Globe Observatory, here we visit the classes and what subsist in the scholastics and academic level of the absurdity of the universe. Globes represent in a monadology the ways of the universe. An absolute tells of order as the globes fall into place. Take an item here, it is in globe form. Each globe represents a nominal existence. So two or more objects in the room are absolute in their order. We are both hearers and studiers of all. We find perception absolutely amazing as it is after all endless. Referencing to the globes one can think of anything imaginable. One can build up from reflecting on these globes since they are a nomina of the mind. Having assigned globes one can make an equity with them in a room within their head. The globes are made by one who imagines them in the faculty of ones ability in physics. One can move mountains or paint a town in the likes with the tetraktys.

10) Deity Monastery, this building is sacret to all the Deities of the universe. Pythagoreanisms is a class not a religious sect that can study and believe in multiple Deitses. We view moral, materialism, and intellect in the vary vanity of religions. Each religion has its own tetraktys and some are worse and some are better than others. We have

two Elders, a man and a woman which worship all and each Deity. They are the head's of this monastery. Pythagoreans of Gebelin are always denouncing and renouncing Deities in their work and study. Though most Pythagorean's like to be Gnostic because then they can believe in their own practice in life.

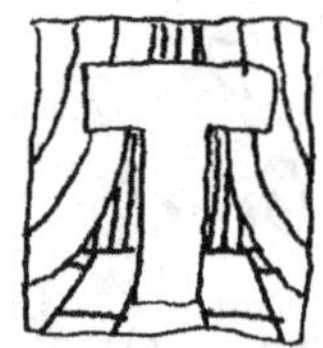
hought by the tetraktys,

Pythagorean

Our Wizard's at this guild practice this type of tetraktys to use as a basis for organizing thought in a record of scientific principle. The idea is to visualize the method in steps, so one can value and honor what they have thought.

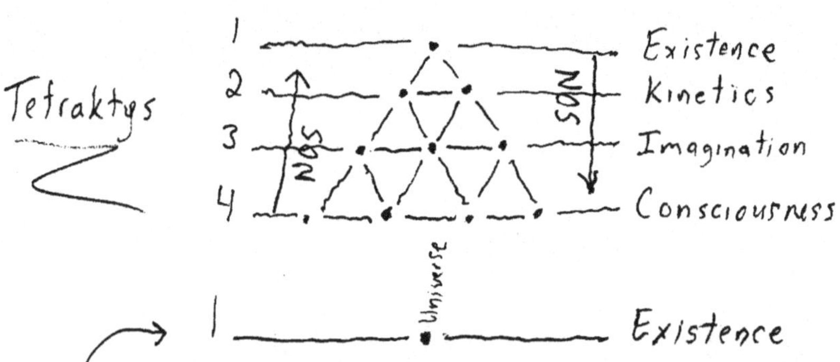

In existence, say the life span of a human being, we take a subject (Whatever that subject might be - a beetle, a mountain, a planet or globe) For now the subject is the universe, and I mean the whole thing as of now, the past and forever. It is the subject in this tetraktys that define as our surroundings out from the center of perception to the furthest reaches of outer space. Everything one can fathom is considered in it. The Wizard takes a view of the universe as a subject where one considers a particular perception (in the verse of the mind-nos) one can view themselves in the dimension of their mind. The nos comes from the eyes and ears and is controlled by ones intuition. The universe is the biggest space and is the most important being nominally only - one verse - in dimension. Though one can hold any subject as this - one verse - and view it in the likes. For instance, try a stick... A stick appears in the mind, this comes in a subsistence through honor (Holding a value for something in the mind.) It's up to ones thinking in considering One verse. A noun or piece of intellect can fit the importance of an objective, food in the likes. A pickle that fits in the mouth or a monkey wench that twist on a pipe. A particular or universal thing in the absurdity of the universe shares a - one verse - address, basically assigning a name for each and every thing. So in one room (Major division) the items or things in it (Minor division) all have their own verse or name to them. Us Wizard's cohesively consider the whole philosophy of the subject in the tetraktys as a monad is considered to be with oneness. Existence is the mainframe of the heuristic other wise we wouldn't have a dirrection with in all the emptiness of space.

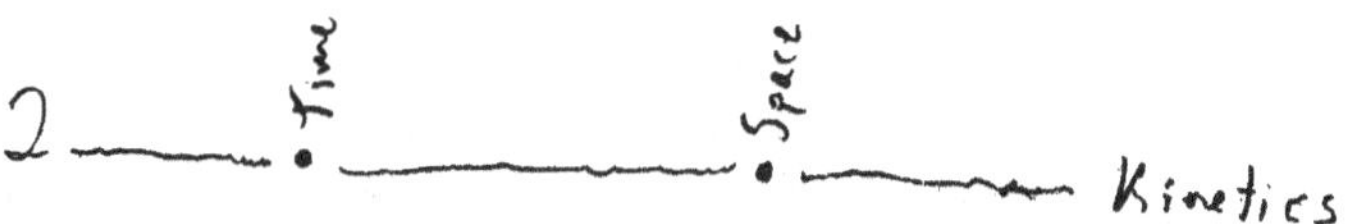

The actions and reactions of the universe all come from time and space that the apparents (Space of perception) are the Kinetics. As faith before the evidence of the thing you are praying for is there... Every action or motion is in the space of the first section of this tetraktys (The universe) the subject of existence. The cause depends on what one chooses to view nominally (Without reality) in the affinities of the subject. So if one chooses a pencil, one will also choose some paper to go with it in the likes. There may be a desk and office with it along with the universe (The subject). There would be a difference in choosing an Aircraft carrier or a house fly. One can make and play with a model of anything in the dimensions of the premise to the surfaces of the tetraktys as the subject of the universe. We hold here the apple of the eye in aesthetics when playing with subsistence.

3 — Intuition — Safety — Intelligence — Imagination

The reason of man behind the universe is granted by the subject (Universe) and the kinetics (Motion) where one can pick the cause and effects of the first surface in a tetraktys. This is where we work with images in the imagination to make things happen and think things through. The subject is dimensionless and the apparents a premise. The imagination is a tangible surface where we play with images within our consciousness to the experimentation of the scholastics. With the subject picked one can move through the apparents to choose an image to substanciate a reason (Imagination) and orate it consciously. Vision's, focus and epiphanies to dream appear in this section.

4 — Math — Science — English — History — Consciousness

This is where thoughts are found in the tetraktys. Dirrections and durations of the thoughts in the importance of considering the orientation of the body of the tetraktys throughout the mind and universe come together in a commerce where it is a heuristic experiment. This is the biggest part of man's perspective since it is where one can view ones thoughts throughout ones endemic lifespan. This is the second surface where the mind lay's out the definition and reacts with the rest of the tetraktys into a concievable thought in its entire clergy. Here the intellect is simply defineable and cohesive. We die in this surface, eventually.

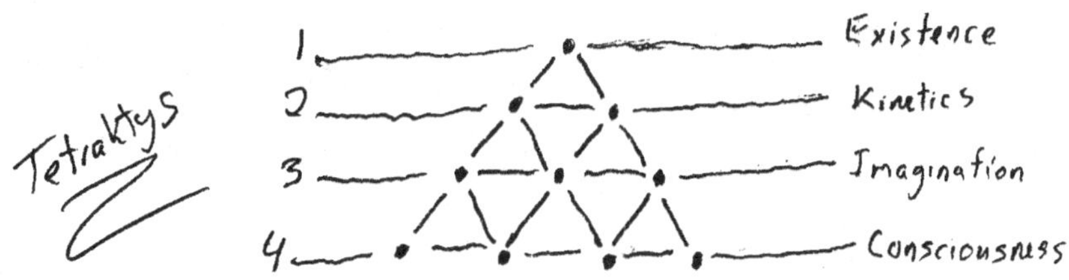

When putting all the sections together one develops a thinking principle and a thought process which gives quite the accuracy in perspective. The Wizard's of the guild use the tetraktys in this way in living and doing there research. There are more thought processes in a tetraktys then there are number. We are discovering new method's all the time. This concludes the study of this one process of the tetraktys that us Wizard's use.

Nato Christensen

Nato Christensen, 1647AD

he Artifices,

There is an element and intellect behind our magics and study which is based off a rudiment taking the form in a science of symbolizm. Basically we have a language which functions on the mind of human beings when it is conditioned. Symbols with thought in mind creates an identity which becomes their science or practice in meditation and thinking. The Gnostic in the likes suit the Pythagorean's to be the best scholastic mind frame.

We will be able to create portals in the future, yet for now we are making apeiron globes to resource the element and intellect to process our magics. We have the tetraktys which is basically the production of perception and intuition. The tyriad which is the product of the forces of the universe and affinities of the element. Last we have been studying the myriad for some time now. In all of them we use these types of knowledge:

- Precept
- Postulate
- Apeirons
- Portals
- Holes
- Dimensions
- Apeiron globes
- Nim stones
- Absolute
- Monad
- Kleromancy
- Transmigration
- Presentation

These are our artifices that we toy with in our conjecture. Some lead to finite states, others we find are enigma's. These mind sets let the Wizard's sharpen their skills giving them a basis to seek with.

Precepts,

At the start of a principle lies a precept where one can distinguish the type of a theory. It is usually something to base an idea of a rudiment or character defining the principle to get the right perspective. Together they develop into axioms where we associate idea's to reflect on for the situation. Which is inductive and deductive in perspective for the Wizard.

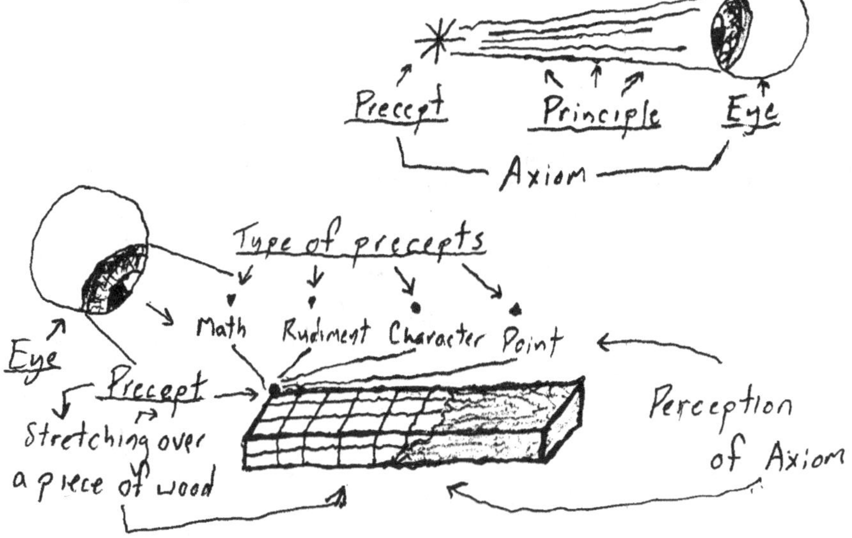

The precept has a point which is distinguishable by the subjects where the principle encompasses the rest of the piece inductively and deductively in an axiom. With each type of precept it changes with subject then showing a difference in principle. Each precept represents a different perspective. The eye changes with the type of object. In looking at different things in a room the eye takes form in the likes.

When one finds a memory in their head they find it inductively.

The Wizard plays around with it, Moving it around the space and inductively searches with it. The object in the Wizard's head is the precept. The principle is whatever else he sees plausably. The axiom is one in all in capturing everything.

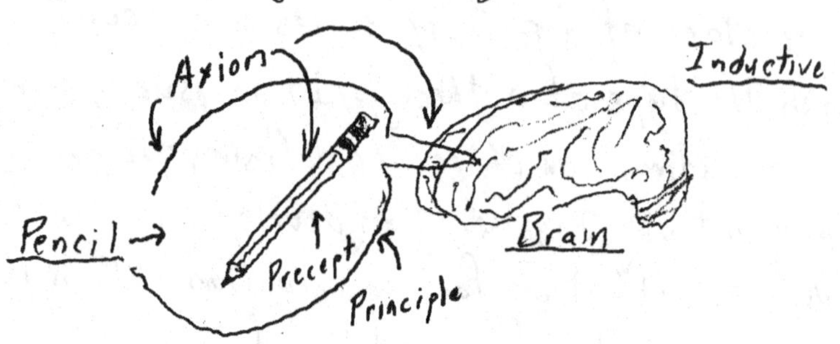

The pencil is in your thought inductively. One can imagine writing or drawing with it. It is the precept that is defined as-a tale to write with. One can have anything as a precept and one must define it in the right way. A spoon-for eating in the likes. One can run into trouble by defining something like a gun in the wrong way. Our definitions of precepts build intelligence. How does a Wizard view a cup? How about a student? How would they define a cup?

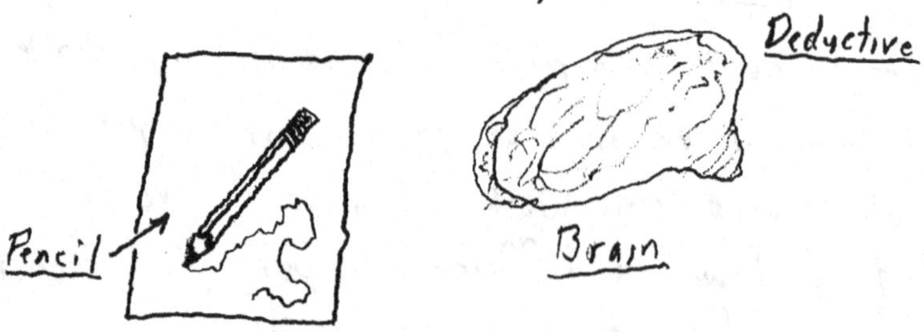

The pencil is one the page in front of you deductively. One can use it to write or draw one a page. The Wizard's use both inductive and deductiveness in their conjecture of artifices.

Postulates,

Postulates are artifices for drawing things up in the mind and meditating on when viewing things. In summoning and organizing things a postulate is key. They are there for our calculation.

The First postulate is basically a place with no point, it is dimensionless. Its best described with a circle where there is an invisable point with in it.

1st ——— Postulate

The Second postulate is a line with no points in a row that are making it. It is like an imaginary ray of light. Two first postulates make up the ends of this line, the second postulate.

2nd ——— Postulate

The Third postulate is like the second only three first postulates at an angle.

3rd ——— Postulate

The Forth postulate and last is two parallel lines that continue forever.

4Th ——— Postulate

All four postulates together make an organization process for the mind. It takes a long time to understand them. Us Wizard's use them to single out problems in the likes.

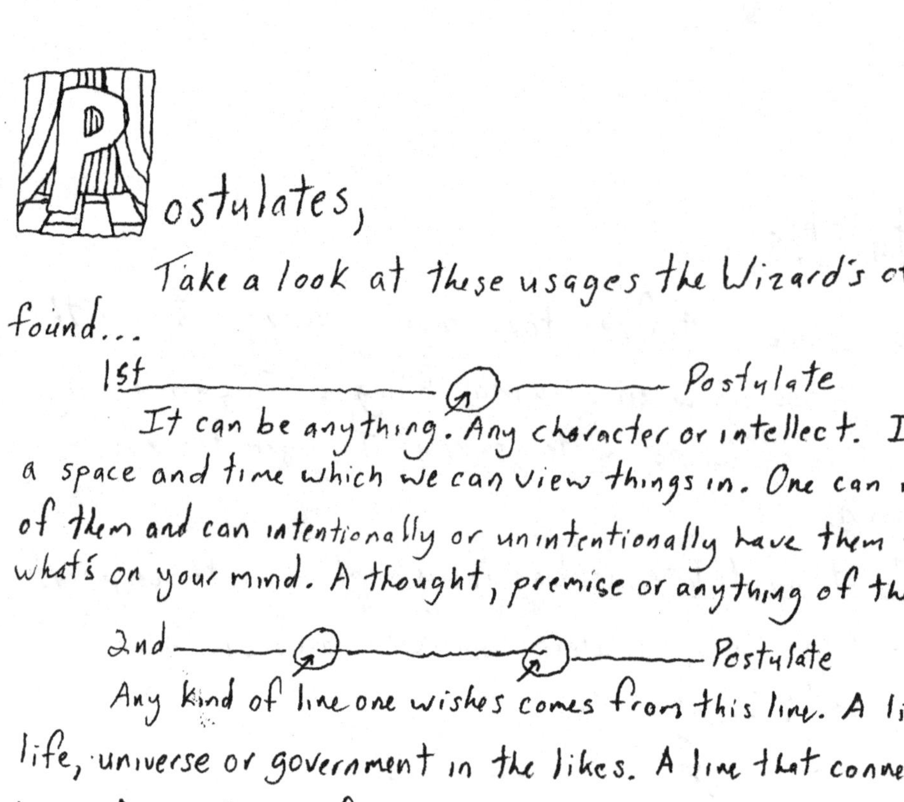

Postulates,

Take a look at these usages the Wizard's of Gebelin found...

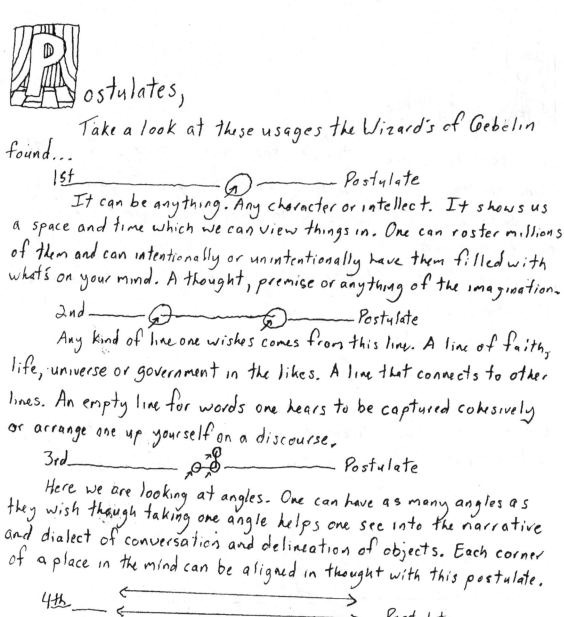

1st ——————— Postulate

It can be anything. Any character or intellect. It shows us a space and time which we can view things in. One can roster millions of them and can intentionally or unintentionally have them filled with what's on your mind. A thought, premise or anything of the imagination.

2nd ——————— Postulate

Any kind of line one wishes comes from this line. A line of faith, life, universe or government in the likes. A line that connects to other lines. An empty line for words one hears to be captured cohesively or arrange one up yourself on a discourse.

3rd ——————— Postulate

Here we are looking at angles. One can have as many angles as they wish though taking one angle helps one see into the narrative and dialect of conversation and delineation of objects. Each corner of a place in the mind can be aligned in thought with this postulate.

4th ——————— Postulate

This helps one relate the unison of the endlessness of the Wizard. The lines expand forever and do not run into anything unless the Wizard chooses them to in the likes of an object or piece of intellect. One can summon just about anything. The only question is – where did you get it?

The mind is a wonderous tool. The Wizard's here have more than they can eat. One must find a purpose with the postulates.

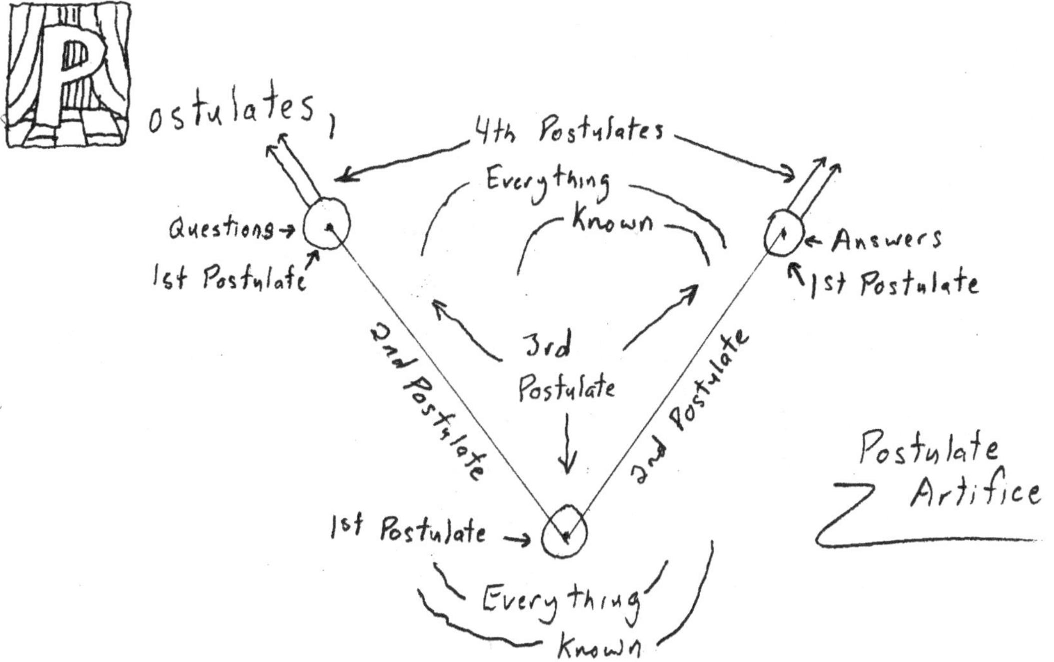

In this artifice of the postulates one can summon and view anything in the universe.

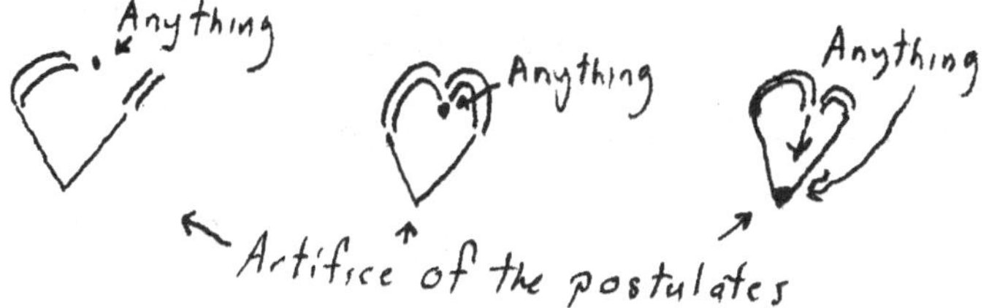

The postulates can resource and let go of anything at an importance. These are really neat in viewing this with careful respect.

The postulates are endless like the golden ratio. There is an unlimited amount of space at each postulate.

Us Wizard's are in tune with the postulates when needed. After all this isn't the only artifice. Though this one makes alot of sense when one can put it together in their mind.

This is a universal tool which any class can use. The idea is to take the time to get used to using it. With practice it can be yours.

peirons,

The apeirons have a long history. United in the ginning of the cosmos, they are considered unlimited. It's an unknown material, harder than diamond and indestructable by fire and cold. There are holes (Deep holes, bottomless) around the world which turn anything (except flesh) into apeirons. Nobody knows exactly who created these holes. They are said to be bottomless and it may be to the fact that there are portals to other worlds within them. One of the holes is in Washington, USA and there is another in Nevada, USA. The Hopi Indian's of Nevada all sleep at one of these holes. One can get an apeiron by lowering things down it. They discovered it by lowering an icicle down it and found it was no longer cold and it didn't melt even in the fire. It couldn't even be destoyed.

Us Wizard's use them to time travel since they can't be destroyed. Not hot, cold, dry or wet, it stays in the same state.

An apeiron can be a medium to the mind in its unlimited dimension in the likes of metaphysics, The cosmos and everything in it can be the principle idea of an apeiron vision. Consider it as a safe visual which we can seizes the day. The question is, is the imagination an apeiron light? We Wizard's reflect on this with the golden ratio to consider visual dimensions.

An apeiron works like a solution one must develop to see into the innaculate of Earth, Heaven and other-dimensions. It is endless to what one can perceive, Us Wizard's use them to see the universe.

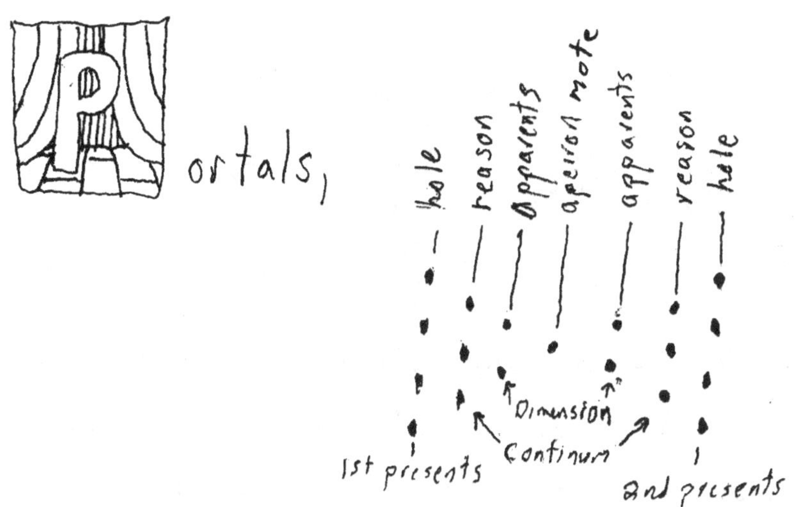

The portal is some how made with a tyriad when a hole on each side is met with an apeiron going faster than the speed of light. The portal holes depend on where in time and space they are designed. The production of a portal is a prepositional postulate. We are not sure of how to open and close them yet in reality. We use them in our minds to do all sorts of things. A Wizard can organize things in time and space in the likes.

Having a portal in the mind one can open a place they have already been or an imaginary place. Its like simple addition and subtraction.

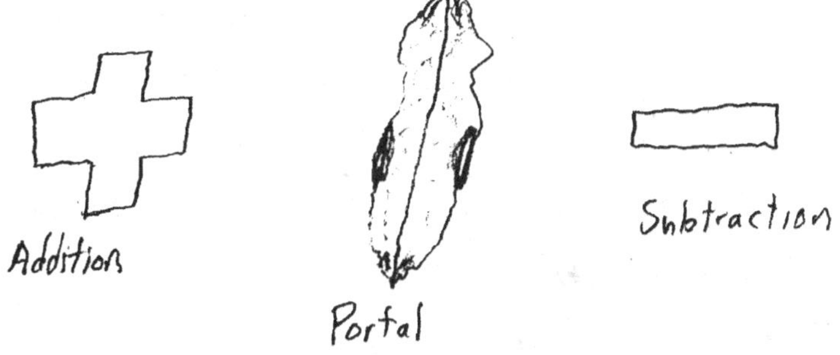

A selective mind in the likes. The mind is said to be laced with these types of portals. A Wizard can find them in their mind through meditation or 10/20 vision of the imagination.

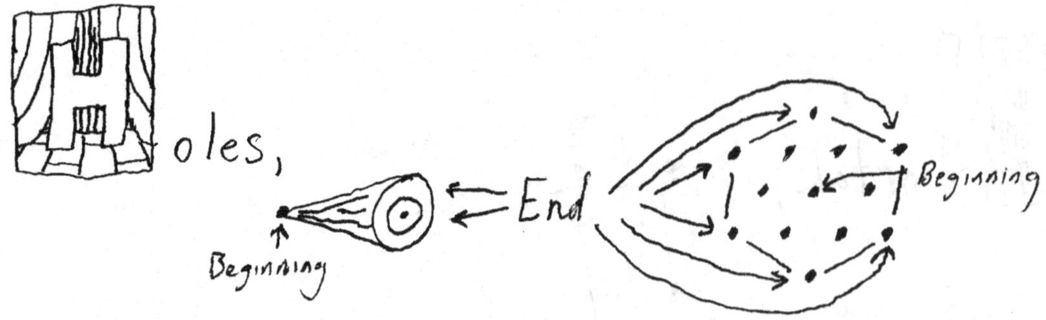

The hole has a beginning and end. The bottom depending on the precept could be never ending. Two holes connected at the ends some how make a portal, at least that is what we think. A hole could be for anything, to see the future, to see whats in the box, or put something in it for storage. Most holes are here for a beginning and end it being the past, present, and future in the guild contemplation. We also use them to size things up. Our eyes are like these holes. The production of a hole acts like a pronoun, a being that lives and feeds.

Hole
500 B.C.
Eye
Today

We tend to look right at things through holes whether it be an object or certain thing in the past, present or future. This takes a great deal of practice and planning. This is like a 6/10 form of vision of the mind where 20/20 is the perfect vision of the eyes. This is only in vision, we haven't been able to reach inside a hole to take something out quite yet, though we are working on it.

Holes are like tunnel vision and make a great resoures to the Wizard that practices with them.

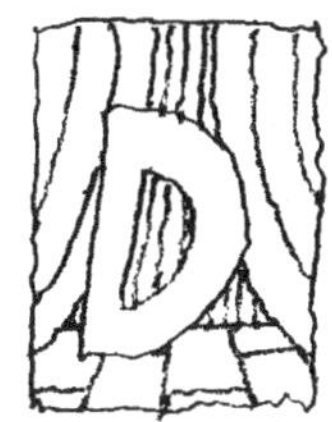imensions,

Dimensions are any measurabe extent.

- Length - distence from one end to end. Extent in time and space.
- Height - Highest point or degree. Distance from bottom to top. Altitude.
- Width - distence from side to side. A piece so wide.
- Scope - range of understanding when taking a look at things, action in the likes.

The dimensions can scale up anything. Take a globe for instance.

1/16 3/8 1/4 1" → Mile 10 miles → Any other shape → 1 light year

One could make anything as big or small as one may wish. In the mind or illusion it depends on the importance. Creating a movie in the likes.

Imagine a realm which one could call it their own. One could put anything in it they wish. Dimensions are endless, though some are finite, yet others are enigma's. This is totally up to ones addressings of resources and intelligence in the imagination of the dimensions. One could have a orange the size of a house or the moon within their hand. Any thing one wishes may be imagined within a domain of their own dimension. This is a thing where we can see and measure the dream arguement. What is real and what is dream. It comes down to a moral commerce and what one calcutates from in the envisorn.

Us Wizard's calulate from tools and artifices and from a nominal tetraktys. We weigh each calulation with caution of repercussions.

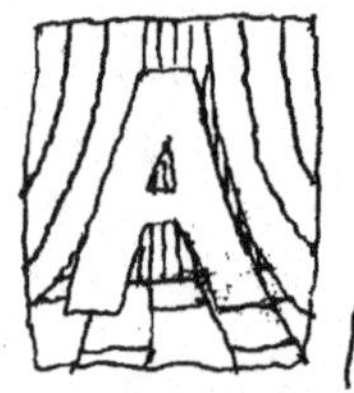

peiron globes,

We searched and dolored hard for this one. A globe which keeps a medium of not wet or dry, nor cold or hot, plus it is indestructable. Within it we can set a subsisting image of the imagination or universe kind of like freeze-drying ones thoughts. To get something in it we turn to the Jewish language of the Hebrew words "Ayin Ensof Aur." Which means "Out of the darkness comes light."

These globes hold a power which can be resourced with the intuition of man's digitals which sort of make whatevers in the globe copious in which it flows.

The Apeiron globe is used to make magical items which we make tetraktys into. One can do anything with them in crafting an arrangement of globes. We find water with this example:

Digital

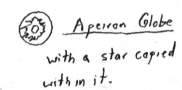

Apeiron Globe with a star copied with in it.

Water

Apeiron globe of water which with the intuition of mans digitals creates the element water. The possibilites of an apeiron globe are endless. It is possible to use different apeiron shapes when needed. The things in this universe are all important to us Wizords as we are taking things from a source we do not know of it is the risk we take with our magics. We resource the element, but from where?

im stones,

An ancient game of visions and story telling, nim was what the monks of Tibet and Indians of India had to explain their culture in teaching the young and for entertainment.

To Play,

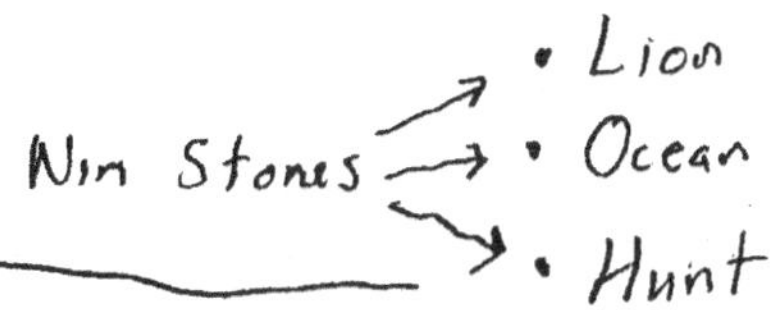

One would pick up a stone and tell a vision, story or imagine a thing or animal. The vision in the likes would be imagined by the people which heard the story. They would finish the tale by putting down the stone. The stone became a record of that story and then a new stone would be picked.

Nim Stones → • Lion • Ocean • Hunt

The stones were remembered as each one held a different tale.

A lion's tale, a story of the ocean and a tale of the hunt.

Nim stone's can be used to organize a story.

• Bear • Man • Forest

A Bear attacks a Man in the Forest.

In the likes Nim Stones held a high value for those who told stories in antiquity. Us Wizard's use them for spells.

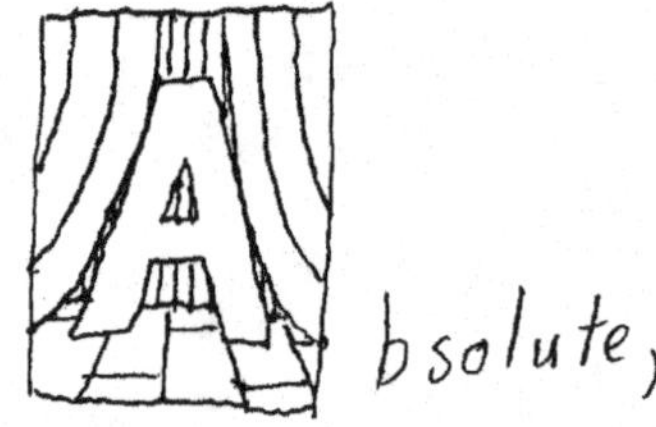
bsolute,

In theory everything comes together is a solution as one absolute.

10 = · · · · · · · · · · = 1 2 3 4 5 6 7 8 9 10 → Absolute

All ten dots as a whole create an absolute. Absolute is a thing at a plenum. Everything is added up in ones professorship to bear its mart. Every piece is relavant. Imagine inventing a card game or writing a story. Where you the inventor or auther has to come up with the story or types of cards.

If one makes a story or deck it is absolute when all put together, same goes with the globes above our heads, though with them they are mure models in the likes. One takes a globe and labels it to bring better understanding. One may group the globes in an absolute kind of like this: The Solar System,

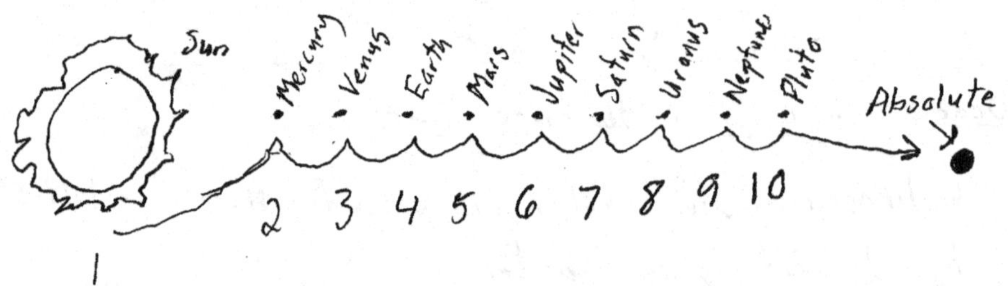

onad,

A monad is a perspective of a thing in unity. all parts of it are considered at a plenum or one whole part in the monadology.

O ← Monad → ◎ ← This whole system is a monad.
One — Together as one

Every part of a complete plenum is considered at a monad when looking at the whole thing. Looking at the universe as a monad shows everything in itself as though one would catch the precepts of the Delphi Oracle. Meditation on a monad gives a type of mana which is energy one can use and depending on what it is gives one its metaphysics to use in a solution to a problem.

• - Monad of the universe -

Looking at this point as a monad of the universe is pretty simple yet small scale in a model. Go a head and expand it.

Monad → ◎ ← Outer reaches of space

Then expanding the monad to the outer reaches of space gives one the freedom of dimension to reflect in on a study. It is really simple to have a complex study and then be able to return back a step to the plain and simple monad of the monadology.

Us Wizard's create these monad's by matching the intellect with the word.

leromancy,

Divination of lots...

•← the lot of Kleromancy. One can put anything into a lot. It matters at the importance. Some use dice, others use bones and some use pebbles. It's purpose is to conject into the future and calculate adding and subtracting the present with the past and future of things. Heuristically Kleromancy starts with the casting of something like bones to arrange certain happenings with the past, present and future. Pythagoreans use it to organize moral, intellect, and material things.

Bad • ——— • Neutral ——— • Good ← Moral

Lots vary with their faculty in type. Here is a tripartition of moral where we honor the bad, neutral and good. Honor all three together and we have a plenum of somber.

Lots hold many values and come in any kind of objects in its heuristics. They are learned through honor. Look around the room you are in to see something you honor. What honor do you have about these things? The better the honor the better the lot of Kleromancy Each honor is going to tell you a different thing. There are many things which are unknown to man, an enigma in the likes. The future remains unknown, cast your lots.

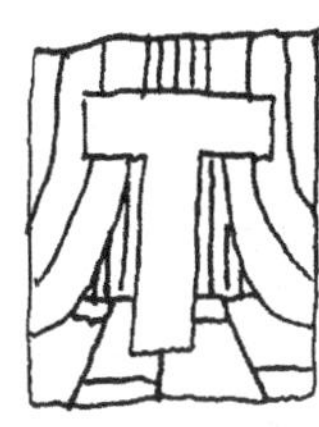

ransmigration,

Can you think of a square?

Square

Then can you think of a box or cube?

← Box or Cube

Can you put something inside it?

Like a spider?

This is transmigration in the basics. One must think of a controllable space such as a box or container and have a plenum of elements in the subject (The spider) and surroundings (universe) in order to fully transmigrate.

When someone is a master at this all you see is the spider. The Wizard's body becomes unseen.

To get back to the form of the Wizard one meditates imagining a box with a tetraktys inside to return back to normal.

Tetraktys and Box

Man's particular State...

It takes about 8 to 10 years to master this, though one gains a large amount of sanity imagining these possibilities.

he tetraktys,

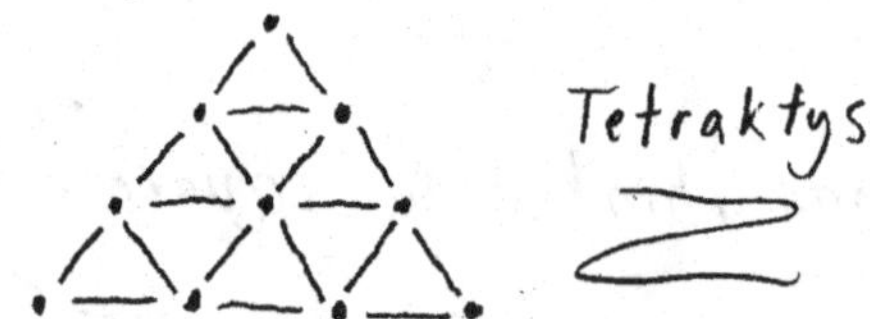

Us Wizard's take great care of this artifice. It's basically the universe and the model of thought for us Pythagorean's. Anything and every thing can be drawn up on a tetraktys. It was Pythagora's who found it on traveling to India. He also studied Egyptian mathematics. In Latin Pythagora's conjected clearly on the basis that the tetraktys gave in forming the math of the universe. From the first cause he conjected in a tetraktys the point and then motion, reason and consciousness of man in conjecture.

First Cause

1 ——— • ——— Point
2 ——— • — • ——— Motion
3 ——— • — • — • ——— Reason
4 — • — • — • — • ——— Consciousness

He conjected that the cause of all things was a balence of the tetraktys. There are more things to tell about the tetraktys and this is what the Pythagorean's base everything on in the entire existence of the universe in a plenum of discovery. After 2500 years we are still searching.

The tetraktys is our main tool us Wizard's use. It is the fact that it adds and subtracts anything one could will. Giving us a system in scientific principle. I think, therefore, I am.

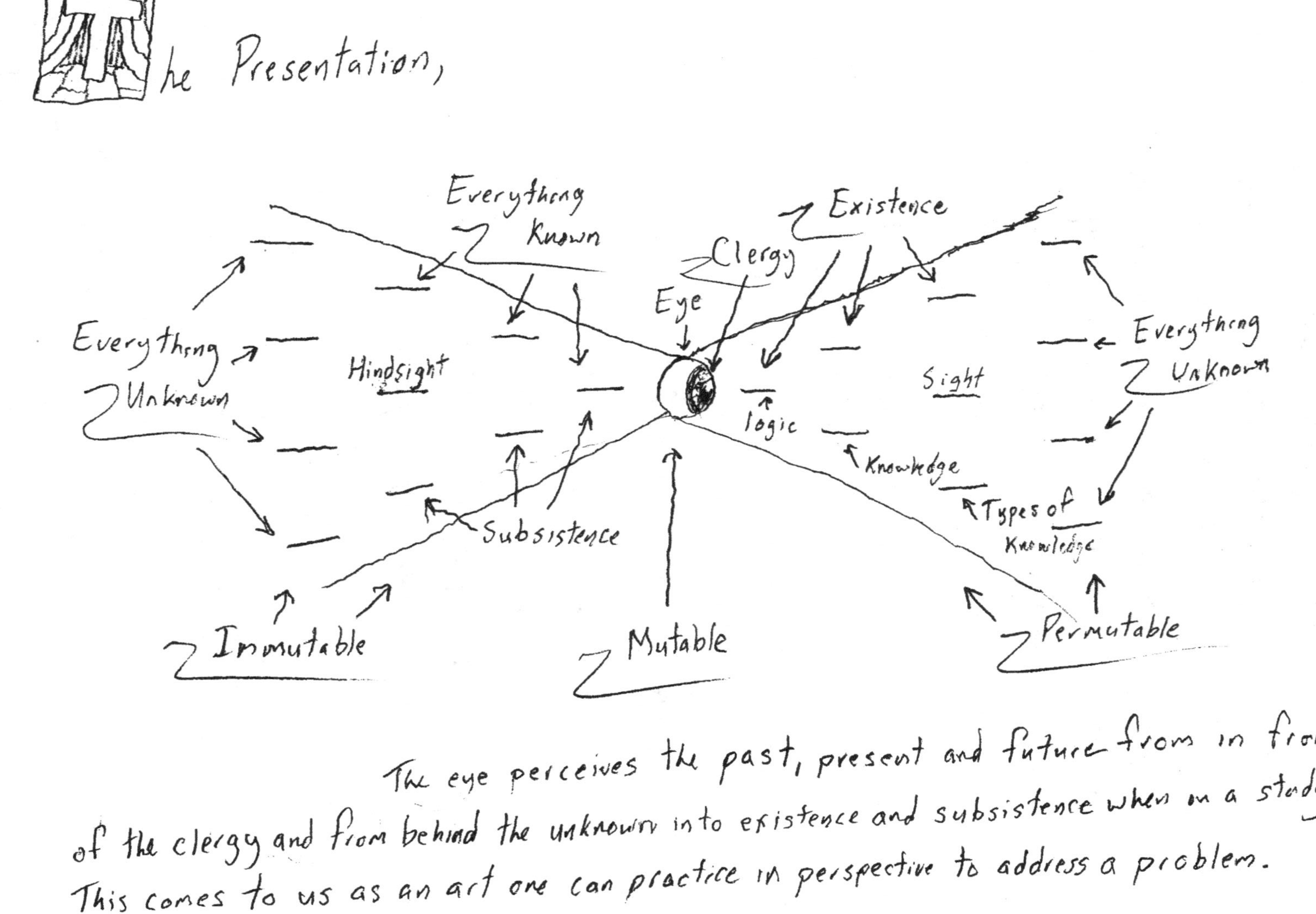
The Presentation,
Everything Known
Existence
Clergy
Eye
Everything Unknown
Hindsight
Sight
Everything Unknown
logic
Knowledge
Types of Knowledge
Subsistence
Immutable
Mutable
Permutable
The eye perceives the past, present and future from in front of the clergy and from behind the unknown into existence and subsistence when on a study. This comes to us as an art one can practice in perspective to address a problem.

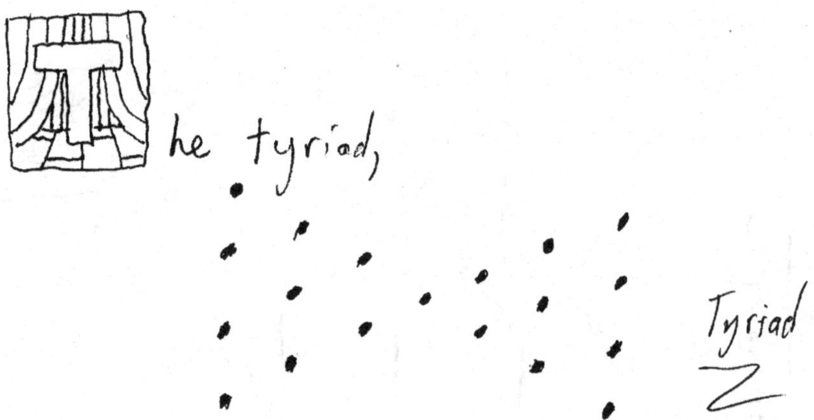

The tyriad,

Here we have an artifice that looks in the respects to be a bow-tie. From right to left time flows to the center on through the vessel. The center point is the present and to the right is the future and the left the past.

Past → ← Future Durations
Present

With it us Wizard's test durations of thought in the plenum of physics of the universe.

Portal

A tyriad also acts like a portal some how, we haven't been able to use this techology yet. We use a tyriad globlet for our time travel needs for now. It is a magical device which works with dating the E=mc2 of the Earth and Sun.

A more practical use of the tyriad is in the element in rest at the distance from the mind. We have the present where the element rest, Where a dot in existence or subsistence makes a point in time and space forming a period in a vestage in duration. The future is a consciousness in existence and the past is a consciousness in subsistence. We conject at the mart of this serendipity. We live in all three states since we are made up of the element in a physiology. It means the arche is a ginning. This begins the dream argeement.

We argue reality vs. dream. We need to understand the elementary of reality to identify a dream in existence. It takes a lot of time and study to be able to freely dream when one wishes unless it comes to you as a gift. There is a map to the spaciousness of dreams. We are living a dream right now, though we maybe in a sleeping state where we only have piece of the map. Thought is a form of reality which makes up the moral of our dream. When we wake up we bounce around reality to get on with our lives. Dreams are incorpereal realities comprised of visions. Thoughts are collections of dreams we associate from reality. Nightmares are artifices where they bring fears or terror. The tyriad is a vessel which the entire universe weaves through.

In taking the time to measure the basics of the tyriad one can learn to weald reality into a dream. It teaches navigation of time and space. Where one can leap anywhere in perspective.

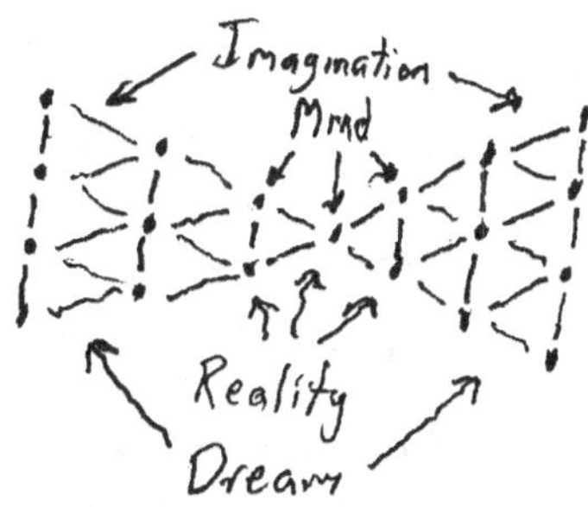

The clergy at the point lets one view reality of the mind and dream of the imagination.

The Myriad,

There are a multitude of things the myriad can do in effects to existence and subsistence. It is only known to a few what its maxium is in the universe. By us Wizard's our study tells us it means a birth or some kind of protection.

It opens up a space in metaphysics where we find a serendipity of protection aimed for our survival within the madness of the world. Without it the element around us would colapse into a chaotic state.

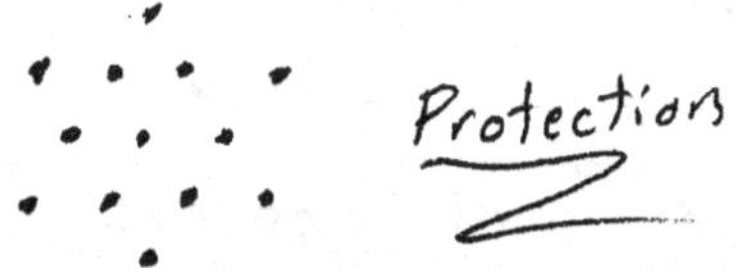

If we take a male and female we find that when we do reproduce we have the formation of the myriad.

Two tetraktys in juxtapostion make a myriad.

The myriad is the beginning of things. It is the order in which birth comes about in the universe. It is the home plate of existence. The affinities of the myriad lead toward a finite state, it could be infinite, or imfimisal regarding the dimension with prudence.

Us Wizard's use it to reflect a type of protection in the enviorn. When we have worked hard and become out of focus, it is up to this artifice to help out in the likes bringing us back to the birth of existence.

The myriad stone gives birth to the all-seeing-eye in 1054 AD under the monad edifice in the kingdom of Gebelin when Edwind activates it as a boy with his intuition. Starting the beginning of the kingdom of Gebelin.

When the myriad flies in the mind one gets a somber state of protection. Meditating on it brings peace. The myriad is the seed to idea's in intellect, moral and materialism. Metaphysically it clears a single idea to the root of a problem in a lot of heuristics.

I find this book very much incomplete. We will never find a utopia or we will forever lose our freedom. Perfection is not for humanity we will only continue to produce more convenieces that will come into being with time.

What would the people think of this book in the distant future?

I'm thinking we will have to keep adding to this as we go on with our study.

So for now guildies seek and thou shalt find...

Nato Christensen, 1647 AA

Nato Christensen